T0367540

Dusk

DUSK

Laura Waltenbury

DUSK

iUniverse books may be ordered through booksellers or by contacting:

iUniverse
1663 Liberty Drive
Bloomington, IN 47403
www.iuniverse.com
1-800-Authors (1-800-288-4677)

ISBN: 978-1-4917-1919-0 (sc)
ISBN: 978-1-4917-1921-3 (hc)
ISBN: 978-1-4917-1920-6 (e)

Library of Congress Control Number: 2013923261

Print information available on the last page.

iUniverse rev. date: 12/20/2016

ACKNOWLEDGEMENTS

Special thanks to all of my friends and family!

PROLOGUE

A child's mind is consumed by playtime, with their belly on the floor, racing cars across a carpeted, very stained floor. They have a complete focus on winning against invisible competitors that zoom around. The car goes for fill up, suddenly a dinosaur, controlled by another boy, takes over, as the boy plops down, growling ferociously. The car turns into a rocket car momentarily, as it shoots to the sky and crashes down on the dinosaur. My, what innocence – to see their minds so focused on playing, making up stories, growling, giggling, and having fun, without the least bit of worry for something more important.

I imagine a time when I had that, a life with not a thought in the world but playing on the ground with my brothers. It was a short, sweet time that I hold dearly, deep inside, safe from the darkness that clouds my thoughts. But in a vivid memory, I remember myself with a genuine smile on my face, a chubby little boy who wanted to do nothing but play. I would stay up late at night, long past when Dad put me to bed, playing with my brother on our beds with airplanes, giggling away until our Dad came in, flicked on the light and looked at us sharply. We were young enough to take his threats seriously, so we'd scurry off to bed and end our playtime. With a parting "goodnight," Dad would turn off the light and go back to his room as my mind floated away into dreamland.

When a boy is just a boy, he can be anything he can dream of, but when that boy witnesses a death by his own hand, that boy will never just be a boy. He can never turn around and know he will have a good life, a good job, wife, kids and a big house. That life will always be tauntingly beyond reach, but forever at the edge of my mind.

If only I could close my eyes and forget everything, leave my life behind and walk away forever, but I can never leave – I've always been too weak, despite my infamous title. I am death and darkness, more evil than what is found in storybooks. I am Dusk, and I am an assassin.

CHAPTER #1

The sun shone through a cloudy sky that threatened to darken despite it being the morning. It was a gloomy Wednesday, with little promise and all the intent of misery. I strode through the labyrinthine alleyways that had long ago been the only roadways when the city Vale Darra, had been but a small town. Originally known as Valley Cove, the village expanded and grew from a small population of just 1500. It continued to grow into a large city and years later was renamed Vale Darra, with it now being just shy of a mega city. Large streets ran through the city, fountains beautified the landscape and statues of angels and baby animals adorned the streets. Trees brought life in two single file rows along the roads. Most buildings had revamped and remodelled, becoming a site of beauty and spectacular architecture. It catches your breath in your throat when you first lay eyes on the city and still does after many years.

Everything about the city speaks quality. The richly fashioned houses spoke of the wealthy and the massive inflow of people spoke of a huge tourist attraction. But within the walls angry black marks marred the city. The people were not all fair or rich, many lurked in the dark alleyways as cut throats, thieves and murderers. They became a huge problem for the once peaceful city, but they were controllable. They were often caught and detained, efficiently dealt with. The assassins were another matter. Hard to capture and confine, the assassins were the real problem.

It was only 30 years ago that Vale Darra met a new kind of terror. A fear instilled in everyone no matter how stubborn they hung on to their ignorance. At that time a young man came into the city, trailing with him he brought dangers never before imagined. His name was Midnight and he was a world famous assassin. By twenty he was killing by the dozens, Vale Darra was not the safe, peaceful place it once was, far from it, it became a dark and dangerous place that no one wanted to live in. It was the worst kind of nightmare where no matter where you ran, death was always lurking right behind you.

Born into a family of murderers, he was one to be feared. He was smart, an opportunist, but most of all he was a planner, and a good one at that. He planned out everything, even his own death. Jotting everything down in a diary. Pages filled with every detail of his life so that one may read about his legacy he left behind.

It was him that turned the world to darkness around me, the sky went black and my hands dripped red with the blood of the people who died by my hand. He was a possessive human who was so sure of himself he feared nothing, he was thought to be invincible until I killed him and turned into a beast far worse than Midnight could ever be. I was fear and darkness at its very essence. Even I feared myself.

He came into my life on a late August day when I was walking with my dad to the grocery store and a man popped out and scared me. I screamed and cried as any five year old would. My father laughing at my fear, comforted me and addressed the haggard man standing before us with polite courtesy, "Sorry sir didn't see you there, come on Khire, it's ok," Dad began to walk on, but the old man spoke, his breathy voice rattling with effort.

"What a cute little boy, I'm so sorry to have scared him," The man said with little sincerity. My father, nothing but kind hearted smiled and nodded.

"Yes, and very easily spooked too," my father joked, and as I continued to cry, he picked me up and carried me away.

"Now now Khire stop crying, everything's ok," my dad whispered into my ear as I watched from over my father's shoulder the man stare after us, a smile on his face. Everything was not ok, despite my father's reassurance, even at a young age, I knew I did not like that man.

☾

Sitting on a blue plastic stool I coloured in a picture of a ball, going out of the lines regularly, my crayon scratched against the paper with a determinism only a little boy can have for wanting to finish a picture so he can go outside and play. The teacher came around to me as I was just about done and smiled.

"What are you colouring Khire?" She asked as she bent down beside me.

"A baaauul," I said and she nodded.

"Well, that is a very beautiful picture of a ball, I think you deserve to go play. Go clean up and have fun," She said patting me on the back. I smiled with pure joy and raced to put away my crayons. In a whirl of movement I cleaned up my station and washed my hands then raced outside. The kindergarteners to grade twos were separated by a fence from the rest of the school, but I could still see the other students. The school went from JK to grade 8, a small school with only about five hundred students. It was a good thirty minutes past Vale Darra's limits, but my father liked us in a smaller school than in a large overwhelming place within the city.

I turned towards a couple of kids playing with a ball, I wanted to play to, but just then my big brother came over to the fence.

"Hello Khire," he said happily.

"Hello Shean," I said smiling widely. Shean was nine now, brown haired and brown eyed, people said he was a spitting image of our dad at that age.

"Climb over the fence and come play with us," Shean said as he looked around for any teachers. While there were none looking this way I began to climb the old chain linked fence.

"Hold it!" Mrs. Derkosk's voice cut through the air, silencing everyone nearby. Cringing, I looked over my shoulder at a very mad Mrs. Derkosk storming my way. I hopped down and stared up at her pouting, belly out and hands clasped behind my back, look of complete innocence.

"Oh don't give me that look Khireal, get back inside," She commanded me and unhappily I went. Turning to Shean who was to slow to get away unnoticed, Mrs. Derkosk sternly addressed him, "Well hello there Shean, not causing trouble I hope?"

"Oh no! I was just talking to Khire, I'm sorry I'll get back to my friends now," He said and ran off. He was a troublemaker, but also a coward.

I sat down in my blue chair and stared at the small desk in front of me. The same teacher that had let me go play earlier came over asking curiously, "Why are you back inside?"

"I got in trouble," I told her miserably.

"Oh and what did you get in trouble for?" "I tried to climb the fence," I told her. She nodded with a sigh.

"Well you could have hurt yourself. You need to listen to the rules ok? Since your inside; would you like to help me?" I nodded enthusiastically and got to my feet and followed her to the door as she continued speaking.

"I have some things in my car that I need help carrying in," She explained and I followed at her heels coming up just past her knees. I was a small, tubby boy, blond-white hair and dark blue eyes, I was told I looked more like a pug then a little boy.

She led me down a green and brown hallway to the outside where her old car sat in the parking lot. After some fumbling around in her purse, she found her keys and opened the doors, reaching in she pulled out a small box. Looking at me she asked, "Here you go honey, you're a big strong boy," she placed the box in my arms and I nodded, only just able to hold it. Although it was small, it was still a little big for me, my little arms unable to comfortably wrap around the box and my protruding belly making it awkward to carry. She smiled at me then dug around in her car again and withdrew some more boxes. Locking up, we walked back to the school, I trying to keep up with her long legged stride.

I discovered after recess was over that the box was filled with toys, to my delight I dove into the box and pulled out an airplane. Running away from the box slightly out of breath, I went zooming around after imaginary enemy pilots. I was shot down by my enemy and crash-landed into a couch then bounced off onto the floor. I became a sweaty heap on the floor, panting to try and catch my breath.

It was a few minutes before the bus came when I noticed the same old haggard man hanging around in the school parking lot. He was smiling towards the waiting kids, but I couldn't tell who he was looking at. After a few minutes he walked over to me and crouched down.

"Well hello there, Khire is it? Nice to meet you Khire. My name is Sinth and I have a problem I was hoping you could help me with?" He asked me smiling.

"What's wrong?" I asked a little scared. He had a large nose and sunken cheeks, with many scars. He also smelled bad and had a weird way of looking at you as if he could see right through you with his pale blue eyes. He wore a long black coat, ripped and patched up in many places. His brown leather shoes were old and scuffed while his black pants were dirt stained. He rested a gnarly hand on my shoulder while he spoke to me.

"You see," He started seeming upset, "my mother is sick and I've been trying to help her, but she doesn't want me to talk to her. I was thinking just this morning when I seen you with your daddy how nice it would be if a little boy came and sat with her and read her a story. She is very old and misses the company of children you see,"

"I can help," I said happily.

I was raised to help anyone in need and judge people later. I had no forewarning not to go with him, no idea that saying yes would inadvertently change my life forever. I was a very stupid child.

"Oh thank you so much, you will make her so happy, you just need to come with me and stay with her. After a few minutes I'll drive you home ok, she just needs to see that she will be ok," I nodded as he grabbed my hand with his knuckled withered one and led me off. For an old man, he walked fast making me having to all but run just to keep up.

It was a quick, but confusing walk through the alleyway ending with a stop before an old stone house. Still by the end of it I was tired and sweating and had lost interest in this adventure.

"You live here?" I asked confused wrinkling my nose.

"No, my mother is staying here, this was her childhood home. She is so sad she came back here," He told me and I nodded. "Now remember what I said, she doesn't want to see me, so I'll let you go in alone. She should be sitting on a red chair, just talk with her and tell her she is ok," The man nodded and I went into the dark house.

The walls were scuffed, wallpaper torn here and there. The windows were so dirty, light could barely stream through while the air was stale and dust particles floated around lazily. I took a deep breath then had a coughing fit as I tried to squint and see down the hallway to my left, but I couldn't see much. To my right was a kitchen that looked unused and forbidding. Winding my way, I discovered nothing but dust. I finally entered a room and found an old lady with a cat on her lap, snoozing in a red chair.

"Umm excuse me," I fumbled as I approached her. The cat, a skinny thing, woke up and hissed at me.

"I've c-c-come to cheer you up!" I tried enthusiastically. The cat growled then fell silent as the lady woke up with a puzzled expression, "Can I help you?" She asked clearly confused.

"I thought you were sad, so I came to cheer you up!" I told her earning an uneven smile full of black teeth.

"Well thank you, what's your name?" She asked in a surprisingly strong voice. She looked haggard and worn, but seemed to be ok despite her age. "Khire," I told her and she nodded, green eyes thoughtful.

"Well Khire, thank you for coming to cheer me up, I'm afraid I've been having the worst time ever," She told me with a sigh, looking at the wall behind me as her eyes welled up. I walked up to her and grabbed her hand.

"Well let's go play, playing is fun!" I told her, tugging on her hand. She looked at me dearly and gave me a sad smile.

"Playing does sound fun," She said and started to get up.

I ran away from her back to the man to tell him we were gonna play. As I came out of the doorway, I couldn't see him.

"Sinth!" I shouted looking around for the old man.

"What's wrong?" The women asked coming up behind me.

"Your son was here, I wanted to tell him we were going to play," I told her then turned around. In her hand was a huge knife.

"There will be no playing today," She told me then lunged at me seeming to have no problem moving quickly. I screamed and began to cry then ran out the door. Not knowing where I was going, I ran as fast as my short, fat legs could move, lungs heaving. Fortunately she stopped at the doorway to her house, still I kept running, tears streaming down my face wanting only to get away.

I finally came out to the main part of the town and turned right, running with the flow of the people, I didn't know where I was, but I wanted to get away from the crazy lady. Suddenly, I was caught from behind and lifted up. I screamed, letting out a piercing shrill.

"Owe! Khire stop screaming it's me. What's wrong?" My father asked as he hugged me to him. I balled my eyes into his shirt. "Oh it's ok, I know you got lost and got scared, but what were you doing running off like that?" He asked me as he began to make his way back the way I had come.

"Nooo," I whined and tried to wiggle free.

"What's wrong?" He asked as he stopped.

"There was a mean lady with a knife, she ran after me," I told him a little hysterical.

"A mean lady with a knife? Well that doesn't sound nice. Don't worry, she won't hurt you, I'm here, nothing will hurt you while I've got you," He whispered into my ear until my crying stopped and I fell asleep in his arms, exhausted from my excursion and comforted by his words. Those words stayed printed in my mind thereafter.

CHAPTER #2

On a beautiful sunny day in late August, when I was six, I had another encounter with the man. He approached me as I was sitting in a cage full of puppies. My brother had picked me up and plopped me in with them thinking it would be funny seeing as I still looked like a pug. Laughing, he told me to play nice with the lab puppies and walked away to look around the pet store. That was Tellnair, he was far older than me as dad and mom had him when mom was 15 and dad was 16. Now 18 years old with coffee brown hair and green eyes, Tellnair was muscular and athletic, a wrestler at his school and claiming several gold medals in various competitions.

He was looking around the pet store, while back for a few days from university he wanted to get a pet. I didn't entirely know why he wanted an animal as he already had a Guardian. His Guardian was a lion, big and strong, the male lion followed Tellnair, his Protected, lazily. When I was old enough to understand about Guardians and Protected my father told me the story of the Guardians. It is believed that a long time ago there was a war between two groups of people. Based on fear, the non-magic users waged a war against the magic users. Finally the war, after thousands of deaths, ended and the people, magi and non-magi alike decided to sign a treaty.

At the time a small animal believed to be some type of cat approached a pair of twins, one being a magic user, the other not. The cat was a special cat and he could talk. He told the twins that he would serve one and only one. He said he would be a Guardian, a protector from harm and in return humans would ally with animals.

This was to create peace. The twins fought, but when it became obvious that neither would win unless the other was to die or give up the twins turned to the cat.

"We are twins and do not wish to harm each other, if you want to be a Guardian then you will have to choose us both for we will not be separated," the twins said and the cat dipped his head in surrender and split into two. From then on magi and non-magi knew peace.

After that animals walked out of the forests, from underground, the air, swimming through the waters to find their Protected whom they would share the rest of their lives with. One animal for one person, at a certain age usually early teens, a boy or girl will run off and follow the voice of their Guardian until they find each other. It can be a dangerous time, some never find their Guardians, dying from animal attacks or hunger, but it is a journey everyone undergoes without question. Not only were people given Guardians, but the Protected and the Guardians were given a special gift called a Wish. It allowed them to do anything, from change your skin colour to talk to animals. It was unique to everyone. However, there were a few boundaries to it, a turtle would not have a Wish that allowed it to fly, but it could have a Wish that allowed it to run fast. There seemed to be no boundaries on human Wishes, but I'm sure they exist.

As I was far too young I did not have a Guardian, but I was not concerned. I petted the puppies as they struggled to climb on me and lick my face or bite me in play. I giggled and squirmed to try and get away, but as I turned, there in the doorway stood a haggard man, tall and scarred. He smiled at me and walked over where he crouched down and let a puppy lick his fingers through the cage. A chill went up my spine, but I tried to just focus on the puppies and not the old man.

"Well hello Khire," The man said. Wary I smiled and tried to move farther away from the man, getting the puppies to follow me. "I am sorry for my mother, she can be very scary, but after she calmed down she was horrified with herself and is deeply sorry for scaring you. She wished you no harm, she was making supper at the time, a chicken and had pulled it out of the oven so it wouldn't burn. She forgot to put the knife down when she came to see what you were doing, that's all," The man said and I nodded.

I hadn't forgotten the lady, but I thought I would never see the man again. Seeing him here though made me fearful.

"She was scary," I said and turned to him. His ugly face was really close to mine, and I could smell a foul smell coming from him. He made me want to run away, but under his steady gaze I felt trapped.

"Yes she can be, but you helped her. She is feeling much better now, but she is still upset for scaring you. She would like to apologize; will you come with me and accept her apology? I know it's been some time, but she just can't get over it. She's gone nearly crazy thinking about what she did. I'll come in with you this time so you won't be alone. She won't be happy until she can apologize to you," The man said to me with a hopeful expression.

"Ok," And he nodded. I was a stupid, gullible child that thought the best of everyone and had no common sense.

"I will pick you up at lunch time on Monday ok then bring you back to school," the man smiled relieved at me.

"Can I bring my dad or my brother?" I asked him. I did not want to go anywhere alone with him.

"Sure," The man said and left.

☾

The next day at lunchtime I found the man waiting for me. I didn't know where my dad or brother was, but Sinth grabbed my hand.

"No! Where's my daddy?" I asked nearly in tears suddenly. I was easily frightened and I suddenly wanted the comfort of my dad.

"Your dad said he'd meet us there. I talked to him this morning," Sinth said and despite his age and my weight, managed to drag me away from the school. Somehow I left the school without the teachers worrying or seeing me. I followed the man back through the maze of alleys to the same decrepit stone house as before.

"Oh and here, I brought these, I think she will love you for them," He handed me a small handful of flowers, pretty as they were, I didn't like the smell of them. "Careful, deadly stuff for a little boy those flowers, but my mother loves them, give them to her," He said and ushered me into the house following right behind me.

"Where's my daddy?" I asked quietly as he pushed me into the house.

"Shhhh," Sinth said harshly and shoved me into the living room.

Stumbling in, I found the same lady sitting on the same red chair, staring off into space, face slack and seeming to have aged twenty years instead of one. The house smelled dusty and stale like the last time while there was an even thicker blanket of dust settling over everything. The women looked frail and tired this time and seemed to be too tired to even breath. Her chest rose slowly, but regularly, a slight rattle could be heard. Her skin was translucent, blue veins could be seen running down her arms and hands. To a small boy, she looked like death and I wanted to leave her and run as far away as I could from this place. Instead with a glance at Sinth who gave me a sharp look, I decided to be brave.

"Hello?" I said, but she didn't seem to hear. "Hello!" I shouted and she woke with a start. She looked over at me and smiled, green eyes warming.

"Oh it's you, why I was so sad when you ran off the other day, I was absolutely upset with myself. I am very sorry for giving you such a fright and look you brought me flowers, how sweet of you," She said and taking the flowers from me she smelt them. "Why these are just lovely, I will find a vase," She said, getting up and walking over to an old dusty table where a few empty vases stood, dusty and empty. She walked slowly and unsteady, her cat watching her carefully, but the lady made it across the room without mishap. She smelled them again, a funny smile coming over her face, then turned back to me. She stumbled, but caught herself before she fell.

"Are you ok?" I asked worried. The other day? It was a year ago? She must really be going crazy I thought to myself.

"Yes just tired, so how about that play date, I have some toys here somewhere. I think if you go upstairs, down the hall and the first door on the right there should be a box of toys. Dig through it and see what you can find," She told me as she sat back down in her chair. I ran to do as she said, but as I was going up the stairs I heard a hiss and a bang, when I looked behind me I watched her scrawny Guardian cat run out the door. I ran back to the lady who lay on the floor.

"Lady?" I asked and as I approached her, Sinth grabbed me by the arm.

"Oh dear, I think she fell asleep again, well that's ok, maybe you can play some other time. Come it's time you got back to school," he took my hand and dragged me away, but I looked back at the women. Something didn't feel right and I suddenly wanted to cry. She was so still and her Guardian had run away. In my mind I thought and knew she was dead, but I couldn't think of why. The last thing I looked at was the flowers in the vase on the dusty table, elegantly positioned in the old vase looking like a black and white picture with the only other colour being the purple, white and blue flowers.

CHAPTER #3

Panting like a puppy I sat on my deck eating a purple popsicle that dripped down my arm. It was an unusually warm day and I had had a good day at school. Coming home, Jakk, my older brother, and I had run around playing for a good part of the rest of the day. Now tired, I enjoyed my popsicle. Jakk was sitting beside me eating a blue one while dad made supper in the kitchen. I could smell the waft of foods coming from the open window nearby and my stomach growled at me. I giggled and finished off my popsicle as I waited impatiently for supper.

"Ok boys it's ready!" Dad finally called after some time and Jakk and I sprung to our feet and ran into the house. We quickly washed the stickiness from our hands then sat at the dinner table. Dad set down a plate with corn, rice, some cut up stake and a small spoon full of mashed potatoes. I, as usual, gobbled down my food too fast and was still hungry afterwards. "Khire, slow down," Dad said as he put some more potatoes on my plate. I nodded, but ate the potatoes quickly anyway. I sat waiting at the table swinging my feet as I waited for everyone else to finish. Dad said it was rude to eat and leave when others were eating and so I had to wait for him and Jakk to finish.

Just as they were about done Shean and Fetcher walked through the door.

"Supper's ready, good," Fetcher said eyeing the food. I groaned knowing I would have to wait even longer. "Khire," Dad warned. I smiled at him and stayed quiet. Fetcher sat down with a plate full of food and knowing it would torment me, began to eat very slowly, stopping to talk frequently to dad. He was 15, dark hair, green eyes, tall and built. He really enjoyed tormenting me. Shean though also enjoying my torment ate fast. He was taking riding lessons at a stable 30 minutes away and he wanted to get there early as usual. He was a good rider, people saying he learned to ride before he learned to walk. I didn't much care, I was afraid of the large animals, they moved to fast and could easily hurt me, and whenever dad took me to the stables I hated it. I did not want to be there and he knew that. Still he wanted me to have a hobby and he liked his kids to grow up with a sport or something. He took me once every two weeks to riding lessons, but I hated every minute of it. When I went I wasn't allowed to do anything. Other kids got to go faster or even lead themselves, but I was always kept at a walk and was lead around by a small girl holding a lead rope to a very fat pony who was unfortunate enough to be paired up with me.

"So are you gonna be going out tonight, should I be worried?" Dad asked Fetcher.

"No, I'm staying here tonight, it's Tonieal's party tonight, but I don't care to go to it," He replied.

"I thought you two were friends?" Dad asked confused.

"Tonieal has a new crowd these days," Fetcher said and dad nodded. "Well I'm so glad you know better than to follow him. I'm very thankful to have such smart children," Dad gloated happily. I looked at him quizzically, but said nothing.

☾

On a cold December morning I was sitting on the couch when I heard a door bang closed. It startled me from my doze and I got to my feet looking around. The house was quiet, Fetcher and I were the only ones home while the rest were out. "What was that?" I asked Fetcher as he looked at me confused. He got up and began to walk towards the door.

"It's really windy outside, the door probably wasn't closed properly and the wind just blew it open," He grumbled and left the room. I sat back on the couch and began to fall asleep when I felt a weird sense of someone watching me. I opened my eyes and sat up, but no one was there.

"Fetcher!" I called, but didn't hear anything. I looked around a little scared and tucked my feet under me. "Fetcher!" "Shut up Khire!" He yelled back as he came back into the room.

"I was scared," I said pouting.

"Of what, you think the boogeyman's gonna getcha? Grow up," He said and sat back down. I didn't say anything else, but from then on I began to get the feeling of being watched and followed and I didn't like it.

CHAPTER #4

It was a little over a year when I met the old man again. I was sitting on a bench in the park when he came over to me. The sun was shining down warmly and I was a little distracted with all the other kids running around playing. I remained on my bench however, knowing my dad didn't like me on the jungle gym when he wasn't here. Still I was allowed to walk to the park to sit and watch as the park wasn't far from my house.

"Hello Khire," Sinth said happily.

"Hello," I said and looked at him unsure of what he was going to say next.

"How have you been?" He asked me as he sat down on the bench.

"Good, how have you been?" I asked him nicely. What I really wanted to do was push him off the bench, but I knew that would be rude.

"Really good and I have a favour to ask of you. You did such a good job making my mother feel better, why when she woke up later that day she was happier then any day I can remember she being. She cleaned the house and took control of her life again. She moved away and is doing much better now," he told me smiling.

"That's really good to hear," I nodded and tried to smile.

"Since you did such a good job and like to make people happy, I thought I'd ask you again if you could help me. You see I have a very sick sister, she has a disease and she needs to take medication, but lately she has been refusing to take it. She has become very ill. Would you be able to visit her and give her medication? It will save her life if you do," Startled by the fact that this was a life or death situation, I gasped.

"I will!" I said with all the determinism in the world. The old man laughed and smiled at me.

"Good, now I will go pick up her medication, I will meet you back here in say two hours?" he asked as he got up.

"Ok," I said without hesitation. He nodded pleased and walked away.

"Khire, who was that man you were talking to?" Fetcher asked as he walked over to me.

"Just some old man," I said enjoying the fact that I knew something he didn't.

"Don't talk to him, don't hang around him," Fetcher warned and I looked at him confused.

"But he's really nice, I like him," I said even though I didn't. Fetcher shook his head.

"He's bad news, do what I say," He commanded and I looked at him, arms crossed frowning.

"Listen to me or you'll regret the day you didn't," he said and if that wasn't foreshadowing then I don't know what is, because I didn't listen and I have since regretted it.

I went back to the park later, slipping away from the house silently. The old man was already there sitting on the same bench I had sat on earlier. When he saw me he smiled.

"Hello," he greeted,

"Hello," I smiled hesitantly, seeing him still sent shivers down my back and I always forgot how much I hated to look at him.

It was four o'clock as he led me down some strange alleyways that I knew were the old streets of Vale Darra. Cobbled and worn, I tried not to fall over the uplifted stones that lay cracked and discarded on the dirty ground. There was a very stale, bad stench in the air and it was colder and darker then it was in the park. I saw people sleeping on the ground down side-alleys laying curled against walls, dressed in very little clothing. Huffing all the way, but trying to stay right beside the old man least some street rat come for me. I found myself tiring and getting mad that I couldn't even keep pace with a decrepit old man.

We finally came out of the alleyways to a big gate, black and threatening, they were heavy set and caught the eye before the big house it guarded. The house itself was beautiful, one of the more wealthier people lived here, with rolling hills in the background, a big garden out front and the big blue and green house in the middle, the people here were well off and happy with life.

"Hello Sinth," A women said as she approached the gate. She laughed and looked me over. Sneering at me, she crossed her arms and looked me up and down.

"I said bring someone capable, not a fat boy," She smirked.

"He is more than capable, just you wait," Sinth growled and patted my head.

I was unsure of what they were talking about, but I didn't like the women. She was hard eyed and her skin looked like leather. She walked with a hitch and half her face didn't move.

"Whatever, it's your head not mine," She said and saying a few words, the gate before me split apart and Sinth and I slipped through, the gate closing up behind us.

"Ok fat boy, here's the bottle. You're going to go in there and smile and give it to the lady, got that?" she demanded.

"It's ok Khire, this is a friend of mine, she is really worried about my sister and she's just trying to help. She can be a little harsh though," the last part he said while glaring at the women. I nodded and took the bottle from the women, it was small and full of a pale yellow liquid.

"She needs to drink it, ok," Sinth told me and I nodded.

I walked away from them towards the big house, unsure and confused. Why was I always going alone into these things? I didn't know what was going on or what I was supposed to do. And why didn't this medication look anything like the medication I took when I was sick? I found a back door into the house and went inside, it was well lit and very warm inside. A carpeted floor led me down a hallway to a staircase. I saw people walking around and began to become confused. Why couldn't they help the lady?

"You boy, what are you doing here?" Someone yelled at me.

"I'm here to help the lady?" I said stupidly.

"They train the servants way to young, but whatever. Go to the kitchen and get the lady's food then take it up to her," The man told me. "Food? Where is the lady?" I asked and he looked at me frazzled.

"Upstairs in her room of course, third floor, it's the only door on that floor it's not that hard to find," He growled at me. I nodded and ran off, not knowing where the kitchen was, but being too frightened to ask.

Luckily it wasn't hard to smell it out, I found it and as soon as I walked in a fat lady turned to me.

"Oh and what can I do for you dearie?" She asked pleasantly. I smiled at her, happy to see someone nice. I thought thinking I should just ask for food for myself and give up on this excursion. If Sinth wanted to help his sister, he could do it himself, but then I thought of the lady dying and felt like I could at least do this last thing for Sinth.

"I was told to get the lady's food," I told the cook kindly.

"Oh ok, well aren't you young, but alright," She said then retrieved a tray from a counter. It was big and I didn't know if I could carry it, but I managed somehow then walked away to where I had seen the stairs. Amazingly I managed to get to the third floor after what must have been an hour. I was huffing and sweating and tired, having to sit on the top step just to catch my breath.

"I'm too fat for this, why does it have to be me?" I asked myself.

I looked at the bottle and then at her food. A glass of something stood on the tray and I poured the vial into the glass, thinking that it would be easier that way to drink it. I didn't feel like talking to someone anymore so I figured if I just mixed it with her drink she would drink it and I could leave. I picked the tray back up and went to the only door on that floor. I knocked and a man opened the door.

"Finally, the Lady asked for food two hours ago. Come in!" He snarled and I followed him inside where I was told to place the tray by a huge bed. In the bed sat a woman, older than I thought she would be and smiling. She didn't look sick, she was smiling and laughing with a serving girl, brown eyes sparkling. She had a few wrinkles, but her brown hair didn't have any grey in it. She turned to me and I put the tray down and smiled.

"Well who's this?" She asked the man behind me.

"A new servant, I apologize for the lateness of the food," He said and she waved him away.

"It's fine, what's your name?" She asked me kindly. I wanted to answer, but I could practically feel the mean look the man was giving me and so I didn't answer her question instead I said, "I brought you your food, I'm sorry if it's cold, but please enjoy," I told her quietly and she nodded.

"Well alright then," She took the glass and sipped from it.

"Mmmm this is really good," She ate her food and drank her drink then thanked me again. The man handed me the tray with the empty dishes.

"Away with you now," He snapped and pushed me out the door.

I dreaded going down the stairs, I was so tired I thought I'd fall down them. After a little while though I returned the tray back to the kitchen then ran for the back door. Legs pumping. I ran across the lawn to where Sinth and the women waited, heaving the whole way.

"I want to go home now," I whined. My legs were on fire, my throat was so dry and my shirt was so sticky with sweat it was uncomfortable.

"Did she drink it?" The women asked me, grabbing my arms tightly.

"Yes," I said and was about to cry when Sinth pushed her away and handed me a chocolate bar. And like that my mind was distracted by chocolate.

"Well done Khire, you did so good. I am so proud of you," He said and took me by the hand as the fence let us out. We walked back to the park where he left me to run back home, the chocolate bar finished by then.

When I got home it was dark and well past supper time. I walked inside and found my dad standing there arms crossed and very unhappy.

"Hello," I said confused. He did not seem happy to see me.

"Where were you?" He demanded. I was so tired of mean people I began to pout and was about to go into a full-blown cry when he picked me up and carried me upstairs to my bed.

"I'm sorry I was just so worried about you, you can't do that to me ok. Don't ever do that to me again. You left and I didn't know where you were," He told me as he helped me get undressed then tucked me into bed. He kissed my forehead then patted my cheek. "Promise me you won't go anywhere without telling me again," He said and I nodded.

"I promise," I said sniffling. He nodded and left me then. Jakk turned around and looked at me from where he lay on his bed across the room. The light from the nightlight illuminating part of his face, making his eyes look big and black.

"Where were you? We were worried," He asked, eyes wide.

"I was helping someone," I answered and he looked confused at me, but too tired to ask more, he lay back down and fell asleep. I was so tired I forgot that I hadn't eaten supper.

The next day I ran downstairs to get breakfast. In my usual hurry I almost tripped down the stairs, fortunately I managed to catch myself on the railing and unceremoniously sit down before I fell down.

"Khire," I heard my dad's voice call from his bedroom. I looked over, confused why he was still in his room and not downstairs making breakfast.

"Yes," I said walking to his room. He sat on his bed, dressed and ready, but not getting up to face the day. "Are you ok?" I asked worried.

"Yes, I am now, but you realize what you did last night was unacceptable? Your grounded, get back into your room and stay there," He told me and I looked confused at him for a moment. He had never grounded anyone before.

"Can I get something to eat?" I asked him and he shook his head.

"Not right now, you will be fine for now. Now get back into your room," He said and got up.

Pouting I went back to my room where Jakk was just waking up. I sat on my bed unhappy and glared at the wall thinking the world was completely against me. My stomach growled in protest and I slouched deeper into my bed. Dad stood in the doorway and looked at me.

"That is not good for your posture," He said finally. Jakk looked at me then back at dad.

"Can't he come play with me?" Jakk asked.

"No, you can come with me, but Khire is going to stay in his room all day," With that he left and Jakk climbed out of bed and onto mine.

"What did you do?" He asked me. "You were gone for a long time yesterday I thought someone kidnapped you," He said though he sounded more fascinated with the idea then upset.

"I was helping an old man. He said his sister was sick and he wanted me to cheer her up and give her medicine so I went with him to his sister's house and cheered her up," I told him quietly.

"Well that sounds nice, but you should never go somewhere with a stranger, you are supposed to walk away from them," Jakk told me, being only 8 yet far smarter than me nonetheless.

"Oh," was all I said.

Jakk got off my bed and left me then. I was grumpy that I had to stay in my room for having done nothing wrong. After sitting for a few minutes simmering in my own anger I climbed off my bed and left my room. Determined to do what I wanted to do no matter what anyone else said.

"You better get back to your room before dad yells at you Khire," Shean said as he emerged from his room, still in his fleece, blue Pj pants.

"I don't want to. I didn't do anything wrong," I said and was about to walk down stairs when dad came to the bottom of the stairs.

"Back in your room now!" he yelled angry.

I stood my ground and pouted yelling back and stomping my foot, "I didn't do anything wrong!"

"Back in your room Khire!" He began to come up the stairs and as scared as I was, I continued to stay where I was.

"I'm hungry," I complained.

"I was going to bring you some food, but as you have shown me you can't behave and I can't trust you I am not giving you any breakfast. Now get back into your room,"

"I didn't do anything wrong!" I repeated.

"Yes you did. You did something very wrong and you are going to stay in your room until you are sorry for what you did," He said and took me by the arm.

"I was just helping the old man," I whined.

"What old man?" Dad stopped and asked me.

"He said his sister was sick and he wanted me to cheer her up and give her medicine," I told him thinking he would let me go if I told him what happened.

"Never ever talk to strangers Khire, never ever go with them anywhere. You understand me? Never ever trust a stranger. What did the man look like?" "I…. don't remember," I said cringing back as dad frowned.

"He was old, I'd say in his 60's," Fetcher said as he came upstairs.

"You seen him?" Dad asked him.

"Ya he was talking to Khire when we were at the park yesterday. I told Khire to stay away from him," Fetcher added and dad turned on me again.

"So you didn't listen to Fetcher and you didn't listen to me. You ran off with some old man without telling anyone and not knowing who the man was. Then I told you to stay in your room, but you disobeyed me multiple times. Khire I think myself a fair man, but your actions are unacceptable. Do you even understand what you did, what could have happened?" I was starting to get upset, but I was also angry I still didn't think I did anything wrong.

"Hey guys! The Duchess of Vloor is dead!" Someone yelled from downstairs.

"What?" Dad and Fetcher said together. Aster, my second eldest brother appeared at the bottom of the stairs. He was a skinny, lanky thing with glasses and the nicest brother I had.

"The Duchess of Vloor is dead. She was found dead in her bed this morning," He responded.

"Oh dear," Dad said sadly.

"What's wrong? Who's dead?" I asked confused.

Dad went downstairs, Fetcher, Shean and I following him. We stopped in front of the TV, centred in the room though pushed to the wall; a few couches and chairs surrounded it. On the TV a news reporter was talking about a death. They showed pictures of a big blue and green house then a picture of the women who died. I gasped once I saw it was the same lady I had given the food and drink to. Suddenly my mind went back to the older lady, she had also died after I had visited her. Upset I ran back upstairs to my room crying. I didn't know why they were dead, but I felt responsible. Dad came back up to my room and sat down beside me, putting his arm around me.

"It's ok Khire, she was a very sick women, she's in a better place," He told me as he pulled me into his lap and rocked me back and forth.

"I killed them both," I whined.

"What?" he asked startled. He looked down at me, but I couldn't meet his eyes.

"The old man asked me to cheer his mother up, I gave her flowers and then she died. And yesterday I killed the lady on the TV," I cried.

"Shhh now, you didn't kill them. That old man is just mean ok that's why I don't want you to hang around him or listen to him. He was probably just trying to scare you by telling you that you were a bad boy. You didn't kill them Khire. You couldn't have," he told me, but I didn't listen. Deep down I knew what I had done.

I didn't see the old man for a while after that, but soon he began to appear everywhere and though I did everything I could to avoid him, he still got to me. I tried to stay with my family whenever I went out or else I would just stay home, but I began to see the man everywhere. Standing in my backyard, across the street as I watched TV in the living room or outside the fence when I was at school and so I became very fearful. I would tell people that an old man was following me, but they didn't believe me, whenever I tried to point out the man he was gone.

After the world's longest stubborn streak my dad finally realized horses weren't my thing and so I started doing gymnastics. I didn't like it at first, I was terribly fat to be doing anything really physical, but I began to enjoy it after a while. I became very good at it and though I was still overweight I was still able to do more than my classmates could. I finally had something that I was good at and I loved it. I got made fun of constantly, but it was a moment in my life I could smile at no matter the criticism I got.

CHAPTER #5

Standing in a dark alleyway, I peered out at the dark street below. It was a cold December night and I hadn't bothered to grab a warm coat thinking I wouldn't need it. It had been a warm day and so I hadn't anticipated that it could get so cold. Across the street people walked on by, talking, laughing, hurrying to get into vehicles and drive away. I stood shivering in the shadows, my magic doing its best to warm me up. I was short for my age, at 10 years old I was still just a short, fat, little boy. I drew a small thin blade from my sleeve and moved into position. I could see a man in a long coat walking down the sidewalk across the street. Separated by two lanes and other people I had to be very careful to get this right. I was perfectly poised and after a few more steps the man turned to smile at a couple walking past. I threw the knife and it whirled through the air and punctured his neck. With a gurgle he fell to the ground and a women screamed. I ran away deeper into the alleyway, my job done for the night.

I was deep in the dark and secluded alleys when I happened upon a friend of mine. Isaac sat on the ground playing with a rat. Giggling, Isaac tormented the dirty animal, poking it, grabbing it and stopping it from escaping. The rat threatened to bite the boy, but Isaac was too fast and with ease, grabbed the rat and tossed it in the air, all the while giggling merrily.

"Hello Isaac," I said and the boy looked at me. He forgot about the rat and in that instant the rat ran for freedom.

"Hello Dusky," Isaac said with a huge grin. His once white-blond hair was now in long tatters, dirty and unwashed for many years. His pale skin was scraped, bruised and dirty while his clothes were torn and filthy.

He had once had a loving family, but the boy was crazy, he was energetic and a complete lunatic. He got angry and violent easily and on a fateful day his brother stole a toy from him, Isaac killed him then burnt down the house. He killed his mother, father, two brothers and a baby sister that day only to be found by Midnight. Isaac was only 8 at the time and now 10 he had two years' experience of being a killer, but he was to mentally unstable to be reliable. Midnight treated him more as a pet then an actual apprentice. Still Isaac enjoyed it, he liked killing and he loved to cause people pain.

With his lunatic laugh, large blue eyes and wide grin showing small sharp teeth, he made everyone uneasy. Everyone, except me. I liked him, despite his evil ways, he was the closest thing I have ever had to a friend and though I couldn't trust him, I still confided in him most of the time. He was a very compatible person when he was happy and I knew him well enough to make sure he stayed happy.

"What are you up to?" I asked him as I came and crouched down beside him.

"I was playing with a rat… where did he go?" He began to look around, "Ratty, rat, ratty rat," He giggled, but then lost interest again. "What were you doing Dusky?" He asked me.

"I had a target, I just hit it," I told him and he began to bounce happily.

"Another one?" He asked and I shook my head.

"Not tonight Isaac I have stuff to do still. What are you doing the rest of the night?" I asked him and got to my feet. After a thought he stood up too.

"I am going to find Ratty," He declared and with that walked away looking for the poor unfortunate animal.

I turned around as I sensed someone standing nearby. "Hello Midnight, how is your night going so far?" I asked pleasantly. I turned around to face the scarred man who had turned me into the assassin known as Dusk. He wasn't all that old, only fifty-five, his face and hands were covered in old scars, while his skin was blotchy and his black-grey hair was always dishevelled. Still he was lively and energetic.

"Good, you hit your target?" He asked happily and I nodded.

"Wonderful, I have another assignment for you to do. Start being more aware of a boy named Gorden Bry. He goes to the school next door to yours actually so it shouldn't be too hard,"

"I already know him. He is a very good student, but every night he goes home and gets drunk. Then he goes out and parties. He's violent and unpredictable. He likes to spend money on things that are illegal, spends a lot of his nights at a brothel named Sissy's and in the morning he goes to school and pretends the night never happened," I said, bored already.

"Very good, well then I expect him to find his grave by tomorrow night then," He said then turned away and left. I glared at him, hating him telling me what to do.

I could never say no to him. Over the years he had stalked me and slowly began to train me to be an assassin. Giving me little jobs here and there; he taught me about weapons. I don't really know how exactly I became Dusk, I just know one day he handed me a knife and I killed a rat that had been unfortunate enough to be in my way. After that, I moved on to other animals and soon people. I think my loneliness and his interest in me slowly drew me to him. Despite my hatred for him, he was the only one to pay attention to me. When I did well he would congratulate me, but when I did bad, he would punish me. Still, the fact that I had someone who cherished me drove me to try hard to make him proud of me.

I meandered my way around the city, slowly going in the direction of home, but I didn't want to go home. I never wanted to go home. It wasn't home to me anymore and many times I had thought of running away. But something kept me there; I would walk away and find myself back home at some point again. My feet would always betray me and when I stayed out all night, sleeping on the streets by morning I would be hurrying home. My family didn't know I was gone I made sure of that. A gifted child I was, a young mage in training. I started my magic training when I was seven and since then have excelled in it. I already had one ribbon I could call upon at will.

Ribbons were a marker for a mage who developed and trained their magic. At some point when they were strong enough, a thin wisp of a ribbon in a unique colour would appear whenever they used their magic and swirl around the mage. It was a sign that the person could do magic. As the mage got stronger the ribbon became more visible and thicker until you became an exceptionally strong mage and the ribbon would split into two, but that was for elite mages. People who studied and worked with magic may never gain two ribbons, but may only get one very thick ribbon. There were also two types of ribbons, those for the mages and those for assassins. Because the two used magic in different ways, their ribbons developed differently. For mages, their ribbon would float around them, circling them lazily. An assassins ribbons twirled and twisted through the air, swirling around the assassins body, going around them, over them, under them, it was a fast and angry movement that lashed out and only got more threatening as the assassin got stronger. Along with that, the colour of the ribbon was more unique, my ribbon was a blue-purple colour, just darker then a wisp, it was a good width for someone so young.

Whenever I did magic the ribbon would appear and I would marvel at my skills. As I grew stronger I knew I would be able to do magic without making the ribbon appear. It would be very easy for people to know I was up to no good if they seen my ribbon, so I never do magic in front of my family. I don't even think they know I can do magic.

Another difference between magi and assassins were the fact that our magic was used differently. Magi were trained by a trainer in a group of other students all of varying ages as magic could show up in any person at any age. The teacher would train out of a book and the students were taught healing, how to find objects and any useful tool that the King of Vale Darra would find useful. Assassins were first apprentices trained by a master, there was usually only one apprentice per assassin and the apprentice learned magic that dealt with death. Our magic helped our bodies when we were hurt so that even if all the bones in our bodies were broken our magic would take control of our bodies and make us keep running. It stabilized our broken bones, stopped us from bleeding to death, provided warmth when it was cold and cold when we here hot. As we became stronger with magic, our magic began to take over our bodies so that it worked better than our own instincts. Magic was everything to assassins. We breathed magic, it was our blood, our heart beat, our very existence.

I found my way in front of the blue two-story house with a pointed roof and front porch. Small patches of grass out front were barely considered a front lawn, but the back yard extended back to the forest that stood just over a hundred yards behind our house. I walked to the side of the house where my open window awaited me. I leapt up, my magic throwing me at my window. It was hard to do considering the extra weight I carried, but I liked to think it helped strengthen my magic faster. Diving through, I landed on the ground silently; using magic to mask any sound and quickly tore off my shirt, pants, shoes and socks and dove into my bed. Falling asleep was my favourite time, it was the only time I had to myself.

Some months after that in April, I woke to the sound of pounding rain.

"Schools cancelled, the bus driver can't see!" Dad called up the stairs. Smiling I snuggled into my covers and let myself doze off. As soon as I was at the place between sleep and awake I heard something. A creak, sock feet tip toeing across my wooden bedroom floor. I pretended to sleep hoping whoever it was would go away, unfortunately it ended up with them throwing themselves on me and yelling "Happy Birthday!" in my ear.

"It's not my birthday," I told Jakk and he snickered.

"Oh yes it is. You're getting up, you're going to get ready and then we are going out!" He said cheerily and I growled.

"How about for my birthday we all just sleep. School is cancelled, let's just take it as a sign that someone wants Khire to sleep," I said, eyes still closed.

"Nope. Not gonna happen sorry," He pulled back my blankets then grabbed my arm and literally started to pull me out of my bed.

"Jakk!" I yelled as the rest of my family came into my room. "Ya know guys I think I'd rather just sleep for my birthday. What better birthday could there be then sleeping the whole day," I whined, finally opening my eyes and looking at my family.

It was a large family and I the youngest of 6 children. My dad and mother had been high school sweethearts and started their life together young, having kids until one day at four o'clock my mom was giving birth to me. Something went wrong and she died and thus I came into the world placed into the arms of a nurse instead of my mother. Living in the hospital a good three weeks before dad decided to take me home. He was still too sad to do much, lifeless he didn't go to work, didn't care much about anything. I began to get sick and that was when a neighbour came and started taking care of my brothers and me. Cleaning the house as well as trying to help my dad, I was lucky I guess for if it wasn't for that kind lady I would have died. Slightly ironic because she took pity on us so I survived to grow up to become a killer. After about a year dad started to get his act together and began to care for us again. He took back his life, got his job back and became a dad once again. His older kids Tellnair, Aster and Fetcher were old enough to more or less take care of themselves. Tellnair even taking care of me, but when dad straightened up, Tellnair was more than happy to hand me over to him. I blame him for making me fat, he felt terrible about neglecting me and so he gave me everything I ever wanted and most things I wanted was something edible.

Back to the present, my family stared at me like I was supposed to do something. I stared back waiting for them to just give up and go away.

"You're getting dressed and we are going out," Jakk declared.

"I thought you said the bus was cancelled because of the weather," I replied as I sat up.

"Pfff it's just rain, besides it's melting all the snow," Dad said waiving my excuses away. I growled, but got out of bed and found some clothes on the ground that wasn't too dirty.

"I got you a new outfit to wear actually," Dad said and left to go get his present. One thing about large families was that you never got a lot of presents, which was usually fine by me. When I was younger I loved gifts, but since realizing my life would never be happy, I began to push every happiness away including presents. I always asked for nothing for my birthday and Christmas and any other holiday my dad bought gifts for.

He came back with a box wrapped in wrapping paper with airplanes on it. I smiled, I had always thought of being a pilot, I loved the idea of flying. He passed me the present and I tore into it, excited despite my earlier mood. Uncovering the present nestled inside I found a blue t-shirt and black khakis. Dressing into them at my father's request everyone including me was surprised to see that they were too big. I was still rather fat, but I wasn't overmuch like I was a few years back.

"You lost weight. Well I guess that's a good thing, but I'd rather the clothes fit," My dad said slightly miserably.

"Oh it's ok, I'm sure I can gain it back," I said rolling my eyes and laughing. I took the clothes back off and found some others that were too big as well.

"We will take them back and exchange them," Dad said happily. He was one of the few men that liked shopping; he loved to be outside surrounded by people. The crowd's dull roar was his sense of peace.

Later that day, we were all sitting at a table in the food court of Vale Darra's mall. Bags lying on the ground around us greatly expressed our shopping spree. Everyone either bought me a gift or told me it was already at home. They also got something else, me asking them to shop for themselves so I didn't look like an idiot bringing home a bunch of bags. I enjoyed a sandwich and fries while others had hamburgers, or wraps.

"So Khire, now that your birthday is over, what did you want for your birthday?" Dad asked nonchalantly.

"Nothing," I said similarly.

"Come on, your 11, how can you not want something?" He asked annoyed.

"Simple. I just don't want anything. I am happy to have a good day with you guys and that's it," I said and smiled.

Truthfully that's really all that mattered. Ever since Midnight came into my life, I felt my life snatched away from me. I pushed my family away from me to try and protect them, but I hated it. I loved them and wanted them to be proud of me, most of all I wanted to be able to tell them about my day without them being horrified or running to call the police. I hated the distance that was wedged between us. I felt like I hardly knew them anymore and I knew they felt the same about me. Many times I had overheard dad talking to someone about me, saying he was very concerned and felt like he had lost me. He blamed himself and I hated myself for making him feel that way. He was the best dad in the world, I was just the worst son.

"Well is there anything you want to do then?" Dad asked.

"Hmmm. Can we go to the beach?" I asked. I loved to swim, I never passed up an opportunity to go swimming.

"Okay!" Dad said practically jumping out of his seat, despite the fact that the water would be freezing, he was very excited for me to have asked for something.

We grabbed our bathing suits from home then headed to the beach. I immediately ran into the freezing water while the rest moved more slowly. We were there for a good five minutes before dad, who stayed by the car, said its cold and that I was crazy. I smiled and got out of the water shivering, but happy.

"We will come back when its warm," Dad said simply with a smile. We got home and walked inside, all of us carrying our bags in with us.

"Ok, I'll get supper going, Fetcher help Aster, he looks lost," Dad said as Aster looked around confused.

"No I'm fine, where's Jakk?" It was at that moment that we realized Jakk wasn't here, he had stepped out of the car right behind me only moments before, but now he was gone. I went to look outside, but didn't see him, his bags lay on the driveway looking forgotten.

"Jakk!" I called looking for him.

"Khire!" I heard my name called from inside the house and I went to the kitchen to see everyone, but Jakk there.

"Yes?" I asked my father.

"I think Jakk has left on his Journey," he told me and after a moment I nodded.

It made sense, he seemed distracted all day and he was at that age where he would leave to find his Guardian. Still I was a little mystified and upset that he was all of a sudden gone.

"Ok," I said and nodded again.

"We still have some more presents and I know where Jakk hid his for you, I'll go get them all," Aster said as he headed to the stairs. Fetcher went to retrieve the forgotten bags outside.

"You know Jakk would never leave you especially on your birthday," Dad said to me as if I were about to cry. I was very confused by the way everyone looked at me expectantly, but I smiled anyway.

"I know," I said meeting my dad's eyes.

"He loves you and was very excited to give you the present he bought you," Dad began.

"Dad I'm ok, I understand. You're talking to me as if I am upset about this. I'm not stupid," I said incredulous. That day was the first time I ever talked back to my dad. Everyone looked at me surprised and wide eyed as if I had pulled out a gun and asked them "any last words?" But I hadn't, they for some reason were just being overly concerned.

"Ok, here we gooo..." Aster trailed off as he came into the quiet kitchen. As much as I wanted to leave the house and just run free I knew that if I left at that moment my dad would think something was wrong with me. That would lead to an endless amount of questions, questions I didn't care to hear and I sure didn't want to answer.

"Ok, which one-first," I said going to a chair and plopping myself down in it, being patient while Aster looked at everyone else confused.

"Ok, you will get your cake after dinner," Dad said and turned to the fridge to start taking out food for tonight. Aster handed me gift after gift and I unwrapped it, smiling, thanking everyone, acting happy all the while. I did enjoy presents, truly I did. Well mostly because someone had thought of me and went out of their way to get me something. However, as I opened up gift after gift I began to struggle to hold my smile. They were presents any boy in this day and age wanted, a console with video games that entailed killing zombies and racing cars. I got a game about flying planes, but as I read the back of it I discovered it was an army game where I was a pilot and I had to shoot down enemy planes. As much as I wanted to be a normal boy, I did not like getting video games that I ended up killing people, even if they weren't real. I did that in real life.

"Do you want to set it up?" Aster asked still smiling. He had a gift for holding a smile it seemed, no matter what went wrong, he always looked happy. I guess that's why everyone liked him so much.

"Sure," I said and hopped off my chair, walking with him to the living room and sitting in front of the TV. I began to take wires, the console, a controller, a sensor bar and other objects out of the box while Aster grabbed the instructions. I had it set up and TV turned on before Aster could get through the instructions manual.

"It's set up," I told him and he looked up from the small white pamphlet.

"Ummm well that was easy," He said surprised. I gave him a quick smile and turned back to the TV, putting a disk into the console and taking a controller back to the couch with me. I didn't see which game I had put in, turns out it was the zombie one. Quickly I shot and slashed every zombie in sight, suffering few serious injuries. I hated that even though this was a game I still viewed it as real life, I couldn't help but think that zombie that had cut my arm would have actually cut off my arm, leaving me vulnerable.

"You don't have to play the game to make me happy," Dad said coming to pet my head and stand beside me.

"I'm having fun," I said unenthusiastically. He sighed and left me then. Tellnair came over and sat close beside me, close enough that I actually lost my balance and ended up getting myself killed. Surprised how easily I died and not liking it at all, I turned to Tellnair to see what he wanted.

"Sorry," he said a little taken aback. I didn't know what my expression on my face was, but it probably said many words.

"It's ok," I said taking too long to reply.

"Listen, why don't we go out and play?" he said, finding that laughable I smiled at him.

"You and me play?" I asked him.

"Or not….. listen I don't know what's wrong and I understand we all go through an awkward stage, but I am your brother and I love you. If there is anything you want to talk about, no matter what, you can tell me," He said so seriously, eyes staring right into me, I opened my mouth to say something then forgot what I was going to say. I sighed and put the controller on the small table in the middle of the room. An awkward stage was not what I was going through; it was so much more than that, I actually wished it was just an awkward stage.

"I'm fine, honestly. I know I am not as excited about my birthday as you guys wanted me to be, but I don't care about my birthday ok and it's not because I'm older and think myself too good for presents.

I simply would just rather have a good day with you. Why does being officially one year older make the day any more special than any other day?" I asked him, blurting it out before I could stop myself.

"It's your birthday…" He began.

"Yes, it is that, but really, just because I'm older doesn't mean I am any more special then I was yesterday or tomorrow. I like spending time with you guys, that's all I need," I told him and was about to get off the couch when he grabbed my arm for me to stay. He kept a hold of me to make sure I sat there while he spoke.

"Ok, and we all have a right to our own beliefs, but we were very excited for you. We had this whole day planned out and you really are a bubble popper Khire," He said making sure I understood.

"Ya I know that, sorry but I will be forever cursed with the bubble popping plague, but I don't care," I said folding my arms across my chest. Tellnair looked at me as if I was a new person and probably to him I was. I had changed drastically over the years being once a happy little boy to being quiet and introverted. Apparently now I was moody and cranky and I understood why they didn't like that, but I wasn't about to change for their sake. If they wanted me they should have fought to save me. The fact that they had left me for Midnight to steal, made me think that they didn't care for me, and I disliked how unimportant I was in their lives. It was at this moment I realized I resented them all and their happiness.

Everyone else had somebody. Tellnair and Aster were very close and so was Fetcher and Shean. Jakk and I were close, but many times these days he left me for his friends, of course no one else knew that, but him and I, but that was the truth of it. Once upon a time Jakk and I were inseparable, but he had made it very clear that I was not to hang around him at school any more. I didn't understand his reasoning so I had gotten angry at him and called him names. Another thing my family didn't know about me was that I had a foul mouth and Jakk got a good brunt of it on a sunny day. He ended up tackling me to the ground and hitting me, then as I got back up he pushed me to the ground again. I stayed there in the dirt until he left, then I got up and went to sit in a corner away from the other kids. I had no friends and I had just lost my brother. Too angry to feel hurt, I sat on a picnic bench in the shade and glared at the kids around me. Not even the teachers cared to come over to see what was wrong. Everyone seemed to forget me and at that moment I decided to disappear in their lives. I was a ghost, I was invisible to them and the only thing they would think about when recalling the little boy that sat alone at school would be a blank thought.

Months past and my relationships with people got worse, I was a ghost, but a hated ghost. Whenever someone dined to recognize me, they learned very quickly to hate me. I was partnered with others in gym class and chemistry, the unfortunate students that would beg the teacher when they were partnered with me to have a new partner. I hated it also, the other students I found to be very dumb, they were simple and a distraction. When I had to do an assignment I did very well on my own, if anything the only thing going for me was that I was a straight A+ student. It was the only thing that I was good at, so I tried my hardest to keep it that way thinking I don't need friends, but if I can be a great student then that was as good as it could get for me.

It wasn't until I was twelve years old that something positive happened in my life. I was sitting in the shade on my normal picnic bench when a group of girls walked by. By luck, fate or chance just as they passed me so too did a group of grade threes. As it had just rained the day before leaving behind many puddles, the girls shrieked with displeasure as the boys splashed mud onto their dresses. Annoyed that a little bit of mud would cause such an uproar I got off of my bench and went to them. Somehow when I spoke, my voice was polite.

"Are you ok?" I asked the girls. They looked at me, gasping as if I had popped up from the ground. Two strawberry blond girls with green eyes and freckles and one dark haired, dark eyed girl.

"Did I hear the wind speaking?" A girl asked. She had pigtails and a low-pitched voice and I wasn't really surprised that was her first remark.

"It must have been," said another of her posse with her pigtails swinging as she shook her head. Only the little girl with dark wavy hair and olive skin answered me.

"Ya we're ok," She said meekly. She looked at me, head slightly tilted to the ground as if she couldn't hold her head up.

"Miranna!" The other girls cried, mad that she dared to speak to The Ghost.

"He asked if we were ok, I answered," She said though with little defiance in her small voice. She wasn't new, just very shy. I remembered her from my younger years, teachers would always encourage her to speak, but the most I ever heard come out of her mouth was the words she was saying right now.

"Sorry to ha…," I began, sneering at the girls as a teacher came over.

"What is all this screaming for… oh ladies how did you get that mud on your dresses?" The teacher asked emphasizing the ess's in her raspy voice.

Without her even noticing me, I knew this would somehow become my fault. She was just one of those teachers that favoured girls. Blond, short hair cut into a bell shape with a long unflattering blue dress. She stood there with her hands on her hips as if this were a real serious matter.

"He did it," One of the girls said pointing to me. Glaring at her I was about to call her a liar when Miranna did it for me.

"It was some grade threes they were running by. Khire just asked if we were ok," She said sweetly. I looked at her completely shocked that she would speak up for me in front of others and know my name. The teacher just as surprised, stuttered before finally saying something coherent.

"Well whatever the case may be, you girls go into the washroom and wash up before that mud dries……. K-Khire," The teacher said, forgetting my name. I looked at her curious as to why she would say my name. "Could you be a gentlemen and escort these young ladies to the bathroom please," She asked nicely though I could tell in her eyes she was suspicious of me. The two girls glared at me while Miranna smiled.

Happy to torment the other girls I nodded and agreed. Following alongside them I began to chat with them, making them hate me even more.

"What a lovely day it has been," I began and the two girls rolled their eyes. "Why just yesterday I was talking to myself how nice the rain looked and the way the clouds drifted across the sky," I rambled on until we came to the girl's bathroom.

"I'll wait right here and escort you back outside ladies," I sneered to them and the two rushed into the bathroom, red faced with fury. Miranna followed after them, seeming not to care. It seemed like forever when finally the three emerged. There was a brown stain on their dresses as well as a small damp area around the stain, I guessed they had used the drier to dry some of the water, but gave up and put on their dresses.

"Hello ladies, don't you look spectacular," I said uncrossing my arms and standing up from leaning against the blue and brown wall.

"Oh thanks kind sir," One girl said sarcastically.

I led them out into the open air though recess was almost over now. The two girls fled from my side the moment they stepped foot in the sun as if I had held them in darkness. Miranna stayed by me though, first a little shy then becoming braver.

"Thank you," She said and smiled at me. I found myself smiling back and then she left me for her friends. After that, Miranna went out of her way to show me kindness and I began to go out of my way to speak with her. I tormented her friends, but was nothing, but kind to Miranna.

It was a few days after that, when I was sitting outside of my house staring off into space that I thought I heard someone call my name. Confused I looked around, but saw no one. My dad was inside cooking and my brothers were out.

"Khire," I heard it again. Someone was definitely calling me. I began to walk away from the house thinking it would be Sinth. He said I had the day off, but he was an assassin so I didn't count on 'days off'. My dad's house was situated on the boundaries of the city in a large subdivision with big back yards leading off into a forested area that steadily went upwards to the mountains far away. I stood before the tree line and heard someone call my name again and in that instant I dashed into the forest and away.

My heart began to beat faster, I don't know why, I wasn't scared, but something drove me on, making me want to move as fast as I could. I hated to run, being fat; everyone liked to laugh at me and smirk, saying "have you ever seen a whale run on land." But I forgot about the other people, I forgot that this might not be something safe. I kept going and soon I was deep into the forest. I ended up being a day into the forest when I had only been running for three hours. My magic had switched itself on and kept me going. I hadn't realized it would have kept me going for so long and for so fast, but I was far into the forest. I was also heaving and drenched in sweat, legs burning and the world seeming to dim a little bit as I tried to hold onto consciousness.

"Khire!" Someone called again. It was a young male voice that much I could tell, but I didn't know where it was coming from. The trees were older here and so much bigger, bushes and fallen trees littered the floor while the canopy overhead blocked most of the sun. I also noticed in that instant that I was cut up. Thorns had grabbed at me, but I hadn't noticed till now when I began to realize how much they stung. I also didn't realize how hungry I was. I wasn't good at cooking, I couldn't even boil water, so I kept walking hoping something would come up. Making my legs work and grumbling at whoever was calling me better have a good reason.

Night fell and I had not eaten anything or drank anything. I knew drinking unfiltered water could be bad, but at that point I didn't care. I was either going to die from lack of water or some bacteria thing, I chose to die being hydrated. The next day I found some water and practically falling into the stream I slurped up as much as I could. I was so thankful for the water, it was funny and I began to laugh. I was hot, sweating, hungry and I was lost, but for all that I was having a good time. I stayed sitting in the water until I heard the voice call again. This time I took it more slowly. I felt no need to be zooming off into the forest like I had yesterday. I didn't feel tired though I probably was, and I knew I had to find something edible soon. That voice however became distracting and soon it was all I heard. The birds chirped and whistled their songs, but all I could hear was my name being called over and over again.

It wasn't that day, but the next day I found out what was going on. I was stumbling along trying not to fall down when a bear jumped out at me. It was a huge black bear, and though I knew that bears on a relative bases are dangerous, I didn't think this one would be. People said black wasn't as bad as brown and so I gave the bear a wide birth and tried to walk away. I was dizzy from lack of food and tired as well as hot, so I wasn't thinking straight. Unfortunately I found out the hard way that no matter the colour, a bear is still a bear. He charged me; a huff was the only warning I got before it collided with me. The wind knocked out of me, I tried to get to my feet when a paw came and swiped at me sending me falling backwards. My ribs hurt and I was still trying to catch my breath as I gasped desperately for air when the bear came at me again. I had a knife on me and I pulled it out to face my attacker, adrenaline kicking in and instinct to live and fight taking over. I dodged the first swipe, swiped at the bear myself then jumped to the side again to miss its other paw.

I heard a crackle of brush and stupidly I turned to face it. The bear however was focused on me and charged me again, knocking me to the ground with a paw. The bear was just about to bite down on me when an animal hurled itself at the bear's head. It was a brown, scraggly cat, too young to be away form its mother, but alone all the same. It ducked and dodged the bear, getting in a few bites of its own. The bear began to get irritated at the cat and it began to back off. The cat pounced at it and gave the bear a good scratch on the nose before persuading the bear to leave. The cat hissed ferociously. Its fur was dirty and unwashed so I could tell that it had not been taking care of itself properly.

Once the bear was gone the cat turned to me. I could now see it was a cougar. Small and unkempt, I don't even think he is a year old. He watched me panting with a steady gaze. I didn't know if I should crawl away, I couldn't run and I didn't think I could focus enough to use a knife.

"Khire," a voice said and I realized it was in my head.

"Y-yes," I said unsure, still looking at the cat.

He came over to me and licked my face and it was then that I realized I was on my Journey. A smile lit my face despite my battered ribs. I put my arms around the small cat and cuddled with him, breathing in his sent.

"Khire, my name is Myre," The cat said in my head.

"That rhymes with my name," I said giggling a little.

"I know that's why I like it," He said and began to purr.

Myre pushed his face into mine and rubbed his face against my cheek. Whispering a name in my ear I instantly thought of a name and whispered it into his ear. When a Protected and Guardian meet they are supposed to give a special name to each other to create an unbreakable magical bond. It's a bond so strong that the two beings become linked. Myre was in my head and I in his. I could hear every thought, know ever thing that he did. Know his likes and dislikes, his actions, his mannerisms. We were one being in two bodies and from that moment on we were inseparable.

"Let's go home," Myre said with a sigh. I nodded and got up slowly and unsteadily, finding if I walked slowly I could move. My ribs protested and left me short of breath as we began to make our way back home, but my magic helped me a lot. Myre was worried about me, he was upset with himself that he hadn't gotten to me before the bear attacked, but I told him I have been through worse.

I still hadn't eaten and had only drank a little water that day. The next day was hard as every pain seemed to flare all day, but I found more streams and sat in them to cool off every chance I got. Remarkably, Myre was able to hunt, but I wasn't good at making a fire. I got a flame started one day and was able to cook some meat though I ended up charring it and nearly setting myself on fire as well as the forest. Still I was able to eat something and I felt better doing so.

I arrived back home a few days later to an empty house. I was a little upset, usually a kid coming home was a huge deal, but I guess it's hard to stay home when you don't know if your kids going to even come home. Still I felt very upset and I let myself think that they'd just think I'd die. I was fat after all and young and to them, stupid. Why would I be able to survive when other kids died?

The door was locked but with a bit of magic I fixed that. I shouldn't have been using so much magic, I was already feeding off the magic as an energy source, a heat source and a pain reliever, but my anger made me ignore that. In the end though, the most I could do after that was collapse on the couch.

I don't know how long I slept, but when I woke up I could hear footsteps. Someone was whispering a little louder than they thought I think and so I heard who it was. More whispers told me even before I opened my eyes that four members of my family were here.

"Khire," I heard my dad say.

"Yes," I mumbled and slowly forced my eyes open. I watched them as they smiled happily at me. Myre was eyeing them from his position on my legs and as they came closer he gave a slight hiss.

"Khire," My dad said again a little sternly.

"Look I'll clean the couch if I've made a mess ok," I whined and began to slowly sit up and get to my feet.

"Well I wasn't going to say that. Your Guardian has been growling at us since we've come in," He said and wrapped me in a hug. I said nothing just hugged him back and let everyone else hug me. Tellnair wrapped me in a hug and squeezed me enough to make me squeak.

"What's wrong, you look like you've survived a tornado," Jakk said. I gave him a look.

"No I got attacked by a black bear thank you and I'm fi..." I started.

"A black bear! Dear me, Khire why didn't you say anything or go to the hospital?!" My dad said. I wanted to tell him that if he cared that much for me then maybe he should have been there all the times I've needed him, but I just shook my head.

"Don't shake your head at me boy, come on," He dragged me to the door and I didn't resist. Welcome home Khire.

Three years past now and I was fifteen, walking down the hallway to the outside as the lunch bell stopped ringing signalling recess. Hand in hand with my girlfriend Miranna I smiled and talked with her, her dimpled smile showing back. We hung out with a small group of friends whom had joined our two-some over the past year. That was the way it went now, ever since that fateful day I began to reappear before people's eyes. I began to talk kindly to people and people began to like me. Most importantly my family relaxed a little, seeing me come around finally after what seemed like the dark ages. We were one of the more popular couples in school and people liked to talk to us. I was still over weight, but not overly so. Miranna was a tall, twig, and strikingly beautiful young women. Everyone was jealous of her and me. Though I wasn't very good looking I was still dating the most beautiful girl and so that gave me popularity points.

I lost contact with Midnight frequently. Declining his missions for me and telling him straight up I was his no more. I finally felt free like I was taking my life back. But happiness for me was always a short-lived thing. I began to feel guilty about my relationship with such a kind person. She shared everything with me and she wouldn't dare even hurt a fly, even if it bit her. I however had been killing people years before, I was a monster and a murderer, I could never be a good person no matter how I tried to change and be nice.

Miranna and I would frequently walk to what we called "our place". It was a little spot by the mall, a bridge crossed the large expanse of water that surged down towards the next town. It was filthy, cluttered with rocks; the water tainted with pollution and the land a hiding spot for old cigarettes, beer bottles and other odd bits. Despite this, we found it a secluded haven beneath the big iron bridge. Miranna and I would sit on a large flat rock, her leaning against my chest as we watched the grey water gush by.

"I love this moment," Miranna would whisper half asleep. I'd pull her in tighter to me and whisper back: "I love this moment with you,"

It was a moment filled with sweetness, both of us young and thinking we were madly and perfectly in love with each other. We would even think of the future and about the names we would call our kids, where we would live and the jobs we would have. Each time we got to jobs I would hesitate and draw away slightly. I didn't know what I wanted to be or even if I had the right to a dream of being something besides a killer. Noticing my hesitation, Miranna would twist around so that she knelt before me, arms wrapped around my neck while one hand stroked my blond hair. She would stare into my blue eyes, her dark brown ones wide and full of love as she would tell me what our life would be like.

Sometimes something would be different, I'll always remember the first time she kissed me, she was as shy as I was terrified and we smiled like fools for days afterwards like we alone held the secret to fixing world hunger. A part of me was still flabbergasted at the fact that I, this fat loner, could find someone as open and beautiful as Miranna. I couldn't help, but question myself and think there's no way this could be real. One day I'll awake from this amazing dream and find everything back to the cold, lonely world I once had.

Over time she became bolder while I still worked up the courage to kiss her. Sometimes at school she would push me against a locker and kiss me as if it was her last day on earth. I enjoyed it, at first I was a little nervous, I knew she had never kissed anyone else, a relationship being new to both of us, but was I living up to her expectations as her first kiss? I thought I was rather good at kissing despite the fact that I had never kissed anyone either. I was thinking I was doing rather well until she told me that I was actually a sloppy kisser, but she thought it was funny. I loved her laugh so I couldn't be mad, but after that I would try to kiss her less sloppy.

I was so happy to be with her every day, kissing her, hugging her, hearing her voice; it turned my world around to the point that I could forget about my old assassin life. I just wanted to be with her every day. But it wouldn't last; she was everything virtuous while I was a lie.

I sat on a bench one day, dwelling on my life, lost in thought I didn't even register that Miranna had walked up to me. She pushed my hands away from my face and leaned in, kissing me smiling and asking me what's wrong. I looked at her and smiled, knowing I would ruin my chance at this great happiness I found. Still I knew I had to tell her, I wanted her to know who I was, who I had been. I was in agony worrying, I desperately wanted to believe she could forgive my past and the person I was. Taking courage from that, I searched her face for hope and said, "After school lets go to the bridge ok?"

I walked with her to the bridge trying to hide my panic the whole way as she oblivious to my dilemma, smiled happily and told me about her day. I thought of all the great times we had. How I loved her smile that would light up her eyes, how she'd laugh at my jokes as if they were actually funny. The future we could have together and the places we could see. Since it was a good thirty minutes from the school, I had ample time, but no time at all to tell the women I loved I was a killer.

Under the bridge, no one could see us and I sat her down on a rock, finding one nearby, I rolled it over and sat down before her. Without hesitating I got right to it, hoping against all odds that our love would allow her to see past my darkness and take me for who I am now.

"I love you so, so much and you've made me such a good person. You're everything I wish I could be, but I have to tell you something. You're not going to like it, but...," I started awkwardly and she nodded smiling. She was just so innocent; she couldn't see the darkness inside of me.

"It's ok tell me anything," She said encouragingly.

"I'm... ok, I'm Dusk," I told her after a moments pause. Dusk. Named by the citizens of Vale Darra because I always struck at dusk.

"What?" She asked, her smile slipping.

"Miranna, I'm an assassin, I'm Dusk. Well I use to be. I'm not anymore, you made me a better person and now I know I don't have to kill anymore," Maybe that last part was what did it, but in any case, she shot to her feet, her face flushed.

"What are you saying?" She demanded in a voice I had never heard her use. Hearing the hurt and anger in her voice made me regret telling her.

"Ok just let me explain. I'm saying that I *used* to be Dusk. I'm not anymore, I will not kill people, I never even liked it to begin with," I ended lamely.

She glared at me, her hands balled into fists, her breathing gone ragged.

"Is this some kind of joke to you?!" She asked me. Confused I shook my head. I could see her so wanting to trust me, she always trusted me, but what I was telling her was tearing her up inside.

"I'm sorry I know I've caused a lot of pain, but I'm better now. Who I was is not who I am now. It's all because of you... you saved me," I told her and reached out to her desperately wanting her to just hug me or say she loves me. I needed her acceptance. I needed her to say that she knew who I was and she knew I was a good person.

In that moment, seeing her fear me, I felt on the edge of an abyss with one foot on solid ground the other over the edge. My heart was beating fast and I felt myself choke up. She doesn't love me. After all we had been through, she didn't see the goodness inside of me. I was a good person, I wanted; I needed her to see that. She was the only thing in my life that gave me hope, why wasn't love enough for her to accept me?

Her hand came very fast, slapping me across my face. I was stunned for a good minute, cheek stinging where she had hit me.

"Miranna," I said haltingly. I actually wanted to cry as I felt my world get turned upside down and torn apart.

"A lot of pain… Khire…. you k-you killed all those people," She whispered in fear.

"No! Khire don't tell me this, tell me it's a lie, this isn't real!" She screamed at me. She was nearly hysterical, tears coursing down her beautiful face.

I stepped back from her feeling lost. Looking back I think I was rather oblivious and stupid, but in the moment I just didn't understand. She loved me, why was she so upset?

"I'm sorry…" I cried, the tears starting to fall down my face.

"No, no, no…. Khire! You were perfect! I loved you, I trusted you!" She glared at me. I wanted so badly to wipe her tears away and take her in my arms, but she looked ready to fight me and my instincts told me to stand my ground.

"I'm a good person! It's not my fault what I've done! You can't leave me, I don't know how to live without you!" I screamed at her, but she shook her head her hands pulling her hair.

"I can't be with you," She said sobbing.

"Yes you can, I need you. Why can't you see that I'm not a bad person? I love you and you love me. Isn't that enough?" I pleaded.

"You're nothing, but a monster!" She ran from me and I ran after her, wanting to stop her and try to work it out. I had to stop her, she was upset now, but in time the wounds would heal. Time heals everything.

I never fully understood what all happened afterwards, but it ended in blood shed and death. She turned around, probably afraid that I was chasing her.

"Miranna! I love you! Please!" I begged her desperately. She stopped so suddenly and grabbed a rock from the ground that I nearly collided with her. I tried to take a step back, but the rocks at my feet were loose and I couldn't get away fast enough before she struck me in the head. I couldn't help myself, I was trained to kill and fight, that instinct kicked in and I lashed out with a knife that somehow came into my hand. Before I knew it her body was draped across my arms, cooling in the shade of the bridge. Horror struck, I stood there for what must have been an hour until finally I fell to the ground. Tears streaming down my face disbelieving what I had just done. Looking down at her I could see there was no bringing her back and it was all because of me.

The water rushed on behind me and all I could hear was its waves lapping against the ground. I opened my eyes realizing they were closed. It was significantly later in the day now, my face felt stuck and I could feel the tear tracks on my face dry now. Miranna was cooler, her blood had flowed down from her neck and had puddled around us. I felt her blood on my hands, arms and my legs. I smelled it, the scent of her blood was overwhelming. It was wrong and I thought I would never be able to forget the smell of her blood. She shouldn't be dead, this is all wrong. I cried again not knowing what else to do. I couldn't move I was paralyzed by what I had done. I loathed myself, I was evil incarnate. I had never deserved such a beautiful creature in my life and now I don't deserve to live.

After a while, I finally picked her off the ground and looked to the river. The water was deep and murky and I walked towards it in a trance. With magic, I created a rope, making it as strong and durable as possible and tied it around a pale ankle, the other end I tied to a large rock. With the help of magic, I threw the body and the rock as far as I could. With a large splash both disappeared within the dirty water and I could no longer see my love. With a heavy heart I decided that I would never love another person, that there was no such thing as true love. Her blood stained my clothing and I knew I should just wash them off then use magic to dry me, but I looked at the blood with little care. Let everyone see what I was, the only person I thought who would accept me no matter what had left me and now I had nothing left to care about.

I began to run as fast as I could back into the city, my mind didn't know where I was going, but something inside of me did and I followed it into the darkness of the alleyways. The stench of them did not bother me, the homeless that shrank away from me, the cats, rats and dogs that lived wild ran from me, growling and hissing as I went by. I ran past old dilapidated houses, rocks tumbled everywhere, blocking other side streets and narrowing the main road.

Suddenly, taking in my surroundings, I found myself in a very old section of Vale Darra, forgotten even by the street people. It was here that the old man stood, smiling as I approached him, but his stance was feral. He was ready for me and I finally for him. Growling I launched myself at him pulling out two daggers from my sleeves. Midnight danced from my reach and evaded me with ease. I hated him even more then, how easy it was for him, how happy he was to have such a miserable, meaningless, painful life.

"You monster!" I screamed at him and he gave a harsh laugh.

"Monster? Now Dusk I have not done anything wrong, I am what I am. What are you?" He stood before me. A withered old man in a long coat, he had a slight limp and was wrinkly, but despite that, you could not tell his true age, his Wish made sure of that. A special gift that all people have, and unfortunately he had a despicable one. He aged slowly, his Wish prevented time to ware on him as it did others each day. Everything affected him less; he had more vitality, more youth to him.

"I am nothing like you! I have a great family, a great life; and you are not welcomed to it. I will have nothing to do with you, we're done!" I turned from him and began to leave.

"You have nothing, you are nothing. But I, I made you into what you are meant to be. You don't even realize it, but you were meant to be an assassin. You have a special gift that will make you the best assassin the world will ever know," Midnights haunting voice caused me to stop.

"No," I said to him and turned to face him.

"Dusk, you were born into this world and you will die in this world, it is something you cannot change. Your life has also been chosen for you, long before you were born and you cannot escape it now. You will kill, Khire. You are nothing, but a killer. Every fibre in your body knows that, your mind is turned, your body works on impulse, your magic is flawlessly perfect for being an assassin and it will only get better as you get older. You will only get better in time, already you far exceed many apprentices," He told me with a weird sense of happiness.

I did not want to listen to him, I'd had enough of him and so I turned around and started to leave, breathing hard and trying to calm down. As I left I could hear him begin to snicker as if something was funny. Losing control I whirled around and threw a knife at him, he ducked, but I ran at him and we engaged in battle again. This time, I held nothing back I wanted so badly to kill him, to hurt him and make him suffer for all the pain he's caused me. I wanted him to beg me to stop and to realize I was too dangerous even for him at that moment. I punched at him, keeping my left arm up in front of my face then lashed out with a kick to his knee. He dodged it and kicked me in the thigh causing my leg to go numb. I stumbled to the ground and tried to trip him. Magic flooding through my veins and allowing me to get to my feet, I dodged to his left then up behind him and jabbed at his kidneys. Making a hit, he grunted and turned to try and grab my arm, but I evaded.

"You are an incredible fighter, and you are something to fear when you are furious. You have death in your eyes Dusk, you will surely kill me one day, but for now boy, I have had enough of this. I have things to attend, enough!" He drew a short sword and knocked my knives away. And in that moment I got lucky. I turned the hit into a turn, twisting so I came to his left side. With all the furry I had left I used it to plunge my knife into his shoulder. He stood there shocked momentarily then his face and ears went red and he turned on me. He bashed me hard in the head and began to beat me. Losing my anger and my sense to fight back, I longed to just go home and forget none of this ever happened, but I couldn't.

When he walked away from me I lay on the dirty ground in my own blood. My nose was bleeding, my head was pounding, the world spinning so much so that I couldn't focus on anything, everything was dark around me even though I should still have enough light to see clearly. My chest and sides hurt, I thought I felt some broken ribs. I lay on the ground cast aside from the rest of the world. I hated that I was left pitiful and half dead. I couldn't move, every movement hurt causing my head to spin more and making me collapse back onto the ground. I closed my eyes and let the world slip away losing any sense to stay awake and find help.

Chapter #6

Some years ago when I was twelve I had been on a mission where I had journeyed to a rich family's house to kill all, but the boy. They lived on the outskirts of the city in a wealthy neighbourhood with huge sprawling lawns and large mansions. The husband and wife were one of the wealthiest people in the city, but I had been watching them for a while and discovered that most of their money came from selling illegal products. Knock offs from high priced companies were imported from another country and these people sold it. Selling it for cheap, they got rich off of it with no one the wiser. They had an easy life going for them money wise, but I didn't like how they were getting it. When I told Midnight about these people he didn't care for my personal little mission I had planned, but then he looked into it and decided it would be a good test. These people had a state of the art security system the best money could buy. Also I feel that Midnight like the idea of me going after what were actually good people. Back then, though I thought they were stealing, they weren't giving any money away to charity or anything, they were greedy people who just wanted more. In my eyes they were bad and I wanted to stop them.

And so I found myself alone one night with my Guardian, standing just in the shadows of a tree. I watched as the lights in the house turned off and everyone went to sleep. I knew they were not sleeping yet, their son would be, but they usually stayed up late, chatting and going over their day. Which would make killing them both easier for me. Slowly I began to get through their security system. Their cameras that patrolled the lawns moved away from where I was and I ran to another dark shadow. My Guardian's Wish made it so I blended in with any shadow and so staying in the darkness I could not be seen by anyone.

Shadow to shadow I got closer to the house, finally nearly to it I stopped and with some magic bounded high over the invisible electric fence, stopping just inches away from another fence. One thing with magic, when putting up barriers there were rules, you couldn't place two boundaries on top of each other because then they would cancel each other out. You had to set them at least a foot apart from each other so that they would function to their full power. Everyone was fine with this because the boundaries that acted as a security system were invisible so no one trying to break in would see them and know where to step and not to step. However, I wasn't just some break and enter amateur. I could sense the boundaries of magic with my Wish which was starting to develop and so I knew how high I had to jump and where to jump to.

I came close to another boundary as I jumped another, sucking in and trying to not hit the invisible barrier. I stopped and stood still as a camera roved over the lawn nearby taking the time to catch my breath. Another thing that many people didn't know about was when you stood between two magical barriers they made you invisible to some things. The cameras mounted on the wall were magical, creating a huge flaw in their supposedly top notch security system. Magic passing through magic, say a magical camera looking at a magical barrier, won't set off any alarms even if someone were to be standing right behind that magic barrier. It was all because it was the same magic. The same person who built the cameras put up the magical fences and so like two barriers unable to be put on top of each other, a magical camera couldn't see past a magical fence even if it were invisible. It made anything on the other side invisible. How no one had figured this out yet was beyond me, but I wasn't about to go tell people.

I had thought I would enjoy this mission, I was hoping it would show off my skills, but the simplicity of it was pathetic. I bounded over the next wall with a flip so that I passed a little farther this time, missing the ground sensor set a foot from the inner most wall. Right at a window now I traced my finger along a seam and suddenly the window opened like a door. It was one of my favourite tricks; it was fun, very convenient and tended to befuddle those that didn't know about it.

I crept down a dark hallway; each footfall was precise and silent. I turned down other hallways to avoid the patrol and slowly, but surly I made my way to the staircase. I ran up the banister and leapt up and over to another room. Diving through the open doorway as another patrol came around a corner. He walked on by and I entered the hallway again, going the way he had come. I took a moment to slow my breathing, I wasn't tired yet, I had enough endurance to get this far, but I still needed to breath.

It took me another hour to get to the right bedroom. Having to go up two more staircases and evading people and sensors. I was right outside the bedroom door where I could hear nothing. I was a little confused, they should be talking and there were no magic spells keeping them hushed and I from hearing their voices. I knew that I could not touch the doorknob for that would set off an alarm and knocking on the door would as well. The door and the doorknob had a sensor on it, as soon as something touched it, say my finger, it would scan me and recognize me for an intruder. It would also send my fingerprint to the police and they would easily find me and catch me. The door had to be opened only by certified people.

I was met with the same problem if I tried going through the window. Barging through the wall would allow me to get inside, they had not prepared for anyone to do that, but then I would have to be really quick, killing them and getting out. While also not getting seen, but the noise would surly alarm someone making me have to run from the cops at some point in time. Therefore, I decided to just let them allow me in. I would speak out their names and they would just have to ask who was there. I had many plans and back up plans should anything happen and I had my whole speech memorized, but as I listened I did not hear them and I began to get worried that I had made a mistake. Suddenly someone was coming around the corner. I ran farther down the hall to the staircase, running up the banister to the higher floor I managed to evade the patrol again. I looked around, this floor was quiet to, but I could sense more people on it. I walked down the hallway and soon enough I heard the man and wife I was here to see, their voice coming through a doorway. It was their son's bedroom they were in and from the sounds of it they were having an argument. I simply opened the door and walked in, the son's room was not sealed and censored like the parents room.

The first thing I did was throw a knife at the crow that turned to look at me. The wife was about to cry out at the loss of her Guardian when I threw another dagger at her. Quickly her husband fell to the ground soon after, his Guardian having lost his Protected, ditched everyone and headed for the doors. When the Protected died that's what usually happened, but it didn't work the other way around. As sad as it was, I didn't care, I didn't have a lot of time, and I could already hear people coming to this room, having seen the man's dog Guardian leaving.

The small boy sat on his bed, pale and shocked at watching his parents die before him. I drew another knife, hidden in a shadow and threw it, but he suddenly moved. He lunged at me and I wrestled with him. I growled at him and he fought hard, but in the end I was heavier, more experienced and stronger and so I won. I pinned him to the ground, but at that moment the door opened up and before I could slash the boy's throat a dog came barrelling at me. I leapt off the boy and together my Guardian and I dashed through the window. We crashed through it and plunged down to the ground below. Our magic stopped us from hurting ourselves as we landed on solid ground and we once again blended into the darkness.

I could hear the alarm sound and I started to sprint across the lawn, jumping over the boundaries as lights flickered on. I just made it into the safety of the trees before I was caught in a light from a nearby post. I knew I wasn't safe yet and so I ran through the forest, jumping from tree to tree, the ground had a layer of magic on it and I knew I couldn't step on it now. I had great balance and magic, but I was also heavier and loosing energy. I was breathing raggedly now and my fear of getting caught was the only thing driving me on.

"Don't get caught, don't stop and don't get caught," I gasped out to keep me going.

Finally after some time I was safe and sound back in Vale Darra's alleyways by three in the morning. I panted for breath and stopped, walking to try and prevent my legs from cramping up. It didn't work and I ended up lying sprawled on the ground. I was panting hard, the sweat streaming down my body, I could smell myself and I wrinkled my nose. It was a warm night, which made it worse for I could smell the stench coming from the old garbage on the streets as well. I managed to get back to my feet and hobble down the street, it hurt, but I made myself keep going. At times I stopped to massage my legs, but they burned and hurt all the more as I squeezed them.

I found myself almost home, when I took another break. I had to get into my room without anyone knowing, I couldn't come in panting and moaning as I had been. Taking a deep breath I stalked forward towards my house. After twenty minutes I was passed out on my bed, clothes thrown in my closet without being properly put away.

I could hear Jakk snoring from the bed across the room and I heard the quietness of the house so I knew I had successfully left and came back with no one the wiser. I did little else to make sure no one knew, as I could not help, but collapse into tiredness after that. My heart beat slowing as I drifted off.

CHAPTER #7

I opened my eyes into the present, but was met with a fuzzy darkness. I tried to move, but my body hurt so much and pitifully I whimpered.

"Don't move," Someone said nearby and I instantly recognized Cadence's voice. Now years older, he was twelve, brown hair and eyes, lanky and tall for his age. After I killed his parents that night he had run away from his inherited home and took to the streets, he had hated his parents and seeing me kill them and with only a little boys knowledge he had searched for me. Luck was with him because the night after he had found me. Midnight had been close by and he found it amusing that the little boy who had watched me kill his parents wanted to join me.

I hated it of course, yelling and screaming at him, threatening to kill him, going crazy with rage on how he would just willingly walk into a life that I was thrust into against my will. Midnight threatened me telling me not to touch him. In the end I quieted down and watched as Midnight introduced us to the new recruit. The boy was named Jade, he was stubborn and mischievous and he already knew his Wish made him move faster than normal. He did not care for anything that pertained to his parents and he was excited about a life of killing and freedom to roam and wander as he pleased. After that day for a month I tried to talk to him, to get him to go back, but he would not have it and Midnight would hit me plenty of times saying I was being selfish and rude. Jade liked me; for all that I had done and said to him, he followed me around like he was my personal shadow. I still had not shown myself to him in the light so he never found me during the day, but he harassed me at night. He had also changed his name, wanting to leave everything from his old life behind. I don't think he really understood what he was getting into.

He had stayed with me all the years and now here he was tending to me and making sure no one else took advantage of a wounded me and kill me.

"Don't move," He said more fiercely.

"What time is it?" I moaned. My head hurt a lot and I felt like everything was spinning, the world moving too fast to be real. My breathing was shallow, but I couldn't take a deeper breath.

"It's one," he said and I nodded. That was ok. At one it was still dark in the city and so I began to get up.

"I better get home before my dad and brothers wake up," I told him, but as soon as I got to a knee my head seemed to spin faster. I gasped for breath wheezing and my body complained to me. "How can I hurt so much?" I whined mostly to myself.

"What? Khire it's one in the afternoon, no one is asleep right now," He said slowly. "You look awful,"

"I'm fine, just dizzy," I said and shook my head. That did not help; it instead made me have to curl into a ball.

"Ok no you're not ok, I'll get a healer," he began to get up, but I stopped him. Despite the fact that assassins were assassins, we did have some rules. If a person, who was not an assassin, was a healer of some sort, they could not be targeted. The healers on the other hand couldn't tell a word to anyone whom they were treating. They had to be open for all assassins who needed them and be able to help them as much as they could. It was a good arrangement; magic bound the agreement so that if an assassin killed a healer then the assassin would be plagued for years then die. The healer if he or she told someone would choke on his or her tongue and die.

The world did not brighten throughout the day and by the next day I began to fear.

"Cadence," I said with dread and he came over to me. I still was terribly sore and now very hungry, but my head still felt stuffed with cotton balls and so the thought of food made me nauseous.

"Yes, can I help you?" He asked kindly. I heard him, but I couldn't see him and with a stone sitting in my belly I told him, "I'm blind,"

CHAPTER #8

When I returned home my dad was furious with me. I told him Miranna and I got jumped. Police had come and listened to me as I told them Miranna and I had taken a walk down through some gardens that were a good distance from the mall. Some people had come out behind us and hit me in the head with something. I didn't remember anything else and I didn't know where Miranna was or what happened to her. I never told anyone else besides Cadence that I was blind.

Over time I began to get use to the fact that I was blind though it took me a while to accept I would never see someone or a flower, or the sun rise and set. Still I had my Wish to thank, it allowed me to sense everything around me and so I wasn't terribly at a loss. The colours were confusing. Everything alive I seen in blue, everything that's dead I seen in black and everything else I seen in red. I could also see through red things just so long as the object was thin enough. I couldn't see detail; just outlines of everything, so a large crowd of people looked like a massive blue, black and red blob. Fortunately with my heightened senses I could focus and pick out individuals even if I couldn't see them clearly. It took me a long time to adjust to this new way of viewing the world, but once I was comfortable and confident enough, it wasn't so difficult. While becoming adjusted to my sight, I spent a lot of time with Cadence and began to think back on some memories. One memory that came into my head was of Cadence.

I hadn't had an assignment from Midnight for a while now and I felt light and free. I was 14 years old still fat and ugly with blond hair and deep blue eyes. The sun was beautiful, a gentle breeze and very little clouds in the great blue sky. I hated the fact that I could see so little sky, but the deep blue that appeared between the buildings made me smile. I had nothing to do, but still I wandered around till I got tired, then I found my way to a park. It was cooler in the shade, but I was still panting and sweating from the heat. Having no money I couldn't even buy myself some ice cream, but I sat for a time looking around.

Some hours later my brother found me asleep on the bench. He poked me awake and I looked at him groggily before his words made sense.

"Hey lobster!" Shean said enthusiastically. He was wearing his usual jeans and a worn and faded green shirt. He smelt like horses, which made me think he had just got back from riding lessons.

"What do you want?" I grumbled.

"Nothing I just thought I'd wake you up before you got baked," he said and started walking away. Out of all my brothers Shean always annoyed me the most. He said very little, but he always spoke with a taunting lilt to his voice. He at this point was on the verge of being kicked out of his second school, but he didn't care.

Knowing it would bug him, I stayed where I was instead of following him home. I could tell as his shoulders tightened that he realized I wasn't tagging along. I smiled and got up just as he whirled around, a sarcastic expression on his face ready to say something to me. I smiled sweetly at him and waved goodbye.

"Where are you going?" He called after me. As curious as he was, he found it beneath him to follow people younger than him around and so when I didn't answer he left me alone.

I was deciding if I wanted to go home when I caught sight of a person rushing towards me. Long brown hair in tangles and brown eyes wide, Cadence came barrelling towards me, a cop running after him. I sidestepped not wanting to get involved, but somehow managed to still get in the boys way. The issue with being part whale. He crashed into me cursing and swearing. I pushed him away before he could think up something and then I moved away. The cop was fighting to get through the crowd, but it was pointless, Cadence was far faster than him. The boy dashed into an alleyway and disappeared. Not wanting to get caught either for whatever reason the cop could come up with, I disappeared into the alley as well. Cadence obviously had the impression no one would follow, as I turned a corner and then another and ran right into him.

"Can I help you?" Cadence growled threateningly. I could see that he was holding a bag of something, probably food, he lived on the street and Midnight didn't feed us. If you wanted to eat you had to find your own way to provide for food.

Before I could answer he ran away, apparently fighting wasn't his first idea, an issue that Midnight would soon solve. I shrugged and wound my way through the alleys to get home. Nestled in a friendly neighbourhood, I found my house and went to the side of my home, magic burned through my veins as I sprang at the open window and through it. I liked going through the window instead of going through the door so that I could avoid any conversations. Landing quietly on the wooden floor I stripped off my clothes and tucked myself under the covers of my bed.

In another clear memory it was a bright, sunny day, and I was sitting on a rock in the park gazing out over the water when I saw Cadence striding through the park. He was dressed in a plaid shirt and ripped jeans, with a frown on his face, he looked menacing as he strode as if he owned the park. I didn't know what he was doing, but I became instantly curious and so I followed him. He went to a tree and began to dig, when he didn't find anything, he began to circle the tree. I realized he was on a mission from Midnight, a mission Midnight had given me years ago. It was basically a treasure hunt, one designed to make us think and problem solve. Cadence seemed confused for a moment then looked up at me and said amused, "You're really fat," I couldn't believe that was the first thing he said.

"Ummm," I began then stopped. I didn't want to speak to him so I walked away.

"Hey wait, I need your help," I almost started laughing at him, but instead I turned around interested.

"I… ah…. I lost something and I am trying to find it. It's a little red thing," He began and I shook my head then walked away. He was smart enough not to attract too much attention in public, but still dumb enough to ask strangers for help.

Later that day I was deep in the labyrinth of the alleys when I ran into Cadence again.

"Hey!" He said cheerily. Just then a group of five people rounded the corner and came up behind him. Cadence really wasn't a fast thinker. The group charged us before Cadence could even figure out what was going on. I felt sorry for him, but stayed back before I intercepted a guy about to slit Cadence's throat. In two minutes I had them all unconscious on the ground.

"Your incredible! Can you teach me that? You know I know someone who could use you!" He said happily.

"Cadence," I said, looking at him incredulously.

"Ya? Hey how did you know my name?" He asked, not ruffled at all, just confused and curious. It was like teasing a young child with a magic trick. He seemed oblivious to the obvious and just awed by what happened. It was ridiculous.

"It's me you idiot!" I snarled at him and he jumped.

"Dusk!" He shouted, his voice going incredibly high.

"Well aren't you a bright one," I rolled my eyes then started to walk away.

"Hey wait! How come you never told me who you were?" he sounded upset by the fact that I didn't find him worthy of my identity.

"I am an assassin, and I am sure that is also what *you're suppose*d to be," I said instead.

"Ok I'm a little ruff, but that's because everyone's ditched me. I'm also only 11 remember. I'm doing good for going it alone I think," he said with what I think was supposed to be self-dignity.

"You're not alone, you have Midnight and even Isaac," I told him impatiently. My day off did not include baby-sitting Cadence.

"Midnight ditched me and Isaacs creepy. Did you know he killed his parents and set them on fire?" He said horror struck.

"And what you do is angelic?" I asked, stopping to look at him. "Look, you have a huge inheritance, you suck as an assassin so why don't you just reclaim your title and live rich?" I asked him.

"Because I want to be like you," He said so simply I was lost for words.

"Why?" I finally asked.

He had huge brown eyes and he stared at me with them as if I had all the answers in the world. I actually felt bad saying all the bad things about him in that moment.

"Because you take care of yourself, you're not even scared of Midnight. You're a great assassin and your young. Midnight speaks so highly of you of everything you do and you have everything," His voice cracked a little and I was worried he'd start crying any moment now.

"I don't have everything and I hate Midnight, I don't like being an assassin. Killing innocent people, even people that have done bad things does not help me sleep at night. I am a killer and that's all I'll ever be because that's all I know. My family doesn't know what I am and I don't want to tell them because not only will they hate me and fear me, but they will reject me and push me away. I know you didn't have a great experience with your parents, your parents were abusive, but I love my family and the only thing I have ever wanted to do was make them proud and I can't do that because I'm a killer," I spat out. I breathed in deeply trying to calm myself down.

"Then why don't you just walk away?" Cadence asked me. I grabbed him by the shirtfront and shook him until his head snapped back and forth.

"You can't just walk away you dumbass! You really don't get it do you?! Once you're an assassin you're always an assassin. No wishes, hopes, dreams are ever going to change that. You can't just erase and forget the things you've done. Life doesn't work that way. It's unforgiving and harsh, it's about time you realized that," I shouted in his face.

"But you don't have to make it harsh, you can still have a good life, it's you that lets yourself live in a life of misery ..."

"I can't be anything else you see, because I am just part of Midnights big plan. I don't know what the plan is or why I am so important, but Midnight has a huge plan for me and I ain't getting out of it any time soon," I told him angrily.

"Maybe, but you can get a job, make some money and buy a house. Live something of a normal life..." "I'm fourteen years old!" I shouted at him.

"Well you're not gonna buy a house tomorrow they're something your kinda have to save up for. Get a job and save some money and in the near future buy a house," Cadence said, his hands waving through the air.

He made it sound so simple and I wanted to believe him that it was that simple, but I had put so many walls up around myself that my life would never be easy. I wasn't ready to break down those walls and realize I could do that. I made myself believe I was under Midnights rules. Though after being with Miranna, I had started to think of a possible future where everything was good and normal. Still, a good part of me held on to all that Midnight has taught me and I still didn't have the courage enough to truly be rid of Midnight. Blowing him off a few times was one thing, but to tell him I was his no longer was entirely different. At that realization I turned around and left.

"Hey wait, what am I supposed to do?" Cadence asked confused.

"Can't you get a job?" I asked him as I turned a corner.

"I'm 11," he told me as if I'd forgotten.

"Well then go to school and graduate that's something that you can do that won't leave you with nothing. There's a school close by that helps orphans," I told him and he nodded.

"But I.... look Midnight left me, can I please just stay with you?" He whined. "You're not some stray animal off the street. I can't just ask my dad to let you stay, he would never let you into my house, I'm sorry. Look... I will sneak food out here for you, I can help you find a place to stay for the now ok," He nodded and I sighed. "Ok, well you can't get a hotel and you have no money anyway, but you have magic, that's better then what most people have. I know a place you can sleep. It's not special, you're a street rat remember that, but it's dry and secluded," He nodded encouraged and I led him in silence deeper into the alleys.

After a time I came across a dilapidated house made of stone. It was a sad looking thing, but it would serve its purpose.

"Here? I'm not sleeping in that, it's going to collapse any minute," Cadence said eyeing it expectantly.

"That's where your magic comes in. Look, I'll strengthen the stone ok, I'll meld it together on the inside so that from the outside it looks bad, but inside you will be dry and safe. No one will trust it so they will leave you alone. Not many people come here so it's quiet, ok?"

"But who lives in all these houses?" Cadence asked gazing around.

"Ghosts. Look this is an old part of Vale Darra long forgotten; I think no one even knows this place exists really. You'll be safe here and I will bring food here every day for you just so long that I can get away from my dad ok," I said and made sure he understood. "Good, now I will get you some blankets I guess too ok?" He nodded and sighed. "I know this is a sucky life, but you don't know what it's like to hide under the covers terrified that your dad or moms gonna come in and beat you. This is the first time I feel in control and that if someone wants to hurt me they can't because now I have the power to hurt them first," Cadence said, his voice full of emotion. Sighing I threw my hands up.

"Ok well your life really isn't too much better right now, really it's not, but let's just try and survive the next few years to actually say we had a life ok. Right now we don't really have anything to show for it,"

"But what are you going to do?" Cadence asked me curiously.

"Go to school, pretend everything is great like my dad does, he really thinks the world is a glorious place. I'm tempted to take him for a walk down these alleys so he can realize that the world really isn't all that glorious. But I will go on like my life is fine and I'll see how far I will get," I told him and he nodded.

"Ok, well goodnight then I guess," He said and before I took a step away he hugged me. I actually stopped breathing, no one had hugged me for quite a while and though it wasn't anything special, it did not make me feel warm and happy like someone actually cared or liked me, I just felt awkward and cold.

"Right ok good night," I told him stiffly as I pushed him away.

The next while after that, I brought him food every day, sometimes twice a day. I got him new blankets and even a mattress, nothing spectacular, but it was softer then the ground. We used some spells to make sure that no rats or mice or any other animal could ruin it. It felt nice to take care of someone and I began to spend a lot of time there. I still would bring up the life that Cadence could have should he decide to return to his old life, but he would always turn me down. He seemed to have this weird idea that I was this amazing person and he actually worshipped me. And after a time I let him help me with my missions. Though most the Vale Darra's citizens hadn't figured it out, Dusk was actually two people.

CHAPTER #9

Back in the present, I returned to life as best I could. It was tough not letting anyone know I was blind, I didn't want to tell anyone. I know I should have and maybe if I did I could have gone to the hospital and possibly got my vision back, but I was afraid and a part of me felt like I deserved to be blind. Being blind was my own personal punishment for all the wrongs I've done. Besides Myre is a great Guardian and we have always been close. We trained together to become the great assassins we are now so I knew I could count on him to be my eyes. And over the years I began to get a better understanding of my Wish. It heightened all my senses and I felt like I was probably better having to depend on my Wish then if I had still been able to see. It wasn't sight exactly, but better as I could sense everything around me, but people don't always see everything around them.

School was a whirlwind for me. I was a fantastic student, it was the only thing I got a choice in, for the most part. I had to go to school, but I got to choose how I applied myself and as much as I hated standing out as a fantastic student, which just impressed Midnight and made him want me more, I hated being called stupid. I was fat and ugly; I didn't need to be called stupid to. At that time that was really the only thing that truly upset me, people could call me anything and do anything to me, but if they called me stupid I hated it. Sometimes I'd scream at them, other times I'd just go off and plan their deaths. I never came close to tears, but it still hurt me to be called stupid. Unfortunately that was practically my nickname.

Despite the fact that I was a straight A student people would called me Dumb-Ugly-Pug.

Everyone all but forgot about me once Miranna disappeared. Everyone was upset about Miranna's disappearance, but for some reason they forgot about me and just focused on her. I didn't even get asked if I wanted to speak to someone. I was once again Ghost. Even the bullies left me alone, I was a perfect target for them, I sat alone, I was fat, ugly, unfavoured, so was any bullies dream of a target. But even they didn't seem to notice me. I almost wish they did, I don't really know what I would do had they tried to hurt me, but at least it showed that someone knew I existed.

It was to Midnights liking that I was left home alone for two weeks. I was fifteen so able to take care of myself. Dad was out of town on a work call, he is a real estate agent and he got the chance to sell a very expensive house. He and some friends packed some clothes and went to get the house ready for selling and showing. My older brothers were away at college, university or some other place. Feeling completely at home Midnight strode through the door right as I was making a sandwich. It had been some time since I had attacked him and I still resented him, but he seemed to have no hard feelings towards me.

"You're not going to eat that are you?" He asked me as if that were bizarre.

"Ya I'm hungry that's what normal people do when they're hungry," I said sarcastically. He rolled his eyes at me.

"You'll just throw it up, now I have a great assignment for you listen," He said and sat down on a chair, after a moment's thought he grabbed my sandwich and started eating it.

"Heyyy!" I said grabbing for it. He swatted my hand away and began speaking.

"Listen, next Thursday there is a very important event..." he began.

"Ya I know the Fair for the Fair, it's a prestigious event where all the rich people come and go hang out at the castle, fine dining, a masquerade ball, some tea in the morning, some sporting events then more food, a meeting where they all get together to talk about money and their land and why there neighbour is poorer than them. It's dumb," I finished much to Midnights displeasure.

"Well in any case you will be there and I don't want you looking like a pig in a suit. I got you for two weeks let's make them count,"

"I thought the whole fat look was good, made me less of a likely look-to person when things go bad," I said crossing my arms.

"Ya well things change. Now I have this great new thing for you to try, you will eat and drink this stuff and nothing else," And with that he handed me a bottle of what looked like purple sludge.

"Oh yummy you find this at the bottom of a pond?" I sneered.

"Almost," He smiled.

I scrutinized it then took off the cap and took a swig. My mind, body and every other part of my being screamed at me to spit it out, but suddenly Midnight was there with his hand over my mouth and on my neck. He was doing something that made me involuntarily swallow the foul stuff. I tried to gage it back up, but he cuffed my ear.

"Stop that. You're going to drink this and in a few days you'll be fit to be seen. It's powerful stuff, in a week you can lose ten pounds. And that's with still eating food, which you won't be doing. Amazing isn't it? It's called Purple Syrup," Midnight said happily. "And unhealthy and the most repulsive thing I've ever tasted. I am not drinking that!" I said and went to the sink. He lunged at me and drove his fist into my stomach. As much as I thought that would be good to help me throw up whatever it is I just swallowed, it didn't. Instead he slugged me to the ground and poured more down my throat making me swallow it. I drank half the bottle before he stopped.

"You will finish this and I will give you more each day ok," He reported. I nodded because it was the only thing I could do.

In just under two weeks I had lost about 30 pounds. I didn't know how, I knew loosing that amount that fast was not good, but I didn't feel bad. I didn't like it, but at the same time I was fascinated. How could I have lost that much weight so fast and not be in the hospital? Midnight was beaming. I tried to put on some old cloths to compare, but the difference was very drastic and I ended up giving up, hoping I didn't look like a skeleton.

"Go shower and I will give you clothes when you come out," He instructed and I did just that.

Within an hour I was dressed in a very fitted suit, hair brushed nicely and even some cologne. I couldn't believe how different I felt. With my blond hair, dark blue-aqua eyes, the aqua tinge from my Wish, I imagined myself to actually look pretty good. I smiled actually happy. I hadn't felt this good in a long time and I felt like I could go to school and stare everyone down. I hadn't been to school for a few days now, Midnight was too worried I'd sneak something to eat.

We left the house at three in the afternoon and arrived at the castle. Large sprawling fields circled the place, with multiple gardens and streams. It was a huge place, the castle every bit of what you'd assume a castle to look like.

"Hello, name please?" a man standing by the doorway asked. He was dressed in a very expensive suit, it made him look taller, but not overly imposing.

"Mr. Jhole and my son James," Midnight said and the man looked on a glass screen he held in his hand, found our names and smiled.

"We are very pleased to have you here with us, please if you are in need of anything do not hesitate to ask," The butler said with all the kindness in the world.

"Thank you we will be sure to," Midnight said and sauntered into the castle. I followed him grudgingly already hating this. Most people liked the chance to get into the castle especially into such a prestigious event, but all I wanted to do was go home and sleep.

It was a beautiful place, driving through archways and a tree lined gravel road to a large intimidating castle. It was old and weathered, but still standing strong. There were banners strung on the wall, the banners flying Vale Darras colours of silver and blue with a depiction of a cascading waterfall and a sun rising behind it. It was a dumb crest I thought, but others seemed to like it.

Walking through the large metal and wood doors, we stepped onto blue thick carpets that stretched from the doorway to the far wall. To my right a staircase laden with a silver rug that draped down it, stretched up along the wall to the higher floors. The front entrance was a large room with a waterfall making up the back wall. Vine plants trailed up the rocks as water rushed down them to gather in a pool. The waterfall started at the second level where people could look down at it or at any newcomers entering the castle. To my left was doorways leading to other parts of the castle.

Sinth, I and our Guardians Sungar- Sinth's panther- and Myre went up the staircase to the second level where most of the activities would be happening in the East wing. A large room where one side was glass, allowing people to look out onto the beautiful gardens below. It was a pale green coloured room with swirls of dark green mixed in to the bottom half and swirls of even lighter green mixed in to the top half of the wall. Large tables with white cloths held food, water and servers brought expensive wine to those that wanted it. Circular white chairs were at the edges of the room so people could sit. In the front stood a raised section where the King would sit and speak from. A slightly less raised section allowed other people to approach a podium and speak their peace.

That day was very long; all day we slipped poison into people's drinks, some just to make them sick. Midnight hated this event and he wanted to make everyone as sick as he could to stop this event from happening. He was doing a great job; many people were seeking bathrooms by the end of the night and a small group even left. The King made an announcement about going out and experiencing the city, which happened, but Midnight was ready. Whatever happened that day, wherever we went, whatever we ate or drank, Midnight was there to ruin it. By the end of the first day, the people were distressed about their lives. The King had a lot of work to do.

Day two was much like day one, people got sick and left, others went out to the town and got shoved, bumped into, even puked on at one time. Midnight was ready for anything; it was fascinating to see him work. I had never seen him so fervent about something before and I began to get a new impression about him. What I wasn't realizing was how different a future I was creating for myself. Though the meeting and gathering by all these rich people was a money grab in and of itself and just a bunch of spoiled rotten people bragging about it, I didn't know how important it was. They were the ones that paid for the big projects in Vale Darra; they were the ones who supported clubs, schools, groups, and missions. They did a lot for the city and that year, we lost it all. The King had to raise taxes by 5% just to keep afloat. I of course didn't feel too much of a loss as I didn't buy much, but I heard everyone else complain about it.

At the end of the week when my dad came home I told him that the King lost the funding as it was by then the talk of the town. He was understandably outraged. He came through the door and stopped. Staring at me like I was a newly found species.

"Hello Khire," He said bewildered and I smiled at him. As much as I felt like flaunting it in his face that I wasn't all that ugly and fat anymore I simply told him about the loss of the money. That took his attention off of me, even off of the fact that he sold a 7.2 million dollar house. It was supposed to be a good homecoming for him, I think that upset him the most; unfortunately I had to literally ruin it. Not just by breaking the bad news to him, but by actually having caused it, I not only ruined his day, but pretty soon everyone realized just how important that money was. There were a few riots, some civil unrest and missing events. Not as many tourists came that summer, but any good King knows how to smile through bad times and any great King knows how to find a solution to any problem.

King Esmir was the greatest King Vale Darra has ever had. He found funding, he found new ways to bring tourists in and soon enough Vale Darra was booming again. It wasn't even a year when the King was already sitting comfortably on his thrown again.

School despite the fact that I was practically a new person on the outside wasn't any different. I did catch a few eyes, but that was about it. I did have someone walk into me and say sorry, which had never happened before. Some people had walked into me, but they never said a word usually or if they did they caused a tantrum and made me apologize to them. By the second week I gave up on making a new impression. Some things just don't change.

It was a few years after that, the day after I graduated I left a note on my dad's bed saying I loved him, but I couldn't live with him anymore. I took a few things with me, a few coats, sweaters and other clothes and stuffed them in a backpack. I was 18 years old, average height, really skinny and I headed to the streets. I wound my way to Cadence's house and plopped my backpack on the ground inside the house. He came into the living room and looked at me.

"You left?" He asked incredulous.

"I didn't know what else to do," I said shrugging and he nodded.

We had spent the last years getting to know each other and training each other. I taught him the most, reading, writing, math, science, I'd bring my homework here and we'd work on it together. I also taught him weapons, balance and other assassin basics. Life lessons and knowledge that would help him. He became a better person and a much better assassin. Throughout this time I seen very little of Midnight, Isaac came around a little, but he didn't like how quiet it was and so he never stayed long, just long enough to spy on us then run back and tell his Master. I assumed Midnight was letting me go, he taught me everything he wanted to teach me, I was no longer his apprentice. I was an assassin now, on my own and picking my own moves, planning my own targets. I liked it if

I didn't think about the fact that I was still killing someone, but I began to get really good at it.

The first year on the streets was hard. Winter was cold and Cadence and I would curl up together and use as much magic as we could to try and create body heat. Food was hard, we tried catching rats, which was easy, but I couldn't get a taste for them. Cat made me feel like I was eating my brother's cat and eating dog made me feel like I was eating my dad's Guardian. So I began to steal food and Cadence got a job. I wanted to get a job too, but I was worried about running into someone I knew. I told Cadence it was so that I could become a better assassin, but really I was ashamed of myself. There is no dignity when you sleep on the streets, I tried to find it and soon I found it just made things worse. The only thing I ended up finding was acceptance, which ended up being all that I ever need. Acceptance is the only thing I have ever needed. If I had found it earlier, I would have been a better person I think, but it took me 19 years to find it.

I was 22 years old when I ran into one of my brothers, I had been doing some running around for a while by the time he stepped out in front of me and caught me by the back of my shirt.

"And where do you think you're going?" He practically growled at me. I was confused why he was so angry with me, I hadn't seen him for years so I hadn't even done anything besides killing people, but he didn't know I did that.

"Well, well look what you've become. Didn't you use to make fun of the police as a kid?" I asked him. He was in full uniform, a flashy badge of Vale Darra's crest pinned on him with the worlds VDP underneath it. "What are you doing?" He asked again.

"Going for a nice stroll, what are you doing?" I began to wiggle, but he shook me.

"What are you doing?" He asked again annoying me.

I was fairly clean, I had washed myself in a stream this morning and wore fairly clean clothes, but a street rat can only get so clean.

My hair was wild and though I had shaved, I had a bit of a gruff still and a few holes in the knees of my jeans.

"Walking, is that illegal now?" I don't know why I was being so defensive, but he got my guard up and I wasn't about to put it down.

"I'm taking you home," He said and started dragging me down the street.

"I have a home," I tried to be as difficult as possible which was working for my benefit as he was losing his grip on me.

"Khire! Stop you're going home!" He yelled at me and pushed me in front of him.

"Fetcher! Let me go!" I yelled back.

A few heads turned our way, but a red-faced cop pushing a street rat wasn't rare here and so they lost interest quickly. I was about to try and break free again when Fetcher opened his cruisers door and threw me in. Myre tried to get away, but Fetchers Guardian who is a tiger, forced him in after me. The cruiser was big, still considered a car, but it was big. The divider between the front and the back was strong and durable so that anyone's Guardian couldn't break it. I sat with my arms crossed as Fetcher started the car and merged with traffic.

It would take us forty minutes at least to get to our dads house, the traffic here was so busy you almost felt like you were moving backwards. So in that time I made sure to glare at my older brother in the review mirror the whole time. He made sure to ignore me and once we finally got to our fathers he got out of the car and quickly opened my door. I kicked at him then tried to push past him, but he was obviously prepared as he dodged my kick then punched me in the stomach. Gasping for breath as he grabbed me by the hair, he dragged me to the front steps.

"I don't have to stay here if I don't want to," I growled at him.

Suddenly the door swung open and our dad walked out into the daylight, absolutely furious. I dug in my heels to try and get away, dad wasn't a violent man, but when he was angry he was still scary.

"Khireal!" He growled. He hardly ever called me by my real name so obviously he was really angry with me in particular.

"Father," I said sweetly. That was a bad idea, Fetcher pushed me towards him and he grabbed me by the neck and slammed me against the doorframe. He didn't use to be violent; apparently if you provoke anyone they will turn on you at some point.

"What?" I squeaked.

"You stupid good for nothing boy!" He spat.

Fetcher and many other people who came out of the house got an ear full with really colourful words to boot for the next while as dad told me how upset, disappointed, furious and everything else he felt about me.

"I am old enough to live on my own, to live wherever I want to," I told everyone listening.

"Oh no you're not, you've had your fun, now it's over, you…" Dad began.

"Fun! Fun. You think I did this because I think its fun? Dad I…"

"Then why? You have a house, you choose to live on the street, and it's your choice. My door has been open this whole time, I haven't seen you in years!"

"You just don't get it! I don't want to live here I don't like living here! I'm sorry I really am, but I don't want to stay here," I said glaring at him.

"Why not?" He slammed me against the doorframe again and my head made a distinct crack as I smacked my head against the wood.

"Owww Dad stop," I said feeling the back on my head with my hand for any bumps.

"You're an idiot, you had everything and you gave it up!" Dad growled. "You're not returning to the streets and if you're not going to stay here you can go sit in a jail cell," He threw me back at Fetcher who caught me and smiled. Despite the fact that I was his brother obviously he liked the idea of putting me in prison.

"But I haven't done anything!" I said trying to get free of Fetcher. He was well muscled and a lot stronger then my scrawny body. He probably had a good 50 pounds on me, I wasn't about to get away from him without using magic, which wouldn't do me good because then I'd just get charged.

"There's a new program, street people will be placed into a house where they will be provided with enough food and essentials to live comfortably. They will be monitored and in return they will work for the city. Until you repay back into the system and are able to support yourself you will live there. Once you are able to support yourself you will buy yourself a new house. It's a great system," Fetcher told me sounding reasonably pleased.

"That sounds fantastic, but I am very happy where I live thank you," Just then I kicked him really hard in the shin then brought my arm up and hooked it under his, I got him flat on his stomach within seconds and was off running down the street. I heard people calling after me, but I got down the street and turned the corner, after a little more distance, I used my magic to propel me faster. Speeding down the laneway faster than cars. I got back into the city and wound my way into the safety of the alleyways.

CHAPTER #10

When the sun had risen well into the sky I was already positioned on top of a tower that reached for the clouds above. Now twenty-three I had the muscle build of a long time acrobat, though still scrawny and rugged looking. The tower stood high over Vale Darra like a large needle. It was grey and weathered, but still a busy building as the people inside rushed around filing paperwork and attending meetings. There were one hundred thirty six employees working here that dealt with paperwork, clients and setting up deals. Eighty-two receptionists, fifty-nine maids to clean the eighty-eight story building entirely each day. Along with twenty-six security guards and seventeen executives.

The building had two hundred and ninety eight rooms from forty-four janitor closets to eight large conference rooms. The building had very thick walls and a strong foundation. It had thick glass windows, a good security system and a backup alarm system. Each room was newly painted a colour to set a mood. The conference rooms had long mahogany tables and hardwood flooring, large floor to ceiling windows and lamps that hung from the ceiling in an intricate vine-like design. The offices varied in size, but each had a top quality computer, a mahogany desk, large windows and cabinets. The reception desks were long and busy and polished to a shine. Windows spaced every six meters, carpets stretching from the revolving doors to the desks with the rest of the room being blue marble tiling. A waiting room off to the side that had chairs and tables with sports and fashion magazines, a flower pot stuffed with dahlias, and old classical books about the West, newer books written by well-known authors and books about health and food.

Despite the elaborate and welcoming decor, I had heard through a grape vine of people, that there were a number of people here who were spies. And so I decided to pay them a visit. I got inside the building through an open window just below me, leaving behind the sun that shone through the clouds to hit Vale Darra. A breeze cooled me down as if to help prepare me for the work I had to do. I went to the staircase and looked down at the floor far below. I waited and listened. No one was in the stairwell though no one really used it any way, as there were four large elevators. I jumped over the railing and plunged down, slipping between the gaps between the staircases. I was counting in my head, falling faster and faster as the floors zoomed by me. I was reaching forty when I thrust my hands down and said a few quick magical words. I reached out and caught a railing, swung over and landed neatly and quietly on a step.

I casually walked the steps down to the thirty-ninth floor then out the door and into a light, carpeted, purple walled hallway. The air smelled slightly of perfume and scented deodorant, the silence filled by many buzzing computers, people typing on keyboards, talking on the phone or using the multipurpose photocopier. I walked down the hallway paying no attention to others with my head held high like I had somewhere really important to be. Several doors down and on my left, I found the door I wanted. I knocked on the door and when I heard a women's voice call, "Come in!" I entered.

"Oh hello. Can I help you?" The women sitting at her desk asked. She was dressed in a tight-knee length, black skirt with a white blouse and black tie. Her long, wavy brown hair was tied in a bun and her thin-framed, blue glasses brought out her two toned blue eyes, her face was thin and long with high cheekbones and a small chin. She stood up and reached forward to shake my hand. She offered me a seat and with a thanks I took it.

"Ok, so what brings you here?" She asked getting straight to the point with an air of authority.

"Well I'm here on behalf of some business. I hear your going away," I started.

"Ok, are you Mr. Hash Phaymar?" She asked.

"No, I'm representing him today, he meant to come here, but was called away on important business. My name is Riley," She nodded along and I continued, "I was told you were going on vacation. Is that correct?"

"Yes, I'm going away," She spoke clipped as if she didn't want to discuss this topic.

"Ok and for what reasons are you going on this trip for?"

"Well I am also involved in other matters, none that concern you of course,"

"Of course of course, but can I ask where you're going?" I pressed.

"I will be doing some work when I travel in a few months' time to the East," She told me thin lipped. I nodded.

"Well is there anything we should know or do you have any questions?" I asked sweetly.

"Yes, I would like to know the reason why you're here?" She told me. Her face was stern and sharp, her eyes piercing me as she sat, stick-straight in a chair that looked particularly uncomfortable. She seemed to be an easy person to read: a dusty, old perfume lingering in the office, a stern person at a very neat, clean desk that was organized down to the last paper clip.

I smiled at her and got to my feet.

"Well when an employ asks for a few months off, we like to see what's going on and if there is any problems involved. We just like to make sure employees are happy here," I said with a smile as I reached out my hand and nodded to her. She stood up on her black high heels, leaned over her desk and gave my hand a shake.

In seconds her body dropped and I was around the desk to catch her limp form before her head could smash into the hard wood floor. Her Guardian, a small bird screeched and flew at me. Myre had the bird pinned to the ground in seconds, but it stared threateningly at Myre and I as we gathered them up. Well at least as threatening a bird can be eye to eye with a cougar. I knew very well who this woman was. The real employee who worked here was a woman named Vasha Snivv who is a typical alcoholic and is now letting one too many drinks sort out her life. The woman before me was a good impostor though. I had no problem with Vasha, she was harmless, but this other women I didn't trust.

I suspected for a while now that there were some assassins here in the city plotting something. I didn't know what, but I being the nosy person that I am decided to find out and kill them if I didn't like what I found. Currently, there have been spies working for people who want to over throw the King. I, though not technically the King's spy, did spy for a royal member of the family and so I spent a lot of time tracking down people who wanted to cause harm to the King.

This woman, whose name was Hollen Baddon, was a spy for someone and she had information that I wanted. I had been studying her for months to learn her targets and motives, but have only learned that she liked impersonating other people and working for big corporations.

I turned to the window and decided the window would be my best bet. As I walked towards it, my hand, with the body on my arms, made a pushing motion and the window flew open. I looked out, down to the streets where vehicles honked and rumbled, as they made their slow progress on the paved road. I swung my leg out the window then jumped out with my Guardian, holding the still furious bird in his mouth, behind me. In seconds my body, along with Hollen and both Guardians, went invisible and we plummeted to the ground. We weren't really invisible, but it was a technique used that made us less of a focus. To some people that actually noticed us they would just see something at the corner of their vision, maybe a bird swooping in the air. With some more magic I slowed my speed and hit the ground light and silent, going into a crouch to absorb the slight impact. I walked off and away, down the alleys to a small wooden building barely standing. It smelled of old alcohol and blood, the insides filled with broken tables, chairs and cabinets.

I set the body down on a dilapidated chair, the cloth eaten away long ago. Hollen lay unconscious as I went around making sure the windows were boarded up and the door shut securely. Ten minutes later she woke up groggy and looked around somewhat confused until her eyes locked with mine. She jumped to her feet and thrust her hands forward yelling out spells and sending them hurling at me. Her magic flowed out in a grey-green colour, curling like smoke, but rushing at me as if a strong wind blew it. I knew if it hit me it might kill me, assassins were trained death magic and though the magic may not be strong enough to overpower my magic, I didn't care to test it. With a slight motion of my fingers her spells died away before even coming close to me, a useful defence magic that basically caused the spell to neutralize itself by turning inwards and terminating itself.

"Now listen here. Where are you going, what are you doing, and who is going with you?" I asked her in one breath. She stayed silent. "And just to speed this up, start talking. You will be surprised how much patience I have, so you might as well just work with me," I told her crossing my arms.

"You can't do anything to me Street rat," She snarled at me. Street rat was a common insult I got, having lived on the street since I was eighteen, I didn't exactly look up to par with Vale Darra's high-class citizens.

"Frightening. Now speak. I can make you do what I want if you don't do it willingly," I told her, my voice deep and cold.

"I will not tell you anything," She growled.

I stared at her expectantly and she stared back thin lipped and agitated.

"I'm not going to tell you anything! Either leave or I'll kill you," She said her voice rising and quivering slightly.

"Now why would I do that? I want something from you, I'm not gonna go away. And besides the probability of you killing me is highly unlikely, it's not even realistic," I told her as if she were stupid.

"Now, you and a few buddies are going *east*, was it? Now I know who you are. You're a spy, and you're here on business. You want information. You're planning something ... But what?" The woman's, eyes locked forward and remained silent, but the lines at the side of her mouth and her stance told me she was very alert and tense.

"Are you planning to kill a particular person? Are you planning your next victims, maybe gonna kill someone or help someone.

"Oh by the way, my friends interviewing your friends right now, they're not far away, I bet if you screamed they would hear you. There's only thin walls between you and them," I taunted. She stayed silent.

"You have some training, but you haven't been a spy long."

"I've been an assassin since I was eight!" She yelled.

"Not a spy? Well anyway, you're a horrible assassin. Now who was your master? You were probably trained by… Hmm lets see… was your Master Zero… maybe Huron… No that wouldn't be it. You were trained by someone here, I know that, ah Scarlet. She trained you wasn't it. Ya she was a good assassin; she liked herself more than anything though. Got caught in a mirror more times than at gun point, but she certainly was someone you would never want to turn your back on. Now, what did Scarlet teach you? She was great with magic, very powerful, and she was very talented in getting in and out of tricky situations. You, however, aren't living up to that, but then we all have our strengths and weaknesses."

"You know nothing about me!" She yelled and lunged at me.

I sidestepped and brought my knee up into her stomach, knocking the wind out of her, then crushing her to the ground as I brought my hand down.

"Just because you're a girl doesn't mean I'll be nice to you. You're no different from others I've dealt with," I growled.

"Just kill me and leave, if you're not going to kill me then leave anyway," She said through gritted teeth.

"If ya want me to let you go, you have to tell me what I want to know first. Or we can keep doing this, your choice." I said shrugging nonchalantly.

"I'll tell you nothing, not now not ever!" she yelled and ducked into a roll and around to my side. She straitened slightly then lunged at my knees to take me out. I pressed my hands to her head and as she did a face plant into the dirty and dusty ground I pivoted around to stand beside her. Her face in the ground, she made an annoyed sound and pushed herself off the floor. She turned around and looked at me.

"Why don't you go ask someone else?" She growled stupidly. "You have others? Who?" I asked innocently.

"You can very well go and find them on your own, now let me get back to work," "Why would I do that? You wouldn't have somewhere important to go now would you?" I sat down on the ground cross-legged, and looked interested in hearing what she had to say.

"Nowhere you need to worry about," She rolled again, coming up on my left, this time kicking out and twisting to punch up into my jaw line. Before foot or fist could connect, I seized her neck and had her in a headlock before she could draw another breath. I sat beside her and released the pressure slightly.

"Now what is it that you want to tell me?" I asked pleasantly. She gave a frustrated half growl and tried to wiggle free. I tightened my hold and she stopped as she gasped for breath with difficulty.

"I'm going to go meet someone. He hired us to get information about you and now we're going back to tell him what we know. He wants to kill you." She said the last part happily.

"Good. See, talking gets you far," I loosened my grip a considerable amount. "Now what else do you know, who is this guy and why does he want me dead?"

With the released pressure she took a deep breath then brought her elbow sharply back into my ribs. I tightened on instinct, but could only wince from her elbow. "I'm not telling you that, you can figure that out by yourself," She gasped, still remarkably stubborn. I looked down and let her slump to the ground.

"You're playing with me," I said as I got to my feet. "You said that as if it was nothing. You have things you can tell me, things you can't tell me and things you are told to tell me to a certain degree. That was something you were supposed to tell me. What else am I supposed to know?"

She panted. "Your life will get more and more miserable over the next few years. He's going after everyone who has had some sort of contact with you and then he will come after you,"

"Anything else?" "Ya, you're a good for nothing street rat and I can't wait till he kills you," She growled at me and I kicked her in the face.

"Well you're a pleasant woman. By the way you make a horrible assassin and he sent you because you're disposable," I said as she rubbed her jaw. She had bit into her lip and the blood dripped down her chin to the floor. She looked like a mad dog without the froth coming from her mouth. When she saw the blood she stared at me and swore, spitting and white knuckled she cursed me and laughed with pleasure at her own foul mouth. Slightly amused I let her ramble then when she was out of breath I said my goodbyes.

"Very well. Enjoy your stay here. You should find everything you need," and I walked away and left her, leaving her to her own devises and a room filling with poison.

CHAPTER #11

I went from one place to another, walking through the alleyways to a small cabin that had bordered up windows. The cabin creaked every time the wind blew. This one was in rougher shape than the one I had just left. There were many holes and gaps in the panels and it was positioned beside the old, dilapidated jail that was falling to pieces. When I was young, I would sneak into it as a test and retrieve an object that my Master hid in there, then kill someone and have to take a personal item of theirs and put it in the jail without being caught and seen.

I looked at the jail as I approached. It was closed down when it was rumoured the jail to be haunted. Long ago, every night a prisoner could be heard screaming at the top of their lungs, crying for help, pleading, hysterical laughing and screams of total agony and fear. And all around the jail people could hear sounds like walls falling down and someone being slammed against something hard. The man who did it all was simply known as Wally. He lived in the darkest cell where he had no windows to see out of and only rats to spend time with. Being a smart man, he was able to get around to all the other cells and torture the prisoners. He didn't do it to seek justice, he liked to create fear and pain and he had a very great love of making the guards watch and turning them just as insane as Wally was. Most of the guards that worked there are now in mental institutes while all the prisoners are dead, their bones hidden in the walls.

I had met him only once, and I wouldn't want to meet him again. He was always hunched over and had long, grey, wiry hair sticking out at odd angles from a very deformed head. His skin was very blotchy, dirty and bruised. Open wounds were badly infected and his bones were jutting out at all angles giving the illusion of skin too small for his body. He was deathly skinny and wore a long, very old, very dirty and torn sweater with equally torn shorts. He was bug eyed and he smiled constantly, though he only had black gums and no teeth. This wreck of a man used to be the most famous and wealthiest person in Vale Darra. He hit his downfall when he was in the kitchen one day and his wife came home after having an affair with another man.

It was a nice day and he was whistling in the kitchen when she stumbled into the kitchen in a tight fitted, black dress. He knew at once where she'd been and he had gotten very mad at her and so with knife in hand, he swiped out at her and scratched her with it. When he seen the blood he became crazy, it was only a little bit of flecks on the steel blade, but it was enough to drive him over the edge. He was mad and he wanted to kill her and so he cut her up, hacking at her body repeatedly until the very ground was covered in blood and body parts. He lost it completely as he bundled up the body parts and put her in the wall. It took at least a year for her body to be found and him put in jail.

At that time the jail was a grand place, thought to be the best jail the city will ever see, the guards were great people that all knew to be fair and just. It had high hopes to last long and contain the worse people in Vale Darra. But when Wally was put into his cell, he at that point was so mentally unstable he instantly started attacking people. Even when he was in his jail cell alone, he somehow got himself out, that part has never been found out how, but he did do it and he would sneak into other cells and slaughter other prisoners, then return to his cell. The guards found no holes in the floor or walls, no loose bars or anything, but every night Wally got out, even when he was guarded, Wally got out and cut up his guard's bodies. I even tried to find out how he escaped, but I never could.

Trying to stop Wally, the cabin was built right beside the jail to put Wally in it, but that proved worse. Though the cabin was built securely and thought to be able to contain even the strongest of magi, Wally was able to get out and kill even more people. And so Wally was returned to his dark cell in the jail. The cabin was never entered into again after one day people walked into it to find the walls blood red and insulated with bodies. In the end, Wally's jail door was cemented shut and no guard or other being visited him again, he was completely shut off from all contact with people for three years. After a time, a dozen guards discovered his body in a wall in the Sargent's office.

I stopped and shook my head, turning my mind from wondering and setting it to the matter at hand as I looked back at the cabin. I felt a shiver go up my spine as I looked back to the old jail. I wasn't scared, but I didn't need to be thinking about it.

I opened the door carefully to the cabin, more hesitant and unsure of its ability to continue standing with the wind blowing on it. I preferred going in this way as appose to using the jail front doors for many reasons, but mostly because I found the jail creepy and this seemed a little less so. I walked inside and followed a dark tunnel dug in the ground, the trap door pushed aside, which took me beneath the jail. The smell of decay was very strong in the air as I approached my apprentice. He looked over and smiled at me.

"Hello Dusk," He said simply and then turned back to his victims.

"Hello Cadence. What do we have here?" I asked him. Cadence was crouched on an old stool looking at his victims steadily. He had a black eye, which told me someone got a hit on him, but he still managed to subdue them. His brown hair was tangled and plastered to his forehead from sweat. He was heavier than me, but with the same muscle build and same hardiness. He is my apprentice; though not a great one, he does have some uses.

He got out of his crouch on his stool and stood on the ground, coming up just a bit taller than me. I met his brown eyes, almost black in the dim light, as he tilted his head to the side.

"I got some information out of him, but nothing much. What about you? You got that girl?" He asked as if we were talking about something pleasant.

"Ya, she's not talking much. Though, something interesting… she's an assassin," I told him.

"An assassin, but I thought she was a spy," Cadence asked confused.

"Ya well she's an assassin," I told him and put my hands on my hips.

"Ok… but she never even killed anyone, how…," He started before I cut him off.

"I know I know, just move on,"

"Well what's the big deal anyway? What does this *assassin* goin away got ta do with us?" He asked slightly confused. "Well she did tell me something. Someone wants me dead and they are first going to kill anyone connected to me," I said darkly.

"Oh that's all?" Cadence sat back down on the stool. "Well that's really nothing new," He said after a moment.

"What else did you find out?" I asked. "Nothing really, they did say some stuff about going to this place called Harrows Peak, do ya know the place?" He said and I thought for a moment.

"I think I remember hearing about some place like that, but what else did they say?" "That they were going to go there in three months' time and do some stuff. They're meeting someone there and are planning some big thing. They were talking about some dumb soundin' stuff, like something bad gonna happen so they were planning how to protect themselves. Apparently someone isn't happy and they don't want to be in the way. They continued to speak about something to do with people from the past coming back to get revenge or something, which doesn't surprise me," He said shrugging.

"Ok, what else?" I pressed getting a little annoyed at him.

"Ahhhh well they said a particular person, who wasn't named, but referred to as 'particular person', should be transforming soon. They didn't really expand on that, but said that this particular person would become a monster. They said it fearfully which makes me think that it isn't a good thing," He said using his hands as he spoke.

"Ok well I'll be on the lookout for monsters, in the meantime lets go see what else we can find out," I said and turned back to the entrance.

Somewhere in the jail panels from boarded up windows were falling to the ground. The nails rusted away leaving the panels to fall to the dust and dirt and send a loud echoing sound throughout the jail. I was happy to leave this place, the wind moaned through the jail and made it seem as if the place was alive which only hurried me out faster.

We walked out into the daylight that shone onto Vale Darra bright and hot. A few clouds lingered in the deep blue sky and the breeze tunnelled through the alleyway that we now left behind for the loud, noisy and very crowded streets of the city. I walked off to my right towards the park. There was one person who could really help right now, and I'd bet myself she'd be there.

It took me twenty minutes to find the right park, but eventually I did. As I got closer I spotted a large owl with piercing eyes that followed me as I walked towards the slouched form on the worn picnic bench. At first it looked like a patchy old dress coat, but then it moved and a face appeared beneath the hood. The owl hooted and flew over to land on its Protected's shoulder.

"Slesh, ahhh Dusk's. What can we do for ye?" The form said in a very lazy drawl. She looked up at us. One vibrant green eye the other an odd swirl of pale and dark blue. Her scraggily white hair fell down to her knees though she was still very young to have such white hair, her face wrinkle free. Her dress coat was old fashioned and fluffed out in random tuffs around her wrists. It was purple, blue and black, random swirls and patterns here and there with a few patches that were of varying colours. She wore worn hiking boots with black leggings on. She had red fingerless gloves and gold and silver hoops around her upper arms. Her skin was tanned and weathered. She was a bizarre curiosity known as Stargazer Sahonnai. Her Wish was that she could look up at night to the sky and see both past and future, supposedly.

I sat down beside her and she stared at me.

"Ah want to know about the past do ye? Well I'll tell ye this, when ye think ye've got the right person, think again. Looks can be very deceiving sometimes and sometimes when ye think ye see one, ye see two,"

"Ahhhh……. what?" I asked completely confused.

"More will come, bad things will happen. Everything pointing towards ye. Someone killin'. If ye don't kill the person that is killin' these people, then you'll die and a great darkness will be cast upon us, but don't lose focus! Ye have a great enemy Dusk. Kill him or y'er life will cease quiet suddenly," "Who is it?" I asked impatiently.

She liked to speak in confusing slightly disjointed sentences. I had once tried to make her talk properly, but she became very vulgar and unhelpful after that.

"No, can't tell ye that, tis something I mustn't tell, mustn't tell anyone, it is tragic I know, but I will say ye will kill the wrong man," She said.

"But beware, times don't always end when the bad things end. You'll also follow a foul trail, go astray and lose yourself. Funny, funny, your life… How cruel it will all be. Tell me which animal are you?" She asked. She then suddenly turned away and looked at Cadence forgetting that she had asked me a question.

I didn't even know what she meant and was annoyed that she might actually withhold information from me that might save my life.

"Ye are a very stupid boy," She said so suddenly I burst out laughing. Cadence looked at her completely bewildered.

"Thanks," He said sarcastically.

"But thank ye for saving the one the world is watching," Stargazer Sahonnai said kindly to Cadence. Cadence nodded, but said nothing, looking completely bewildered.

"Ok we're done here," I said and grabbed Cadence by the arm. I led him away and kept hold of him until we got far away from the crazy lady.

Cadence continued to look back at her until she was out of sight.

"What did she mean, she...?" He started.

"Shush," I said as I watched someone dressed very nicely walk into the alleyway farther ahead to our left. I walked along the cracked sidewalk, passing the storefronts. People paid us no mind as we followed the man down the alleyway. He had his head held high and his hands in loose fists as he strutted down the centre of the alleyway; his long strides carrying him as he stepped over anything questionable looking and dead and continued walking like they were nothing more than gum stuck on the ground.

I watched him. His focus seemed to be set on something, but I didn't know what. And for some reason he seemed familiar. He didn't look very young, but certainly not old. He had dark hair and eyes and equally dark skin. He was wearing a black jacket over a pure white pleated shirt, black pants and a black tie around his neck. From his neatly brushed hair down to his polished black shoes he looked every bit a high-class citizen and a wealthy man. He had a very confident stride and a charm that drew all eyes to him. It was odd to watch all six foot five of him walk so comfortable down the dirty and rotten alleyway.

"You lost?" I asked him and he turned. He looked at me then continued to walk away as if I was of little concern.

"Come on, leave him, he's weird," Cadence said.

"You go. I'm too curious," I told him not turning away from the man. Something about him caught my attention and gave me a weird vibe and I wanted to know why.

"Ok whatever, see you back at the den." He rolled his eyes and walked away.

"Yup," I said waving over my shoulder at him, but still not looking at him. I followed the man for a while. He seemed to know where he was going. He would turn left a few times then right a few times till you felt you were just going around in circles, but he continued on, determined and silent.

I anticipated the gangly forms that hung in the shadows, lurking there as they waited very patiently for a person to come by. They acted more as a pack of wolves than of people, and though they were wearing clothes, they were more wolfish than human. Their long matted hair hung down their backs, yellow teeth, filed to sharp points, eyes watching every single move anything made. They were haggard and dirty, clothes badly torn and black from dirt. They were hardly recognizable as people with their curved claw-like fingers and lanky bodies. An animal-like look in their eyes as they watched from the shadows of the nearby buildings. They crept, crouching slowly towards the man; looking so intent on him they didn't notice me at all. They slowly circled him, ready for a fight, their fingers twitching.

They were coming closer. The man seemed to have taken notice of them, but he continued to look determined as he walked on. The wolfish humans snarled and growled, exposing more of their terrible looking black and yellow fang like teeth.

"You've tried this already and you lost then, let's just say I win again and you leave me alone. How does that sound, mutts?" The man suddenly spoke, his voice very deep and rich and though it sounded annoyed it had a tone of amusement and a very thick accent that wasn't from here.

"No," One human-wolf growled. He seemed to be the alpha male as he came forward faster and soon they all lunged to attack the man. The man's Guardian acted the fastest, fleeting around, biting the wolf Guardians and making them yelp in pain. The wolves backed off from the strange Guardian, it was some type of mongoose. It was fast, zooming around, causing the wolves and their humans to hesitate. The man however didn't, he seemed to become something else. He acted as if it was even simpler than breathing. He flowed from one move into the other darting in and out of the humans, causing bloody noses, black eyes, sending people to the ground, winding them and turning them into a bunch of very untrained pups. He straightened up and looked down at them, smiling. He had single handily taken the nine humans within five minutes. And he fought not to kill, but to hurt. Every movement was precise and instinctual.

"Over the hundredth time you've tried that and I still beat you! Maybe it will teach you for next time we meet, but you know what they say, 'you can't teach an old dog knew tricks'," The man said haughtily.

With that the man kept on walking and I took a moment to look at the sprawled and tangled figures on the ground, then ran to catch up with the man.

"Hey, what's up with you?" I asked him now walking beside him. He looked over at me and smiled.

"Wondered when you would come out of hiding," He said casually and looked forward again. "You're a young one aren't you," He didn't sound like he was looking for an answer.

"Ahhh ya? What's your business here?" I asked him.

"Business as usual," He said so calmly it actually made me tense.

"Business and what business would have you down these streets?" I questioned.

He grinned at me.

"Just business," He answered with a slow and careful tone.

"Listen people like you don't just come strutting on down here for *just business.* Your gonna tell me what you're doing here or we're going to have a problem," I threatened and suddenly his hand was around my throat and he had me slammed against a wall before I could defend myself. He was fast, almost too fast for me. I kicked him in the leg hard enough to break his grasp and make him stumble. I brought out a knife and shot forward.

The fight was quick that was for sure, he dodged my moves and I dodged his. We seemed to be equally matched except for one thing, he seemed unable to do magic or else he just held out while I had no qualms using my own magic. I had him pinned against the wall unable to move.

"So your Dusk, well now it's nice to meet you. I'm an old friend of your Masters," He said smiling.

"What does he want?" I growled.

"Nothing that I know of, I haven't seen him in a while, but I'm sure he'll pop up at some point in time. Now you let me go," He glared at me, his dark eyes taking on a new edge.

"What's your business?" I asked keeping him pinned with my magic against the wall.

"I'm scouting, that's what I do. I haven't been here in a while and I thought I'd check things out. Now that Midnights gone off somewhere I don't have to worry about him coming after me," He said simply. "Now will you let me go and let me be on my way?"

"No I think I'd rather speak to you some more thanks," I continued. "Well then how is your day?" The man asked companionably.

"Lovely couldn't be better, how about you?"

"Rather lovely as well," He replied.

"Who are you?" I asked squinting as I looked at him.

"I have had lots of names. Right now I am Duke," He told me thinking slightly.

"Umm ok, Duke, you've obviously been here before though I've never seen you before, and I don't entirely believe you," I told him thoughtfully. "You're a quick one. I was born and bred on the streets far from here and you should never trust another human, we aren't the truthful type," He said with a hint of amusement as if something were funny.

"Tell me do you know what you are?" He asked and I laughed.

"Ah I'm human and I lie?" I said thinking he was leading on to say he didn't trust me either.

"I guess you don't know who I am, but I know who you are. Tell me have you discovered just how powerful and bloodthirsty you are Beast?" He said sneering.

"Who are you and how do you know me? And I am not bloodthirsty. Midnight might have made me who I am, but I am not a beast," I told him coldly.

"One day I am going to kill you Beast and I will make sure I will make you scream," He said, his features turning darker if that were even possible.

"Great looking forward to it, why are you telling me this?" I asked ready to draw swords.

"Because I want you to be prepared. You have so much farther to go before you know what you are. I want you to know why your kind should never exist, and I want to be the one to exterminate you," He said with a smile.

"But why go through all that trouble of waiting? Why don't you kill me now?" I asked him.

"Because I want you to see what you are and feel it and know that I need to kill you. I want you to want to be killed by me," He told me seriously.

"What am I?" I asked confused.

"You will see, you're more then you even know, more than the world has seen. But in time you'll find out and when that time comes, I'll be here waiting patiently to kill you myself," He said almost gleefully.

"Great, but what makes you think I won't kill you first?" I said then dove at him. Suddenly, the wind was knocked out of me and I landed flat on my face on the ground. When I looked up the man was gone.

The life of an assassin always came down to one thing: death. Death was the way that things were ended, and so death it would be, by my blade or his, someone would die and the better assassin would be left standing. I just hoped it was me.

I turned on my heels and walked away. I had work to do and so I pushed the thoughts of the bizarre man to the back of my mind and prepared myself for my next victim. What was going to happen in the future I would leave for the future, I'd worry about it when it became the present.

CHAPTER #12

Like all teenagers, there is always a dark time in your life, mine started far earlier and went later than most, but I got through it like usual. I didn't fare so well after Miranna's death, the fact that it was my fault near suffocated me. At times I wanted my pain to end, I figured dead people couldn't care about the living, they couldn't care about life, they were dead, whatever dead was.

On a bright day when I was 16, I walked into darkness seeking out a quiet place. The world faded around me, becoming distant, irrelevant. I left it behind along with hopes, dreams and every bit of happiness that ever bloomed within my heart. In my hand I held a gun, it was my companion like my blades were, but it would be my friend for now.

Each step I took was followed by another and each step closer; I let go of life, the living world, willing my beating heart to be still. It would not and I continued to walk until I stopped before a fountain. An angel spread her arms towards me, but her grey sad face did not call me into her arms. As the water streamed out from her palms I approached. In the silence and empty street I stepped into the coolness of the water. I looked at my reflection and knew if I could see, I would see a blond hair, blue-eyed monster staring back. I tilted my head, it would tilt it's. I pointed the gun at the monster and shot, but it stared back at me in mockery. I sneered and pointed the gun again. This time I wouldn't miss. And with that thought I pulled the trigger.

My first thought was pain, which was not what I was expecting and not what I wanted to feel. I wanted nothingness, no sense of anything and yet I felt pain and coolness. The water, the water was washing over me. Could I have missed? I thought myself a terrible assassin if I couldn't even shoot my own head.

Slowly I opened my eyes. The sun glinted off the red water. I hated the blue, red and black shapes I saw and I hated the pain, it meant I was still alive. Suddenly I felt arms around me, they had been holding me the whole time, but I only realized it now.

"Whaaa," I stammered.

"Shhh," A woman's voice whispered in my ear.

"What did you do? You stupid women," I growled.

"Stupid? You stupid boy!" She snarled and grabbed my chin, bringing my eyes to hers. Myre was nearby and he was talking to me in my mind trying to sort things out. Green eyes glared at me with pure hatred. Her black hair streamed down in waves around her small face and I realized who it was.

"Princess Shirra," I said in greeting. She frowned displeased.

"Never call me that," She said and then began to pull me out of the fountain.

"Why did you save me? How did you save me?" I asked incredulous. I believe I had died at least for a short time, how did she bring me back to life?

Princess Shirra was a doctor and third in line for the throne; she had joined the working force and preferred it over her royalty. She was also a very gifted healer. Shirra's Wish was that she could heal wounds and apparently bring people back from the dead.

"I don't know how I brought you back and frankly I don't know why!" She growled at me as I unwillingly scrambled over the cobbled side of the fountain still dizzy.

"Well throw me back in!" I yelled back.

"Ya likely," She quipped.

"Look, you don't know me so I'll be nice. Let me die or I will kill you and then I'm just gonna shoot myself again!" I shouted as I gained my sense of balance. Shirra looked at me, sighing she placed her hand on my shoulder and pain shot through my body making me collapse onto the cobbled ground. I gasped for breath, confused and wondering what happened.

"You even try it and I will have you drooling like a baby from pain," She threatened and I groaned as she knelt down beside me.

"What do you want?" I asked her through gritted teeth.

"Nothing from you street rat," She sneered.

"Then why?" I whispered in pain.

"I told you I don't know!" She stood back up and began to walk away, then turned and walked back to me. She took my gun and with some magic broke it. Then frisking me, she found all my blades and broke them to.

"What are you doing?" I screeched and lunged at her, not even getting to my feet first. As I came close she once again put her hand on me and I once again found myself twitching in pain on the ground. I half growled half yelled in frustration.

"You stupid boy," Was all she said and then she walked away.

I laid there for a while thinking I could try and find another weapon, the fragments of my weapons were too small to grasp and kill myself, though there was a piece I could use to hack away. I didn't like messy work and I didn't like the thought of a slow painful death, despite being an assassin, I still didn't accept death could happen to me. It was a problem and a weakness and right now it made me angry and want to kill myself slowly just to prove to myself I could. Betrayed by my own body I slowly sat up and stayed like that for a long while, not touching the small fragment a foot away from my hand.

Getting back to the present, I circled around the major part of town until I came to a small building attached to a very large skyscraper. I walked in the back door and through another doorway of the small building until I came to the back room. A teenager was leaning against some boxes talking to another employee when

I walked in. They both looked at me, half asleep and not surprised, with little care for anything around them.

"Where's the boss?" I asked and the teenager pointed to the roof. I nodded my thanks and went to the stairs and up. They creaked and I glared at them as I took each step. I didn't like that they made so much noise and announced my coming. I got to the top of the stairs and looked around. It was dusty and the light was dim, though I couldn't see anything. Myre, who followed closely at my heels, told me all there was to see, which wasn't much: merchandise and a lot of boxes, but that was it. I walked to another room and found a man sitting talking to two women. They all looked up at me and stopped talking when I walked into the room.

"Yes what can I do for you? Is there a problem?" The man asked, confused.

"You were out last night away from your family drinking. You came home then you beat your little girl. Of course I have a problem. You," I told him then with a flick of my wrist, the blade up my sleeve fell into my hand and I dragged it across his neck. The women didn't have time to scream before I was drawing my blade across their throats. They had to die, no one could see me and know that I had killed someone. They all went black before my eyes then I left them and went down the steps. The two employees didn't even look at me as I walked by them and out the door.

Back in the sunlight I looked around and decided to go east, traveling along a worn path in the uneven ground. The sounds of Vale Darra's busiest streets met me before the sight did and as I walked onto the street I turned north. I weaved my way through the crowd of people walking this way and that, people yelling over the multitude of other noises to be heard.

"We were talking the other day…" "Ya I just come back, it's so nice out there…" "Well that's what I said…"

"Oh it's such a nice day…"

Everyone's voices were full of different emotions. Some people were nearly skipping as they walked while others were slouching along the sidewalk dragging their feet and looking around at everything half asleep and depressed.

"So, what you up to today?" A voice asked me and I turned to look at a cop.

"Just walking around," I told Fetcher. "You're out on duty today?"

"Ya, well I was doing some paper work, but then one of our guys got hurt and was sent to the hospital so now I'm filling in, by the way I don't like hit and runs" Fetcher grumbled. "Oh what happened?" I asked interested and ignoring the last part.

"He was walking when a cat jumped out at him. He's really jittery. He fired his gun and it ricocheted off of something and came back and hit him. Got him in the arm. He's alright," he said blowing it off.

"I see. Are you working all day?" I said to change the subject.

"Ya, right till eleven," he huffed and rubbed his eyes. "I haven't had much sleep. Work's been kinda hectic," "Why's that?" I asked curious. "Oh, we've been talking with the police over in a few other districts; we have quite a few people come over from some distances away. We're all discussing Dusk and what to do with this new killer. You've heard about that right?" He asked yawning, but trying to stay grim. I shook my head.

"I heard that some people are dying, but that's it. There's a new assassin?" This wasn't entirely new to me, but I still didn't know much about this new assassin. "Ya. We don't know what to think at this point. It seems all the people who are dying are either from Vale Darra or from the surrounding area. And there's no pattern to the deaths. We can't find any lead, but… we'll get him, just like we'll get Dusk one day. By the way, what are you doing in the alleyways? You know you shouldn't be in there?" He spoke to me as if he were my father.

"I was taking a shortcut. Sorry," I mumbled.

"Well sorry isn't gonna work if you meet Dusk or someone else in there. The police aren't as common in those alleyways. No one will be able to help you if you need it," "If I come across anything I won't need any help," I told him in all seriousness.

"Sure, anyway, go see dad he misses you," He commanded.

"So he can beat me up again, no thanks I'll pass," I said sarcastically, once again my guard was up.

"He was just happy to see you and a little upset,"

"He has a weird way of showing it," I grumbled.

"Well whatever, go!" He commanded sternly.

"I don't want to," I said walking faster.

"Well you don't have a choice, I can't take you there this time, but I think you at least need to talk to him. He deserves that much at least," He said grabbing my shoulder and stopping me.

"I don't want to talk to him," I said to him slowly, crossing my arms and looking defiant.

"Fine then go stare at him, listen to him speak. Just go home, what are you getting out of living on the streets really? Trying to prove that you're some kinda tough guy?" He asked me.

"No not at all, I just never got along with dad like you guys did. And I like living on my own, I think I'm doing well all things considering. Besides I do live in a house. It's a little dilapidated, but there's four walls and a roof over my head," I told him truthfully.

"Ya ok, but why don't you try to reconnect with dad, he's not asking for much. Visit him once a week, that's it," He said sounding tired.

"I'm busy," I said crossing my arms.

"Fine do whatever you like, just visit him at some point in time," He said. "I should charge you for running away from police and hurting me," He grumbled.

"Well you had no right grabbing me and forcing me to go to dad's against my will in the first place," I told him simply.

"Just trying to help you out with dad that's all, go see him before I change my mind and drag you there myself," Fetcher said.

"Fine," I said and waved goodbye. He nodded and turned to survey the crowd around him.

I walked away and thinking about it I ended up standing before my dad's house, travelling around in a wide arch just to get there. He still lived in the two-story house I had grown up in. It had a nice green lawn and healthy garden. It was a well-cared-for house. The inside was spacious and homey and family pictures hung on colourful walls. I walked up to the front white door and knocked. It wasn't long until Dad opened the door and smiled at me.

"Khire! It's so great to see you!" He said happily, his tired eyes crinkling as he gave me a hug. I hadn't seen him since he threatened me, but lately something had been drawing me back home and so finally I gave in.

"How are you?" I mumbled as he squeezed me tightly.

"Good, good, how are you?" He said tiredly.

"Fine, what ya doing today?" I asked him.

"Nothing. Why don't we go for a walk to the park?" He said and yawned. He was still dressed in his pj's and his greying hair was untidy.

"Sure," I shrugged and he nodded.

"Ok, let me get ready," He said.

I followed him in and sat down on the living room couch as he ran upstairs to get changed. I couldn't really see anything so I had nothing to do, but sit there and wait. Pictures of my five other brothers, my father and my mother that died when I was born hung around me. Magazines lay on the long, wooded table before the couch. A large flat screen TV was off and sitting in the exact same spot it has sat for the past ten years. Hardwood floors worn smooth from many feet while the door to the closet wouldn't close properly. Many visible signs showed the years of many people living in this house. I smiled as I remembered the abuse and love the house endured from six children.

Sighing I leaned back and contented myself by talking to Myre.

"Well we have to still visit a few more people," Myre said, his deep voice echoing in my mind.

"I know, but let's just rest a bit, maybe when we're out at the park we'll come across some more information. We might find something interesting," I told him. *"Maybe, but what are you doing? This is a bad idea,"* He told me growling slightly.

"I know, I… I just wanted to see him again. I…. let's just make him happy then we can go. I still want to have a good relationship with my family you know how important they are to me," I told him as Myre looked at me, his head rested on his paws as he stretched out on the ground beside me.

"This is such a mistake," He said with displeasure.

In twenty minutes dad was back, dressed, shaved, hair and teeth brushed and ready to go. I got to my feet and followed him to the door.

"So what have you been up to these last few days?" Dad asked as we walked towards the park.

"Oh nothing, visiting people, I'm going away for a few days, but I'll be back soon. There's some friends I want to visit off in another town," I said simply. "Ok," He said and nodded. I knew he wanted to ask more questions about it, but he knew that I wouldn't tell him. He was probably also wondering who my friends were as I've never really had any friends as far as he knows.

"What made you want to go to the park?" I asked him suddenly.

"I just thought a walk would do some good on such a nice day," He said with a smile. He seemed tired; his age was starting to get to him. He was slowing down, not having the energy he once had to get through a full day of work. He was grateful to find a bench in the shade to sit on, though he wouldn't say so.

We continued to talk about the day and the weather as we sat in the park. It wasn't nearly as crowded as the streets, but it was still busy with kids running around screaming and playing. Their parents were sitting on benches talking while dogs ran around off leashes chasing each other, barking and growling. The swings creaked a little and I could hear the kids as they literally jumped onto the slide and went down it laughing and screaming. Kids climbed onto the monkey bars while some nervous moms held their arms up ready to catch their kids if they fell. Some dads threw a ball around with their sons while a Labrador retriever sat in the middle trying to get the ball away from them all. Large yellow sand boxes sectioned off the play areas while green grass sectioned off areas to play ball.

"I miss bringing you boys here," Dad said wistfully.

"Ya I remember you bringing us here. I remember running here as fast as I could from home and trying to beat everyone else," I said thinking back.

We would all play till curfew then run as fast as we could home, not because we were scared, but because we always liked to race each other and see who would win. My oldest brother Tellnair usually won, but now and then my second oldest brother, Aster, would and afterwards they would tumble around in the grass wrestling with each other on the front lawn. We use to have a dog that would whine when they did this then come running up to them growling and barking, nipping them till they stopped fighting. She would lick their faces then lean against them as we all sat in the grass.

It was a fun time. We would watch the stars and for a moment everything would be perfect

"It seems long ago, but you're all grown up now so I guess that explains it. I miss having someone to care for," Dad told me sadly. "Really, you like caring for others?" I asked him, turning partly so that I could look at him as I sat there.

"Ya, I do. I like the feeling of having someone that depends on me. What about you?" He said smiling then asked as if it were a simple question of having someone's life in your hands. "I don't know, I guess in some cases it's nice, but in other cases not so much," I shrugged and looked at him.

"Hmmm," He said and then changed the subject. "Well I'm glad you could come see me. I was wondering where you went off to." "I'm not that far away, you really have no need to worry about me," I told him tiredly.

"I will do what I want thank you very much, and I will worry as much as I like for whomever I please," He said sounding every bit like an old, grumpy man.

"Ok, but I just don't want to see you get all stressed out about me. You have enough grey hair as it is," I told him jokingly and he smiled.

"How can I not get stressed out about you, you…. you're not what any of us expected you to be. We had such great hopes for you. Did you know that before you were born, when your mother was pregnant with you she said to me, these exact same words, 'I can feel this baby will be special, I know this is someone who'll go far'. She told me that about you!" His said, his voice rising.

I put my hands on his shoulders and tried to calm him down, taking a deep breath and counting in my head to ten before answering.

"No I didn't know that, but I know I'm not what you expected or wanted. I'm not successful like the others. I don't have a nice big house with a girlfriend or wife and kids, but please, stop worrying so much. It's not worth it ok. I'm still trying to find my way, but I'm doing ok," I said trying to sound reassuring.

"Why don't you tell me about yourself a little? Give me something to feel like I know you." He pressed.

"You do know me, I'm your son," I said frowning.

"No I should know you because you're my son, there's a difference," He told me firmly.

"Ok fine, ahhh ok here my favourite colour is orange and I love pasta. I hate leeches so whenever I go swimming, which I love to do, I use a spell to keep any leeches away from me. I like getting up early, but I don't like staying out late. Ummm I like being around people, but I don't like to have all the attention on me. What else?" I asked him.

"Thank you, see that's not that hard. What are your hobbies?" Dad asked nicely.

"I love learning new languages, I like doing anything that uses my mind," I told him folding my hands in my lap.

"You were such a good student, you know that. I was so proud of you. I would talk to your teachers and they would always say good things about you," My dad said, a huge grin on his face.

"The teachers never even noticed me," I said quietly.

"Sure they did, they just didn't know how to talk to you. They would always say that you were so intelligent you just didn't know how to express yourself. There was so much going on in your mind, it closed you up to me," He said sadly.

"I wasn't closed up to you, I was just, ya I had a lot going on in my head, I couldn't get it out," I said struggling to make sense.

"Well in any case, do you have a lot going on in your head right now?" He asked me meeting my eyes.

I didn't like it when people tried to meet my eyes. I was able to see them a bit and sense them so I did a good job at pretending to see, but with him sitting so close, trying to meet my eyes I knew it would be too easy for him to see that I couldn't focus completely on him. I looked away to avoid his gaze.

"Ya I guess so," I said shrugging, not so sure.

"When you're ready to open up, I'm here you know that right?" He said grabbing my hand.

"Yes I do Dad and I love you for that. I just don't want you to worry anymore, you have to many wrinkles," I said smiling.

"And I am proud of each and every one!" He said smiling back.

We spent a few hours there, talking and watching the kids play before we walked home.

"Will you stay for supper?" Dad asked me and I began to shake my head, "Oh come on Khire, it wouldn't kill ya to eat with me,"

"I can't I have other places to be, I'm sorry," I told him. "Khire!"

"Dad," I complained.

"Eat here. Then go, all right? It won't take too much out of your time? Your skinny as a rake, you need to eat something," He said angrily.

"Fine," I sighed and crossed my arms as we walked into his house to the kitchen. He followed me and began to prepare supper. He already had steaks out on the kitchen counter ready for the barbecue. One thing I like about him, he always made extra because he always said you never knew when you would have a guest over.

I sat on a stool as he cooked them, then I got up and got out the lettuce, Caesar sauce, croutons, parmesan cheese and bacon bits. I washed some leaves and made a Caesar salad for us to eat. It was done a few minutes before dad came in with the finished steaks. He set the plate down on the kitchen table and took out two plates from a cupboard and handed me one. We had a silent supper, talking very little as we ate. I wanted to eat fast, but amazing even myself, I restrained myself. Living on the streets, I was more than happy to be sitting here eating good food, but what made me want to go was not that I had places to be, but rather that I could never have what my dad had. I didn't want to feel like I owed anyone anything because I knew I would never be able to pay them back.

"Please come visit me again soon?" Dad told me as we both rinsed our plates then put them in the dishwasher.

"I'll try," I told him and gave him a final hug before turning and heading for the door.

The sky was a bruised colour and there was a slight breeze that blew through my thin and worn clothes, but I continued to walk down the road back to the main part of Vale Darra. My night wasn't done yet, but I felt better at having seen my dad, but a little guilty as well. I hated feeling guilty, being with my family made me happy so why did I also feel guilty?

CHAPTER #13

At dusk I was running along the rooftops heading towards a house where a young man waited for me, unbeknownst to him. I leapt through the open window of his bedroom and found him with his back to me. He did however see me in the mirror that was positioned in front of him. A look of surprise and confusion came across his face as I walked up to him. I pulled out a knife and before he could make a noise I jammed it into his back. The blade punctured his heart and blood flowed down his clothes as I pulled it out and with some simple magic, I flicked my wrist and the blood on the blade dripped off the knife onto the carpeted floor. His body fell to the floor, becoming black as his life slowly spilt out of him.

I looked down at the mess then left back out the window and jumped to a nearby house. I caught a windowsill and climbed up, hoisting myself the last couple feet to the roof. I climbed the shingles until I was on hands and knees at the very top. I could see people turning to look at me as I stood. I stopped for a moment to watch them, thinking what might be going through their heads. Arms crossed and weight on one hip, I watched the people of Vale Darra as they stared up at me. Did they fear me, hate me, did they wonder about my life? I turned from them and ran off to the den as more people gathered outside.

The first gunshot split the sky with a loud crack that echoed in the silent night. Everyone stared up at the shadowy figure that dashed across the rooftops; they didn't know my real name or what I looked like yet they still knew me all too well as the assassin named Dusk.

I didn't like the name, but I liked killing at dusk. It seemed like a good time to strike and a good way to end the day. Still, I didn't think I killed often enough at dusk to have gotten named for it. As an assassin, I plotted my targets well, trying to not make patterns. Nevertheless, I wanted them to fear me, maybe if they called me Dusk they learned to fear the coming night, which worked for me.

I ran along shingles, darted around chimneys and leaped from roof to roof. All the while people called out Dusk with mixed emotions. I was just leaving the busier part of the city when I found a good spot to make my escape. I came to a thin slit between two houses and jumped down between them. I was only a few feet away from slamming into the ground when I used some magic to slow my fall and land lightly on the balls of my feet. In one motion I absorbed the impact by going into a slight crouch then lunging forward and running through the alleyways. Around trashcans and over obstacles on the ground, I turned down different alleys, making it hard for people to follow me. I passed homeless people that sidestepped out of my way. A few cats hissed at me, but soon the noises of the city died away.

The moonlight hid from me as I ran through shadows. Panting and heart beating fast with my blood racing through my veins, I smiled as the cool night air blew me forward as if urging me on. The thrill of a chase is a beautiful thing. The knowledge that I got away again and all the people feared me made me like being an assassin, but I was a bit at war with myself. I loved the hunt and the chase, but I still didn't like that I was forced to become this. I don't know if that was because I didn't like the thought of someone forcing me into something or the fact that I didn't become an assassin on my own. That question bothered me. Would I have become a killer without Midnight? Were people simply born to kill or were they thrust into the position and then had to adapt or be killed? There were things I would always hate about my life, but I did love how capable and alive I felt. I loved learning about someone and hunting them, seeing the fear in their eyes or the acceptance that they are going to die.

Those that accepted their death right before I killed them always intrigued me the most.

I came to a three-way intersection and took a right, passing along rows of boxes and blankets that lined the walls. People stuck their heads out from under blankets and openings in the boxes when I passed, but they had little reaction to me. It was common to them to see me dashing through. They did nothing to stop me. Instead they moved aside, giving me room to pass. If and when the cops came, the box dwellers would not give me away. Like them, I was a street rat, and though we didn't have much to be proud of, we were loyal to one another. It was a weird street-rat-family pack, but it worked.

I looked back to see if anyone was behind me. Through the red walls, I could see the blue uniforms running around still trying to look for me in the far distance. I slowed down; breathing hard now and soon was walking towards my home. I walked up to what was mine and Cadence's home or what we would also call our den as it was dark and smelt strongly of dirt. There were some weeds growing in cracks and some insects could be found crawling or flying around here. It was secluded just the way we liked it and with all the stone the sun could beat on them and heat them up for the night. They didn't do much for the winter months, but we were used to it by now.

Chapter #14

As I was sleeping a funny memory entered my dreams, where dreams usually change things, this one was as real and precise to the actual event. Pain radiated throughout my body as I lay on the cobbled ground in a pool of my own blood. I breathed deeply and reached over to where I felt something sharp, a thin blade, black and shiny glistening in the night. I slowly brought it to my heart, I didn't plan on killing myself today, but something's just come up. I had been crouched waiting for the night to come when I had gotten jumped myself. Stupid me for not watching my back. Now dying in the deserted alleyway I figured I was half way there anyway. With that I plunged with all my strength. The black blade biting into flesh, muscle then my heart. Severing something major and causing a gush of blood to swell and pour over my chest, down my ribs. My magic was already working hard to keep me alive from my other injuries, with the blade cutting into my slow beating heart, I could feel my magic gushing through my veins trying to save my life, then slowing, losing strength. I began to lose consciousness when a shadow came over me. My toes and fingers were so cold, my head pounding with each slowing heartbeat. It felt like I was dying slowly, but pretty soon my heart stopped and my magic gave one last attempt to save me before that too gave up.

But I should have expected more. That shadow, be damned I should have killed her when I had the chance. I knew her even before I took my first breath. Smelly air leeched into my now healed lungs. I growled and sprang at her, but like before I fell to the ground trembling in pain.

"You stupid bit…" I began and was wracked with pain; I bit my tongue and cried out.

"You never learn you stupid boy!" She screamed close by. She knelt down and grabbing my chin, she turned my head to look at her. "I will not let you die," She said determined. "I will forever stand in your way of death," She let go of me then turned and left me. It was a quick meeting, but I was left in a great amount of pain for a long time, still confused, but angry that she would save my life again.

This memory followed to the next day. I was sitting in a garden when a black haired, green-eyed girl approached me. She sat down beside me, the garden deserted, but for us.

"This is how it's going to work, I will pay you to keep my family safe. You get me info, you stop assassins from killing my family. You let me in on the underground doings and in return I will heal every wound you get. I will save you from death until my last breath and I will allow you to live in luxury," The Princess said as seriously as ever. She was not one for seriousness, but a fun loving person who lived carefree and did as she pleased. At the moment however, her green eyes held so much sincerity in her words and her voice was strong with deep emotion, I knew she wasn't joking around.

"We have a deal," I said and with that, I left her. From that day on, I would find her or get word to her of what was going on. I would stop poisoners from poisoning the King, Queen or Princesses. I would stop plots to overthrow the King, or to destroy the city. I made it my mission to do anything and everything that Shirra asked and in return I was healed and I was paid. I put it all into my bank slowly and saved it. I used some for food and was able to buy new clothes, but I didn't want to leave the streets. I could have bought a house, but the streets became my home. I felt like I belonged there and I seen no reason to leave anyway. I now had money so was able to make the den far more comfortable. This arrangement carried on through the years but it was on one fateful day where it took a turn for the worst, or the best, I'm still unsure.

The sun's rays crept across the awakening city and the people dwelling within it began to stir, waking up to another crazy day. I had woken early morning and felt the sunlight hit me as it lit the beautiful city and shone down on it. I leapt from a rooftop to a nearby window. With magic I opened it and jumped through. I knew to expect a group of people, but what met me was more than that. Even before my feet hit the ground I was being attacked. People everywhere it seemed poured into the room and threw magic or weapons at me. Doing my best I deflected, maneuverer, jumped, turned, twisted and even rolled around on the ground, trying not to get myself killed.

I threw a blade at someone, cut another's throat and went wild. Killing everyone in sight. The ground was slippery from the blood; it splashed up as we moved. Someone slipped and I plunged a knife deep into their chest then moved to swipe the blade across another's throat. There were so many of them, but they couldn't all get into the room and it was so crowded they hindered themselves.

I was a sight of pure murder, blood covered my body painting me red and giving me a badge of death. Every motion was death itself and soon I was lost in the frenzy that had started to come over me every time I got into a fight with someone. I loved it, I breathed in deeply, the smell of the blood, the fear in their sweat, and I imagined the look of their frightened-angry eyes as I drew my blade across their throats. It was times like these that loved what I had become, I was lethal and swift, a nightmare more nightmarish then what a child could dream up.

Quickly the people began to thin, the bodies that stood, hearts beating in their chest soon kissed the bloody, gory floor and met their end. I growled and stabbed another, he shrieked and tried to run, but I was too fast. My knife cut his throat and he fell to the ground, fear plastered on his face. I took another deep breath and whirled on another group of people, they were smarter, but they were still too dumb. They could not best me in my own game. They could not harm me; they had no power here, no life, no value. They were bodies that turned the world filthy and rotten. I pounced on them and with a yell cleaved someone's head in two as I drew a sword from my hip. I cut them up like I cut up the others and everyone died screaming.

It was over all too soon and I was gasping in the end for breath, for more death. I was still crazed from killing and I needed more. There was movement to my left and without thinking I swung my blade. It drove deep into the child's head, dropping him to the ground as his mother behind him screamed. I jumped at her and as she got into the hallway I stabbed her. Suddenly, the ground heaved and I was thrown into the roof. Splinters bit into my body and I turned on them. Hacking at my wooden foe. I fell to the ground below; it was on fire, great flames reaching up to burn the house to the ground. I wandered through the fire, feeling invincible as my magic stopped me from catching aflame. I went through the house, looking for more people when suddenly another explosion went off and this time a small group of people jumped out at me as I was regaining my feet. They swiped at me and I at them. Their limbs flew off and my blood streamed from my body as we engaged in battle. There were more people then I had thought, I felt a knife slice into my back, a cut to my thigh, my head. I felt weakened and suddenly I didn't feel so invincible anymore. With one last attempt, I whirled on my attackers and slashed them down.

This time I left, running out of the fire and the burning house into the bright morning light. I ran down the alley nearby and went deeper into the darkness there. I was bleeding badly and I was tired, but I had to keep going, if I could just get to a healer I would be ok. Suddenly others came out and I found myself on my back on the ground trying to get out of the way of swords swinging towards my head. Someone drove a sword through my chest; I felt it dig in between two cobbled stones beneath me. I roared in pain, but tried to keep fighting. It was hard, but I managed to cut off some hands. As they began to back away I threw all the magic I could at them.

Then feeling hopeless I threw more magic at them, thinking if I died then I was going to bring them down with me. They were all dead soon and I wasn't though. Instead I was left to die in pain and misery on the dirty street.

I smiled when I heard the approaching footsteps. I was too tired to do anything, but turn my head in her direction. Cursing myself for not knowing if she were my curse or good fortune. It had been a while since I had seen her last; I had become a very good fighter and needed less and less healing each month, but as she knelt beside me and looked me over I felt like it had been just yesterday since I'd last seen her. I smiled wider, closing my eyes waiting for the relief from the pain I felt.

"What have you done?" She gasped. I opened my eyes. In my daze I thought I saw a halo of light around her head even though she was a blue blob to me. I even imagined beautiful white wings streaming from her back as she grasped the bloody sword. With what strength she had, she managed to pull it from my body with a horrible sucking sound that made me grimace more from the sound then the pain it caused. Still the pain sent a spasm through my body and I yelled in pain as she slid her arms underneath me and made me sit up.

"Stop!" I gasped. She cradled me to her body and in that moment I knew I was in trouble. I couldn't bring myself to hurt her, I couldn't think about it. I wanted to kill whoever dared look at her the wrong way. She was everything to me. She gave me breath, a beating heart, warmth. She cradled my bloody, dying, pain-racked body with compassion. She promised to save me and she held her deal. My body began to heal as a pink white ribbon of magic floated around us. I was weak from the loss of blood, but my wounds were no more.

Her body trembled from fatigue and as she began to slouch I caught her.

"Thank you," she whispered. Then I did the worst thing I could have done. I tilted her chin up and kissed her. She didn't move at first, but then I felt her lead me back and soon I was laying on top of her kissing her fiercely. She pulled me closer to her as I kissed her. It was hard, my body needed sleep, but all I wanted to do was love her. I didn't want to stop, but then she pushed me away.

"I…. need……. a-air…" She gasped and I looked down at her. Some blood was on her cheek, but when I tried to wipe it away I accidentally put more blood on her.

"Sorry," I said as I began to shift off of her. She smiled.

"No," And then she kissed me again. Pulling me closer to her as if lying on her was still too far.

The next time we pulled away was for me to breath. I still lay on top of her, breathing in her ear as she lay breathless beneath me.

"I love you," I whispered into her ear and I felt her tense. She smiled then and kissed my lips.

"I love you too. From the first day I did," She said and I kissed her.

Telling her I loved her wasn't enough. I wanted her to know how much she meant to me, how much I cared for her. She was the reason I was alive, whether I wanted to be or not, I owed her my life. And so I gave it to her. When we meet our Guardians we speak a special name that only the Protected and their Guardian knows. You choose your Guardian's name and your Guardian choses yours. Together it creates the bond that allows you to speak with each other mind-to-mind. It was a deep connection that made you share thoughts, feelings, emotions and even senses. That name was precious and not to be given out to just anyone. With all the love in my heart, I gave mine to Shirra. I whispered it into her ear and I shuddered. Speaking my name out loud felt strange, bizarre and it left me feeling dazed and confused. Shirra turned to me again. She whispered my name to me and my body shuddered again, closing my eyes I let the euphoria spread through my body. Slowly, she flipped me onto my back. Now lying on me, she kissed me from my lips down my jaw line to my ear and whispered it again. I was lost in a sense of nirvana as she whispered it. Then suddenly she told me hers and I gasped. Suddenly every thought she thought, every emotion she felt, everything that was her, flooded me. I felt her heart beating as my own, her breath entering her lungs as it entered mine. I could feel her, be her. She smiled down at me in her own captured state of euphoria. In that moment I saw through her eyes, I was covered in blood, but she loved me and didn't see me as monstrous or dirty.

From then my sight improved. It was even more confusing than when I was blind, but it did help sometimes. I could see everything, though everything was very blurry and I couldn't focus on things well or see small detail, I could make out something's like what people wore or if they had long hair. Fused in with the blue, red and black that I typically see in were other colours to. It was like looking through 3D glasses and staring at a rainbow. The rainbow appeared before me, slightly blurred, but I could see it. The colours however, weren't there regular colours. Without my Wish, everything was dim and blurred and made getting around hard, so though using my Wish still complicated things, I did prefer it over not using it.

Our Guardians nearby snuggled together licking each other with affection. We lay, her atop me, smiling at each other for a long time. Lost in our own and each other's pleasure. We loved each other more than can be proven by marriage. I vowed to never hurt her, to always protect her, be there for her, love her with everything I had. She vowed to bring me back to life when I died, heal me when I am wounded and love me with everything she had. Our vows floated through our heads and with them a sense of completeness. Finally I had someone who saw me and did not run from me, but smiled and loved me for who I am. I was now happy my life was whole.

As the sun rose, turning the sky red, I yawned and stretched out, back in the present. My limbs cracked from staying still so long. I opened my eyes and looked around. No one was around besides Cadence and our Guardians. Myre lay by Quirktick, Cadence's cheetah, curled up and sleeping deeply. Quirktick twitched his ear as a mosquito came to investigate the sleeping cat. With a huge yawn Quirktick pawed at his ear then when he found he wasn't going to be left alone, turned over, rolling into Myre and causing him to wake up. Not wanting to do anything, but sleep, Myre growled and turned away to curl up somewhere else. When he sensed that I was awake he came over and curled up against my stomach and dozed.

"Get up you lazy kitten, there's work ta be done," I told him and he gave a slight growl at me as I poked him. He finally turned over and tried to bite me. I avoided him, yawned and got slowly and lazily to my feet. Still tired I stumbled a bit when I straightened up, then looked down at the three lazy figures.

"K well I'm going for a bath," I told them and walked to where a stream flowed down from a bigger bed of water far away. It wasn't too big, but it did just fine to lie in and wash. Being far back as it was, only Myre, Quirktick, Cadence and I used it, so it wasn't as dirty as some of the other streams that most of the homeless people used. I scrubbed all the dirt away and cleaned my hair then lay out in the sun to dry before putting my clothes on, shaving the light scruff from my cheeks using a straight knife with some cheap shaving cream. I was surrounded by dozens of long abandoned and dilapidated, stone houses and felt calm in the cool air. I left to find the others.

When I got back to them, Cadence and his cheetah looked like they were going to sleep for the day. Myre came over and licked my hand then looked up at me.

"*Shall we go?*" He asked. "Ok," I said and with a goodbye to the sleeping forms we walked down the alleyway that began to light as the sun climbed higher and higher into the sky. It looked like it was going to be a nice day and so I headed straight to the North gate to leave. I made my way there slowly, not caring when I got there or how much time went by. It was only a small trip so I took my time.

I came closer and closer to the main streets of Vale Darra and could now hear people talking and car engines running. I could see it all as I turned right and walked along the sidewalk passed statues towards the North gate. The doors of the large gate, though sturdy and durable, had never been closed before. The thick wooden slabs with intricate metal frames hung on polished and gleaming hinges, standing thirty feet, but did nothing other than add to the looks of the large archway over the wide road. The archway had to go over eight lanes of traffic. Each pillar had a metal framework that twined and twisted into a picture around and up the pillar. With the pillar white and the metal framework black, it gave it a contrasting, but formal design. The pictures themselves were of angels on all nine pillars, each in a different pose. Each statue was over a hundred years old; the metal work on these pillars even older and this gate was the same gate that was built when Vale Darra was first inhabited or so it's believed. With it in mind that Vale Darra would one day become big, the gates were created to match. No additions have been done to them since they were built.

I walked up to the window of a small cabin beside the far side of the gates and waved at a guard. He nodded at me and I went into another cabin just off from the first. There was another guy standing at the front desk though he was nearly asleep.

"Working hard I see eh Marko," I joked. The man jolted up with a start then looked around frantically.

"Oh it's you, Khire…" He began to laugh at himself. "Well I'm guessin you're lookin for a horse, right?" He asked, smiling widely with big, white teeth. He pulled out some papers for me to sign and I paid the required fees.

He got to his feet, tall and muscled; he had come here only ten years ago after his farm burnt down. He was weathered and ruff looking, but he had a very friendly nature. His black hair was receding back and his black moustache was peppered with grey hairs. He had a confident stride and I had to speed walk just to keep up with him. I followed him into the barn next door. The barn had a high ceiling and was strongly built, with enough stalls for twenty-five horses, swept clean and kept in good condition; it smelt accordingly of horse and hay. Stonework made up the lower half of the outer walls while all the stalls and inner walls were wood.

"How about Era?" He asked me and I nodded. I grabbed her tack and a grooming kit and set the tack on a saddle rack and the grooming supplies on a shelf. Marko and I walked back outside to a pasture that held a heard of horses. We went inside it and over to a brown mare that lifted her head from grazing.

"Come on Era," He said to the mare and she flicked her ears forward. She sniffed his outstretched hand and let him halter her. She calmly followed us back to the barn while her pasture mates continued to graze. He cross tied her and turned to me.

"Well I don't need ta be doing anythin', you know what to do," He told me and I nodded. He left to go help some other people who had just come in while I went through the motions of getting Era ready for our journey.

I didn't have to spend a long time on her, the currycomb picked up little hair and she was hardly dirty. I saddled her as she stood patient and silent like the well-trained horse she was. She was a beautiful twelve-year-old quarter horse standing fifteen point two hands high. She use to compete, but the family that had her before got a new horse and so Era came here. She would have been better off going to another family who would use her in competitions, but she did make a good trail horse. Despite the fact that I was once afraid of horses, I learned that they could be reliable and handy at times and so I made myself learn to ride. Era had a very forgiving nature and loved to be doing anything with people, which made it easier for me to like her.

When I was finished her grooming and tacking I unclipped her and led her outside. I passed by the helmets without grabbing one. By law everyone 16 and under had to wear one, but as I was older I didn't have to. I just let my magic protect my head.

"Where ya off to today?" A guard asked me as I mounted up.

"Heading to Dunskin," I told him and he nodded.

"Well I heard they just got hit by a tornado, a few actually. Be careful," he squinted up at me.

"Did they?" I asked looking surprised as I mounted.

"Ya. Got hit bad. People are still out of power. Some say it won't be back on till sometime next month. About thirty-eight buildings destroyed and twenty-four other buildings that need repairing. Twenty eight or so dead and another seventeen injured."

"Wow, that bad?" He nodded as I said this looking down at him.

"Ya it's bad, so be careful. Have fun." He said with dry humour.

"Bye," I nodded along and rode out. I went into a trot to put some distance between us and the city as I thought about other things.

I wasn't actually going to Dunskin, though it did sound like an intriguing journey now. Instead I traveled along the road until I came to some smaller roads. The large highways for vehicle transportation were far off in the West. Though it seemed unreasonable to host stables where people could 'rent' a horse and go for a ride, it was very convenient. The program was going to be eliminated, but so many people complained, the King kept it going. There were rules to it, obviously, not just anyone could take a horse, there had to be a background check. So what they came up with about me was my brother was Vale Darra's greatest horse trainer and I came from a well off family. It wasn't a thorough background check obviously, it was just to make sure you knew how to handle a horse or if you would require a guide. There was also magic spells set in place so you couldn't kill, hurt or steal the horse as well as the tack.

Era was a great horse, she loved to run and stretch her legs. Despite the fact she had an annoying fear of water that seemed to come and go, she was willing to jump anything. We ended up in a small town the next day where I walked into a merchants shop. The old man there gave me a mean look as I walked over to one of his daughters.

"Hello Khalita," I said happily.

She smiled at me, fiery red hair, blue eyes and lots of freckles. She was a polite person, but get on her bad side and she could turn your world upside down. She was temperamental and didn't care for kindness when it came to people she disliked. She was blunt and sometimes a little too forward, but she was a great saleswomen. Her Wish also allowed her to scry.

"I brought you some little trinkets," I said handing her a bag.

"What do you want me to see?" She asked.

"Someone is coming after me, I have a few suspects, but I would like to see if you can find anything out about this person?" I told her. Her ability to scry wasn't just viewing people. I told her what I wanted and she could find people even with little information on them. Even people that I don't name.

"Ok," She said as she looked over the items in the bag. She went over to a brass bowl full of water and stared into it. Twenty minutes passed and she came back to me.

"So here's the thing. I see many people who want to kill you though that's nothing new. However, I see one man with two faces, I think he has a twin, but they go by the same name. A black man also wants to kill you, but I see him as an old man one time and a young man another, maybe someone from your past then. He's very handsome though, if you see him give him my number would ya dearie? " She said smiling happily.

"Hmm well I don't know anybody with a twin that's trying to kill me and I think I already ran into Mr. Handsome just the other day," I told her and she nodded.

"Keep an eye on him, I see him a lot in my bowl, but he always looks different. He's old one time and young the next and seems to be getting younger as the time goes on," She told me and I nodded.

"How?" I asked very much confused.

"I don't know, it could be like someone from your past is trying to reach you or they're returning to their childhood home. It's a symbolism thing, maybe something to do with the past or it could be a generation thing. Something people are passing on to the next generation," She said with a shrug.

"Anything else?"

"Nope," She said.

I wanted more from her, but I could tell that she wasn't going to say any more so I thanked her and left. She would ponder on it and later on I could return to see if she sees anymore. With of course something for her to get her talking, but that's the way she was, she worked to get the best deal possible for herself first, the other people were second.

It was a short visit, but unfortunately for her to scry for me I had to be there and so with that I started the long journey home. It wasn't long before I ran into trouble however. The day was hot and I had to go at a walk for most of the day, which meant slow progress. Even cutting across the countryside, I wasn't getting anywhere quickly.

Bandits were an anomaly here so these guys that came out at me were a surprise even to me. Dressed in black and riding large horses they charged me. Black and orange magic sparkled past my head as they tried to fight me with magic. I turned in my saddle and shot a bolt of purple-blue magic back. It hit at the feet of one horse who reared in protest. I could feel Era tense, her stride became choppy, but I tried to encourage her on. Squeezing my legs to send her forward, she spooked and went into a run. She was too frightened to listen to me, her prey instincts telling her to flee. I used magic to create a shield, I was terrible at making shields, holding magic and making it tangible enough to block magic and objects was something I had to focus on which was very difficult on a frightened horse. We entered a forest and leaping off my horse, I jumped onto a branch and got out of sight, Era running on.

As the last guy ran past me underneath, I jumped on his horse behind him and slit his throat. With a gurgle, he crumpled to the ground. I produced a gun from my belt and killed two more guys before the other four turned around on me and spotted me. I was confused on why they were chasing me, I started to think maybe they were hired to kill me, but I couldn't piece enough information together to get a picture. I brought my stolen horse to a halt, they doing the same.

"Why are you attacking me?" I asked them.

"Just give us what you have then we'll let you be on your way," One guy said in a very deep voice.

"I don't have anything. Why are you attacking me?" I asked again.

"Our town is destroyed it's either starve or rob," The man spoke again. He was really hairy and I think he smelt bad; fortunately the wind blew in my favour.

"You're from Dunskin," I said to them and they nodded. "Well men, how about this, why don't you go back and help rebuild your town and then live like good decent citizens instead of harassing people. I am on my way their now, I will help you rebuild," I told them.

"What's in it for you?" One man asked, this one a peppery haired man.

"I had friends there, I want to visit them," I lied. They thought about it for a moment.

"I'm also a strong mage so that might be useful," I added.

Without them knowing I used some magic that made them not forget about the fact that I killed their friends, but just get confused. I wasn't good at making people forget events, so I had to make do. The brain wanted to make sense of information and the fact that their town was just devastated by a tornado directed their brain to most likely think that their friends died in the storm. It took a lot of magic and concentration so the guy had to repeat himself a few times before I could clue in on what he was saying.

"We will still starve," The first guy said.

"Your right, how about this, you keep doing what you're doing and then the police will find you and put you in jail and then you don't have to worry about starving, how is that?" I said, crossing my arms on my pommel.

"Let's go," The first man said and with that we began to make our way to Dunskin. As we got a little deeper into the forest, I shot the other four and tracked down Era, I had seriously debated letting them live, but I did not like being surprised. With that I gathered all the horses together then took off their tack. I shouted at them hoping they'd run home together. With their tack off I hoped that whoever found them would think their riders had been sleeping and their horses had just gotten loose. A tacked up riderless horse would instantly bring searchers and I wanted to get a little farther away before people came looking around.

Lucky for me Era hadn't gotten too far; a cold stream of water had distracted her enough from her mad dash away from the magic throwing people. "Hello good girl," I crooned and an ear flicked my way as she slurped up the water.

I was thirsty as well and with a little bit of magic I cleaned the water enough for me to drink.

"What do you say, go home or do you want to see this destroyed town?" I asked the horse. She ignored me, finding a patch of green grass that was to her liking. "Ok, home it is," I said and mounted up to begin the long ride back.

CHAPTER #15

When the sun dapples the sight
Your gone and never found,
An evil being walking in light.
And to the King crowned
You leave great sorrow
Waiting for the deaths of dark tomorrow.

Hidden in the darkness with the clouds covering the moon, the city was lit with street lamps and front store lights. There were some sections of the city where there were no street lamps which made that part look invisible. I stared at the city with squinted eyes as I crouched down by a wall. Myre and I were on the roof of Vale Darra's tallest building. It was here that people came to do work, file papers, sit in chairs in their small cubicles and stare at a computer, call people or photocopy more paper. I had just come from the old cabin, the woman was found dead by Cadence and so I left him to deal with the body while I came here. We'd gained little information since talking to the women and other people. They had something to do with the person who hired Duke. The peak was three days from here, I had visited it and found nothing, but plants and rocks, no doubt though that was where they were meeting and making plans.

I decided I would wait until I found more information about the problem I was in so I could face it knowing all I could. That way I wasn't jumping into something blind. In the mean time I continued to kill my victims. It didn't take a good listener to hear some of the bad that went on in the dark alleyways, or the houses that were sprawled out around the city. It wasn't hard to find out who did what, where someone is, what someone was doing and whom they were friends with. It took however a talented person to find some more personal information. I knew a lot of the people of Vale Darra back to front, knew them for their worth and knew just how bad or good they could be. For the most part, all the people here had a dark spot, everyone here can relate to doing something they shouldn't of or being somewhere they shouldn't be, but lots of people go a little farther then committing those little crimes of offence.

The building I was on was a very busy building, it held many offices including financial offices, an insurance company, and accounting offices. It was also here where I found many people living two lives. I loved to kill these people, some were very talented at being two faced and I found them interesting to talk to. Though I didn't enjoy prolonging ones death, I much preferred to talk to these people just to see what I could get out of them. However, I don't always get my fun, I wasn't to kill anyone at this point, instead I came here to learn something.

The building itself was eighty stories tall, the sides reflective, with a bluish colour to them. With its large panelling, it wasn't the most beautiful of buildings and reflected the sun's rays on sunny days making it literally an eye soar. It dominated a huge area of the city and had the best view of all of Vale Darra.

When the sun was sinking down, Myre and I had snuck in and got up to the roof where it was all cement with three foot walls around the edge, a small room that stored tools such as a shovel and a pick, and in the far left corner from where I was positioned, smoke slowly curled from the chimney stack. The wind blew the smoke away from me while a dull hum could be heard from some machinery in the level below me.

I stared at something far below, it looked like a large circle with red and black dots randomly scattered in the middle. I studied the shapes and tried to find the pattern of the dots. The circle was red, blood from the dots that were actually bodies, cut to pieces, limbs hacked off and tossed recklessly anywhere and rolled till they came to a stop. The bodies were of twelve males and twelve females, being made up of twelve children the youngest was three while it randomly climbed after that to the oldest adult who was 82 and lying on the ground in a lot of little pieces. It would take a good few hours to even try to put them back together. They were all of different statuses some were low class people, or street rats while a Duke and Duchess lay there amongst them, having suffered the same fate.

I did not feel sorrow for them, nor disgust for looking at their crumpled, bloodied bodies, just as I sat there I felt nothing that showed they meant something to me. They didn't of course, but still I knew who each person was and what they did. A little girl who only a few days ago had just turned eight, a boy who just had his first kiss, and the Duke and Duchess who had gone off on their honeymoon to die with a quick slice across their soft necks.

I stood up slowly to my full height, still gazing at the circle, Myre and I jump off the building and plummeted towards the ground. I thrust my hand forward sending my magic out. Just as I was approaching the ground, I saw some movement from an alley and turned so that I was facing it. Two blue-purple ribbons swirled around Myre and I making us slow down and hit the ground lightly on our feet. I bent my knees then sprang forward, still consumed by the ribbons. I was a blur to the eyes and so was able to jump the gang in the alleyway with no one the wiser. They had trapped a woman and her two young daughters and were now tearing at them. I came up quickly behind them and jerking my arms out to my sides I release the knives that I had strapped to my arms. They slide out of my long sleeves and into my hands. I crouch and readied myself for what was going to be a very easy fight. These people had no chance of living for another ten minutes, though they didn't know that.

They were so concentrated on their prey that they weren't paying attention to anything else.

I was as silent as the dead as I came upon them, my breath was quiet and even, my heart beating slowly and rhythmically, my feet stepping lightly and my whole body attuned to what I was about to do. I stabbed the first one in the back and he jerked forward, a small noise coming from him as the blade sliced through fat and muscle then pierced one of his lungs. The knife was long and slightly curved, the hilt easy to hold so I could twirl it around any way I liked in my hand. In one motion, I jerked it into his heart, blood gushing out over the blade and down his clothes to the ground. It seeped to the ground, bright red and warm to form in a small puddle by his body on the ground. It is the last warmth he felt as I watched as his body died slowly, with only a few spastic twitches.

His gasp had alarmed the others of the danger nearby, making some turn in my direction. I smiled at them, but they are much to slow and in seconds I slice at another's neck, turned and stabbed another in the chest. Their bodies falling instantly, crumpling to the ground, dead with their blood cooling in the air and gathering around them. The others ran at me, but I kicked one in the head effortlessly, sending him into the brick wall behind him. I punched another, stabbed and sliced the rest and within five minutes they were all dead, lying on the floor lifeless and growing cold in the warm silent night.

The women and her girls stared at me frightened as they sat on the ground holding each other close and shake uncontrollably, with tears streaming down their faces. They couldn't see me, Myre made sure of that, but they could see my silhouette and they know who I am.

"Dusk," The women said breathlessly, "Please, don't hurt us, not my girls," She pleaded before fainting suddenly much to her children's horror.

Her children started screaming and crying, desperately trying to wake her up, but they were in the wrong part of town. The only help they'd get would be the attention of more gang members and that's not what they needed right now. They weren't going to get away if they ran and they seemed to know that as they sat beside their mother desperately trying to wake her up.

"Your mother will be fine, get up and walk," I said, trying to sound comforting. I walked towards them.

"No! Don't touch us, don't come near!" One said still on her knees, trying to sound brave.

"Take me to your house and I will carry your mother there, I won't hurt you," I told them tiredly. I picked up the limp form on the ground; she was a small, slim woman fortunately so I was able to carry her. The children gazed at me terrified as if their lives were in my hands, but they led me to their home walking in front of me and constantly looking behind themselves to watch me. They let me in their very dimly lit home and I set their mother on the couch in the living room.

I turned for the door as the children curled up on the couch trying to be as close to their mother as possible.

"You are very lucky to have a loving mother, you are both great kids. Just be careful and stick together, you have a great opportunity ahead of you so don't ruin it," I told them and they nodded, sending their braids in their hair to swinging wildly, seeming to understand. They have a mother and a home, but they were only young now and they were growing up in a rough neighbourhood. If they wanted to survive they'd better follow their mother or I'd be coming after them. They very well knew that too, as they stared after me with terrified, round eyes.

A cold breeze met me as I walked outside, the moon was coming out behind a large cloud letting the moonlight shine on the city. Myre could see stars twinkling overhead, blue in colour against the dark black sky. This city was spectacular at night, the lights that lit the street were designed to light up the city, but not prevent people from viewing the night sky. It was a great advantage when everything was run by magic. We weren't sufficient without it, this city was very dependent on it in order to thrive. There had been a time where technology with electrical energy was being used, but everyone much preferred magic and so the majority of the city was run on magic and the majority of the world did also. This was a magically advanced world despite the fact that non-magic users dominated the world population.

I returned to my circle of death and looked at the people. I put my hands on my hips and just stood there staring at it thinking. They weren't people I killed, and I didn't put them here. And why were they cut up? I recognized whom the job was done by and I thought it definitely would be a good idea to visit this person, but that would have to wait until later. One thing that did occur to me was that all these people were or had the potential to be strong magi. I walked to where I had killed the gang members seeing motion over there. There were three new guys looking around for anything they could steal from the bodies.

"Dusk must've got em eh?" One said.

"Ya an' it looks like not too long ago either," Another said understandably frightened.

They were oblivious to me, though a dark shadow in other dark shadows, they had no chance on being able to detect me. I stepped out and drew a knife as I walked towards them.

"Guys!" One had turned around and had spotted me. This one was actually a girl, maybe seventeen, tall, skinny with burnet hair. She wore a tight black shirt and black short shorts with fishnet stockings. The other two were dressed nicely in clean jeans and t-shirts. I debated about letting them live, but when one of them drew out a gun, I decided. I moved faster than they could blink and in seconds the girl was lying on the ground dead, then the two boys were lying beside her with a cut on each of their throats. I checked to make sure no one was watching and left them to bleed as they pleased onto the cobbled streets.

A cloud covered the moon again and I turned a corner that led me away from the busy parts of the city and deep into the bad parts of it. I used magic to clean my knives as I came upon a small stream. The water was cold, but refreshing and I took a drink then washed my face.

"How was your night?" A voice behind me asked. I didn't flinch.

"Great, but I think we should lie low for a little while. Let's scout for a bit. How many people did you get?" I asked.

"Three," Cadence told me and I smiled pleased.

CHAPTER #16

We scouted for a bit, listening in on the doings of Vale Darra's citizens. Almost a month after I found the death circle, I found myself hunting down some prey. The sun was very warm, cheering me up from my grumpy mood from having to sleep through an unusually cold night. I got up slowly and went to the stream to clean myself. The water was cold, but after a hurried jump in and scrub with some soap I got out and dried off in the sunlight. I carefully shaved, trying not to nick myself with my knife as I got ready for the day.

I walked through the alleys casually, taking my time and making sure no one was watching me. There were some other street rats running around, but I took the alleys that kept me distant from them and so I did not meet up with anyone, which is the way I preferred it.

"I think today will be a good day," I told Myre. He looked up at me then up to the sky.

"But always, only for a moment," His voice rang in my head. I nodded in agreement and made my way to a street that ran parallel to the main streets of Vale Darra.

There were a lot of vehicles driving and horns honking, trying to get through traffic. The sidewalks crammed with people all talking simultaneously. The dull roar droned on making the city alive and noisy. I liked the city, at night the lights were pretty, but I hated the crowded streets, the backed up traffic, the overwhelming noise and the stench of too many people in one place. As much as my den was in shambles and I didn't have electricity or hydro, I love to retreat to my private little piece of paradise. There were few trees and not much wildlife, but it was better than being elbow to elbow with some cranky person trying to rush off someplace.

I avoided the main streets; staying on the narrower one way streets to get to a small shack-like building squished between two large buildings. There was a wooden sign that hung from a wire. A small stone path lead to an odd looking door. It was wood with brass vine like wires running up it. The brass gleamed in the sunlight and gave off green, brown and gold colours. This place was out of character for this street with its standard brick buildings, but it was creative. And outer appearance really wasn't the most important thing; the important stuff was what could be found inside.

I walked up to the door and opened it with a loud crack as the door broke off its hinges. There were multiple holes in the doorframe where the door had broken off previous times. I walked inside then pulled it back into the doorframe to let it lean against it.

"Hey who's stealin' my door?" A man yelled coming out from the back room. "Oh, just you," He said then walked away to place a pot on a shelf nearby. "What can I do for ya?" He asked leaning on the old counter.

He was a middle-aged man with a bald spot on the top, a huge gut and nose, sagging cheeks and watery eyes. Wearing a typical dirty white t-shirt and green pants with floppy shoes that looked too big for his feet. He wasn't the most impressive of people, but I still found him fascinating. He had only one good eye and currently two different coloured socks. "I am here to get some water," I said looking at a weird shaped pot. It was an olive green colour with bumps and dents everywhere.

"Ah water, the good stuff or the tasteful stuff?" He asked going to the back room again.

"Both, a bottle each," I said and followed him to the back room.

"Good, remember to bring back the phials and I can refill 'em for ya," He handed me two small phials and I smiled.

"Glade to," I said slipping him some money before leaving the store.

The phials didn't really contain water, it looked like water, sometimes smelt like it, if you can say water has a smell, but it actually wasn't water. It could take on almost every characteristic of water, taste, smell, and colour, but it was poisonous. Which was very convenient for poisoners.

I put the phials in a pocket of my shirt and walked through the alleyway this time entering the busier streets of Vale Darra. I could see some policemen standing around looking for any trouble, but not one of them looked at me. They seemed busy with trying to keep an eye on everything going around them, but I always worried one of them would spot me and single me out. When it came to humans, you didn't know what magic they could do or what their Wish was and so I was always extra cautious around policemen.

I walked to a store where they sold herbal medicine and went in.

"Hello, I'm looking for some pain medicine," I said to the cashier. She nodded then walked around the store and pulled a few leaves from some drawers and put them in a brown bag.

"Here you go, that all you need?" She asked.

"No, I also need some cinnamon and a few pieces of Ivy," I told her and again she nodded and got what I asked for. She came back and again asked if that was it, when I told her she registered it into the cash register.

"Five eighteen," She told me and I handed over the money. I smiled at her and said goodbye then left and followed the crowd down to where a huge building towered the herb shop some blocks down.

I snuck into a dark alleyway and added the pain medication, which comprised of a few different types of herb leaves, and the cinnamon to one phial and the ivy to the other phial. The one with the ivy would be used first; it was in the poison that was tasteless. I had added these ingredients because the first person I was to kill was great at sensing such things as herbs, added vegetables and other such edible things to liquids and foods. Interestingly enough though, Ivy was one substance that the person had trouble on. I could smother a carrot in Ivy and the person wouldn't be able to tell it for a carrot. So with the Ivy added to the poison, the person would think nothing of it. The other phial had cinnamon and pain medications for similar reasons. The person was great at knowing what was painful. The medication would prevent the person from using that ability while the cinnamon, a flavour the person deeply enjoyed, would make the liquid seem more enjoyable to my victim. With that I went back to the streets and continued my way.

There were people everywhere, the streets were overcrowded with pedestrians and cars sluggishly tried to drive down the four-lane street. Traffic lights changed and cars surged forward hoping to get out of the thick mass of people. A large group of people crossed the street stopping cars from turning and causing frustrated drivers to hit their breaks and wait for the next light. In all the cities craziness people thrived here with its large ever-growing mass of people and for some reason they still called it home.

I felt a little claustrophobic as I weaved through the throng of people, getting jostled and bumped into, tripping over small children and getting glares from angry parents. People spoke on the phone to others and lost focus to their environment, crossing the street when they shouldn't and nearly getting run over by vehicles. Other people huddled together as they walked so they created a wall of people I had to step out onto the streets just to avoid. A few people ran, some elders walked, some street people could be heard singing and playing their homemade instruments somewhere nearby. Cigarette smoke drifted in the smelly city air along with exhaust and the typical city stench. The city was considered a clean city, but the over crowdedness made it have a constant smell of sweat, smoke and gas.

I didn't like the noise and I didn't like being elbowed in the ribs repeatedly. I also did not like getting stepped on and having to fight just to walk anywhere. People became accustomed to shoving others back and saying a few quick words to someone who bumped into them. When I was younger I was really good at pit pocketing, this type of crowd being just the perfect target. But my hands were ready to catch any boys or girls who tried to steal from me as well as be ready to push my way through the crowd. I learned that a punch was unacceptable, but a jab was fair game.

It was very hard to go in any direction except the direction the crowd was going in, so getting across to the building I was trying to get to was a challenge all on its own. In the end I did manage to get to the rotating doors of the building and get inside. There were people in here who were on phones, computers or doing other work that distracted them from realizing someone was in the building that didn't work here or wasn't interested in buying anything.

"Excuse me, I'm here to see Mr. Crayblery," I said to a person who had just hung up. "One second please sir," She said and went on her computer. "Ok I don't see any appointments for him today," She told me.

"Oh I'm not listed," I told her acting as if this was natural.

"Oh ok, then is he expecting you?" She asked me and I nodded.

"I'm here to drop off a resume. I ran into him yesterday and he said just to pop by today," I told her shrugging.

"Ok take the elevator to the top floor," She said smiling cheerily.

I took the elevator and smiled and greeted anyone who came in, but didn't talk much to them, just some small talk. Some people came in and went out without even saying a word or showing that someone else was in the elevator with them. Others were all smiles, asking questions to any new face.

"Hello young man and who are you?" An old lady asked me.

"I'm Archer," I said smiling.

"Archer, are you new here?" She asked confused. She was ball shaped with small green eyes stuck in her head and a short stubby nose to go along with it. Her dull brown hair was in a messy bun, but she was dressed nicely in a blouse and skirt.

"Ya, just looking around, is the jobs good here?" I asked.

"Ya, you'll like it here, Mr. Crayblery is a nice man, I'm sure he will higher you," She said then with a bye left me to ride the elevator alone.

The top floor had an open concept flow to it with tiled blue floors and a white-blue ceiling. The walls were all windows making the tall room look more spacious. A few cubicles divided some workspaces, but for the most part it was one big room with a large desk, three computers on it and many filing cabinets off to the side along a glass wall. The centre of the room was dominated by a pond, which was strange, but I refrained from commenting about it. The fact that there wasn't even a fountain or fish in it also made no sense to me, but I was here to kill someone not criticize the decorator. Positioned on the far side of the room was a large table probably used to hold food and drinks when there were buffets and pot-lucks. It was a nice room, but slightly dysfunctional and for the most part ineffectual due to the lack of organization.

I tucked the phial into my sleeve and loosened the lid then stepped out onto the top floor. There were a few people walking around, but it was easy to find my victim. He stood by his desk looking out a large window, looking at what I assumed was other buildings and a mass of people. He was a tall man, slight build and had coffee brown hair. He had a small bald spot on the top of his head and laugh lines streaking from his eyes, but he wasn't that old. In his later 40's, he was well established and completely comfortable in his skin. Confident, he was a decent person and all right character, if it weren't for his recent activity I wouldn't have mind letting him live. Unfortunately, life liked to be cruel to those that could do well in life.

I approached and leaned over to pat him on the shoulder. As I did so the phial slipped out a little from my sleeve and the liquid poured into the drink that sat half empty on his desk. "Mr. Crayblery?" I asked and he turned around.

"Hmm, oh, yes?" He said focusing on me.

"Hi I'm Archer I was wondering if I could get a job here?" I asked seeming confident and casual as I shook his hand.

"A job, ok let's talk, here sit please," He said gesturing towards a chair. I sat and so did he. He glanced at his watch then at a calendar on his desk before grabbing a clipboard, a lined sheet of paper and a pen. Finally seeming ready to have an interview.

"Ok, Archer, what kind of a job are you looking for?" He asked me taking a drink. It was just that simple and in three days he would be dead.

"Well I'm good with people," I told him sitting straight and smiling like any one would who was trying to get a job.

"Ok, have you had any jobs in the past?" He asked folding his hands on his desk, his brown eyes tired, but thoughtful.

"Yes, I use to be an assistant manager at a retail store, I volunteered at a Childs hospital, just some cleaning and spending time with the kids really, and a few other more on the side jobs," I shrugged and he nodded along.

"Ok, what hours are you prepared to work?" He asked after writing some things down on a clipboard.

I knew many places you had to get an appointment; fortunately, this guy hated appointments and hated making others wait. He was to the point and quick about things, so I could get in and out of here soon. These type of people were more to my liking, every time I had to make an appointment to kill someone I though it a little funny and not very convenient.

He asked multiple questions and wrote down some notes, but mostly focused on me. I made sure to keep my answers simple, but still give some detail to them. The whole interview took about ten minutes and ended with me shaking his hand and telling him good day. He told me he would get in touch with me at the end of the week to let me know his answer.

He was a friendly guy and all about giving people chances so I knew he'd be an easy one to get. However, he was also working for a man named Zikeil who was trying to overthrow the King. I've been slowly working away at killing Zikeil's henchmen over the years and he keeps employing more. I've also been trying to find Zikeil, but he was proving to be very difficult to find and I didn't know if that was because he was multiple people or was someone using an alias. In any case the throne was as safe as I could make it right now.

I left the building and returned to the streets and the huge mass of people. My ears hurt with the roar of the crowd and it was hard to ignore and block them out so I walked with them until I could duck into an alley and run off to someplace quieter. Unfortunately, I couldn't get away for long, I still had other business to attend to.

I cut across and came out on the other side to walk along the streets and towards a park. I could see a woman standing by a tree with her Guardian, they were both looking up to the sky.

"Hello," I greeted and they looked at me.

"Hello," The woman smiled and came towards me. She was a little shorter then I, with wavy black hair and startling green eyes. Her skin was slightly tanned and she wore a light blue long sleeved shirt under a white vest with faux fur around the hood. Along with dark wash jeans and black heels. She was pretty in a simple-is-more kind of way.

"The king should sleep soundly tonight. What can I do for ya?" I asked her. She smiled, a warm and full of love type of smile that touched her eyes. As our minds were connected, I could hear her thoughts, which was comforting, but seeing her was far better. I gave her a warm smile back, hoping no one was around to see us or recognize the princess talking to some street rat.

"I heard something the other day I thought you'd like to hear it," She walked up to me. I could feel that she wanted to give me a hug and a kiss. She wanted to wrap her arms around my neck and pull me close to her. I wanted to love her the way she deserved to be loved, but we were in public and there were too many eyes watching. Seeing each other, even briefly, would have to suffice.

"Ok, what is it?" I put my hands in my pockets and slouched.

"Well apparently Miss. Sashess Flake is having her eighth birthday party, she's a cute little girl with short, squirrelly, red hair and beautiful green eyes, but her fathers a little bit troubled. He's been coming home drunk. His daughter's big birthday wish is that he doesn't come home at all, he beats her and she is terrified of him. Can you fulfill that wish?" She smiled hopefully at me slightly rocking on her heels and leaning forward. "Ya," I nodded and with a bye I left.

"*Love you,*" she said to me in my mind.

"*Not as much as I love you,*" I told her back and I could sense her smile grow bigger.

I couldn't help the birthday girl now unfortunately as I still had one other place to go, but I would do it tonight and so with that, I set off to go to the scariest part in the city. The people of Vale Darra called it Spooker's Corner, though its real name was Woodburrow. It was still part of Vale Darra located on the outskirts of it right in the trees. Some of the houses had trees growing in the walls or even in them as this use to be a huge woodland where people came hundreds of years ago and made tree houses. It used to be filled with bears and wolves so everyone lived in tree houses. There were even rope bridges running from house to house, but now they were old and falling apart. People had added additions to the house so now they sat on the ground.

It's called Spooker's Corner because a marsh lay on one side and fog usually spread throughout the forest. Some wolves and bears still lived here though were usually not a problem to the people living here as all were hunters and generally dealt with the problem animal by themselves. The people were a little strange, but were overall friendly.

It was amazing the city still aloud this place to exist. There were people fighting to make it its own town and it looked promising that it would become its own, but it was a long process and the people of Spooker's Corner were well known for taking their time on things.

The whole tree house town comprised of a population just above 6000 full time residents, a few 1000 more were seasonal. There were multiple buildings clumped together and large planks of wood nailed together to make decks that served as roads. They were strong and well protected by magic so vehicles could drive on it, but mostly people walked or road bicycles here. It was like its own little world full of trees, moss and mud.

Over the years the marsh had dried up so it was only about 20% of its original body, but in most places the mossy ground was still spongy. Marsh plants grew around buildings as if they were gardens and moss grew up the trunks of the many trees. The air smelled a lot cleaner and fresher then the city and it was a lot quieter here, but it was dark, dingy and dirty. A strange little world sitting on the edge of one of the biggest cities in the world, it was a little out of place, and yet it still existed.

People were walking around on the boardwalk going into wooden stores and checking out the town. I wasn't a big fan of this place; I wasn't big on falling into soft ground that I couldn't get out of. But with Myre at my side, we entered a house that was almost camouflaged with its surroundings. The houses surprisingly had electricity, fresh water and heating as well as the other usual stuff a typical house has. It was very clean and it didn't smell bad, woodsy, but a very nice smell. This building served many functions: a bar, a house and a hotel. There were many chairs on one side around multiple wooden tables. On the other side was a long wooden table to separate the bar from the dining area. Rows upon rows of alcohol were organized neatly behind the bar and taps for beer were positioned regularly down the bar table. Old wooden stools welcomed the lonely wonderer to a drink. The smell of sweat and alcohol became more distinguishable from the woodsy smell I had first smelt as I approached the bar.

"Hello," I said to a few people and they greeted me back.

"So Dusk, what ya need?" One said to me.

"Nothing, I'm here on business," I said.

"What ya doing here?" One asked. He was very short, only five two, with brown hair and brown eyes, but he was a good assassin, and his height helped him a lot. He looked like he was fourteen, but he was actually twenty-five, and he had a very thick accent.

"I need to know something, Dracula," I said to one of the assassins in the room.

Though I didn't like people just calling me Dusk out in the open this place was strictly forbidden from people and only admitted assassins and similar type people so it wasn't as if these people didn't know who I was. And as odd as it was having so many assassins here, it was also kind of nice; we got a long as far as assassins could anyway. And it was a great way to get information. The assassin I spoke to was called Dracula, given to him by the media because when his victims were found they had almost no blood in them and two bite marks on their necks. He didn't actually drink their blood, he was a blood mage, but his Guardian was a Vampire bat and he liked the name. It terrified a lot of people and made great scary stories that were good for scaring children. The other assassins were of varying ages from late teens to early fifties. Some weren't too good, but a few here I actually admired. They were a funny bunch though. Chummy drinking buddies, but lethal enemies at the same time. I nodded to a few and greeted them all, some taking their hands off of hidden weapons and taking a swig of beer instead.

"Yes, what dya need?" Dracula asked in his gruff voice.

"There's some people giving me a headache, one of them is your old apprentice. Where is he?" I asked and he nodded.

"The fool ran off some months ago saying he got a better master that would someday be the most powerful mage in the world. He went off to try and become a better mage," His black eyes stared calmly at me.

"But you don't know where he is?" I asked again.

"No, but I'd be happy to help find him with you. Got a few words I'd like to say to him," He said and took a swig of his beer.

"Ok, anyone know something I should know?" I yelled out to the others.

"I hear someone's trying to kill you," Someone chimed in.

"Does anyone know something I don't know? I already know people want to kill me, heck you people here want to kill me," I said and they all laughed. I smiled and I shook my head.

"Something's up, I just got back from Gyro, some fifteen hours from here and the people there are very sensitive to magical changes. They think there's an imbalance and someone's hoarding all the magic," Another said eyeing me weirdly.

"Well don't look at me, do I look like I'm glowing with an abundance of magic?" I asked annoyed. He just shrugged his shoulders and drank his beer.

"I don't know what's up, but if you're thinking there's someone up to no good, there usually is," Dracula said to me.

"Right well, while you all are getting fat and drunk, I'm going to go do something before someone blows up this planet," I said and turned to leave. "Bye, guys," I smiled and they nodded back.

"Bye, Dusk," The six assassins there said in unison.

"Have fun, let us know how it goes!" Someone called behind me.

I left Spooker's Corner and went back into the city. The sun was diving down to the horizon as I went to deal with birthday girl's father. I found him slouched drinking from an empty beer bottle in an old tavern. I had to walk half an hour through the alleyways to get to the place, but eventually I got there. He was far past tipsy and though his beer bottle was empty he kept sipping from it thinking it was full. His hair covered his face in long ringlets. He was a huge ox of a man, and had the experience of bull riding and boxing, but he had now turned into an abusive father and heavy drinker.

He was drooling a bit, but didn't care as he took another drink. His shirtfront was wet and his pants were worn at the knees and seat. I reached over as if to call the bar tenders attention. "Hey," Xerk slapped my hand away and got to his feet. He swayed then fell to the ground with a heavy thud. He was dazed and unable to speak clearly.

"Youuu, whuuut yeee wannnta?" He pointed a wobbly finger at me.

"Sorry sir, do you need help up?" I asked nicely.

"Nooo!" He roared and rushed to his feet. He steadied himself and tried to take a drink. "I don't neeeeed nobody, bu'ha me," He wobbled then threw a punch at me. I simply stepped back and rolled my eyes.

"Ok, sure thing big guy," I walked away and went outside as he swore at me and called on a fight.

I waited by the door and he came raging out like a mad bull, eyes wide. He seen me as I walked to the alleyway and with all the stupidity of the world, he followed me to his death. When we were out of sight of prying eyes I turned around to face him. He charged me and I gracefully stepped aside, a knife falling into my hand and going deep into his heart. He didn't even recognize his own life spilling away from him as he stumbled past me. He turned to face me again and I pulled the knife out of him. He stood there moments after before collapsing in a heap on the dirty and stinking ground. Sashes' wish was granted.

"Happy birthday girlie," I said out loud to myself.

With that over with, I left to go home and see if Cadence had food. Almost all my jobs for the entire week were done. I usually didn't do a lot of killing, but I wanted to keep up an appearance to see if I could get a reaction out of whoever was trying to kill me. Usually I only killed maybe 3 to 6 people a month, on special occasion it would get up to 9, but for the most part I kept it to a minimum. I didn't want to get caught, already I was walking on thin ice so I didn't need to start hacking away at the ice more. I just wanted to kill the bad guys then disappear.

CHAPTER #17

The night was very noisy as people walked on the streets to a midnight fair that went on every year. I, like everybody else, was crammed waiting for it to start. The gates were large enough to let the people walk in a large line, but not everybody, and everybody was excited to get to the fair. They had all been in their homes, probably jumping out of their seats until midnight. Now everybody seemed to be out and headed to the fairgrounds.

This fair was something that had been going on for over sixty years in this city and for the most part it was a time of fun and laughter. There would be rides, chances to win prizes like toys, bicycles, and even cars. There was also a circus, a large toddler play area, a mini petting zoo and food vendors. It sprawled on the East side of the city close to many cookie cutter houses. Some permanent buildings were stationed on the fair grounds to store maintenance supplies, hold items for staff as well as serve as ticket booths. Some temporary structures were also put up in neat rows for people to get inside out of the noisy chaos.

I had gone to this fair as a child and found it overwhelming, but enjoyable for the first few hours. It always started at midnight, though an inconveniently late night for some it had started as a small tiny fair on the outskirts of a desert city. Run by three people who decided to run a small fair with few rides and some camel rides. It was only open to family, but slowly someone new took over the fair and bought more land to make it bigger. At some point it grew too big and a new area was bought and established as the new fairgrounds. It had been decided that hosting it at midnight would still happen because at night it was cool and people didn't have to be out in the heat all day. When the owners moved, they had come to Vale Darra and had established it in Vale Darra. Again it started small, but the King at the time liked the opportunity it held to bring his people closer together and so, buying the rights to it, it became tradition that the fair would be held at midnight each year. The day of the fair changed each year, but mostly it happened in late spring or in autumn.

I stopped and slid into an alleyway to let a bunch of people who were sure they were going to bulldoze through everyone right to the front. They ran past, jostling others, pushing some, knocking small children to the ground and sending them screaming at the top of their lungs. It just added to the chaos and several people didn't approve as they turned on others and started yelling. I shook my head, wondering how a simple act such as waiting in line could bring out the worst in people.

A fight was bound to break out as a teenager continued his way to the front, pushing whoever was in his way or slipping in between people. A big man grabbed his shirt and threw him backwards.

"Hey!" The teen shouted and turned on the man. He was tall, well above six feet, with dark hair and eyes. He had a few scars on his arms that were bare to prove he wasn't one to mess with, but he was lean and not very muscular. The man he glared at was even taller than him, dark hair and green eyes, and very muscular. He crossed his arms and planted himself in front of the teenager. The teenager sized him up and walked away to wait like the rest of them for the gates to open.

I walked out and weaved through the rows seeing a familiar face amongst the crowd. One of my brothers was standing, leaning against a wall with his wife and adopted son and daughter. They looked somewhat bored by the long wait, but Jakk's, wife was always a bundle of energy ready to explode. Always ready for any new excitement or a chance to be out and about. It had been her idea to adopt, not my brothers. She had come home one evening about two years ago with a seven-year-old girl and a thirteen-year-old boy and so he had no choice. Even though they were very young, my brother's wife was a flamboyant and spontaneous person and had all the requirements to prove she could be a wonderful parent. Also as she was unable to have children of her own, she was near desperate to find other ways to start a family as soon as possible.

Though I was a little unsure of walking up to them I managed to weasel my way through the crowd to them. Jakk looked very surprised at me as if a ghost had risen up from the ground, but Vesper, seeing his face elbowed him in the ribs changing his expression to a grimace. He gave a weak smile, but I could tell he was studying me and looking me over.

"Hey," I greeted. I had never met Vesper, but I'm sure that Jakk had filled her in on stuff about me. Dad and Fetcher probably had updated everyone on my latest appearances and so I'm sure they half expected to see me. Still, seeing me was obviously something of an anomaly by the way Jakk was scrutinizing me.

"Vesper this is my younger brother Khire. Onica, Iyen, this is your Uncle Khire," Jakk introduced us.

"Oh, Khire! Well hello, haven't gotten trampled I see," Vesper said humorously as she gave me a big hug. She was tall, almost as tall as her husband beside her. With spiky red hair and blue eyes, she was spunky and wild, and really fun. Complete opposite to Jakk who was more relaxed and chill. She wore blue jeans and a black tank top with running shoes. She was practically bouncing up and down with excitement as she waited for the fair to start.

"You actually showed up? If I had my say I'd stay home," Jakk said unhappily, arms crossed. I smiled at him.

"Khire came cause he knows what fun is. You on the other hand Mr. Funnless don't, but don't worry, when we get home, I will make it up to you," Vesper said winking at him. He rolled his eyes not interested and huffed.

"So why'd you come?" Jakk asked me. There was no "it's so nice to see you, you look great,", but I didn't expect anything from Jakk, we didn't have a great relationship and he was more focused on his work then just about anything else anyways.

"Meet up with some friends," I said and shrugged. The gates would be opening soon and as the street lights turned off and the fair lights turned on, the city got very bright and loud. Sirens went off and there were fireworks in the distance. It was a little tease before the clowns opened the gates. When everything went quiet, the King got up to a podium to speak.

"Ladies and Gentlemen, tonight let us have fun, we deserve a great abundance of joy that can't just be given to you in a night, but here, have fun. Let the gates be open!" The King said short and sweet as he raised his arms and everyone screamed at once and pooled forward. To get in was free, but to play games or ride attractions you had to pay, which, having no money, looked like I would only be a bystander. It didn't matter to me, I was only here to do a job then leave; though some of the rides did look really cool.

The fairgrounds were huge, off on one side were rides like roller coasters, swings, bumper cars, Ferris wheels, merry-go-rounds and more while on the other side there were games to play like catching real live fish or squirting at clown faces to make the balloon reach the top. Small and large stuffed animals hung around the games to tempt everyone to try and win them. People were already hurrying over to try their luck at darts or archery while others went directly to ticket booths to get on the rides. There were a few new ones here this year that even I wished I could try out.

With all the hustle to get into the fair I was shoved right into Jakk's son, who was then shoved into a huge women and her husband.

"You kids, watch where you're going!" They screamed together. "Watch where you're going you great blubbering whale!" Iyen yelled back. Jakk grabbed his son by his shirt and yanked him back.

"Iyen, shut up!" Jakk said, yelling to be heard. Iyen crossed his arms, but went quiet. The husband jabbed a finger into Jakk's chest. "That boy of yours deserves to be in jail for all the trouble he's caused!" The man growled. He was rolling with fat, and glaring at Jakk with tiny pale blue eyes. His balding head was glistening with sweat even though it was a cool night. His t-shirt was damp under the arms and along his back and well worn. An almost musty smell came from him making me a little cautious and wondering if ever I smelled that bad.

Iyen laughed and his sister, Onica bit her tongue to try and stop herself from laughing as well. Iyen had done nothing wrong so I knew this man was just starting a fight for the sake of starting a fight, with no real accusations to go on, he simply came up with whatever stupid accusation came to mind first.

"Ok," Jakk said trying to sound reasonable, but not at all taking the other man seriously. The man was not pleased.

"You…" He wasn't able to finish as my eldest brother came up behind us and looked at the man. He rested his hands on Jakk's shoulders as he contemplated on what to say. I noticed then that a large crowd of people were watching us, not to see a fight, but just because the man was blocking the way into the fair. "Umm excuse me you're blocking the people from getting into the fair, please be so kind as to move so we can get in," Tellnair said very sweetly.

"He is no good," The man pointed at Jakk again. "Yes we know that, he's horrible and a complete disappointment, we're very ashamed of that. However your still in the way," Tellnair said as he nudged Jakk to the side trying to get us around the man.

There was just something about the man none of us could take literally. The man was not happy about being humiliated in front of a large crowd, so he huffed and turned and walked through the gate. I guess it was mean to make fun of obese people, you never knew if he had a condition, but this guy was fat and each step he took caused a huge wave of motion that looked very much like ocean waves. He actually got stuck in the gate and had to be shoved through by a huge guard who wasn't pleased to touch him.

"So little boy, you ok?" Tellnair said looking at Jakk. Jakk wasn't a little boy, he was tall as well as muscular, half ox to be exact. Jakk smiled and shook his head at Tellnair who liked to pretend we were still children.

"Can we go now?" Onica asked annoyed.

"Sure we can, your dad will be with his brothers while we take his wallet and have fun," Vesper said pushing her kids forward. "And who said you could have my wallet?" Jakk asked, but Vesper already stuck her hand down his pants pocket and got it.

"Well now it's in my hand and you can't get it back," She smiled and they went off to see the attractions.

"Ah, I hate when these things happen, everybody is so crazy for them, but I think it just causes a bunch of people to come here and scream, little kids to eat junk food and be sick all over the place and old people to complain," Tellnair said.

"Well now you're complaining does that mean your old?" I asked walking through the gate.

"Ha no, come on lets have some fun, there's that new roller coaster that's calling my name. By the way Khire it's nice to see your doing ok, we've all been worried about you," Tellnair said giving me a playful shove.

"Nice to see you too, but sorry I can't stay. I have to go find somebody," I said and started to sneak away. "After, right now we have a date with Gun shot," He grabbed my arm and pulled me to the line up to the roller coaster.

"I can't I didn't bring any money and we don't have tickets," I said and tried to pull away.

"The others are grabbing tickets and I'm paying so I don't know what your money has anything to do with it. You can leave your money anywhere you like for all I care," Tellnair said barley giving me any attention.

"Tellnair, if Khire's scared don't make him go on the ride," someone said and there was the rest of our large family coming over. I huffed a little taken off guard by their sudden appearance.

"I'm not scared, I have things to do, there's a difference," I crossed my arms and looked unhappy, but stayed where I was while they talked and Aster sauntered over to give me a hug and smile, scrutinizing me.

"Your too skinny," He said looking me over.

"I'm fine," I said defensively.

"I'm just saying, but you look great otherwise, how has things been?" He said smiling warmly.

"Oh fine, enjoying life, how about you?" I replied with a shrug.

"Oh just living the dream," He answered back.

"Jeepers everybody was so excited about this, and you know what I am too! I thought I wouldn't be, but this is so much better than last years," Tellnair said looking around eyes wide.

"Oh my… Tellnair you know…" whatever Aster was going to say was lost in a scream that rang out louder than the rest. It came from one of the riders who was on a roller coaster. She was having a lot of fun, that much any one could tell, but her companion wasn't as the coaster reached its max point and zoomed down.

I turned to look around me, but the person I was out to find was still a no show, I knew she would come, but she would have to be found later. The coaster came to a stop with a jerk then zoomed backwards even faster than before making the people scream their voices to a rasp.

Time was going by fast and I didn't like how much time was being wasted to just stand in a line while your ear drums went deaf, your eyes were blinded with so many lights and people had seizures with all the blinking and flashing lights. I watched as a little girl fainted right as she was walking by a clown who jumped out at her. She didn't even scream, she just looked over to her right and collapsed. The clown was sent into a panic as the little girl's father rounded on the clown. The clown was a young man about eighteen with light sandy hair and blue eyes and he stared terrified at the man who was threatening to sue him. Another clown stepped up behind the clown-which was his identical twin brother-and talked to the man.

"I'm sorry Mr., honestly, our mistake, she must just be overwhelmed by all the attractions. There's a room in the back where you can set her on a couch, it's better than the ground, follow me," As the clown turned to the younger one he glared. "What are you doing?" He asked keeping his voice low.

"Sorry, you said be a clown, I didn't mean to scare the girl," The eighteen year old said apologetically, but also a little mad. The elder one, though only a half an hour between them, shook his head and guided the father who carried his daughter into a tent with pin stripes.

I was pushed forward so I couldn't see what happened to them, but I knew those two boys, though they were in disguises, I knew who they were and they weren't clowns. I was going to step out of the line and go to them, but I was dragged into a cart and strapped in by Tellnair as if I were a little boy.

"You know I might be too young for this ride," I said annoyed.

"I don't care, you're going," He said strapping himself in beside me. It wasn't really strapping, just a bar that went across your thighs, but it added more thrill to the ride.

I was just about to unbar myself when everyone gave the signal they were ready to go and the cart jolted forward. I slammed forward and as the bar caught me, I slammed back into my seat, my head bouncing off the back of the seat.

"Bet that felt great," Tellnair said trying to reach over to my head. I swatted at him telling him I was fine and to leave me alone. We were going down into a tunnel as if in a barrel of a long gun, then the opening appeared and we zoomed out into the night sky, up and up at a very steep and fast rate.

I looked down at the tent, and could see through the tent at the man sitting on a bed while his daughter slept on it. I watched as the two brothers talked quietly outside the tent to each other. They were all growing smaller as the coaster continued its slow, carful climb up the tracks. I was very high off the ground, and only getting higher till suddenly the cart reached its height and careened down. Other than me, everyone screamed and threw their arms up. The night air went by us very fast and we were approaching the ground very quickly, but the tracks pulled up and as the train followed the tracks we were going upside down and turning as the tracks veered to the right sharply. I heard someone throw up and grimaced. I didn't feel anything, but I could imagine it and as we were suddenly plunged towards the ground and into a tunnel that led underground, I heard another person throw up as well. We came up faster than we did the first time to the right and the tracks continued. The coaster sent us one way then jerked us another way making you feel as if you lost your stomach. The tracks took us to great heights to just plunge us down to the ground and into more tunnels and loops that went straight down then sharply bent upwards and back out and up to the stars.

I didn't care for the ride; I jumped off high buildings a lot so the thrill wasn't all there for me. Instead I looked out for the two brothers and anyone else who was working here. This ride was deeply cutting into my time I needed to do other things, but it was fun, and my brothers were enjoying it so much as they closed their eyes and screamed, throwing their arms up as we made another dip. I did want to have a little fun still, I couldn't help but think about the father and daughter. They were in danger and right now the one person that could really save them was stuck on a roller coaster called Gun Shot.

I thought the ride was nearly over when the train jerked to a stop and reversed. Everyone was enjoying themselves, but I was ready to get off, I had work to do and I had finally spotted who I was looking for. A tall, long, dark haired woman, with mischievous jade coloured eyes. She was wearing a skimpy dress that showed off too much of her curvy body and drew everybody's attention and gave her, her name Temptress. She was skinny with a flat stomach and had the body all women dreamed about. Small waist, large chest and wide hips along with a natural looking sun kissed tan. It wasn't her real name, just her job name, but it fit.

Soon the coaster stopped and we all got off. "Ok next ride," Tellnair said and everybody started to go off to go elsewhere. "Ok, well I'll have to catch up with you guys later, I have to go somewhere," I told them. "No, please, Khire, a fair comes to the city and you're doing work, honestly do you know how to have fun?" Tellnair asked turning to look at me.

"Yes I do, but I told a friend I'd meet up with her so I have to go, bye," I said and with a wave I left them. I heard Tellnair yell something after me, but I didn't catch it. Myre was happy to be at my side again, Guardians couldn't come on the roller coaster and some of the other rides though he would have enjoyed it. Still he was happy to stay where his paws met hard ground.

I wandered around seeking out the women when I felt arms wrap around me and a chin rest on my shoulder. "Hello sexy?" She asked kissing me on the cheek. She pulled me closer, smiling at me and pressing her body into mine.

"Chris and Tylar are here," I told her ignoring her attempts to flirt with me and unwrapped her arms around me.

She let me go and we went to the circus tent. I went in the back way, but I was too late, the man and his little girl were already dead. The girl still lying on the bed, stabbed in the heart and the man, stabbed in the back crunched over on his chair, leaning over the girl's body. I checked for anything else, but found nothing. I tried to leave, but the woman was standing in the doorway.

"Well this is cozy," She said and walked over to me.

"Honestly?" I asked annoyed and left.

I turned to do my other business and Temptress and I split, she going her own way towards the target while I circled around towards an alley near the far side of the fair. I didn't like working on certain special occasions, I would have liked to enjoy myself, but Temptress had asked me for a favour and she had helped me out so many times, I couldn't say no. And so my hunt continued.

☾

The people were all having so much fun, busy with their carefree fun to realize the danger nearby, they had no idea Dusk would kill tonight and they would all be involved. It was my job to get the target away from the people and to a private place where Khire could do his work. This was normal for me, I rarely killed myself, instead I just attracted attention and got the targets away so the assassin waiting to kill him or her could do so. It was a great job because I got to have all the fun I wanted with the victims before they died.

I wound my way through the crowd happy to be getting all the stares I was getting, I wore my favourite party dress for this location, and was happy I did. It made me look great and on any other person they would butcher the look, but I pulled it off. It hugged my body in all the right places, but gave a little flare out from my hips. With a plunging neckline and the cleavage to pull it off. I had put a few strands of hair up, but let the rest fall down in long wavy black curls. Some makeup that made my eyes look bigger and some jewellery, I was a flawless diamond among rhinestones.

I smiled teasingly at anyone I met eye contact with then found my target and walked confidently up to him. He looked at me and smiled.

"Hi darling, you don't know me, and I don't know you, why don't we solve that right here right now," I said smiling as I put my hand on his chest. He smiled.

"Would love to Sweetheart," He said.

"How about a quieter place hun," I asked him, brushing my fingertips up one of his arms and leaning towards him.

"Lead the way gorgeous," He said and followed me to an alley.

"This is just a faster way to my home, do you mind?" I asked looking under my lashes at him. He shook his head.

"Nope," He said and followed me into the darkness. It was the worst thing he would ever do, but he just followed me smiling. Stupid boy not thinking with his brain.

Silver reflected in the moon light, then the silver was suddenly red and dripping and the air was fresh with the smell of blood and a thump sounded in the night, but no one else heard it. Khire stepped away from the body and came towards me. "Good job," He said with a smile. I smiled at him and circled my arms around him, grabbing his ass in the process.

"Seriously?" Khire hissed at me.

"Well no time like the present," I teased as he wormed out of my arms.

"Go!" he demanded and with a sign I left him. I found a girl this time and stumbled up to her slightly crouched.

"Hey, sorry, could you help me with some girly stuff?" She was confused, but nodded and followed me. As we were walking by the alley hands reached out and grabbed her, before she could make a noise her throat was sliced.

That was two and there were still five to go. I had a lot to kill tonight and I wanted the job done quick. I didn't care to kill so much in one night, but these people had irked me for some time and I was finally able to get Khire to help me. I went out and found a couple, a boy and a girl talking with another man, they were all targets so getting the men's attention was easy while the girl came along because she was jealous by the women randomly stealing her boyfriend away. I led them to another alley and Khire made a quick job of dealing with them. One boy actually screamed and jumped back, but Khire quickly grabbed his head and gave a violent twist.

I pushed the frightened girl at him and he grabbed her and stabbed her in the heart then did the same to her boyfriend. It was going well, but soon there would be screams and not from people having fun.

"How do I look?" I asked Khire as I twirled slowly.

"You don't have any blood on you if that's your concern," He said and I waved him off. I went out making sure I had no blood on me and got the next two people, they were brothers and they were the last kills. They were both boxers and I was really excited about these two. I enjoyed watching a good fight, and I knew Khire was an excellent fighter that could pummel these two into smithereens in seconds, but maybe he would have some fun and kill them slowly.

They both were talking, but stopped as I laid a hand on one of them, I was being coy now, but my actions told otherwise as I looked at them with a small smile and narrowed my eyes.

"You two fine gentlemen wouldn't be interested in helping me now would you?" I asked them.

"No not at all, what d'ya need?" One asked.

"Oh something, I need help lifting this thing into this other thing," I said acting stupid.

"Ahh ok," They said confused and followed me as I sauntered past a ride that was a big cylinder that turned fast enough to press everyone to the sides. I turned and they easily followed me into the shadows of a narrow alleyway. It wasn't very narrow, three people could easily walk side by side, but it didn't matter. This was the best alley way and one that many would use to get back home. I wanted everyone to know these boys were dead.

Khire jumped out and punched the first one then reached around and stabbed him in the ribs. The man punched forward and his brother came at Khire from behind. Khire jumped up on top of one and took out a gun to aim down and shoot. The sound was small, only a little snap, but the force was lethal. The man dropped to the ground and his brother furious lunged at Khire and grabbed his arm and twisted. Khire manoeuvred to avoid getting his arm broken and came around the other man, stabbing him in the wrist then the ribs then the neck. The man was twitching, but he tried to grab Khire again and pin him to the ground, he did manage to get a good kick to Khire's ribs, but not enough to save his life. Khire simply did a high kick to the temple and the man dropped like a stone. Khire stabbed him a few times to make sure he was dead then we hurried away to where we could be alone.

He used magic to get any blood off his clothes until not even a stain showed, then smiled at me.

"Thanks Temptress good work," He said with a smile.

"Thank you," I said giving him my greatest smile. I put my arms around him once again and gave him a meaningful look.

"Now how about you come home with me?" I said with a smile. "I bet I can give you a better night then what you could have here," I turned on my charms, using some magic so that I was even more attractive. On any other guy I'd have them literally drooling and crawling after me. Unfortunately for me, Khire was not just any guy. He was sexy and a fantastic assassin, a great hit, but somehow he was unaffected by me. No matter how hard I tried, I couldn't get him to sleep with me. He wasn't interested, instead he smiled and unwrapped my arms around him then waved goodbye and returned to the fairgrounds, going a different path then the one we had just come from. Pouting, I watched him leave trying to think of what to do now that my fun was over. Those stupid people were finally taken care of for the rest of my life and I hadn't made any other plans for tonight. With little else to do, I decided to leave to find someone to amuse me. Maybe I could catch up with another assassin and see if they needed help with anything.

CHAPTER #18

I walked around looking around till I coincidently walked right into the two people I wanted to see.

"Hello, you two having a good night?" I asked acting like we were just having a casual conversation.

"Oh wonderful," Chris or Tylar answered smiling. "Adding to the record are we Khire?" He asked.

"Got a few accounted for, how are you two doing, other than the two people I already know about?" I said smiling. "Ah you ruin our fun," Tylar/Chris said acting upset.

"Ah sorry, but what are you guys doing here?" I asked now confused. "Well there was a fair, fairs are our greatest hits and our favourite," One said. Natural dark eyes, dark hair, tanned skin; though in disguise now, I could still recognize them easily, but not differentiate which one was which. They had very straight noses and high cheekbones, they loved to be in disguise, but liked to show off their good looks too. They worked as a team on their assassinations and had a lot of fun doing it together. Sometimes they got into fights, but in the end they worked well together.

I stood cross armed before them smiling amusingly at them as they spoke.

"Hey are you guys staying here long?" I asked looking around.

"Nah, we just came for the fair then we'll be packin it up to go back home," One said and sighed with a shrug. "We have a little friend, she's quiet nosey and well, she's got herself into some business that she doesn't need to be in. We were gonna give her a visit to show her why she shouldn't be doin that, but maybe you'd like ta do it for us?" Tylar/Chris asked questionably.

"Tell me about her?" I sounded a little interested. "Well she is a social butterfly, always out and about, always seen at Jakkie's on Sunday morning at five drinking a coffee and eating a bun. She then leaves at five twenty to hang with three of her girlfriends who always take her to the mall. They go to the same stores, except when there's a new store that has just opened and it is interesting to her. Sometimes she buys something, but she always checks out the men, you could be an easy catch, just go there and she'll be sure to notice ya," They told me.

"Hummm well I think I know who you're talking about, I don't really do dates, but I don't see how she's a threat," I said confused.

"It's simple, she knows too much," They said in unison.

"Ok, I'll deal with her, but later. I need to keep a low profile for a few days. I've got where she lives and I know what she does during her days so I can come up with something that's best suited for her, but do you plan on having any part in her?" It was always nice to stay on people's good side, especially when they could potentially be your enemy. Besides, Vale Darra was my turf, I didn't like too many assassins competing with me.

"No just want to see one more name added to the obituaries thank you very much," They smiled and turned to give their attention to a little girl who was brave enough to approach the clowns. "What can I do for ya sweetheart?" One asked kindly. I'm guessing it was Tylar because he was the nicer of the two.

"Can you make me an animal balloon?" She asked a little shy.

"Why sure I can, what would you like?" Tylar crouched down and stared up at her while she thought.

"A cat," She finally said and Tylar took out a balloon and went to work making it into a cat.

Chris turned to me.

"It be better sooner rather than later. We have reason to believe she up to know good. Deal with her tomorrow and then lie low. She knows info that could be far more of a problem for you if she tells anyone," He told me.

"Fine… tomorrows Sunday, I'll take care of her tomorrow and be done with her ok, but do you know anything about the red circle in the news?" I asked him.

The circle I was looking at earlier had been on the news for a while so if he was watching TV, he would have heard something about it.

"Ya why?" He was confused.

"Well I'm looking around to see who killed them and why? It appears all those that died were either strong magic users or had great potential to be strong magic users. I want to know what someone's got against magi," I whispered.

"Oh, well I heard a few things, but now's not the time to speak of it. I'll get you some more information and see you tomorrow night at eleven by the Docks, ok?" I nodded and he turned to his brother. Tylar was just handing over a pink cat balloon to the little girl who took it with a huge smile then she ran off and Tylar turned back to us. "Anyway, thanks for doing this for us," He said already knowing what he missed. They were twins and were good with telepathy so all the information that just passed through Chris and mines conversation would have gone through Tylar's head, he didn't need to be filled in.

We split as a siren went off announcing someone won something big. I wandered around on the fair grounds and found my way to a ride where I could see my family on. They were in these turtle shells that turned, flipped and rotated. The ride was connected in the center that reached out with six arms to six huge turtle shells where people would strap themselves in. It went faster and faster and the arms lifted you up and down, I could hear people screaming, but they were all just having fun.

I stood there watching them when I heard a little girl beside me speak, "Mom, that little girl over there is staring at me," I peeked over to see a small girl staring at another little girl. She was all tattered and rugged, but she seemed not to care.

"Ok honey come on," The scared girl's mother took her daughter away, obviously unnerved by the other little girl. The tattered girl turned her large eyes to me. I smiled and un-afraid I went over to her, I knew right away who she was.

"Hey how's Tykkie?" I asked crouching down. She smiled a creepy, sharp-toothed smile. I could see she was already much like her master.

"Great, he's upset you haven't visited lately, how come you don't come visit? You don't like us?" She had that hypnotic mousy voice that was so like her masters it sent chills up my spine.

"No, but I'll visit soon, promise, what's up?" I asked her with a nod of my head as I met her eyes, one dark brown, the other a light blue.

"Master wants to know how the fairs going, he was happy to come, but he couldn't so he told me to come and enjoy it for myself," She gave a large creepy smile. She had large long braided black hair, dark skin and a small round face. She would have been cute if she didn't look so creepy, but I being blind could only take Myre's word on it that she was a sight. I couldn't see her and I was use to her master more than anyone else, so I wasn't taken aback by her.

"Well are you enjoying yourself?" I asked crossing my arms on my knees. "He he, yes, but I wanted to go on a ride and they wouldn't let me," She seemed very upset about this.

"Ah what ride?" I said cocking my head. "Gun Shot," She said like I was stupid.

She was probably eight years old and short for her age no wonder they didn't let her on. "Ya they won't let you, these citizens here are a lot more soft. There not use to the upbringing our kind are used to, but don't worry, you've heard of the Nights Party right? Some people are putting on a little fair over in another town. It's not for the public, just for a few selected people only so you won't have issues not getting on to any ride you want there. It's in a month, how about I meet you and your master there ok? Then we can have some real fun," She smiled hugely again. "Ok, I'll tell master and he'll be rrrreeeaaaal happy," She ran off and dashed into the nearest alleyway, out of sight. She would pass it on to her master Isaac.

I smiled happy that Isaac had a little protégée of his own. He wasn't one for followers, but he did like people. Tykkie was his real name and I used it when I was around people that might over hear. If I had said Isaac people would have freaked.

"Khire," I heard someone say from behind me. "Yes, Fetcher?" I asked the cop behind me. My family stood there staring at me strangely and I gave them a weird look back.

"What's wrong?" I asked confused.

"Who was that little girl? How do you know her?" Fetcher asked. I knew he knew that little girl too, he didn't know as much as I did, but he did know that she was crazy and dangerous.

"Oh, she's my friends little girl," I answered and walked over to them. "How was the ride?" I asked to change the subject.

"Good, we were gonna head home, you comin?" Tellnair asked.

"Ya," I walked beside them to the gate. Jakk's family was with him and his wife was animated in all her excitement, the rest were tired, but smiling happily and Onica was holding a large purple rabbit.

"Find whoever it was you wanted to?" Aster asked me. "Ah ya, tonight went well, it was a good time to catch up with some friends. I found a lot of them here, so we went and got pizza. We were..." I was cut off which was ok because I was just filling in the silence. People started running around screaming as now people were discovering the bodies in the alleyway.

"What's happening?" Fetcher asked. He left us as he seen a squad of policemen run by towards the first bodies.

"There's been a killing," We heard one say to Fetcher. "Oh, Dusk, well great now the fair is ruined, great, thanks Dusk," Aster said sarcastically as if he knew Dusk was listening. I looked at him and so did everybody else. "I'm not actually surprised, come on lets go home, we'll see it on TV," Jakk said and steered his family out the gates and down the street to their homes.

"Khire, come home please," Dad said walking beside me. "I am going home dad, you should go home too," I said wishing he wouldn't do this.

"Please, just for tonight, please just come home," Dad didn't like the fact that he didn't know where I lived. Worse if he did know he really wouldn't like where I lived. Little did he know my life would only put him in more danger if I were to live with him. So I slept in an abandoned somewhat dilapidated house and I dealt with all the problems it gave me much to his displeasure.

"Maybe another night dad, I'll be fine," I said trying to end the discussion.

"You need to come home look at you, you're thinner than a rail," He told me gesturing to me as if I hadn't noticed myself. I was still very self-conscious of my body, though I wasn't fat and ugly anymore I still felt uncomfortable in my own skin. I didn't want to talk about how I looked and when someone tried to, I got very defensive.

"I'm alive alright, just leave it alone," I snapped and he looked at me hurt. "Fine, then I will see you for tomorrow morning," He said sure he was going to get me sometime.

"Can't I have to work," I told him as we walked down the street towards his house.

"Why can't you just come by for a few minutes?" Dad was upset more because he didn't even know what I did, and he worried a lot. I hated that he cared so much, it wasn't like we had a great relationship when I did live with him.

He cared too much for his own good and I wanted him to stop. I didn't know if he truly felt bad and wanted to make a good father-son relationship between us or if he was just pretending. He was really close to all his other sons maybe he wanted his youngest one back, but I wasn't ready to give him a chance. I still held him responsible for a lot of my troubles and I didn't entirely believe him that he cared that much for me. Besides I was an assassin, I didn't need a weakness. Maybe he wanted a perfect family, my dad was always striving for perfection and was a very vain person. It made him a really great realtor, but I always felt it was one of the things that spread us apart. I kept going back and forth between trying to figure him out and convincing myself I didn't trust him.

He never cared about me the way he cared about his older sons. He was with them every minute, gave them everything that they wanted and loved them like they were the most precious things in the world to him. I guess he blamed me for killing the love of his life, but it wasn't as if I had meant to kill my own mother when she was giving birth to me. Still I didn't want to hurt my dad, he loved me in his own way and I loved him back, but my life was, I knew, short. I was expecting death to meet me around each corner I turned, and I faced it determined to get past it and live another day. That stubbornness or any name you could call it helped me to survive each passing day, but there would be a day where it would just be too hard. I didn't mind dying, I had tried to kill myself so obviously it never worried me, but after reconnecting with my dad I felt a little better about my life. However, despite not being the greatest fatherly figure to me he was still my father and I couldn't let that go. My feelings seemed by polar or something with all these mixed feelings about him, but I really just couldn't figure it out.

"Dad, I have to go to work, but I will stop by after ok. I have something in the morning, but it will only be a few hours I will be at your home for ten ok, I can't stay all day alright only two hours max," I was putting limits on our time spent together, I already had a busy day and I didn't need it any busier.

"Thank you," He said smiling. He hugged me and turned to go down his street to his home, while I walked with Tellnair and Shean to their homes. Shean lived a little farther away so he probably had his car at Tellnair's.

Shean lived near the outside of the city on a large 250 acres of land. It made sense since he trained horses and was an instructor as well as held competitions. He also grew his own hay, which actually made me a little jealous. He wasn't your typical city dweller, but he had his life going for him and still dad loved him. However, heaven forbid I decide to leave the city dad would be upset and disappointed as if I were betraying him. I frowned as I dwelt on how unfair my life was, getting totally distracted in my own moodiness to realise Tellnair was talking to me. He gave me a poke in the ribs to get my attention. I was about to swear at him when he spoke first,

"You know you could make him very happy and just talk to him a little more, he loves you so what's wrong with staying over at his house or staying a few extra hours? Seriously, you pick *work* over your family all the time," Tellnair spoke, he wasn't that emotional, but right now he seemed upset.

"I know, but there's things I just got to do, I can't expect you guys to understand something you don't know, but..." "Don't know, Khire we don't know anything about you because you just ran away. You lived with us until you were old enough to move out then you left and now we know next to nothing about you. We don't know where you live, what you do, what you like, who your friends are, anything! We know your birthday, we know your name, but the list ends there. You're our brother that's not a good thing if we know so little about you. We need to understand some more things here, tell us something," Tellnair said more as a command then a question. He had a point, but it still wouldn't convince me to tell them anything.

"I never had a great connection with dad, I'm not like you guys. I'm not successful, I don't have a nice house, a wife and kids. I don't have your life and quite frankly I don't want it. I live very simply so I don't know what's the big deal that you don't know that stuff about me. It doesn't affect me so why does it matter that you don't know about that stuff. You know what counts that should be good enough," I said getting more irritated.

"Khire we're not judging you and belittling you because you're not… you just have to be a little more open that's all and not so secretive. Why not share the little things about you, sometime it's the little things that mean the most?" Tellnair said and Shean nodded along.

"Ya well like I said you know what counts that should be good enough. Goodnight," I said, but before I could walk away Tellnair grabbed my shoulder.

"What?" I said with a huff.

"Your our brother so you matter and I know we all got a lot of attention and you got the short end of the stick, I've always known that. When I was younger I was selfish and I didn't care, but I care now and I think we've miss treated you. You have such great potential, why can't you just let us help you?" He asked pleadingly.

"Because it doesn't make a difference now," I said trying to hold my temper in check. I swatted his hand away and walked away from them not caring if they were offended or not.

I went down the street until I could hear nothing but Myre and I breathing. We walked for a bit to cool down before turning down a side street and following it back to the city. The city was noisy with people talking, crying, yelling, fighting and doing anything that made noise. The streets usually always had someone on them, but I managed to find one that was empty. I walk down it for a while thinking to myself. I was suddenly in a grumpy mood, but didn't know what to do about it. I eventually found my way home, Myre forever loyal at my side as he brushed up beside me to help me manoeuvre around obstacles on the street.

CHAPTER #19

When next I wake, the sun is just rising. I slowly got up as my body began to warm up. Leaving my home, I went for a little walk to stretch my legs before starting the day. I found myself standing at a little river deep in the warrens of the deserted section of the city, which I occupied. The water was freezing, but better than nothing and after getting changed into clean clothes and shaving, I readied myself for the day. Everyone was still sleeping, the silent and rare peace greeted me, but as I made my way closer to the city I began to hear the sounds of engines running, people talking and the city awakening. I heard a bird singing its tune in a park nearby, and little kids running around screaming as they chased the birds that landed on the ground. They were laughing as they ran and they were completely happy, no care in the world for anything else, it was just them and the pudgy birds that swooped down to land.

I couldn't help but stare; I didn't remember a time when I was that happy and I didn't even remember something that could get me some of that happiness. I had a hard lonely time growing up. It surprised me how sad I must have been and how much everyone else must have talked about me. A kid who walked around, un-smiling, able to do lost arts that caused death, able to move faster than the eye could see, have the knowledge and capability to kill. They of course didn't know I knew all that and more, but they knew something because they all stayed away from me. I had friends, but slowly each one drifted away till I was left with only my shadow.

All these flash backs were going through my head. I was an eight-year-old boy walking down the street, everyone was so sad, they were all crying or had been crying. Their eyes red and puffy, hair messy, clothes wrinkled, walking around listlessly. The Kings father and mother had died as I had just killed them the night before and now in the morning when the news was spreading, everyone was so hurt and it was all because of me. I knew it was because of me to, but I didn't cry. I knew that I was the reason they cried so much and why Vale Darra had permanent bloodstains on its streets and homes.

I was young and I understood everything even when I walked past all those people and got to school. Everyone was there, but no one was in the mood to teach, instead we all just talked. The younger kids, the ones that didn't understand, played outside in the schoolyard while everyone else sat in the large gym to talk. I sat there for hours listening to teachers and students get up in front of everyone and cry and talk how the deaths of these people hurt them and what the people had meant to them.

I couldn't cry, the only thing that went through my head was that they're dead, I killed them and I killed them because I was told they were bad people. Teachers came up to me and took me to a quiet room, it was just me and two other teachers and they cried and talked and asked me questions. They thought I was so upset by the deaths that I was just in shock, and so they were trying to help me, but I was mostly helping them. One got sick and I called the doctors, the other was weeping so much he couldn't get off the floor and so I had to talk to him. I didn't like it. All those people crying and pain written on their faces so that all could see and feel it too, I couldn't handle it so I had run away that day. I kept running even when I reached the forest, I tripped a few times and when I went down and couldn't get back up I just laid there, but no tears came. My eyes weren't even wet; I just stayed there until a dark figure came up to me and kicked me gently in the ribs. "Up," That voice said and I got up instantly hating myself for obeying.

I stared at my master as he stared back at me.

"You understand what's going on; do you understand what you've done?" He asked, but he wasn't mad.

"Yes, I killed the people that everyone loved and now they're sad. Everyone is crying because of me, because I killed and now people are without so much… They weren't bad people, they were loved," I told him quietly.

"Yes, you did so much, well done," He started to laugh and that made me flinch. It sounded so cruel and evil and I didn't like it. It scared me and I got mad.

"You made me this way! I'm broken because I killed and now I can't cry!" I yelled at him and he stopped laughing, but he was still smiling. "I made you into the killer you are, but you still have far to go. You will become so great already I can see your worth. You have the potential to do so much; you are growing into someone so dangerous. Soon you will be on your own, no one beside you and all you do is kill. You will be the best assassin the world has ever seen," He sounded crazy, getting crazier with his fantasy. They were always about me and how great I was and how much more greater I would become.

He could be so cruel and so heartless. At times I didn't know if he was even human, I couldn't believe someone could be so cold. I wanted to run home and feel safe and warm in my house, but that house was not a home to me anymore. I was all alone in my world ruled by a cold, heartless monster that wanted to turn me into a monster too. It made me feel lost and unsure of who I am. Somewhere, a chubby, innocent little boy was devoured by a homeless, killing, lonely monster. I had fought so hard to push Midnight away then my family and be myself that I pushed too hard and lost myself as well.

That memory flowed into another memory, one where I was nine. My brother Tellnair picked me up and carried me inside a building. We went into a pet store where he set me down in a round cage full of puppies that came up to me with their tails wagging frantically so that their whole bodies wiggled and their tongues egger to lick me lolled out.

The owner of the store came up to us and smiled.

"Hello Tellnair, hello Khire," He greeted warmly. He was one of the nicest people I knew, with his tall figure, thin, wiry body and silver hair and kind brown eyes. I enjoyed his company. Tellnair began to talk to him, but my attention was turned elsewhere when an old man bent over and petted a puppy then left. As his hand slipped back into his long sleeves he dropped a small piece of paper beside me and turned for the door.

I looked after him, recognizing him then took the paper and opened it. It read:

Kill Mr. Harpres Valany

I looked sadly up to the storeowner; I didn't want to kill him. He not knowing any different came over to me as I tucked the paper away in a pocket.

"So, how are you doing?" He asked me smiling as he tried to pry open a puppies jaws that had latched onto my pant leg. He was always a nice person to me, always smiling and there was always a sense of kindness around him. I always felt safe and relaxed with him like just so long as he was smiling, no evil could get me.

"Good," I said though I probably didn't sound good.

That night I was supposed to go and kill him, but I didn't want to, instead I hid in my room. Sinth found me in my room the next night, put a hand over my mouth, dragged me through my bedroom window and away to someplace quiet.

"Why didn't you obey?" He asked angry. Even in the darkness I could tell he was furious. He was pacing in the narrow alley, going one way then sharply turning around and going the other way then rounding on me.

"I don't want to kill him," I whined.

"You have no choice, you are a killer! The only thing you are good for is causing people to die and others to cry," He hissed and grabbed my wrist tightly. "I'll teach you why you don't disobey me," He threatened.

I was taken to a back street where no one would ever hear me no matter how loud I screamed. Sinth turned to me, when he was mad he became violent and the expression on his face was a black storm cloud. I tried to run, but he grabbed me from behind and threw me against the wall. The next thing I knew I woke up to a cold morning, the sun still rising and my body in a painful torment that left me gasping for breath if I tried to move. I cried a little then, not from the pain, but because I felt that I deserved the beating. What good was I, I was trained to kill and yet I didn't want to. My life didn't belong to me and I had no way of taking it back. That was the first time in my life I had thought of suicide, I thought of many ways I could do it, but I just laid there in my own pain and misery until the sun had risen some more and I convinced myself that I should get up and get home before anyone the wiser. I did so and when I got home I had stopped crying, but I was still hurt.

I had returned home, snuck in and went directly to the bathroom to go for a quick shower. Sinth was very good about not hitting me in the face and not breaking bones so I just had to hide my bruises from my family. I was sore for a long time, but no one noticed. It was a busy time for them, but at that point I began to hate everyone. I began to hate them more then I hated Sinth and I began to blame them for everything, if they loved me they'd open their eyes and help me, but they never did.

Memories that hurt when they were happening brought fresh pain to me now and I stopped walking and stared into some water from a fountain. I peered at my reflection, but I couldn't see myself clearly. Everything's a weird blur around me, colours were hard to make out. I decided it was a good image of myself, my reflection the reflection of an undistinguishable person, blurred and fuzzy around the edges, stared back at me.

I sighed and kept going. My life was something I tried once to leave and found I couldn't. The only thoughts that went through my head were how to survive in this life, and how to kill. Worse I now accepted what I was, I felt I could do something and I felt like I could take control of any situation, or I could handle any hardship. Most importantly I felt dangerous, like I could get through any obstacle and come out on top. I wasn't going to be bullied anymore, I wasn't going to feel stupid or unimportant. I felt somewhat free and I liked that I was well trained. I liked the feelings I got when I killed someone, bringing justice to a system that was built on to many laws to bring real justice to anyone deserving of it. I was an assassin and though killing is still hard for me, I liked the thought of being powerful. I wouldn't tell many that, no one would understand me, but I didn't care.

The sun was shining from higher in the sky and I smiled at it as I walked to the small building where a girl sat drinking her coffee. I casually walked by it and out of the corner of my eye I could see her head turn, following me. She was interested and now that I got her attention, I would find her in the mall later on and that's when I would strike.

It was a twenty-minute walk from the coffee shop to the mall, but it was still a lot faster than driving. People were beginning to crowd the street and the mall doors were being opened up ahead. I took my time getting there though and so looked around as I crossed the bridge. I stopped and looked out over the water, down by the edge I use to go and have a picnic with my girlfriend. She was the greatest person I had known, and it was where we spent so much time. Talking with her and laughing, telling jokes, skipping rocks across the water and talking with other people. We had a lot of fun, and we loved to spend so much time there. Funny how her body now lies at the bottom of the stream, even I can't see it from here. I had loved her, I still miss her and she still haunts me, but it was I that killed her and I that put her there. I can't take it back and though I had cried so much I know it wouldn't have ended any other way.

All those good times I had with Miranna, smiling, talking with her, being normal, were gone, because I killed them. Stabbed them till they bled to death and dumped them in the river then foolishly cried about it. The water rushed by faster than my memories could let her go, and the river was colder than me, but still I killed her and I killed hundreds after her. So I was so much more worthless then the cold water that was now polluted with the cities toxins.

People had tried to kill themselves in this water when their life got too hard, but someone had always saved them and took them to the hospital where they could be treated for toxicities, but no one had found the body that I had put there. No one had stopped me from killing the love of my life. The body was probably eaten away and swarming with algae so much no one would recognize her, but I knew I would. It was one of the last things I saw before I lost my sight.

I could hear people talking behind me, one voice in particular. "What's wrong with him?" I turned and there was Onica staring at me with her head tilted. "Hey Khire, you ok?" Vesper asked, smiling comfortingly.

"Ya, sorry, just got lost in thought I guess. What are you guys doing here?" I walked over to them. Now I could see Jakk and his son walking towards us from the car, they were yelling at each other and everyone around them were giving them space and looking at them weirdly.

"We just came to check out the new store," Vesper said shrugging. "Do you want to hang out with us?" Onica asked smiling widely at me. I gave her a smile back. "Nah sorry can't, I've got stuff to do. I'm meeting someone here," I told her and she looked disappointed.

"Ahhh, please," She begged. "Dads boring, you're so much better then him," She pouted. "I heard that," Jakk said coming up to us. "Maybe your boring dad won't buy you those nice things you want," "Please, I'm sorry, jeepers, can we just go already," Onica said sounding annoyed. She would be nine in a week and she was already acting as if she were fifteen. Trying on makeup and wanting to only wear the latest fashions.

"Ok come on, so what ya doing Khire?" Jakk asked me.

I walked beside them as we made our way towards the mall. "Oh, I'm meeting someone here, somewhere," I shrugged. "Well that sounds fun, way more fun than my job. I'm just here to buy things then hold them as they walk around to make me buy more things to hold," He put his hands in his pockets and stared at the mall, but he would be buying something for himself too and I knew that would make him happy.

"Do you need anything, we could get it for you why'll you're busy Khire?" Vesper asked turning her head to look back at me.

"No I'm ok, thanks anyway," I told her and she turned back to talking with Onica.

"Are you going to see dad?" Jakk asked me then. "Yes," I answered frowning. "Are you going to stay with him?" Jakk had a lot of questions today; it was starting to annoy me. "No," I said bluntly. "Why?" He asked looking at me annoyed. "Because I already have a place to live," I made sure I didn't sound mad.

"Sure… Ok, but can't you spend some time with him? You know how much you hurt him when you go off?" He told me as if I didn't know already. "I know and I'm sorry, but I got things to do," I said tiredly. "And so you pick your *work* over your family?" He said accusingly. He made the word "work" sound as if what I do isn't actually work. I don't think anyone believed me that I had a job, even though technically I didn't. "No!" I yelled and looked around as people gave us weird looks. "Sorry, no….I just… I am trying to get my life to a place where everything's just going great, I just can't juggle everything like you guys can," I said sounding calmer.

"Ok, makes sense, but if you think we got our lives all fine and dandy then you're wrong. Our lives are a juggle to, but seriously you should think about staying with dad, he is so upset you keep saying no. And we're confused why? You're not fooling anyone you know? You live on the street, you think your classier then the rest because you wear better cloths, speak better, actually have the chance to live in a house and have a job if you want. But you're not. Your just the same as the rest of the street rats," He explained.

"Gee thanks," I said my self-confidence doing a face plant into the ground. I had actually felt good about my appearance today. I had taken some time to look really good and now my own brother was shooting me down.

"Look, I am safe, I'm alive, I'm standing right next to you heart beating fine, not a scratch on me," That last part was a bit of a stretch, I've seen better days. "You may not see me as anything, but I actually think I'm doing ok,"

"That's not all…it would be easier if you had kids then you'd understand," "Oh well sorry for not being on your level. I'll just go out and have kids then, I'm sure that will make my life turn right around," I crossed my arms now and didn't look at him. "No… I'm not asking you to start having kids, I'm asking you to get a life, you obviously have stuff going on that's taking you away from having a life and that's what everybody notices. You don't get it, dad is just trying to make it easier for you by inviting you to his house. You want your life to get someplace, you try, you make things work, but you're not even trying and when someone tries to help you, you freak at them as if they insulted you. You live on the street, getting help is not insulting, it's getting help. Also you could get a girlfriend, I know you're still upset about Miranna, but get over her, she was just…" "Don't, I don't need to hear the rest of that," I stopped him my voice coming out a little deeper and threatening then I intended.

"Khire, you need to get over her, she's been gone for like eight years, get over it, let go, go find someone else," I grinded my teeth and stared forward at the mall ahead. We just entered through the doors and now I was in a huge building with a lot of shops that took people two full days to just go through them all.

Many people poured in around us, the sounds of all of them talking made it hard to have a comfortable conversation with others. Exotic plants adorned the centre of the mall and a fountain with fish brought more life to this place. It was a very beautiful building. Designed so that everything flowed. The entire place was colour coordinated and the rounded archways attracted the eyes. Despite the craziness of it all, if I could imagine the place for how it is without the people, it would have been the most beautiful building in Vale Darra. The people, no matter how decent a citizen they were, ruined the glory of the tall, sprawling building.

"I am over Miranna, I just don't want to be with anyone else!" I yelled to be heard over the crowd.

"I don't believe you!" He yelled back.

"That's not surprising. I got to go!" I left Jakk even as he tried to stop me, I didn't care if he got mad at me for walking away, but he shouldn't have said those things and so I just kept walking. How dare he say that stuff to me?

In just one hour of the mall being open, people had already crowded in and started to shop. I, frowning, kept my hands at my sides trying not to punch or push anyone away from me who threatened to run me over. I also kept getting stuck in the flow of traffic when I just wanted to slowly walk around. Somehow I managed to meandered around somewhat leisurely until I found the store where my victim was. I actually dreaded these date-kills. I was bad at flirting and after the talk with my brother; I wasn't feeling up to this anymore. Nonetheless, I slowly walked by and pretended to notice her. She smiled at me and said hi. I said hi back and kept walking. "Who is he?" I heard her say to someone behind me.

"I don't know," Was her friend's response. I walked to the back of the store where there were guys clothing and began to look through the racks pretending to be interested in the jeans.

Out of the corner of my eye I could see her constantly looking over at me and soon she was walking over to me. “Hey I’m Dwyet,” She held out her hand and I took it smiling. ”Boe,” I said and she smiled. ”Boe, that’s a nice name, where ya from Boe?” She asked politely. Standing beside me casually with one hand on her hip, she gave me a huge smile, showing off white, clean teeth. She was pretty, she had a good modelling carrier, and knew some very impressive people, but I didn’t care.

“Ceptun, I’m here for a few days,” Luckily Vale Darra was big and had a lot of large surrounding towns, so it was impossible to know everybody.

“Ceptun, oh that’s nice, I’m from here, how about we get a coffee? I could show you around?” She pointed with her thumb behind her. “Sure, where can we get the best coffee?” I asked as we left the store and walked to the food court. ”Well not here, but there is this one place in the mall that’s rather lovely,” She told me as she led me out of the store. ”Nice,” I said, inwardly dreading this ordeal.

As I walked I reminded myself why I hated dates and why I had to dress up and look my best for them. Outwardly, I smiled pleasantly and tried to listen to her. I told myself I was doing this for some friends to stop Dwyet from getting involved in business she doesn’t belong in. I just had to slip her some poison and be done with it.

We went to a restaurant at one end of the mall and waited to get our seats. It was a fancy restaurant and so she was probably trying to impress me because it was hard to get into this one. She smiled at the waitress who took us to our seats that, as I noticed, were away from everyone else. It was very nice, music playing softly in the background, dimmed lights, soft colours. Everything set up to make people’s days calm, romantic and settled.

“Hello my names Stephanie and I will be your waitress today. Can I get you something to drink to start with?” The waitress asked. “Coffee please,” Dwyet answered.

"And for you?" The waitress asked eyeing me. "Um the same," I said and she walked away. I don't actually like coffee, it was disgusting, but most people drank it so I went along with it.

"So, do you have any family here?" She asked. With big brown eyes and cacao brown hair, she was good at positioning herself even in a chair so that she looked her best. It wasn't hard for her I guess being who she was. A good career and many years ahead of her to become more successful, she had life handed to her on a golden platter.

"Ya my grandma. I just came up to see how she's doing," I rested my chin in my hand. "And?" She nudged me. "She's sick, either my family and I move here to be with her or she moves into our home," I sighed acting upset.

"Ah what's wrong with her?" She said and actually pouted her lip.

"She's really old and in a wheelchair, now she might have cancer," I shrugged and acted somewhat indifferent somewhat saddened by it. "Oh that's so sad; I hope she's ok, do you need a place to stay? There's a hotel near my place. It's so nice and it's close so if you need help with anything I could help you," She snuck in and I knew she had been waiting for the right moment to say that.

"Maybe I don't know, I think my dad is just getting us a hotel close to my grandma," I said and the waitress came over and gave us our drinks.

"Here you go, now can I get you anything to eat?" She asked, giving her friend a quick smile before turning towards me.

"No," Dwyet answered her quickly. "No I'm fine thanks," I smiled and the waitress nodded and walked away.

"So…" She started, but then her phone rang. Perfect distraction. "Oh I'm so sorry I have a call," She looked upset at me.

"That's ok, I'll wait here, please take it, it may be important," She smiled and left.

I looked around to see who was around us. I had come in already checking out the room and had noticed that we were in a spot where the lights were a little dimmer and we were away from most of the others in another room. There weren't even cameras and only three other couples who were engrossed in each other's company. I simply reached over and poured liquid from a small phial into her drink. The liquid was tasteless and disappeared into her drink instantly.

I drew my hand back as the waitress came in. She smiled at me. "Sorry I felt so bad, I know you guys didn't want something, but the cooks here are the best in the city, I just couldn't let you starve," She placed a huge plate of steaming food in front of me. I swallowed and tried to find my words as my mind focused completely on the food.

"Oh, really, well then I might just have to eat this," I said smiling and restraining myself with an impressive amount of willpower I didn't even know I had. I wanted to eat it all right now before I had to deal with someone else, it smelt amazing. It was chicken smothered in a pesto sauce with fettuccine noodles. There was also a freshly baked multigrain roll topped with a very creamy looking garlic sauce and extra cheese.

"Pasta, you must be a mind reader. I love anything fettuccine," I said truthfully.

"Well we only serve the finest foods and pasta certainly tops the list with me. It's on the house," She smiled at me and turned to see Dwyet coming back in.

The two girls scowled at each other and the waitress left. My chance to eat my food undisturbed vanished, I tried not to whine, but I was a little annoyed she came back. I wasn't that good looking, couldn't she have just left me alone instead? "Sorry about that, it wasn't important so I said goodbye, but where were we…did she bring you that?" Dwyet asked noticing the food.

"Ya, she said the cooks are the best here, she couldn't let me starve. Would you like some?" I asked stabbing a piece of noodle and offering it to her.

"Umm no thanks, the food is good here, but something's aren't if you know what I mean," She took a sip of her drink. "But then again, the coffee's not bad," She shrugged and took another small sip before she put the cup down. Now it would take two days, the poison slowly eating up her bodies supply of oxygen. It was a really cool poison, it made the person lethargic in a day, by day two, the person would fall into a deep slumber and eventually the heart would just stop. The body running out of oxygen and unable to be supplied with more.

I took a bite and it was just as good as I imagined. It was really difficult for me to eat in public; all I wanted to do was stuff my face. I hadn't eaten something this good in a long time and I wanted to eat as much as I could before anything else happened. I was trying to make taking huge mouthfuls look good, but Dwyet was looking at me somewhat bizarrely so I knew I was pushing it. "Well it's not that bad, but it's better than my mothers," I smiled and she laughed.

"Better than my mother's to, she can't even cook, we have a cook to do it all for us. I swear if my mom cooks she'll have accidentally poisoned the food and kill us all including herself," Dwyet was one of those that talked with her hands and made big expressions. I smiled and sat quietly adding a few words every now and then. "Have I been talking all this time, I'm so sorry, let's talk about you, like what's your last name?" She reached over and took my hand as if that was casual. I looked down at our hands and smiled up at her, she smiled back and waited. I had been slowly depleting the food on my plate, but was a little stuck now that I had to talk. "My last name, its Gorvin," I just putting letters together.

"So Boe Gorvin, I like," She smiled then put her hand to her stomach. "Are you ok?" I asked actually a little surprised.

"It's nothing, I guess I just have a cramp, it will go away," She took a pill from her purse and took it with her coffee then returned her hands to mine.

That didn't last long; she slouched slightly and then kept her hands around her middle.

"Ok how about I walk you home, we can talk tomorrow maybe," I helped her to her feet, just as the waitress came. "Oh hey sorry she's not feeling well, I left some money on the table though, thanks," I told her and she nodded and went to clean our table a little bewildered.

I helped Dwyet put on her coat and leave. She had a car, but I told her I didn't have my license on me so I couldn't drive. We walked over the bridge and I had a sudden flash back of dumping a body off this bridge. "You sure you're ok?" I said to draw my mind away from the thought and keep it focused on her. I was trying to think of all the possible explanations for this. Did I give her the wrong poison? Was this actually her not feeling well?

"Ya I'm fine, let's just get to my house," She said hunched over.

I heard a car approach from behind me and turned to see my brother and his family who recognized us and pulled over.

"Is she ok?" Jakk asked concerned.

"No, I don't know what's wrong with her?" I said honestly. She went limp, but I caught her before she could smack into the ground. Bad timing for me, but I had no choice just to play along with it. Mentally I was cursing myself. What was going on? "Get her into the car, we'll take her to the hospital," Jakk got out and opened up the door so I could lay her in the back. "You coming?" "Sure," I said and got in.

The back was now crowded, there were two seats in the middle plus three in the back, but it was a narrow three seats. And now it was filled with an almost nine year old girl, a fifteen year old boy, a nineteen year old girl and me, a twenty three year old. Plus a cougar, a poodle, a bear, a ferret and a bird. Vesper's Guardian snuck up to the front, but the rest had to squish together. Jakk got back in and drove faster than the speed limit allowed all the way to the hospital. Once there, I picked up Dwyet and carried her into the hospital where a doctor rushed towards us with a stretcher. I actually felt kind of strange handing a girl I just poisoned to someone intent on saving her.

Others came and took her from us. Before long police came up to us and began to question us, but it was me that they really wanted. It happened really fast, usually someone being carried in was taken seriously as people were always worried it had something to do with Dusk. So as I had carried Dwyet in, people immediately thought Dusk, which ironically was actually me in the flesh.

"I don't know what happened, I met her in a store and she invited me to have coffee with her. I said yes thinking nothing of it and we went to that fancy restaurant in the mall and she got a coffee. I had a coffee and food, but she didn't eat, but I think she may have gotten something before we met. She had said something about there being a place where you could get the best coffee so maybe she got something there," I told them, which was all the truth. "Oh, but she had left at some point in the restaurant to get a call. She was back a few minutes later, and she said something that she might be having cramps and she took a pill, but I don't know what it was," I added as if I had forgotten. The cop took notes as he wrote it on a piece of paper and nodded along.

It was now a waiting game, fortunately the poison was undetectable until death so they wouldn't be able to know how to save her until she was dead. Just so long as it was the poison I thought I had given her anyway. I had no idea and no way of checking. I started thinking about any possible way I could get out of this should she suddenly walk away from this.

"Are you ok?" Jakk asked sitting beside me.

"Ya why?" I wasn't even acting confused, I already was by his question.

"Well you know you walked off angry at me than you have a date and she dies, that's a little much don't ya think?" He raised his eyebrows at me.

"It wasn't a date, I don't like her," I said sounding stubborn.

"Sure, anyway, I'm sorry for what I said. How about we get out of here? I'll take you to dads, there's nothing we can do here," I nodded, but then the doctor came out.

"Are you the family of Dwyet Hannsin?" We shook our heads.

"We were the ones to bring her in," I told him.

"Oh, ok, well I can't release too much, but I will tell this. We couldn't save her," He frowned and bobbed his head then walked away to find Dwyet's family. Now all I had to do was get out of here and wait to make sure no late suspicions arise about me.

"Ok, let's go," Jakk said pulling me away.

"Hold it!" Fetcher called, coming out of nowhere and startling me. "Sorry, can't let you leave, we are checking this out we believe someone poisoned her, Doctor explain," Fetcher came and stood beside us as the doctor came back.

"It's true we have checked and there was poison in her system, but we haven't discovered what type yet," He explained holding a chart.

He was really old, white hair, that was thin and only around the sides of his head leaving the top a shiny bald. His face was thin and wrinkled, but he looked capable of being a good doctor.

"Ok, so you think someone else is involved?" Jakk said. "This is going to take a while," He sat back down. Fetcher shook his head and looked at me.

"Go over everything that happened, right from when you woke up," He told me and I sighed.

"Ok well I woke up and I was going to the mall to meet a friend, only he didn't show, but I did meet Jakk before going into it, but I left him then I was looking in a store and I met her. She asked if I wanted to get a coffee with her and I agreed. We went to the restaurant in the mall I think it's called Kiwikiis, and we were seated…" "Where?" Fetcher said before I could finish. "Ah in the restaurant," I told him stupidly and he rolled his eye.

"Where in the restaurant?" He asked annoyed. I could tell this was going to be a very irritating conversation. I tried to be patient, talking with Fetcher was important. I had to convince him that I wasn't the poisoner.

"We were brought to a separate place, I think Dwyet knew the waitress and she brought us to a private place. Dwyet ordered a coffee and I did to,"

"You don't like coffee," Fetcher added and I scowled at him.

"Well I could start," I growled then continued. "Then we were talking, but she got a phone call. She left and when she left the waitress came and brought some food, she said it was on the house, she said the cook was the best and she couldn't let me starve. Dwyet came back, they looked at each other weirdly..." "How weirdly, describe it?" Fetcher said still writing everything down. "I don't know, like they were asking each other what are you doing here? I didn't catch it and the waitress left and Dwyet sat down. Some minutes later she started to feel sick, she was holding her stomach and I asked her if she were ok. She wasn't so we left and as we were crossing the bridge that's when we met Jakk. She collapsed and Jakk brought us here," This was the second time I explained the truth and I really had things to do, but it wasn't getting done which was starting to irritate me.

"Ok, what time did you meet her at?" Fetcher asked.

I was a little annoyed by him always showing up where I didn't want him to be. "I don't know um I got to the mall sometime after it opened then I wandered around and found her maybe an hour and half later, so like nine thirtyish,"

"When did you arrive at the restaurant?" "Um ten... twenty maybe, I don't know, we went there right when she started speaking to me," Asking a lot of questions must run in the family or in their training.

"Did anyone see you with her?" "The waitress and when we were in the store she was talking to a friend or two, but I don't know about anyone else. I also happened to be in a mall overcrowded with people if that helps," I was getting tired of this, my plan for the day did not include being interrogated. I was just going to take her to her house and leave her there to slowly die.

Fetcher had a lot more questions to ask me, but he told others to go and find some witnesses.

"Ok, where you going now?" Fetcher asked me though at this point I really wasn't going anywhere. "Well I'm still talking to you, but once this is done, I was going to dad's," I told him tiredly.

"Ok, are you staying there?" He tapped his pen on his clipboard.

"I thought you couldn't question me because you're family?" I asked instead.

"Just answer the question," He responded, smiling at me. "No, I have to go somewhere else after I visit, but I'll be there for at least two hours," "Where're you going afterwards?" He asked me looking at me closely. "I have to go see a friend,"

"You have a lot of *friends* to *meet.* Who?" Fetcher asked.

His questions were getting personal.

"Just my friend, why does it matter?" I crossed my arms.

"An accomplice maybe," He said in all seriousness.

"Oh right I forgot I get a kick out of going to the mall and killing girls, silly me," I said sarcastically.

"Just so that we have a number to get a hold of you if we need anything else," Fetcher said sighing. "That's it for now, you may go," He said finally. "Thank you, bye," I growled and Fetcher said bye, but didn't look up from his clipboard.

I walked towards the door with Jakk and his family who had remained silent or whispering quietly to each other.

"Uncle Khire, what's wrong?" Onica asked walking beside me. "You were upset this morning…" She shouldn't have said that. Fetcher heard us and as soon as he heard it he yelled.

"Khireal! Come back!" I stopped and went back to him grumbling to myself.

"Yes," I asked impatiently.

"You were upset this morning why?" He asked taking a step towards me as if he were too far away. I was tempted to push him back, but refrained.

"Because I have an annoying family that likes to ask questions and get into my personal life," I answered quickly.

"Khireal, I am serious," He looked at me sternly.

"Because I was passing the bridge I was staring at the bank," He looked at me knowing why I had been looking at the bank. My whole family was use to me walking by someplace that brought good memories and me stopping and zoning out.

"Are you ok? Maybe you need to see someone. Here, here's a number," He gave me a card.

"Oh great so now not only you think I like to kill people, but you also think I'm mental, no thank you," I said reading the card then handing it back, but he wouldn't take it.

"Just try her, I think it will be good for you," He said looking at me as if I were a child. "Well maybe, but we'll never know now will we," I said and tore up the card then walked away. Luckily no one said anything and so I climbed back into the back of Jakk's car and once everyone else got in we headed to dad's house.

CHAPTER #20

"You know, I'm fine with walking," I told Jakk when the streetlight turned red and a huge crowd of people surged forward to get to the other side of the street.

"No its ok, we're almost there," Jakk said determined to drive. I didn't know if he didn't trust me to go to dads without him or if he just really wanted to drive, in any case I wasn't getting out of this traffic any time soon. The mass of people finally passed and the light turned green allowing us to slowly creep forward until we got to the next red light. I really didn't understand why anyone drove, walking was much faster, though would probably include getting jostled and stepped on, still I much preferred walking to driving.

I tried to think of something pleasant. The storefronts would be colourful with fresh flowers. Young bushes were growing in clusters on the strip of grass that divided the street and the sidewalks. Every now and then there were statues of people. This was a newer part of the city so everything would still look clean and colourful. Not like the older parts that looked worn and tired. I tried to imagine how this place looked like compared to the older parts, but it was hard to imagine it all. Even the architecture was different here, the buildings more rounded and modern compared to the sharp pointed rooftops of the older buildings that were brick, cement or wood. I tried to look out the window and glimpse it all without the crowd of people, but even if I could see it all clearly it was too hard. I could see the buildings well enough to see some details like the windows and the doors, but I couldn't imagine this place without the people.

I sighed and decided to wait it out; today was already a long day. The car stopped again as a person walked in front of the car. It was either Chris or Tylar, I smiled at him and waved. He mouthed an apology to Jakk who waited patiently for him to move. As Jakk drove away I seen Chris or Tylar go to his twin and nod smiling.

Their problem was solved, good for them. Jakk drove slowly, similar to that of a fat caterpillar. Sometimes we weren't moving at all, but soon enough I could see dads house and shortly after we were pulling into his driveway. Dad came out flustered. "Khire you said you would be here for ten, it's quarter to twelve," Dad was angry at me, by the hurt I heard in his voice, he was trying to hide it, but failing.

"Sorry, I was with someone then she died, then I was with Mr. Questioner Fetcher and then I was with Jakk and we were stuck in traffic," I complained making my day sound horrible.

"Your friend died? Oh I'm so sorry," Dad now looked sympathetic and a little shocked.

"She wasn't my friend, I just met her," I said and Jakk shook his head.

Dad didn't know what to think as we all entered his house and went to the living room.

As we came in, I looked over at the table to stare at the pictures of mom and the rest of the family. Dad caught me looking and sat beside me. I hadn't been in the house in what felt like forever, I wanted to sit and try and remember all the good memories, but found myself just thinking about how empty it felt in here now. I frowned at that thinking dad probably hated living here now with everyone gone.

"Are you ok, son?" He asked, sitting way to close to me. "Yes I'm fine," I said turning to him while moving over slightly.

"You have gone through a lot, it's ok if you're upset and need someone to talk to, but honey, to get over this I really think you need help. You know I love you and will help you how ever I can," He said with sincerity. He brushed his hand across my head, flattening my hair as if to calm me. "Thanks dad, it means a lot to me, but I'm fine," I said more calmly and grabbed his hand. "Really I'm ok," I said and patted his hand to reassure him.

Dad smiled at me and turned to Jakk. "How are you?" Dad asked him.

"Good, I have to get going to work, but I'll be back tomorrow," Jakk said as he got up and left, kissing Vesper goodbye.

☾

Today I knew would be long, right from the minute Onica, my daughter, came shouting around the house for everyone to get up.

"Dad let's go!" Onica yelled happily.

"Come on Jakk honey you promised," Vesper said to me as she got out of bed beside me.

Yawning I climbed out of bed and got ready for my day. I had to start work later and would be gone till tomorrow morning, that being so I had promised to spend time with my family in the morning. We left for the mall planning on spending some few hours there before I took them to my fathers. I found a place to park after driving around for a bit looking for an empty spot. I ended up on the opposite side of the mall I wanted to be on, right near a bridge, but I knew better to take the spot I found then try and find another. This place was just too busy for people to expect to get good parking.

"Ok let's move out people!" Onica yelled and raced out of the car.

"Onica honey, slow down and watch for cars," Vesper said and Onica stopped and waited for us impatiently.

"Hey there's Uncle Khire!" Onica said pointing to where Khire stood on the bridge staring at the water.

"Iyen I'm only mad because you lied to me. I trust you, if you want to go out and have some fun then fine, but just tell me or your mother where you're going. Keep us up to date. And I told you not to go to that party. You know I don't like those guys you hang out with, they got charged last week," I said trying to keep my temper down.

"They're my friends and if I had told you that's where I was going you'd never let me go. If you trust me then actually trust me. I won't do anything that'll get me into trouble ok," Iyen said annoyed.

I was about to say more when I realized what Onica had said and looked over at Khire. I huffed.

"Great another problem to fix today. Come on, let's go," I said and walked over to my brother. I tried to talk to him as we made our way to the mall, but I hadn't the patience today to deal with him. I couldn't understand why he wouldn't just move on and why he would want to continue being miserable. It seemed he didn't believe he could succeed in life and so instead of feeling disappointment, he gave up before he tried to have a good life. It always seemed he just wanted to be angry at the world.

He had gotten better when Miranna was dating him, but then she disappeared and Khire seemed to fall into a black hole. After graduation he ran off, which I can't say I was overly upset about. He never wanted to be in that house anyway. I was a little upset that he never turned out right, but I figured there was always one person in the family that was different. When dad started talking about him being around, I was a little sceptical. I didn't know if it was a good thing or a bad thing that Khire was coming back into our lives. Seeing him I felt only pity for him, but I didn't know how to talk to him. He was easily offended and always on the defence, he didn't seem to want us back in his life so I couldn't figure out why he would come back into ours.

He was so skinny and rugged, nearly unrecognizable since last I seen him. He had changed so much I couldn't believe it. I wanted to help him, which is why I decided I'd talk to him now and try to be straight with him. I ended up driving him away, which angered me, but I wasn't about to make a scene and so I let him be for now.

"Why can't Khire just go live with dad and sort his life out?" I said frustratingly to Vesper once Khire left.

"Khire isn't like you and I think he is trying to sort things out, he just does it differently then you," She said and took my hand. I smiled at her, but inside I was still concerned about Khire.

"I just think everything could be real easy for him if he'd just listen and stop being so proud," I said irritated.

"I don't think its pride, I actually think it's the opposite. Your dads really hard to please, he always wants to be perfect. No he does, face it. Khire likes to test the waters first, he's young and he got sidelined a lot so he's just use to going it alone. He's trying to make you guys proud by showing he can make it, but he just needs more time. I think he needs a friend not a bossy older brother," She said simply.

"Well whatever," Was all I could think of to say.

I went with my family and bought clothes for Onica and Iyen. As punishment I took away Iyen's cell phone. He complained a little, but then gave up and walked beside me, not saying anything not even looking at me. Vesper sighed, but said nothing and soon distracted herself with shopping.

Onica ran into a store and stared at an outfit for a few minutes then tried it on, then stared in the mirror just looking at herself for some time. I really didn't know how she could just stand there gazing at herself, but I didn't bother to ask. "Can you buy this for me pleeeeaaaassssse?" She begged. "Nooooooo," I told her and she unhappily put it all back. That happened a few more times, but I eventually bought her a new outfit. I also found a store to my liking.

"Ok Onica I bought you some clothes now how'd you like to buy me something?" I asked jokingly.

"Ummmm, not very much," She said crossing her arms. "Ok, looks like you're getting nothing else," I told her smiling and she sighed and though she didn't buy me anything in that store she did buy everyone ice cream afterwards.

We left the mall and packed everything in the trunk. We started driving when I noticed Khire half carrying a hunched over girl across the bridge. My bad mood was instantly taken over by worry as an image of Khire and Miranna came to mind. I pulled over and asked if she were ok, confused Khire didn't know what was wrong, but was willing to come along for the ride to make sure she was ok. We picked them up and after the long time in the hospital I took Khire to dads and left him and my family there.

Now I had to work and it was going to be even longer. The traffic was bad so as I was making my way to the castle I was constantly looking at the radio clock and looking around. Walking would get me there faster, but I may need my car later. I stepped lightly on the pedal and I began to pull forward, but someone pulled out at the last minute and cut me off, making me slam on my brakes and nearly hit them. I was passing the hospital, trying to take the shortest route to the castle, but it was proving to be the slowest route.

"Watch it!" Someone yelled angrily at me. I sighed and waited for the car to move, the person gave me a mean look then drove away and I continued on my way. I was making slow progress when the light went green and in one big rush everybody hit the gas and shot forward.

People had some place they felt they needed to get to so we were all going down the street a little too fast with all the people around us. I knew something bad was going to happen so I began to slow down and try to set a good speed. It was going really well, but then I heard screeching tires and my car slammed forward. I wanted to scream in frustration and curse the idiot that hit me. I glared into the rear-view mirror and gave the guy behind me the dirtiest look I could give.

I wasn't hurt, mostly jerked and the air bags didn't even go off as my car went into the car in front, but I now had a huge headache.

"What did you do that for?" Someone yelled behind me as people began to get out of their vehicles to survey the damage. I had gotten rear ended by a car, making me rear end another car, which did the same to another car ahead of it, in total five vehicles were damaged, and now I was going to be really late. This is why I hated driving in Vale Darra, the traffic was beyond terrible.

I got out and looked at the front of my car then at the back, nothing too bad, just a little dent in the back and a scratch in the front. More people were complaining all around me as others still driving waited to pull out into another lane to continue on their drive.

"Why did you slow down?" A person came up to me angrily.

"We were going too fast, so I slowed down, I didn't want to hit a pedestrian," I said, but no one liked that excuse. "This is all your fault, now I'm gonna be late," The man said throwing up his hands.

"You're going to be late? So is the rest of us!" Someone yelled from down the line.

"Good job crashing, you do us all a favour!" Someone yelled.

I sighed; today was not a very good day for me. The police were coming and I could see Fetcher leading the squad. He looked at all of us frowning. How was it that in this big city I ran into him twice? "Who caused this?" He asked as he approached.

"He did, arrest him!" The first man said pointing at me. Fetcher looked at me amused.

"We were all going too fast, I tried to slow down then you hit me," I said turning on the man.

"Oh sure, you weren't paying attention to the road!" The other guy retaliated.

"Ya I was, if you'd have known where to find the break we'd all be ok. Hint, the break is beside the gas," I said angrily.

"Ok, ok, we don't need to start an argument," Fetcher stepped in. Why did he have to show up here? I wondered to myself. How was he always the one to respond?

The man huffed and sat on his car's hood.

"So now what, I'm late, and now I have to wait here talking to you guys?" He said as if he was the most important person ever to walk on the face of the earth.

"Well sorry, but we all have places to go!" Someone yelled up ahead.

"Ya sure, where you're going can't be any more important than mine?!"

"I have to pick my daughter up!"

"Well I have an appointment to talk about my divorce!"

"And I have to get to work, why don't we all shut up so we can leave!" I added and everyone glared at me.

"Not helping Jakk," Fetcher said as he started writing on a notepad.

More questions were asked and I stood there still a half an hour later answering them. We were going around in circles, everyone accusing everyone else till Fetcher and the other cops just charged us all. I took the slip of paper with the fine and got back into my car. It started and so did the rest of the cars and we all drove off still angry. Before going to work I paid the fine, then got to the castle as quickly as I could.

My car needed to get repaired, but I would have to call a body shop later. The sun was moving across the sky faster than I would have liked and when I finally got to the castle it was three quarters across. Parking in my designated parking spot I rushed to the door to get inside.

"So why are you late?" Someone asked me.

"Because man made cars and people got fat and lazy that we couldn't walk!" I said as I walked away from him. His name was Vurt and he was my friend, but he was also my boss.

"Ok, won't ask than, just go find the King and stay with him!" Vurt called after me. I waved my hand at the grey- brown haired man who stood by the castle's East main entrance.

Vurt let me through and smiled as I stomped my way up to the double doors. I pushed them open and entered the castle. Maids were going around cleaning everything to a shine and others were going around doing other work. Dressed in either pants or skirts with a white blouse, they looked like they were having a good day as they dusted, swept and washed everything. Walking through thick, hard doors you were met by a large room with a partially carpeted and partially tiled floor. There was a grand staircase leading up to the higher levels at the far wall on the left, many doors and hallways leading off to other rooms. Paintings hung on the walls and writings of history or of important persons were set in little alcoves along the walls. There were large, vine like fans hanging from the beautifully painted ceiling where you could gaze at golden meadows and a beautiful sparkling sea. The walls were a light silver blue that made everything look more grand and spectacular.

I quickly went to the guard's rooms and got dressed into my uniform. Black pants, a silver t-shirt and blue vest. A thick black belt went around my waist with multiple pouches for bullets, a gun, my stick, a pen and small notebook as well as magic spray. The vest had a few buckles on it to strap on other weapons should I need them, but as I was in the castle, I wasn't allowed to wear any weapons. The uniform was very comfortable, made to be flattering, but also practical. If I had to go racing off outside, the clothes would protect me from the elements while my pants and vest were made from a strong bullet-proof material. Despite that, the uniform was light and though a little too warm, it has proven useful in the past.

Once dressed, I left and went towards the throne room that was located closer to the other side of the castle to find my King. The entire castle was split into sections. There was a section for offices, with the biggest one having a large wall with a painting of the world on it and another showing the Kingdom of Vale Darra. The city itself was sectioned into five dukedoms, with Vale Darra the centre city being where the King ruled from. The divisions between the dukedoms were represented by different coloured boundary lines with a legend on the right bottom corner to explain the symbols scattered across the map. There was also a large wooden table with more maps on it and in the far corner against the red walls there was a table with a bunch of drawers storing anything that had to do with maps.

The next section had a large glass door leading to a large room filled with paintings of the royal family. On the far side were more large glass doors that opened out onto a large veranda where you could sit in the metal chairs and eat, talk or gaze down at a beautiful garden below. The room smelled pleasant from the flowers blooming from the garden. The room never got too hot or too cold and the large glass doors let any sunlight beam through. There was a glass table in the center with swirls of green, purple, pink and blue. The table symbolized a flower holding up the glass tabletop. The plant spread across the underside of the glass and cupped around the edges to hold the top in place. It was beautifully done with grace and style to make it as flowing and beautiful as a real flower. There were other smaller glass tables just like it around the room where potted plants sat. The room was a light faded blue and it worked well with the mood of the room, it made it look more open and brighter. It was also reasonably called the Glass room.

I went down a hall with a long, thick, floral green carpet with more paintings hung on golden walls. I passed through several arches and then entered into another room and after that another hall. Finally I came to large double doors that were opened by huge guards on either side of the door. I nodded to them and entered into a large room. There were several balconies going up on either side of me so spectators could watch the King make decisions as he sat on his elevated throne. There was a huge carpet that covered the entire floor in a lush silver blue colour. Then at the far end right in front of me was the throne situated on a higher level. Going up five steps to get to the chair that was metal with royal blue cushions. There was a small table beside it that right now held a glass of water and a few papers. The King wasn't in the chair though; instead he was walking around staring at the writings that hung on the wall. They told stores, like Vale Darra's history and past Kings.

"Your Majesty," I announced and he turned to me.

"Ah Jakk how are you doing?" He asked coming over to me. I bowed to him and smiled. "Fine your Majesty, I am sorry that I am so late, the traffic is horrible," I didn't want to get into much detail and take a lot of the attention from the King. I hadn't been in my position long and was still amazed at the fact that I was one of the King's personal guards. I was never a bad kid, but I didn't care for politics and least of all a kingdom. But I found my wish to be one of defence and I was a natural fighter. Though young, my wish made me a very good guard.

I had started studying law and then policing then somehow came upon an old guard who was looking for young people to take on. Signing up on a whim I not only became a Kings Guard, but I became the Kings personal guard. "Oh, did you make through it all right?" The King asked curious. "I did, but my car didn't," I said frowning. I felt comfortable talking to the King and the King told me many times that he much preferred being talked to like a man then a King.

"Oh, well we shall have it repaired. I have been meaning to talk to you for some time, do you mind coming with me to my office?" He asked politely.

"I don't mind at all my King," I said smiling.

My Guardian, a small Black Bear named Chicoah, and I walked through several more rooms passing through offices filled with documents, a computer room, a room just filled with filing cabinets and finally into a room with a bunch of long tables and shelves. This was the King's section. These areas were only accessible by the King so I was actually familiar with these rooms. The room we were currently in was large, though crowded with a bunch of tables and a few sinks. The room was called the Kings Laboratory, because he liked to experiment in here, nothing too scientific as he was no mage, but he played with a few trinkets here and there.

I looked around thinking he wanted to just stop here, but then we turned right and left that room to the connecting room. The room was large for an office though still not a considerable size compared to the other rooms. It had white walls and white tiled carpets. Off to the right corner there stood a large desk holding two monitors, a computer and a keyboard and mouse. There were bookcases off to my right as well as some plants scattered around the room on small tables. It was a very simple room, but the King liked it as he said the white walls were like his blank canvas ready to give him new ideas.

"Please sit Jakk, I want to get right to it. You and I both know that Vale Darra is a crumbling city. No need to defend it, I see people every day to give final blessings. More and more people are dying and it appears there are more and more assassins each year. Assassins are still a very big problem for us and it looks bad that they can still be at large and the police not one step closer to catching any of them.

"Vale Darra has so much potential I just don't want it to just fall. I have spies that have been keeping me up to date with the happenings and there appears to be a few people that we are noticing are causing some issues. One person in particular I worry about. It appears my daughter Shirra is spending a lot of time with a boy. He seems like a very nice person and they get along, but he is a very powerful mage and… well I can't say I trust him. I am sorry to say that it is your brother Khire. I like to think well of him as he is your brother, but I do not think it appropriate for them to spend so much time together.

"I have been looking for a suitor for Shirra, but have been having very little luck. My other daughters are easy to find suitors for them. However it seems my youngest daughter is a bit of a challenge. She is rambunctious and intimidating for many. I like that Khire can put up with her and see no reason to split them up. I think it is very important for Shirra to have male friends… I guess I am going about this all wrong. It is just hard to believe that I can't find someone for her and yet your brother seems to have befriended her so well. I think Khire is a very nice person, I hear that he is nothing but respectful, he doesn't push Shirra. They're casual and it's strictly a friendship relationship. However, I have heard Shirra speak about Khire a time or two and I can't help, but worry," He said a little uncomfortable.

"Yes I have heard Princess Shirra bring up Khire and I know Khire is friends with her, but Khire lost his girlfriend some years ago and he's still having a hard time getting over it. He's moody, he's secretive, he likes to keep to himself. I know he isn't looking for a relationship. I do think it's something to look out for, Princess Shirra is very much a go getter if you don't mind me saying so, but I don't think Khire can let go of things very easily. He can be very sensitive at times which really stops him from finding another girlfriend. Khire also lives on the street so I think Princess Shirra takes care of him so they've become very close. Khire likes going out, he doesn't party, but he always ends up with a cut or a bruise or some type of injury, so I think Princess Shirra acts as a healer," I told him honestly.

"Well I'm glad she is watching out for him, but why does he live on the street?" The King asked sitting back in his chair.

"I don't know he's just always been a little different. Growing up wasn't the easiest for him, no one really accepted him into the family. We were all just so busy so Khire learned pretty quickly how to take care of himself. He ran away from home at a young age and doesn't want to go back. It's only recently that he's starting to talk to us again," I told the King regretfully.

"Well that's a bit of a sad story if I've ever heard one. I wonder if there's anything I could do for him?" The King said rubbing his chin.

"Khire won't like that Your Highness. He is very accepting and though I did say he was moody, he's a really nice guy, but he just doesn't like people interfering with his personal life. I think it's his own way of trying to cope with everything and live at the same time,"

"Kind of like he is punishing himself?" The King asked and I nodded. "Well in any case, I do have spies looking out for them both. He is a very powerful mage. Somewhat of a threat. I'd like him to join my King's Mages just to keep an eye on him better,"

"Khire doesn't like being tied down to rules and laws, Your Majesty. I don't think it would be easy to convince him to join the King's Mages knowing it was just so you could watch him," I told him with a shrug.

"Well he's too dangerous to be left to his own devices, even if he does mean well. He is close to my daughter and I have to be a father first and a King second, I do not trust such a man so close to such a… head strong young women who still needs to learn her place in life,"

"And another thing I wanted to talk to you about, I have been dreaming a lot. You know that my Wish allows me to dream possible events that might happen or allow me to understand things that should be. I have been seeing this boy, I think it's Dusk, but it's not the same Dusk as everyone thinks of him. In my dreams Dusk is crying, he's begging someone not to make him kill. He gets beaten up a lot and tries to kill himself multiple times. This little boy seems to have just been given a very unfair share of life's turmoil's and I can't help, but want to help him. I know I can't just call off the search for Dusk, but I keep seeing the world as a dark and evil place, but standing in the middle of a large field I see a bright light. I know that light is coming from a person standing there and I think it's Dusk. I can't understand it, but Dusk standing there is making the darkness go away and is healing the world. I see other things were Dusk dies, but then the world turns black.

"I think that though Dusk is evil, he needs to live until he can do whatever he needs to do that stops the world from going black,"

The King said in all seriousness. I looked at him until I could put my thoughts together.

"What do you suppose we do Your Highness?" I asked. I had no idea what to think.

"That Jakk I don't know, but we need to do something and soon. Something is coming and I don't know if Dusk is ready to face it yet," The King said gravely.

A bell rang signifying the Kings presence was needed elsewhere and thus ended our discussion. I bowed and left the King to see to his duties, but promised I would see if Khire would come in to talk to him. As I was walking past the main entrance I heard something that sounded like a dish crashing to the floor.

"That's the third plate today! What happened to all your *talents*, don't they at least include being able to hold onto a plate?" A familiar voice screamed, but the next voice was new.

"Actually, my talents include something else that's hands on. Something you wouldn't know anything about little girl," The new voice said smartly. "Why don't you be a good little princess and let your big daddy find you a darling little prince and leave the men for me. By the way I was out with a lovely young man the other day. Can you guess who? We work great together, I'm a better match"

"Ha! You guys would kill each other!" Princess Shirra said laughing. I entered just as a dark haired woman picked up the broken dish on the floor. "Oh who's this?" She asked eyeing me.

I cleared my throat trying not to stare, which was very hard as she stayed in a crouch picking up broken pieces of glass. Her clothing was far past the line of modesty and completely inappropriate. I cleared my throat again and knowingly the women gave me a big smile and stood up, one hand going on her hip with her head tilted as she regarded me openly. With long wavy ebony hair and large green eyes, she had tanned skin, a toned body, and full lips. She was tall, but not overly so, about the right height to easily kiss her... I couldn't help but stare at her.

"Hello, ladies, may I help you with something?" I asked looking over at the other women. Princess Shirra, sat at a table eating ice cream. I couldn't tell if they hated or liked each other, but in any case I was thinking of an excuse to separate them.

"Oh I know who you are, I'd know the brother of..." The women started then Princess Shirra smacked her in the head.

"Hey! Abusive much!" The women exclaimed with a glint in her eyes. I was ready to step in should the women strike back, but then she gave the princess a light elbow in the ribs and smiled pleasantly.

"Oh your no fun, I was just going to compliment...," She began. "Not important, this is Jakk, a guard here," Princess Shirra said pointing at me while glaring at the other women.

"Hello Jakk, I'm Caprica," The women said extending a hand to me. I shook her hand and gave her a polite smile. "Nice to meet you Caprica, I haven't seen you around here?" I said to be nice. "Oh no, I'm new here, thought I'd try being a maid for this castle. I'm great friends with Princess Shirra, we share the same interests," She said her eyes mischievous, hinting at a secret.

"An interest you will think to not even go near again, understand, he isn't yours and he doesn't even like you," I didn't know the Princess had a boyfriend and from what I could see she was jealous of Caprica, for obvious reasons. The Princess was pretty, her sisters were far more beautiful than her, but Princess Shirra had a natural charisma that made people like her. However Caprica seemed like a goddess with no one coming close to compete with her.

"Oh you're too possessive of your things didn't your daddy tell you to share and play nice with the other kids. He's his own person and not yours Princess. Just you watch, he'll come around and realise that you don't have the time of day for someone who deserves better. He'll come right to me," Caprica seemed not at all intimidated for talking such a way to a Princess.

"You don't want him, you just want to sleep with him," Princess Shirra sneered.

"So? What's the difference?" Caprica asked with a shrug.

"Do you not hear yourself?" Princess Shirra said glaring at the other women.

"Ya I want Khire, plain and simple. Khire needs a real women to show him what love is," Caprica said with no shame making Princess Shirra laugh. I choked on my own spit and tried to take a deep breath before speaking.

I shook my head wishing my little brother luck in dealing with Caprica.

"Listen I have work to do, but I am not comfortable with you two together, may one of you come with me please?" I asked.

"Oh, Jakk you don't have to worry, we'll be ok, we fight, but we actually are friends. It's a love hate relationship," Princess Shirra said waving her hand at me.

"Ok," I said giving them a weird look, I would never understand women.

"Princess Shirra, if I may say so, while he is my brother and I do think highly of you, I'm just not comfortable with you seeing my brother especially since I work so closely with your father. Khire is nothing, but trouble I hope you listen to my advice when I say you're better off staying away from him," I told her and she sighed. Caprica shot her a funny look.

"That's what I think, totally agree," Caprica said smiling.

"Thank you Jakk, I appreciate your worry, but we're not actually dating. I just really care for him and don't want to see him with someone who doesn't deserve him," The Princess said eyeing Caprica who smiled angelically.

"I think Jakk, you'd find me a much better partner for your brother," Caprica said and Princess Shirra burst into laughter.

"We just discussed that you just want him for one thing, I don't think Jakk wants his brother being a toy for your amusement," She said elbowing the women gently.

"Well I have to go, both of you stay away from him," I said pointing to both of them. Princess Shirra smiled, but Caprica waved my warning away and threw the broken glass still in her hand in a nearby garbage can.

"I am only a servant with many talents, I do what the master says," She spoke sneaking a mischievous glance towards the Princess.

I shook my head, but left them and wandered away.

"I like him, he's..."

"Shhhhhhttt," The Princess's voice followed me out the door. Other maids and servants rushed back and forth as I walked around and walked up staircase after staircase. I met a maid who was carrying a basket from a room.

"Donta, hello," She was Princess Shirra's personal maid and though I had questions I'd liked to be answered I wouldn't ask Donta to answer them. It was between the Princess Shirra and myself.

"Well hello Jakk, how's your family doing?" She was one of the nicest maids here and honestly loved her job. She was always smiling, sometimes singing to herself or just humming. She has a pleasant demeanour that made people relax around her.

"They're good. How's yours?" From what I knew she had four younger brothers, a sick father and a mother who stayed home to watch her husband.

"Well my father's back in the hospital, but other than that we're doing fine, thanks for asking," She had stopped on the stair to talk to me, but as another maid was coming up the stairs Donta began to move away. I turned to see who it was and found Caprica smiling at me.

"Well 'ello," She said winking at me.

"Oh Caprica thanks for coming to help me you're such a doll, come on, I hear sheets just screaming our names," Donta said smiling at Caprica who looked annoyed at her.

"Bye Jakk," Donta said as she walked past me.

"Oh ya bye Jakk," Caprica said waving at me. "Tell Khire that I love him," She called as Donta grabbed her arm and pulled her away.

"You are being rather rude, I didn't even give him my number what if he wants to call me later?" Caprica said to Donta who looked flabbergasted at her.

"Ok, bye," I replied amused. Now the King's worries started to make a little more sense to me. I made a mental note to myself to tell the King that it would be best to keep good spies on Khire and Caprica.

I walked on till I was on the sixteenth floor and I met another guard.

"Hey how are the upper levels?" I asked looking at him. He would be sixty-two this year, working here for over forty years and was now white haired, but was muscular, fit and very tall.

"Nothing to report, how are the lower levels?" He said his voice gruff.

"Same. What do you know about the new maid Caprica?" I asked.

"That she is going to be nothing but trouble and she is bringing Princess Shirra down with her, though at this point I don't know who is more the instigator," He said and shrugged.

"Have you over heard them talking about anything?" I asked him curious.

"Yup, Caprica is a talker. She's already given her number to Brent, a new young guard here. She has hit on the other men, young and old including me, you will probably be next. She has told the cook boys she loves a particular type of desert which I believe is now being made for dessert tonight and she has told me personally she loves to go shopping and dress up," He said looking a little irritated.

"Great thanks, I just met her. She was talking with Princess Shirra and they seem to be very well acquainted," I told him and he nodded.

"Yes, I think it best to keep two eyes and ears on that one," He said raising his eyebrows.

"Agreed and thank you, I will continue on," I told him and he nodded and moved on.

I walked through a white room with several bookcases around me, it was the library, but it was the children's library so it had a bunch of statues of animals posed around the room. The statues looked very real, there was a lion cub getting ready to pounce, a cheetah licking her cub while her two other ones played near bye. A small heard of zebra with three foals pretended to graze in the corner while a number of different types of birds, all carved in stone and painted to look real perched around the room.

The Princesses would come here when they were younger to read books or be read to. I smiled, wishing I could do that with my family. Vesper was not able to have kids, her body for some strange reason couldn't support one. After having tried for a year now we had finally accepted that having a child of our own was never going to happen. I loved her still and was happy to adopt, but I knew she felt terrible about herself saying she could never be a good enough wife. I sighed as I left the library.

☾

The worst thing about having people around you was that you could never yell at someone without attracting attention. Worst yet was being a Princess who everyone thought must always 24/7 act calm and in control even when you have someone right beside you who you would like to tackle to the ground and yell at. Being closely associated to an assassin, I had already plotted many ways to dispose of Temptress, never really wanting her dead, but still thinking some days would be better without her. Temptress wasn't here to cause any trouble, I actually think she was here to keep an eye on me and try and glean some information about the going-on's in the castle. She was an insider, which was helpful to me and most importantly she was loyal to Khire and I.

At the moment however she was annoying me and making me mad. Right now her mind was set on my relationship with someone else, a particular someone else I was very protective of and though I trusted him, I didn't trust Temptress as far as I could throw her. She saw any guy as fair game even if they were married. She had no shame stealing some guy away from another women just to have sex with them for one night and then never see them again.

I couldn't completely blame her though; she had a very hard childhood. Her father had been a carpenter, her mother a florist. Her younger sister had a rare disease that put her in a hospital bed for life when she was five years old. By the time Caprica was six, her father lost his job and her mother gave up on life and started doing drugs until she one day killed herself. They were evicted from their house and forced to live on the streets for a time until Caprica was old enough to get a job and make some money. She left her father, a shadow of his former self, and became independent. She got a job at a bar being a dancer some nights and a bartender on others.

After some years she was able to get an apartment then later a house. All the while her younger sister, whom Caprica loved dearly, lay in a hospital bed wasting away to a vegetable. Caprica visited her very frequently, but no one was able to help Cassa, as her muscles broke down and her bones turned to liquid. Everyone was surprised when Cassa lived to 17. After her funeral, Caprica took on a more direct path in life. She would get every amount of pleasure out of every moment. Her master, an assassin named Pandora trained her from the age of 15 to be what Caprica is today. She wasn't trained much to kill, but mostly to be a distraction and a really good spy.

Now 22 Caprica still struggled in life, but was determined to make the most of it. She had very little education so didn't have very many options in life, though I and Khire did help her out and Donta taught her to read and write as well as do math. With some adult classes she took some nights, Caprica was able to get by, but it will always be her looks and her fierce attitude that will get her far.

I considered her not only my friend, but like a sister, as she knew me for who I really am. Her and my personal maid Donta were the only ones who knew I had a life outside my princess life. Not dressed in gowns and tiaras, but in the dirty, grimy, dark and damp alleyways running around at night. I love being a princess, but I love to be able to be my own person with my own motives once in a while.

I was once a snuck up little girl in frilly skirts and carrying a wand when I was younger. I was now a young lady waiting for her father to give her hand to someone rich and marry him and give him children. A life living in a beautiful house with servants at my beck and call. It was a life I thought I always wanted, but I became a doctor when it was discovered my Wish was healing. Due to that fact, I was immediately forced into medical school, all kids with a Wish that could make them a good doctor or nurse were forced to go to medical school by law. They had to serve five years, it was almost cruel, but the lack of doctors and the many sick people required harsh laws. Beside most people found enjoyment in the end with what they were forced into.

I did love my job; I was a doctor, a very famous doctor as I was Vale Darra's best healer. I loved the feeling of going to work one day not knowing what I'd have to deal with, but knowing that I could handle it. I liked to put people at rest whether it was heal them or allow their last minutes to be peaceful. It also allowed me to be very independent. I was third in line for the throne so I didn't expect nor didn't want to be on the throne. With a successful life I could do well on my own. Still I cared deeply for my family and wanted them to live long happy lives as well. Which is why I approved of having Khire and Caprica around to deal with any potential threat

When I saved Vale Darra's most infamous assassin, I knew I was crossing a line. But looking at the blond boy who lay on the ground having given up on everything including life, I didn't see a murderer, but a misunderstood person that needed someone to talk to. I chose to save his life; feelings I still do not understand, compelled me to heal him even though he had been dead. Somehow I had reached out and brought him back. After that I devoted myself to saving him, from others as well as himself. It started as a business transaction, but it grew quickly to something more personal. I felt safe with Khire there behind the scenes protecting my family and I. However, I also love Khire and being able to go and see him, let him wrap me in his arms, I feel like I could be who I really am. I feel like I could make mistakes, be foolish and have fun without him judging me or telling the media. He was everything to me and I didn't know how to live without him now.

His love for me showed in how he spoke to me, stood beside me, went to the extreme to make me happy and in his protectiveness over me. Though I did not receive flowers and gifts like other couples do, I got a life full of love and safety, knowing my family was protected. Everyone who knew of us knew I was his and he was mine, the only thing saving me is that I am a healer and by *law* no assassin can kill a healer outright. Caprica was the closest thing I had to a best friend despite the fact that she got on my nerves and tried to get into Khire's bed, I liked her. She and I had many chats about Khire, life and girl stuff, it was nice. I trusted her and she trusted me, as much trust as you can give to an assassin anyway. She always told me how much Khire did and knew, she marvelled at Khire and I could see why. Khire was a great person, but I stood from a different viewpoint. Khire and I knew each other's real names so we were connected, I could feel his emotions and desires. However, because of that I could also feel when something was wrong with him.

Lately that bit of goodness in him that I always felt, was starting to disappear. Khire was becoming more confident and though he was still good in the sense he only killed bad guys, his mind was starting to turn to killing and plotting and planning. He is a very intelligent person and he uses it to greater himself as an assassin. We use to try and find something that used his skills, but made him something other than an assassin. I thought he could be a private investigator, but he didn't like the rules and laws he'd have to follow. There was a drive in him to be his own person and it kept him apart from getting a legal job. Slowly I have been feeling it growing in him, a dangerous evilness that would consume him if I couldn't save him first. It worried me and each time I tried to bring it up he would smile and say that as long as I was in his life, there would always be a light shining in his heart to chase away the darkness.

I sighed and continued writing my documents.

"So what are you guys doing tonight?" Temptress asked looking up from picking up more pieces of the broken dish and throwing it in the trashcan. "Tonight?" I asked confused.

"Ya you know for your guy's anniversary, you've been together for six years, you guys are practically married," She said and swept the ground. It was funny seeing her do such chores, as I knew she hated doing almost anything that required work.

"Ya… I don't know I guess we'll see," I shrugged and smiled.

"You guys could elope, I would come and be your witness," She said suddenly.

"Oh because that would go over well with my father," I said and despite myself I pictured myself and Khire running away and finding this old little house where we could live in secrete. I could sense Khire's amusement and I mentally sent him pictures of us walking down the aisle hand in hand, walking towards a priest who would marry us.

"Ya see, you like the idea. I think you should just do it, get married and go live your life. Your older sisters will still be here to take care of everything," Caprica said and it was so tempting.

"Maybe one day, for now let's just get through each day ok," I said and sighed.

Another thought came into my head. Jakk would most likely go home and tell his family what happened and they would all want to know a little more. It would be too close to drawing attention to Khire and me. It would put everyone in danger, most of all me despite the law, I would be a weakness. Khire would hate to leave me, it would hurt us both, but he feared for my life. If I became a target because of him, he'd leave or kill himself. If people found out about who he really was he would also leave or kill himself. It was a very disturbing realization and I began to fear the worst. Jakk knew something was up, I could see it in his eyes. It would just be a matter of time before he put the pieces together. He would find out though, then he'd tell my father and mother and sisters. They'd be shocked and ashamed. The public would find out, everyone would turn on me, on the entire royal family. My family would be kicked onto the streets to live like scum. We...

My mind kept racing until a voice settled me down. Khire sent calming thoughts to me through our link and I began to breathe easier. I told him how much I loved him and how much I wished he were here right beside me. I could feel the love he felt for me through the link, it nearly drowned out any thought I had, but then I became aware of another voice.

"Shirra......Ssssshhhhhhiiiiiirrrrrrrrrrraaaaaaa," Someone was saying.

"Oh, yes, sorry, what?" I asked looking around, but it was just Temptress.

"Hi, how are you today, how was space?" She asked pretending to be pleasant.

"Oh wonderful, stars are so pretty, what would you like?" I asked resting my chin in the palm of my hand as I sat in a chair. I felt warm all over and wanted nothing more than to sit and drown in Khire's love.

"Well ya see I had asked you a question," She told me simply.

"Which was?" I asked stupidly.

"What are you guys planning?" She asked and I nodded to keep myself focused on her.

"Well I don't know, maybe we'll go out. I don't really care what we do or where we go, just so long as we are together," I told her.

"Awe you're adorable. Well I was thinking, I've got to go to a party tonight. Would you guys like to come?" She asked, a challenge in her eyes.

"Sorry, but I am so tired right now I think I'm going to have to go to bed early. I really don't think I feel much like partying," I said. There were people around us and people eavesdropping, so we had to be careful. When I say I have to go to bed early, it means, I will be in my room early, come to my room and we'll talk then. She knows how to get to my rooms without being seen and working here she has access to my rooms at any time.

"Oh you old fart," She said frowning at me.

"Hey I am your princess you wench," I said mockingly. "I am off to go for a walk, away with you," I said and got up, grabbing the papers I was working on.

"Okie dokie bye," She said waving at me and leaving to do other chores.

"Don't forget the huge dust ball under the staircase maid!" I yelled to her.

"Yes Lady!" She said waving over her shoulder at me.

I walked around until I found myself in the garden room; I went outside and just sat in a chair listening. It was so quiet and the air smelled so good, the breeze was just right and the sun that beat down was so warm. I was falling asleep and let myself drift off to sleep. Dreaming of Khire and a life where everything was as I wanted it to be. Khire picturing everything for us in his mind.

CHAPTER #21

The moon was up even before the sun could get three quarters across the sky. Having finished all the business that needed to be done, I headed to the docks. Vale Darra was huddled around a large bay, deep and wide enough to let large ships come in and out of easily. The harbour stretched along most of the bay, large wooden docks streaked out into the water to allow boats to tie up. A few wooden buildings were situated at each dock to allow captains of ships to register their merchandise or report anything. Slabs of stone laid out pathways where forklifts would drive on to move cargo. The place was kept relatively clean, but it was always busy. Just one street over was where all the vendors sold their fish, lobsters, crabs and any strange creature that some fisherman pulled out of the water. Other merchandise like cloth, spice, food and other goods were taken deeper into the city or sold out of the captain's own house that usually was not far from here.

There were already a multitude of boats and ships tied off, people going around with clipboards to write everything down. Some bringing merchandise onto ships while captains inspected everything. The smell of fish overrode the other smells of sweat and blood. I looked at the ships with somewhat dislike, I did not like the large water or the thought of being stuck on a ship for weeks on end. I was a land mammal and as such I had no desire to ever step one foot on a ship or boat. Though obviously people didn't share that same dislike as a great many stood waiting to board a cruise ship to go to some far off place. A sign welcoming all passengers with "Welcome to the Dreamers Fantasy Cruise to Spry Island and Fenlon

Mountain Resort" hung on a post. I didn't know those places; well other than they were a huge tourist attraction and therefore probably some sunny paradise with large beaches and spas.

I turned away from the crowds of people and went to a small wooden pathway that led to an old shack that was very nearly going to fall down. It was an old storage shed, probably once used for keeping scrolls and reports. It wasn't used much now since the development of magical devices that could scan everything and enter itself into a computer. I went inside and encountered only dust and some mice looking around for food. I went to the back corner where beams that had helped support the roof lay across the ground broken and dusty. They were extremely heavy and after some grunting and heaving I was able to use my magic to move them over to get into the door at the back. This led me into a little closet where the trap door was rotted away leaving behind a large hole in the ground. I jumped down after a moment's hesitation, my feet sunk into mud immediately. Myre walked ahead of me to try and find someplace drier while I plodded along sinking down to my knees with each step.

I soon found planks laid out to walk on and gladly stepped onto them out of the mud. Crossbeams supported them, the ends buried into the walls on either side and supporting them well above the mud. There were torches jammed into the dirt walls all the way to a large room casting a spooky glow to the earthly place. The room also had torches in the dirt walls and a weird chandelier hanging from the ceiling supported by a large beam running along the dirt roof. Despite the secrecy of this place, this room was used very frequently, so was set up to be comfortable. Currently two people sat in two cushioned chairs that were positioned around a very old table.

"Ok, so what do you know?" I said and claimed an empty chair as they turned to me.

"We don't really know much, but something bad is coming. We've been keeping an eye out for anything, but we haven't come up with much. We've been talking to other assassins and they say they're all avoiding the city. Someone is threatening them to go elsewhere," One of the twins said.

"Threatened? By who? Who would have that much power?" I asked confused.

"Someone very strong and important definitely. The other day I felt this large wave of magic hit me, it was actually kind of scary being hit with that much magic. I don't know where it came from, but it felt kind of familiar. Kind of like I knew the mage, but didn't" Chris/Tylar said.

"Ok, well Khalita said something to me about seeing two people with the same face and name. Stargazer told me I'd also follow the wrong trail and I would kill the wrong man," I told them.

"Twins then!" As soon as Chris or Tylar said that I laughed.

"Like you guys?" I said and they realized what they said and laughed.

"Well besides us. Maybe there's two people out there, one is trying to kill you the other is not. Maybe you end up killing the one that's trying to help you? And as a disguise the one impersonates the other," They said shrugging.

"Which by the way wouldn't be us just so we're clear," Chris/Tylar said putting up a hand and I nodded.

"Maybe, but I don't know who's trying to help, so far everyone's either against me or wants nothing to do with me," I said throwing my hands up in frustration.

"Well I will work it out later. Now, what do you know about the circle?" I asked them after a moment of silence.

"Well Isaac chopped them all up and someone had a thing against magi," One brother said and I nodded.

"I haven't seen Isaac in a while, but I plan to visit him soon. Maybe he could fill me in. He could be mad at me, but let's expand on the other idea. He hasn't been killing up until those people and that's strange for him. If he was told by someone not to kill… I don't think he'd even listen, but if someone did then they must have something on him that even he doesn't want to test," I said to them as I thought it through. "Then maybe someone is trying to weaken something or make enemies of someone. What if someone is trying to get all the assassins out of Vale Darra so they can get in?" Chris/Tylar commented.

"Get in? But why would he want all the others out? Have you guys been threatened?" I asked puzzled. They shook their heads.

"I talked to a guy named Duke, but he didn't warn me to stay away, he just said the flow of magic is moving in a different direction. A direction that might possibly lead to the extinction of all life on earth," Chris/Tylar said. "Huh, well I had a lovely chat with Duke as well. He told me he was going to kill me one day he was just waiting for me to beg him to do it," I told them rolling my eyes.

"Oh really?" They both snickered.

"Well, when we find anything else out we will let you know. In the meantime, stay on the lookout for anything odd. We will be boarding a ship in a few days, but we will be back later in the year," They told me together and I nodded.

"Ok, see you guys later," I said and we left it at that.

I thought about what they said. Everyone knew that magic flowed freely in the world, it was in everything, an unlimited source, but also uncontrollable and unobtainable to humans. If, and that would be a big if, the flow of magic is now flowing in a different direction it could mean anything. I tried to look at it like the ocean currents. I thought magic could flow as it liked in any direction and change at will, but if it flowed similar to the ocean currents, then there could be potential harm in them changing. I didn't know what could happen, but decided whatever was going to happen was probably something I couldn't control and so I tried to focus on the next issue. I wanted to find who was threatening other assassins and why.

I was waiting in my room when Temptress knocked on my door. I quickly opened them up and ushered her in.

"Ok, tomorrow night there is a party, the twins are going and they need dates. Obviously your truly beloved is also going to be there once again heroically defending the crown from those who wish to knock it off the good Kings head," She got right down to business, she told me everything quickly and quietly. I managed to keep up with her and nod along, but for the most I was just expected to show up and look pretty. Soon after giving me the details she left, taking with her a few sheets to look like she was doing some late night laundry. I closed the door and went to bed. When I woke up the next morning I would get ready for what was to come.

☾

The sun disappeared behind a tall building turning Vale Darra crimson against a purple and red sky. I could feel the rays on my skin and knew it would have looked picture perfect. I could partially see the buildings and trees, but the fine detail was lost to me, lost in a blur of shades of red. With the sun slowly sinking and the temperature noticeably changing, I gazed out at the scene before me, trying to piece together what I thought Vale Darra would look like right now. I knew those buildings were made of many little bricks, the roadways were cobbled and the trees would be a thriving, vibrant green.

I crouched low and waited until I could hear the sound of someone coming down the street. This was the richest part of the city and was home to about twelve percent of Vale Darra's population. Here the men wore tux's, ironed daily with shoes that were polished to a shine. Their hair was brushed and lightly jelled to stay as the person wished. They walked all similar too, a confident, long stride that kept their heads up and their backs straight.

The women wore long flowing dresses that puffed out from the hips and came down to nearly drag on the ground. Their feet were slipped into high heels while their hair was twisted and twirled to be pinned up in an elegant style to show off slim necks. The style that was most fashionable of late was long gowns with large skirts. Long sleeves draped over the hands that were decorated with rings. The top was to be tight and flashy, the skirt embroidered and heavy looking. The colours that were really in were green and orange though yellow and violet were also popular. To me these colours did not match and I couldn't picture how the dresses would look, but fortunately I didn't have to worry about that.

These were the rich people that had servants to do work for them. Wealthy beyond belief, these people have never worked a hard day in their lives. They ruled this section of the city as if it belonged to them instead of the King. They expected the best and had very high opinions of themselves. They were the brats, the aristocrats of this city. They thought themselves so highly prized; you had to be born in the family in order to live here. Marrying in was a huge ordeal and all others were outsiders, allowed to come and gaze at the richness of this place, but never to own any of it.

They all lived in large mansions. Spectacular green lawns sprawled around each one interrupted by rows of flowering trees, large, extraordinary gardens with rare and exotic flowers. Statues and fountains set the scene and made it look like a storybook. Large gates prohibited people from venturing onto the lawns while the magic running along the top of the fence prohibited people from climbing it. The houses were made in the old style with a step or two leading into a large open porch then under a grand entryway into a large boot room. The main theme of the houses was old and rustic, but with a hint of modern and classiness. The typical "Beware of Dogs" sign hung on a post outside each house warning intruders of trained guard dogs. Which from experience were actually very well trained and extremely dangerous.

The houses looked like something out of a magazine. Everything was made to be picture perfect down to the smallest detail. Stone work was done on some of them so that the bottom half of the mansions were done in stone while the upper portions were done in a dark wood. Set back from the paved road, each driveway had their own names, usually named after the occupants of the house.

This section of the city was marred by the fact that it was close to a middle class section. Some old buildings and some new buildings sat across the street from the breath taking houses seeming almost to be in opposition with the finer folk in this city. It was here that I was waiting in an old vacant building, sitting in a windowsill watching others walk along the street towards a mansion that was to host a ball tonight. For the most part, the guest list included all the rich people on that side of the street. Still, there were some merchants visiting here that were looking to sell precious items.

Only on the odd time did I come here to kill someone. They were rich, they had servants, but they didn't beat them, they didn't treat them unfairly, they paid them well and were, other than snobby, really good people. Still there were some people that every once in a while liked to cause trouble. I was here tonight because some people were getting a little too in over their heads thinking them better than the King. They wanted to split from Vale Darra and create a dukedom. Most of the residences were fine pretending to be their own Duke and Duchess of their own place, but a few were whispering about demanding their own title and larger lands. They were becoming more and more demanding as they become more greedy from wealth.

I could sense the next women coming down the street and as she turned the last corner, she came into full view. She wore her hair up into a tight elegant bun and wore a long black dress with flecks of gold around the hem. The dress, like others, was tight around the torso, a modest neckline, no sleeves, but she wore gloves that had the same gold flecks on the back of the palm. Heels gave her an extra inch in height, but it was the way she held herself, her head up and all the confidence in the world. She looked stunning and I marvelled at the sight of her. Her hair was black and her eyes were a lovely hazel. I could almost see her clearly though the picture I formed in my mind did not do her justice. She was far more beautiful than my imagination could piece together.

Another woman came up beside her and looped arms with the other women. She was wearing a beautiful dress with the bottom frilly and layered. It had off the shoulder sleeves, which drastically opposed the latest fashion. The colour was white with little gems in it, flashing beautifully in the skirt of the dress and on the gloves. She wore her hair into a bun, but had a few strands down, her hair was red and her eyes flashed an icy blue. Freckles dappled lightly across her nose and down her arms. She strutted down the sidewalk as if it were a catwalk.

I knew who they were immediately as they passed by, though they did not look up at me. I smiled and looked back the way they came as two more people came walking towards the ball. A husband and wife, married for twenty years now and wearing a black tux with a silver tie and the women a silver dress that had a high neckline with a bow which tied at the back and streamed down. The dress was stunning on her and the stilettos matched nicely, but this woman who carried herself as if a Queen looked a little green. Her make-up looked rushed and her hair was down in curls that frayed. She almost looked nice, but she wasn't complete and her slightly nervous smile gave off an air of incompetence.

They passed by and I turned and dashed into the room, I stretched and walked around to loosen up my muscles. I was getting ready to play my part. I walked out of the room and into the deserted hallway. It was a nice hallway, light blue with a darker blue border. Old wooden floors showed years of many footprints walking up and down these halls while the old shutters and rounded archways showed how historic this place was.

I made my way to the stairs and got to the bottom then turned to Myre.

"How do I look?" I asked turning. He looked at me amused.

"Dashing," He said then smiled. I petted him and smiled back. "Hey so do you, and you smell nice from your bath," I said rubbing him behind his ears as he growled softly at me.

"You ready?" He nodded. His fur was groomed, a good bath and lots of soap even managed to make him smell nice. I tied a black silk ribbon around his neck the same way I had seen others tie ribbons around their guardians neck. I didn't really know the reason behind it, but as it was the fashion of today, that is what I did. The ribbon had a slight gold sheen to it to match my black tux with a black tie that had the same sheen of gold. I didn't like the clothes, though they were the nicest things I've ever worn, I found them to restricting. They were too tight and not meant for lots of movement. They made me a little self-conscious and I wanted to put on my old ragged clothes just to feel better.

"You look fine, just relax. No one knows you so here's your chance to be the stuck up snob you've always wanted to be," Myre told me in my mind. I glared at him not thinking him very funny, but relaxed a little anyway.

I walked outside and met with another man who smiled at Myre and I. His Guardian, a monkey, sat on his shoulder and pointed at Myre. The two Guardians spoke to each other, but we couldn't hear them.

"Ready for our little fun?" It was either Chris or Tylar, but I didn't know.

"Yup, you?" I asked back and he nodded. Myre told me he too wore a tux, but instead of gold it was tiny white spots that fringed the edges. His hair was a nice brown while his eyes were a dark chocolate brown. He smiled a charming dimpled smile. For the most part, he was not disguised, his tan skin, beautiful accent and fluency of making conversation was normal. Sometimes the best disguise was no disguise at all.

"Here," He said and I put the wig on. My hair went from blond to black and I put in the contacts that turned my eyes a dark brown. I smiled and turned around.

"Well you aren't much to really look at, you look good, but you're a street rat. Your too skinny, your unclean and you have no manners. What can I say you're lucky you have talent and brains to pull something like this off," He teased.

"Well thank you, and while we're complimenting each other if I may add, you don't exactly have manners either and you aren't really high quality," I told him putting my hands on my hips.

"I'm higher then you," He told me as his twin came up who I thought was Tylar.

"What are you guys talking about? Chris you are about as high as the bottom of the ocean and about the same quality as a flee," Tylar said straightening his jacket.

"Ha ha that was so funny," Chris said sarcastically, turning towards his brother and completely forgetting me. "I know, I'm hilarious," Tylar smiled as he put his hand on his chest and stopped before us as if posing. He was dressed in the same outfit as me: the same wig and the same contacts.

"Well you know…" Chris started then was cut off. Music started and we all turned towards where the ball was held.

"Looks like we're on, Chris and Tylar, no goofy stuff," I said acting like the adult.

"Ok, Mr. Zervanick, say where are you from?" Chris asked smiling brightly at me.

"Well some place far away now, Tylar you know where to be. We have over a hundred people involved, it's us three with the two others, and we have the eight plus yours, alright, let's get on with it," I said and changed my voice to be accented of some distant land.

We walked towards the giant hall and as we got close Tylar moved off into the shadows of a building and hid there, his part would come later. Chris and I walked, backs straight and heads held high towards a stream of people dressed as nice or even nicer then us. They turned at our approach and began to whisper amongst themselves. They had never seen us before and new faces were something that attracted everybody's attention. Soon Chris and I along with our dates will be the center of attention and everyone will be coming up to us to get information on us.

We met up with Temptress and Shirra, Temptress turning, smiling and waving at us as if we were distances apart.

"Well don't you two look handsome, come on we're late," She said.

I offered my arm to Shirra who quickly wrapped her arms around me and gave me a kiss. Lingering a little longer than necessary, Temptress had to tug at Shirra's arm to get her to let go of me.

"Sex later, party now," Temptress said and Shirr shot her a dark look. Chris gave a bow then kissed Caprica's gloved hand. She smiled, her eyes twinkling as she gave a little spin making her dress spin out around her. Temptress and Chris looked ready to cause chaos, a glint in their eyes told me they were up to no good. The two of them were well matched, both were overly flirtatious, shameless and overly confident. They were a dangerous pair when they worked together.

My date and I were more reserved, we smiled and talked to each other. I acting like a gentlemen and her acting like a polite, young women. We were more the charmers and the others more the attention seekers. We two were to figure out who was out to unsettle the crown while Chris and his date took to the dance floor and had fun. They had some targets themselves, but they were here mostly to have fun and make a scene so that Shirra and I could snoop around.

The music wasn't my taste, but it was Mr. Zervanick's, a fictional man I made up so that I could come here, and so I had to become him. I smiled as I gave my invitation to a well-dressed boy waiting by the doors. He smiled and nodded his head then announced our names.

"Mr. Morjin Zervanick and Lady Cathalis Crinne!" His voice wasn't deep yet and his face was round so he was still very young, but he stood tall and expectant as if older. His hair was brushed to the side in brown wavy locks while his brown eyes were sparkling with excitement, but held no mischief. I nodded at him earning a happy smile from the boy and together Cathalis and I descended the stairs and onto the main level.

Around us couples danced or talked and ate. The main floor was huge with a stage on one side where a band played and a large tiled floor for dancing dominated the other side. Off to the right along the wall of the dance floor was the food table where all types of food were steaming or chilled on plates, in bowls or pans. There was a white tablecloth that reached all the way to the ground with another sheet of white underneath it. Anyone could hide under that table comfortably as it was high off the ground and wide enough. It stretched from one side of the room all the way to the other with plates stacked high alongside cutlery and napkins at regular intervals down the table.

There were stairs on either side of me, slanting up to a higher level where people stood or sat in metal dainty chairs. The levels went almost a quarter of the way out so people could peer from the floral balcony at the dancers below.

The scene before me was full of colours, fine music encouraged people to dance slowly in another's arms. Dim lighting around the band and the food made the dance floor the focal point. Many people were already dancing, the sounds of their shoes hitting the tile added to the music from the band. A quiet hum was all I heard from the many people talking in the corners and along the walls.

I circled around and went up the stairs to the second level. Cathalis and I smiled at people who smiled at us and greeted whoever greeted us, always being very polite and kind.

"Young man, where are you from?" Someone asked me. He was old with glasses and a tux that was too big for his thin frame. He smelt funny too, but I wasn't about to tell him that. His grey wispy hair reminded me of dandelion fluff, but his kind brown eyes and his warm deep voice made his question more friendly then rude.

"Well I am from Tallfetia," I said with an accented voice trying not to wrinkle my nose at the sudden smells that hit me.

"Tollfaychia?" The man tried to pronounce it. "Almost, it is a far off place, a great place really. We hardly have a day to call bad, the sun shines and is always warm. We are close to a sea and it is good to us, keeping away real hot weather and snow in winter," I told him, rambling.

"Ah sounds lovely," He said as he took a thin, crystal glass from a waiter.

"And where sir are you from, may I ask?" I waved a hand to the waiter and he left, I wasn't here to drink.

"Well, I live here, but I have another home down in Shaythings. Darling place that is," He took a small sip. "So what brings you and your young miss here?" He asked eyeing Cathalis.

"Oh Cathalis and I were actually traveling apart, but we met a few months before. Then we heard about this great ball and decided a trip to Vale Darra together would just be wonderful," I smiled and nodded towards the women beside me. Cathalis smiled and looked up at me.

"Cathalis is it? You are such a darling young women, where do you come from?"

"Well thank you, you're too kind. I am from Tallfetia's sister land, Zullmayia. We live in the mountains with the snow. It is such a magical place, the ice crystals gleam so brilliantly," She said her voice accented beautifully.

"That sounds like such a nice place, my darling wife and I must come visit some time," The man said with a smile. "Oh certainly, my maids are most kind especially to have a chance at impressing such fine people in their company," Cathalis said. She was very good at this, being born to the hierarchy; this was a normal day practically, while I was having difficulty finding the right words.

"Just keep smiling, you know how many wars can be won with just a smile? You're doing well, relax," Shirra's voice echoed in my mind and as she sent calming thoughts to me I could feel my body relax. I didn't know how tense I had been until I realized my back was getting sore. I nodded at her as I let a breath out and tried for a more pleasant smile that showed I was more relaxed then I actually felt.

Cathalis looked so at ease, a smile on her lips all the time without seeming to be fake. Everything about her seemed charming and elegant, the confidant way she spoke and the effortless way she moved around everyone drew the eye as well as a smile. She looked very pale with just a little colour on her cheeks. Her eyes were the most beautiful green and I could see others staring awed by her. She, like Chris, went with a little disguise, preferring to depend on magic to kept people from knowing she was really Princess Shirra.

"Glad we will be honoured most gratefully, but up in those mountains, would they not be most horrible? How cold it must be and dark?" The man said shivering as I came back to the conversation.

"Yes, but our people believe, when one is cold we embrace it, and when darkness comes we know that light will follow. We take it as a lesson for all to strive for greatness. You can only be great if you can face great things. So we embrace our lands with pride," She said that as if she has believed it for years.

"Wow, great words from such an astounding young women," The gentleman said smiling.

Then his wife came, she was the opposite of him, where he was lean and tall, she was round and short. She had squirrelly ginger hair that was short and stuck out from her head in all directions. Her eye shadow was different shades of green that made her green eyes look huge. Her dark red lips were full and pouty, her cheeks powdered though not enough to hide her many freckles that covered her face.

She could have been nice looking if it weren't for the ball shaped body she had. She did not have the self-confidence to pull off her shape and I felt a little sympathy for her, having been in the same position once before. She wore a deep forest green dress that touched the floor at the back and went up into a slit to her knees; she was about eight years younger than her husband, though looked just as old. Her feet were in thin straps, which were green as well, and she wore a light green veil across her arms and slipped behind her back. She held out her hand to me and I smiled instantly. I took it casually and carefully leaned forward and kissed it much to my dislike.

"Well good evening, Miss, what a lovely dress that is. It brings out your eyes in such an astounding way," I complimented.

"Oh aren't you just charming," She giggled and I smiled back relieved she was easily flattered.

If this were all I was doing, I would hate it. I did not care to meet and greet people with fake courtesy, smiling warmly at them and act as if we were all long lost friends. I was getting anxious, shoving my hands in my pockets to keep from fidgeting with a button on my jacket. Cathalis grabbed my arm and stood closely beside me to better control me.

"Just wait a little longer, we just started," She said with more patience then I deserved.

"I just can't seem to settle down," I told her truthfully. I felt like a bundle of energy and didn't know if it were nervousness or something else that was making me like this.

"Well young Lady, you have got yourself a fine young gentleman, how long have you two been married?" The other women asked tuning to Cathalis.

"Oh we're not married, just two people who happened to meet on the road," She said smiling up at me. I gave her a warm smile back actually wishing we had made it seem as if we were married.

"Oh, well you to are such a darling couple I just thought…" The older women started.

"No, no, it's fine, we have become great friends in the small time we've shared together. Maybe it will lead us somewhere farther down the road, but for now, a friendship is our connection," She nodded and gave a small smile and shrug.

"Well I hope you two a life time of happiness. Come darling, let's not bother them over much," The women said turning to her husband. He nodded and smiled at her.

"Pardon me," He said to us then they went off to the dance floor.

"Would you like to dance?" Someone said coming over to Cathalis.

"Certainly," She said and took his hand. They went off talking and went to the dancers along with several other couples.

"Don't just stand there awkwardly go find someone to dance with or go eat something," Shirra instructed. I nodded and turned to find someone just as out of place as me. Most people seemed to be very comfortable here; many were gathered into large groups talking while others danced.

"Oh darling that girl leave you all alone, come dance, with me?" Another women said coming over, her accent thick. I recognized Temptress immediately as her and Chris came over to me.

"I'm dearly sorry Anatya, but I simply mustn't," I said smiling, instantly relaxing.

"Ah what a pity," She pouted. She seemed to be having fun, her cheeks were flushed from dancing and drinking, her eyes twinkling with excitement. Myre commented how funny she looked in the red wig, but I didn't tell that to Caprica. She had always wanted to be a red head and apparently she didn't much care if it suited her.

"Time be getting late," Chris said in his accent and I turned to the huge clock at the front of the hall above the entrance. Surprisingly an hour had already gone by, but I hadn't found out nearly as much as I wanted.

"Yes in deed, but give a few more hours, excuse me, I must go to the food," I said and left. I didn't know what else to say that sounded like an excuse you would usually hear at these types of parties, so I just settled for the food.

I went down the stairs and worked my way through the thick crowd to the food table. "Well what a fine young gentleman," I heard some women say to my left. I looked at them out of the corner of my eye. They were in their late fifties, wearing a purple and pink dress, white hair in a bun, and ear lobes hanging with heavy earrings. They wore bracelets, rings, and necklaces all shining with gems. I acted as if I didn't hear them and moved on.

"Oh this party is wonderful, the guests are so lovely and seem to be having so much fun," I heard one of the hostesses say. As I moved closer to the food, the quiet hum became a dull roar.

I was almost to the table when a woman stepped in front of me. "Well where are you going?" She asked. She looked about fourteen though very tall for her age. Her frilly dress made her look like a little bird and her heart shaped face, pouty lips and pixie hair cut proved she was young.

"I am going to the food, I am famished," I said acting hungry. "I heard the food was wonderful here, and I just couldn't resist," I said smiling at her. She smiled back and followed me to the table.

"Well yes, my cooks prepared it and they only prepare the finest foods," She seemed very proud.

"Well I hope you're right," I said and grabbed a plate.

"So who are you with?" She grabbed a plate too and started moving down the line after me. I was a little surprised looking at her as it was hard to believe she ate anything at all, she almost disappeared when she turned to the side.

"A friend of mine, Cathalis," I told her as I reached for a bun.

The food smelled so good my mouth watered, I was not leaving this place without a few napkins full of food. I piled my plate, attracting attention to myself, but I didn't care, this was heaven to me and I was going to take advantage of it.

"Oh, she's just a friend?" She asked curious.

"Yes," I told her then picked up the long tweezers and piled a few types of vegetables onto my plate, leaving the salad because I didn't like salad.

"Well that's nice, do you come from far away?" She asked and took the tweezers to get some lettuce.

"Yes, I live in Tallfetia," I told her and she looked confused.

"I'm sorry, but I haven't heard of a place like that. How far away is Tallfetia?" She had some trouble saying the word, but managed it better than I expected.

"About four days away," I answered.

"Four days, so how did you come here, in a carriage? Why did you come here?" She was being really nosey.

"I came on horseback, Cathalis and I met and we heard about this ball, we thought it was something we must see," I grabbed a big fork and put some type of meat on my plate then dripped gravy over it. My food at this point must not have looked at all appetizing because everyone was staring at it disgusted and at me very confused.

"Ummm, you know we do allow seconds?" The girl said beside me, giggling.

"Oh, well that's ok, where I'm from it is rude to go for seconds and rude to leave even a portion of your plate clear," I said before I could think. "I would hate to seem rude," I said not even half way down the table.

"Ok…Here I know where we can get some seats," She said and I followed her looking back at all the food I hadn't gotten to. I sighed and followed the girl to where there was a little platform and lights were strung on fences that caged in an area for people to eat.

Already people were in seats that were metal twined with plush gold cushions. Not all the chairs were filled and I could tell it was reserved seating, but I followed the girl to a seat as if it were nothing.

"I am so sorry, I haven't even introduced myself, pardon me. I am Cateik," She said and smiled. "It is nice to meet you Cateik, my name is Morjin," I announced and nodded towards her.

"Morjin, that's a nice name, does it have a story behind it?"

"My grandfather was named Morjin, he died when I was born and my father was deeply saddened, the only thing he could think of was his father. My mother wanted to call me Maynuik, but she loves her husband and so named me after his dad so my father could think of him when he thought of me," I said coming up with that lie on the spot. "Ahh, that's such a nice story, my mom named me Cateik because it reminded her of a kitten," She said rolling her eyes.

"Would you like to dance?" She asked me suddenly. She smiled widely, showing very straight white teeth, but what must have worked for others did not work for me. She was blurry and hard to focus on with her quick sudden movements; I had no interest in dancing with her nor even talking with her. Though her mother was an issue, this little girl had no idea about the rude and cruel ways the world worked.

"Ah," I said nearly choking on my food.

"Don't worry, your food will be wrapped up, and I gave orders to make more trays filled with the rest of the food, maybe you can bring some back to your home. Then you will have a taste of us with you. It is seen as polite here to want seconds," She gave her best smile hoping it would convince me.

"The truth is I don't dance, at all," I said looking apologetically at her.

"Oh well that's ok, I'm not a very good dancer myself, come on, there is a first time for everything is there not?" She got up and extended a hand towards me. "Well I guess I must then, but please give me just one moment to wash my hands. I would hate to spill gravy on such a lovely dress," I turned and left her looking at me smiling.

I wound my way through the crowd till I came to a servant who stopped me. "The Lady Cateik asked that I had these prepared for you," He said and held up three trays full of food. Each tray was made of Styrofoam and wood. It was about eight inches in length by six inches wide and six inches deep; opening it up you had two layers and wooded bars to keep certain foods separate. I really couldn't care if my food was one huge pile, but I didn't tell them that.

"Well I am most pleased thank you," I said taking the trays. The waiter smiled happily then walked off.

I looked around, seeing Cathalis leaning on the balcony looking over the crowd with Chris and Temptress on the dance floor spinning and having a lot of fun. They attracted a lot of attention and weren't really dancing like the other dancers, but they were having more fun than the rest. Temptress's dress was spinning out as she twirled and it showed a little more leg than expected, but with a devil may care grin, she danced without care.

I turned and left them then, heading towards the doors. "Just going out for a little walk and some fresh air," I told the boy at the door. He nodded his head and continued to stand there as tall as he could be. He hid a yawn by pretending to wave at me, but remained on his feet.

The weather had gotten bad unfortunately. Rain pelted down, but the doors were already closed behind me and no one was around. I walked into the rain and went into the closest alley I could find.

"Hey Cadence, here you go, take it to the den and don't eat it all," I said warningly. He smiled and grabbed the food greedily. He was very skinny with little muscle tone and long hair. His skin was dirty from not being washed and having been bombarded by perfume and air fresheners for a while he smelled horrible.

"Go get a bath and get your hair cut to," I said motioning with my hand for him to go. "Why? I like my hair," He said sounding pouty.

I went into an abandoned building and pulled up a plank, under it was a bag, which I pulled out. Inside were cloths, a wig, contacts and shoes. I quickly changed my disguise and stuffed the old stuff back into the whole and covered it over with the plank. I was now a green-eyed older man with greying hair. I was dressed in a dusty grey, un-fitted suit. Magic changed my features so that I had a gaunt face, grey blotchy skin and gnarly fingers. I went from a young man to an old man who walked stiffly and slightly hunched.

In order to set up tonight we had to limit just how many people were involved. That's why I and Tylar were playing the same person. Morjin had to stay in sight the entire night as he was a key person in our charade. He was the prince charming with lands, estates and a history for being very generous with the right people. It had taken us some time to create such a character, but now many people were somewhat familiar with the name and his reputation. We were hoping that having him out and about we would have some people seeking him out looking for ways to fund their own underground businesses. Having set the stage for him, I was now able to hand that over to Tylar who was really good at reading people and getting information from them.

I went back inside to the party told the boy a different name, he announced me and I walked around along the wall till I came to the staircase. Once on the second floor I found the bathrooms along the far wall. One was empty so I snuck in and closed the door slowly as if movement hurt. Well I thought it was empty. Temptress popped out of nowhere.

"Well hi ya!" She said and hugged me, pushing me towards the wall.

"Oh for the love of God, leave me alone women!" I said, trying not to yell. She gave me a peck on the lips and smiled up at me.

I pushed her away then jumped up onto the toilet and shoved at the ceiling to remove a panel. A hand reached out from the darkness and I took it and was hoisted up to the ceiling.

"Ok, I met a women, named Cateik, she's a hostess dance with her. I met another gentlemen and his wife, they live around here, have a house in Shaythings, here you go," I handed a phial to Tylar and he nodded and took it. I hopped down and Tylar peeked his head down at my companion.

"Well, well, well, look what's going on here?" he said much to my annoyance.

"Would you both stop?" I snapped. Temptress blew Tylar a kiss and left. A few minutes later I left, hoping no one had seen us. He would sneak out and get in through the front door to keep up the image of Morjin. He was supposed to have scouted out the crowd and take his targets out then change to Morjin to let me get my own victims. Whether he did or not, I didn't know yet, but I was too occupied with sorting my own victims out right now to care.

This next act, I played a grouchy old man who had lots of money and hated to spend a penny of it. I was to be rude and abrupt, but very concerned with the world and interested in doing what I could to make the world better. I was little known to these people, as I tended to be more solitary then a social highlight.

Many were dancing, while others were talking in little clusters of people. One woman, dark skin and long dress got up to the stage and began to sing a fast song. Her voice rose and carried without the use of a microphone very well throughout the room. She wore a white glittering dress, with diamonds in her hair. She had no trouble hitting the high notes as her voice carried effortlessly around the room. It wasn't a song I knew, but it was very catchy and beautiful to listen to.

I went to the food tables again, this time taking very little food. I ate slowly, picking up the food and inspecting every bit of it as if I despised it. Checking the clock, I waited a few more minutes then went back up the stairs and all the way to the top floor, running up the last flights of stairs that were restricted to all party guests. I got to the top without being spotted and turned down a hallway glistening with sparkling objects from around the world. They were quite the collectors I noted, but I stayed focused as I rushed down the hallway and came to the grand bedroom. I slipped inside soundlessly, but stopped just inside the entryway as I heard voices. I eased the door closed glad these doors were noiseless.

"Mother, I met this darling young man, very handsome, can't remember his name though," It sounded like Cateik, and I had no doubt in my mind that it wasn't. She must be talking to her mom I guessed. I had hoped that Tylar would have distracted her and kept her downstairs, but as that wasn't the case I had to adapt my plan.

I circled around the circular room till they were in view. It was Cateik, her mother and two maids. Cateik was looking in the mirror fixing her make-up; her mother was in another mirror doing the same while the two maids went around cleaning the room. The two maids looked like they wouldn't be leaving anytime soon and neither did the daughter. I surveyed the room to see how best to make my move without creating more casualties.

The room was large with a vanity curving around with the wall and a large bed covered with blankets and small pillows. The room was a rose pink with white tiled flooring. A large window was on my right while the daughter and mother were on my left. The maids were in front and slightly to the right of me. The vanities were not pressed all the way to the wall, a small space just wide enough for someone to slip behind them proved to be the best way for me to get into position, but there was no way for me to get behind them without being seen.

"Well that doesn't help me if I don't know his name. I can't get him to marry you if I don't know the easiest thing such as a name," The mother was saying.

"It's not my fault, he has a weird name, and he's from a far place. How am I to remember all these people's names here? There are hundreds here mother," Cateik whined. Cateik turned to the maids to address them and I quickly scooted over to the vanity. I managed to get behind it before Cateik turned back around, but it was close. I took a moment to assess my situation and then very carefully and slowly made my way over to the mother. I very carefully lifted up part of the older women's skirts to reveal one of her legs. I quickly poked her with a poison filled syringe and backed out using a large amount of magic to leave the room without being seen.

I gave a little sigh of relief, impressed at myself and swearing to never have to do that again. I had to stop for a few minutes to catch my breath. Having used so much magic all night and hide myself as well as continue to use magic was starting to take a toll on me. I had a terrible headache and I was dizzy enough that I couldn't walk fast even if I wanted to. So playing the part of an old man, I very gingerly went down the stairs. Each step made me feel like I was going to fall forward, but with a white knuckled grip on the railing, I managed to get to the bottom without falling. My back was a little stiff from being so tense, but I still had a part to play. I had spent almost forty minutes dealing with Cateik's mother and now had to deal with some more.

There was still seven people here to kill now, the rest were all from other places, all conveniently placed in the palm of my hand. It wasn't very often I had people from around the world all in one place. So despite the fact that I wanted today off, I couldn't miss this opportunity. However, something I had to keep in mind with killing so many targets was to be careful not to make it look like everyone died from this ball. So all the poison I used today would slowly kill people. Some would die next week, while others in a few months' time as their liver slowly failed. Two of the poisons I will use are crafty little things designed to only kill the person if the person ate a particular type of food. This way it looked like the person was dying from an allergic reaction and not from here.

I casually went down the staircase when Cathalis walked in front of me.

"May we dance?" She asked. I nodded and took her to the floor. She looked a little relieved to see me as I held her arm and patted her hand to reassure her and myself. At her touch she sent some magic into me to give me strength. My headache and dizziness went away and I smiled gratefully at her.

"Mr. Buikson is walking by the drinks, he is with his son and daughter," She whispered into my ear. "Miss. Sharonna is walking outside for a smoke while Miss. Sadish is flirting with Tylar over by the food. Leave Cappit and Musgin, I want to watch them longer. I don't entirely think they are up to no good," I nodded and waited till the song ended to move.

I left her as she went over to another man, Mr. Weskit, a son of a Duke, she could handle him while I handled the others. She was easy with him, flirting and seeming to enjoy his company then asking him if he wanted to join her on a walk. She took him outside where Chris was ready to kill him.

I got to Mr. Buikson and his son and daughter walked off as I approached.

"Hello, Mr. Buikson, I have heard so much about you. Your paper about the lost planet was superb," I complemented, smoothly directing all attention on him and demanding he talk to me. I shook his hand with a stiff, quick shake and managed a thin lipped smile.

"Well I didn't know I was so appreciated," He smiled pleasantly. He was a big guy, bald with big brown glasses. He was an absolute genius, and if it weren't for the fact that I wanted to kill him I would have loved to talk with him and pick his brain.

"Oh yes, I thought differently at first, but after reading it, it changed my whole point of view on things. Tell me what further research have you since done? Have any more planets been discovered?" I asked him kindly, but with a sudden directness that was verging on being rude.

"Well I'm glad you enjoyed it, I'm sorry who are you?" He asked. "I'm Falcon Breesh, you can just call me Falcon though," I said and smiled again.

"Ok, Falcon, I have done only little research since that paper. Unfortunately, most others do not agree so heartedly as you have to my ideas. The idea that there are more planets outside our galaxy is too much for them. Yet I am determined to see it through. My team has finally invented something that we can send out to outer space and travel around in search of other planets and most importantly other life," He spoke with great enthusiasm, fully believing in his ideas.

"Do I have to kill this guy? He's too smart, it's a waste for him to die," I said mind to mind with Shirra. I sensed her frown.

"Do you think he's innocent? He helped fund some people who wanted to shoot my father," She said unhappily.

"Only because your father is being very close minded about some things," I retorted.

"I say kill him, he's a lovely man and a genius, but we can't afford to leave him alive. He's too dangerous," She said and ignored me.

I knew Mr. Buikson's ideas were routinely shot down; we lived in a world obsessed with the notion that we were the only life forms on any planet. To believe otherwise was to think that there might be something better out there. I myself thought it very possible for other planets to sustain life, however, I did not care to go out and seek them so determinedly as this man has.

"Very impressive. I have been tinkering myself and think I can help with that project if you are interested in a partner?" I asked him, taking out a small booklet from my jacket.

"I would be very interested to partner with you, let's see what you have to offer?" He said and I led him to a quieter place.

He called for a drink and within minutes he was drinking wine. Perfect. I handed him the book to peruse. Only about the first ten pages were used with drawings of oddly shaped vehicles designed to fly as well as go over uneven terrain. Some notes were scribbled in the margins, while arrows pointed out certain aspects of each drawing. Shirra had made this not too long ago, mostly taking the drawings from other people's ideas. He turned as someone bumped him, Cathalis, and I quickly poured the phial that was up my sleeve into his drink as I pretended to reach for him, but decide not to and draw my hand back.

He took a sip, and kept reading. A few minutes later he put it down. "It is incredible, however, this is a rather large operation. I am not sure about some of your drawings and calculations," he told me kindly.

"Well we all can't be geniuses like yourself now can we. If you don't like my ideas then I will be off with them and my money," I said and grabbed the book from his hands and walked off with them.

"Hello Miss. Sharonna, I must say that colour green brings out your beautiful eyes. It makes them a jade colour and one so beautiful I know that no stone exists to match that beauty," I layered the compliment thick; I only had a few minutes so I had to work fast.

"Thank you, and you are?" She asked pleased. The man next to her turned away in annoyance as the women gave me her full attention. She was a scary looking thing, thinner than even I was, with a fur veil and green dress that showed off just about every bone in her body. Her brown hair was the only nice thing about her though she had it pinned up in a ridiculous hairdo at the top of her head.

"Oh, Falcon Breesh, Miss," I said and kissed her hand. It was as simple as getting my previous target. I was on my next person when Chris bumped into me.

"We gotta leave, someone's catching on," He whispered.

I apologized to the person I accidentally ran into, slipping a small pill into his wine then found Cathalis. They all left shortly after while I made a fuss about the food and the wine not being good enough for me. I left outraged that no one would see to my demands. They were happy to see me go as the rest carried on in their merriment.

Out of my eight I got four, with Cathalis's help two others were left alone to be monitored for further evaluation. The others got almost all of their people, and could get the rest at a later time. In the end we did well. We snuck into a building we're we changed into our usual attire.

We left to go home with a quick goodbye and a wave. Cathalis gave me a quick kiss then ran down the alleyway practically skipping. I shook my head and smiled, I had a good night. With that I went to find Cadence.

For the rest of the month, I did nothing, and it wasn't until three months later that Cadence and I awaited our next target. We circled around a dusty orange saloon surrounded by old brick buildings. A few dogs barked in nearby backyards, but the streets were empty save for some parked cars. Cadence circled around where a victim waited in the saloon, singing to everyone as she sat on a stool. Smiling happily as she looked around, the light catching her brown eyes and voice rising in tune with the music. People watched and listened happily. She turned to include the whole room and smiled a wide dimpled smile. She looked lovely in her silk purple dress with her wavy short hair. The light streamed down on her soft and slightly dimmed. The small room with only thirty-two seats was crowded with people. The brown walls and grey tile floor was very boring, but tonight this was a lively place. Pictures of people from the past hung on the wall, but the history of the saloon wasn't what had brought everyone here tonight, though that was something of an interest to tourists. It was the young women on the small stage that had gathered this crowed together. She was very talented, with the potential to go far with a great singing career, but only if she could have just stuck with that.

I recognized the song as an old tale about two people who went off to war and fought each other only to find out that they were both twin brothers. It has a sad ending as the one brother kills the other. As the brother lies dying they learn of their birth and so the other brother kills himself and they lie on the field, side by side while the war rages on. People are so caught up in her voice that they pay no attention to me as I enter. I join in with the crowd making sure no one's suspicious of anything and as I look around I can see people with tears in their eyes or tears streaming down their cheeks, focused only on her. The room was so silent, with the girl's voice going soft and sweet; everyone was so still as if all were in a trance by her voice.

...And the brothers laid their heads
And the war went on and on,
Down on a soft grassy bed
The brothers slept on and on
No one seemed to care.
The dying found their rest...

When the song finished she thanked everyone and left. The room filled with chatter, people getting back to doing their job as some left and stools were rearranged back to the way it was before the performance. The singer went to the back room to gather her stuff with Cadence right behind her.

"I give one chance," He said to her in a dark and threatening voice. She turned quickly on her heels and gasped, fear written on her face. Her large eyes were so big, her Guardian, a bird, looked like it would die of fright.

"Who are you?" She asked backing away. Her hand felt behind her, finding nothing but a table that was nailed to the ground.

"Last month you were caught stealing from a grocery store, last week you did it again and just the other day you did it again. I am giving you one last chance to stop and make things right or else," He said frightening her.

"I will! I won't steal anything ever again I promise! Please don't tell the police!" She said already in tears. Cadence was great at scarring people, that's why I mostly made him give people warnings, they tended to listen to him better than me. Something about a tall black man with black eyes and scars all over his body just struck fear in people. Funny thing was of the two of us, he was the nicest. He didn't like scaring people, but he also didn't always like to kill them either. So I gave him these little assignments. Mostly thieves and people who started to interfere with something I didn't want them interfering with.

He left her then, his job done. He came out to where I still sat and smiled disarmingly, shrugging off the experience as if he had been discussing the weather with someone. He strolled out of the building casually, his long strides carrying him past the slower older people. I waited for a bit until I saw the singer rush out, pale faced and eyes red. Her mascara had left tracks down her rosy, blotchy cheeks, but she avoided every ones look of confusion and fled as fast as she could. Then I left. Cadence was good, fortunately the girl didn't see him the previous night laughing and drinking with some buddies.

Chapter #22

The next night I had my own little target I wanted to get rid of. I found her in a dance studio and waited patiently for the right moment. The room was alight with lights hanging from the roof, the walls were white, while the floor was hardwood and one wall was a complete wall of mirrors. A gold beam ran horizontally along the mirrors at waist level and twelve women danced in the room to the sound of music. A woman in the front dressed in a tight black shirt and black tights with a green sash strung with coins on it showed the others how to do a move. This was dance practice and they were all being taught by the women in the sash to become belly dancers. They moved across the floor double stepping and moving their arms and swivelling their wrists. They held scarves that they swirled around them and together they did a dance, all trying to move with the music. They had only a certain amount of space and with that they moved in tight circles trying to mimic the teacher. A younger woman, only nineteen, turned to another and smiled, they were better than the rest, but they paid the teacher little attention.

I sat on a beam high above them looking down. The teacher looked like her dancing days were long past while the group of girls were a mixed group of really skinny to overly plump, but who was I to judge. They were trying, and it was probably good for their self-esteem. Maybe doing this would make them feel better about themselves. And this was probably their most sociable time they had, except for the two teenagers, the rest looked like people that didn't get out much.

I didn't get the music, it was odd, ranging and changing to random tunes, there were no words, just music, and though it seemed to work for what they were doing, I didn't care for it. All I cared about was my victim, right now she was expertly mimicking the teacher, she was slightly off with the music, but she got the move right. She turned to her friend and rolled her eyes, watching the person to the left of her out of the corner of her eye. Her friend laughed at her and they both turned to the awkward girl who looked at them a little upset. The girls looked apologetically at the other girl and started talking to her. The awkward girl nodded and smiled at them then did the move again and looked at the other girls for encouragement. The two girls smiled and nodded at her, but when the two girls turned to each other they continued to talk about her and snicker.

An hour and a half later everyone began to leave, the nineteen year old bent down to do her shoelaces up and as she was getting to her feet, everyone else gone, I jumped down and stabbed her, killing her instantly. I caught her and quietly lowered her body to the ground then, looking around and listening for any noises, I left.

The moon was just coming up as the sun was sinking down making the sky red and purple. The waning moon added little light to the fading day. I walked to a nearby bar and peered in, not seeing someone I was expecting, I went around back. The man was leaning against the wall smoking and talking to another man who held a beer. They were talking quietly, but as I came up they stopped and looked at me.

"Hey bud, what's up?" The man with the beer asked.

"My patience. You've been sending threatening messages to people to try and cause discord in the castle. That ends now. You will never harass, rape or steal from anyone. You will neither have any power nor influence over people weaker then you. Do I make myself clear?" I asked them and I watched as they both sized me up and shrugged.

"And who are you to tell us what to do, boy?" The guy with the cigarette asked. He was my initial target, boyfriend to the girl I had just killed, but I didn't like his friend either.

"That doesn't matter to you now…," I said and threw two small knives at them. One knife I aimed perfectly, it hit beer guy in the throat. Blood gushed out as he fell to the ground and slowly died. The other knife I had thrown with my left hand hit the smoker just above his left collarbone, nearly missing him entirely. He flinched, but roared and came at me with a knife. With a quick motion, I grabbed his wrist, twisted sharply then brought his hand up to stab him in the face with his own knife. It went into his eye causing him to scream horribly as I pushed him to the ground.

I could hear people coming, but managed to stab the guy before someone else came into the alleyway. I turned towards a young man who had just happened upon the scene. He stood horror struck at the silhouette of a man holding a knife above two bodies. He couldn't see my face, but almost as if he spoke the word, he seemed to say Dusk. He collapsed to the ground and I snorted.

"Maybe not the best choice to send out to see what's about," I said and left him.

I went home, jumping onto a nearby house with a low roof. I saluted the nearby townsfolk who gawked at me then ran off to my den. Myre trailing behind me as we ran from house to house and then into the labyrinth of alleyways. Myre settled beside me when we finally reached our den.

"Tomorrow is just another day, we will be sure to see it," He said and rested his head in his paws and slept.

The moon rose higher into the night and I stayed up long enough to see Cadence return home then fall asleep. I woke the next day with the sun still rising above the horizon. I went to a nearby stream to get cleaned up as best I could. I used as much soap as I had to and a very bristly brush to clean myself. Scrubbing till my skin was red and my hand soar from holding the soap so tightly. I took more care with my hair. Scrubbing with shampoo and conditioner till I was sure I was free of any dirt. I was thorough in my cleaning, making sure I was as clean as possible. I didn't want anyone thinking I had just slept in an abandoned house even though I did.

I never wanted anyone to look at me with disgust for being a street rat so I even took some time to clean the dirt from under my fingernails and toenails. I shaved the scruff off my face carefully using the water as a mirror. My magic kept my clothes clean and smelling nice though I gave them a quick wash anyway. Once clean and dry I left to snoop around.

The sun was bright and the air warm, people were walking around doing their day-to-day things, while police officers on horses patrolled the streets and buildings. Their Guardians prowled around their Protected with a trained police dog at their side. Some policemen and their Guardians stood on the ground or drove in their vehicles. There usually were many policemen in one area at one time; though I was still a little surprised just how many I spotted within the first few hours of the morning.

The roar of the crowd was nearly deafening, and with so many people you had very little elbowroom. Unless you shoved at everyone who came into your personal space, you were going to be besieged with other people, getting stepped on, elbowed and pushed. I walked through the crowd getting jostled and pushed around a little as I grew frustrated. By the heat already in the air, I knew it was going to be an unusually hot day. I hoped it made people get off the streets and go elsewhere, but knew better than to count on that. I got an elbow in the ribs and pushed the guy hard into another.

"Hey!" The guy yelled, he rounded on me, but I glared at him and he backed off. I continued walking, very aware of everyone who came within five feet of me. I hated walking in the city, I always became far more angry then I had reason to be, but I was already in a mood and didn't care. I stalked through the crowd determined to walk in a straight line even though the people and even bench's and trees were in my path.

I spotted my brothers talking and headed over to them.

"A little moody today Khire?" Tellnair asked smiling sympathetically at me.

"Why does everybody have to be outside right now?" I asked them annoyed.

"It's the city," Tellnair said as if I had forgotten.

"Ya I know, but it's also seven o'clock in the morning, don't people sleep? What the fuck? What's up?" I grumbled crossing my arms to try and prevent people from elbowing me in the ribs again. I was ready to start punching someone even with an officer standing right in front of me.

"Oh just another killing, but don't worry, we've got private investigators, hired some very important people. I know we'll find Dusk sooner or later," Fetcher said.

"I just hope that when you catch him, you let him live, you guys would be dead without him," Tellnair told him. Tellnair always liked Dusk, always looked up to him and seen him as a hero for doing what no one else had the guts to do.

"Hello Tellnair, how's Mellony?" A man said as he walked over to join us. He was an old friend of Fetchers, I hadn't seen him in a while and by the looks of his tan, he had just come back from someplace hot. "Fine, she's not happy right now, I'm on another run, have ta get her chocolate and some marshmallows," He raised his eyebrows and huffed. His wife, married five years ago, was almost six months pregnant with their first child. She didn't like me and I tended to avoid her. Even when not pregnant, she was a hard person to deal with. She was a handful and very high maintenance. She was uptight and she didn't like when I came to her house for fear I brought in diseases and flees.

"So Fetcher, another killing?" Tellnair asked.

"Yup, this time a young girl," Fetcher's shoulders were slightly drooped showing just how tired he was. With large bags under his eyes, hair rumpled and clothes dirty and wrinkled. He wasn't as clean cut as he preferred to look in public. Tellnair sighed but nodded.

"That's too bad, but anyway I better get going," He said then left after patting my arm. "Cheer up," He said as he passed me and I gave him a fake smile in return. Fetcher's friend left as well with a quick goodbye.

"What are you doing in town?" Fetcher asked turning to face me.

"Oh, just walking around," I shrugged. "Here I'll let ya get back to work," I said and smiled.

"No it's ok, stay, please, I'm going to fall asleep if no one interacts with me, just talk to me for a bit. Vale Darra is so boring, don't get me wrong, I'd rather have it this way then being in the news, usually if it's in the news it's bad. I don't need any bad coming to Vale Darra, but I do wish there was something else I could do," He yawned again and looked around at all the people.

Everyone was talking loudly, trying to be heard above the rest, and doing anything else that caused noise. I didn't see how I talking would keep him up when he stood right in the middle of a noisy crowd.

"Well maybe one day, but for the now it's just boring old Vale Darra and its nosy sleepless residence. It's kinda good you're not involved with it, cause you'd probably be dead if you were," I slipped my hands in my pockets and stood casually beside him. That made him laugh.

"Well yes, I guess I would be dead thank you for that cheery thought. So maybe that's a good thing that I'm only a cop that knows only the information cops usually know," He seemed to awaken a little.

"Hey you joined those ranks," I said putting my hands up.

"Ya getting on the inside of the justice system has a way of making people deaf and blind to society," he mused.

"Funny how that works," I teased him.

"What do you know?" He looked at me curiously, but also amused.

"Oh nothing, just that I think there has been very little killings lately," I shrugged again and looked at him simply.

"Very little why'd you say that?" He asked puzzled.

"Well there are other people here that kill besides Dusk, yet it seems they've all disappeared," I told him. I didn't want to give him too much information, but another person on the lookout was good.

"True," Fetcher said thoughtfully. "What else do you know?" He asked me suspiciously.

"Not a whole lot, but I think there's a person who is targeting strong magic users or people that have great potential," I told him honestly.

"You know more, tell me. How did you figure that out?" He asked complete attention on me now.

"Well Dusks still out there, but the other assassins the city usually deals with aren't, they're a bit of a no show these days. Usually people would think that's a good thing, but I'm thinking something's up. Assassins don't just walk away, there's someone out there that's scaring them off. Assassins won't put themselves into a situation they can't handle, there gonna leave while they still can. Or die trying, but in this case no bodies to show for that. And if you look all the people that have died come from families that are known for being powerful magic users or they have potential to be strong magi. Someone has something against magic and they don't want anyone in their way," I told him seriously. "They also have a lot of power if their getting all the assassins to leave,"

"So what do you think should be done?" Fetcher asked curious to see what I'd say.

"Well he's targeting magic users, that's a very interesting target. The world runs on magic, if too many people who are strong magic users die, the world is either going to crash and thousands die or a black whole will be formed. Either this guy just doesn't like magic users or he's a diabolical genius intent on destroying the world," I said.

"So warn all strong magic users and start making magic reserves in case there's an unbalance," Fetcher said nodding.

"That's a start," I said agreeing.

"But?" Fetcher asked me arms crossed.

"But it still won't be enough. Say this person who has something against magi and something against assassins are the same person. He or she has that much power to tell a bunch of assassins to leave, warning people isn't going to faze him. And creating reserves is a very temporary fix, it won't support the world for more than three months if that. You need to find whoever it is that's doing this and stop him," I told him, almost saying kill, but stopping myself before I got that serious.

"I still have the feeling you know something more," He said eyeing me suspiciously.

"Ya well if I told you all my secrets then you may as well retire and let me take over your job. I have to give you something to do, just think it through," I replied.

"Hm, fine… get gone and let me think," He said almost grouchily.

"Ok," I said smiling and left.

I walked with a carelessness that told others I was merely wondering about, but I did have a street in mind that I intended to go to. It was a busy crooked street that out dated many parts of the city. With cobbled roads and old style lampposts, it felt like you were walking back in time. The shabby little buildings that squatted right up to the street stood slightly skewed as the old timbers gave way to time. Shutters banged loudly in the wind and doors creaked eerily with the slightest of breeze. Still, the roar of the crowd and the little room to move about proved that this strange little place thrived with life.

The street was overcrowded with people all trying to hurry with their shopping. The shops here offered anything the mind could think up and even the most imaginative was impressed by the splendour of all that was offered here. This street simply called

Crooked Street was a place for the rare oddities, trinkets that can't be found anywhere else.

The people that sold the items were strange and peculiar themselves. They all had a weird way of talking, slightly disjointed, but kind and friendly. They were frustratingly so in your face and adamant that they could help you yet had a way of getting acquainted with anyone that you thought you'd been friends for a long time. I believe they had come across seas to Vale Darra some years ago and settled here finding it to their liking. Instead of taking up our ways however, they stuck with theirs. Strange though they were, I had very few issues with these people and only usually came here to hear gossip and plan new targets.

Many times I had to fend someone off trying to sell me some item that was sure to make my day easier or relieve stress. I came up with the weirdest excuses and randomly walked away from them as if I had instantly forgotten someone was standing right in front of me. They all simultaneously left me alone after the third time I did that and then I could think and observe everything around me.

In Vale Darra, each street had a variety of little to big box store buildings selling an assortment of merchandise. Vale Darra was very wealthy because it offered so much to life; it was well developed and always changing. Excluding a few sections of the city that liked to keep its heritage status, most people liked to remodel on an annual basis. Still there were some buildings that were old style buildings and the date that they were built was engraved in a plaque on the side of each building with a little description about the past owners. They were now surrounded by newer businesses that had really turned this place into the city it is today.

Most of the old buildings were in this section so the streets were cobbled and uneven. Streetlights were shorter than the new streetlights. They reached up and sprouted into three lights that spread light across the buildings, street and side walk. The paint was pealing leaving a dull gray behind. The little vines that crawled up the posts streamed high overhead from building to building and post to post. Though it was nearly suffocating here, the beauty of the place still drew photographers.

I looked up to the sky and the sun continued to rise higher in the sky, growing hot and humid as it beamed on everyone. I walked down the busy street and came to a group of street people sitting or standing in front of a store singing. They were regular singers here, always singing about the going-on's in the city with their handmade instruments. Dressed in worn, dirty clothes that barely deserved to be called clothes. Some wore old chains around their necks as if they were necklaces or plastic rings on their fingers. All had greasy beards and hair, some had teeth and one had shoes on, but otherwise they had nothing to show for their livelihood. They could however sing, and by singing here daily they made enough money to survive on. Despite their rustic ways, they were nice people and did work towards a better future for themselves. I stopped for a moment to listen to them sing.

...When darkness is calling out in the night
answer back whence comes the light
If darkness threatens to be too great
leave your life then up to fate

If all is well deep within you
then light within will shine like new
It will turn the gloom into light
and send it back into the night.

The song went on and their voices rose and fell in unison. It was a catchy tune and soon enough I had it stuck in my head as I continued on my way, humming it quietly to myself. It had a very happy rhythm to it that made me think of trumpets. Other people around me seemed to think the same as they continued to hum it as well and add a little skip to their walk.

Some people dropped money into a case by a beggar's foot who smiled thankfully at them. I left them and walked to a fountain nearby, fish swam peacefully in the large tank, completely dependent on their feeders. They were well humanized and didn't initially spook as I approached. The water was heated and maintained at a specific temperature, cleaned routinely and everything checked up on regularly. The sunlight shone down and glittered on the pebbled bottom. I walked away from the fish and the singers thinking how everyone and everything was dependant on something.

I went from stand to stand, I had no money to buy anything, but it was the casual thing to do and as I reached for an item on a stand I looked at it pretending to give my full attention to it. People gossiped a lot here and listening, I was able to find a lot of information. I continued to listen and move along to other shops until a couple of voices caught my attention.

"Did you hear about Vurla?"

"No, but Hoken found the thief that stole some of his money,"

"Really what did Hoken do to him?"

"What do you think, what would be the Dusk thing to do?" That was now a famous saying "what would be the Dusk thing to do" it seemed that everyone had a problem with the world kill, let rest or any other words with the same meaning. Even though it all meant the same meaning, it somehow sounded nicer.

"No, but...seriously...wow, how many is that he's...?" "I don't know, he came home the other day all bloody, I think he was with his ex, but I'm not sure," "You know he's living a dangerous life..." That was the end of that I now had a target.

By midday, the heat from the day seemed to leave all at once, leaving a chill in the air. The moon rose as the clouds drifted away promising a crisp clear night. I stood in an alleyway wearing only a long sleeved shirt and pants. Temperatures could be as hot as 40 degrees Celsius here in the summer and in the winter can be as low as -40 degrees, we got usually more sunny days then wet and a lot of snow that every year usually got to the height of three meters and a minimum of one meter. Freezing rain would come and go and everything would freeze in one night then melt the next day making the streets washed out and slushy.

It was a harsh reality for the street people, many had never known the life of living in a house, but some did. Some came from good families brought down in harsh times. Reduced to scavenging and thieving. Human morals quickly forgotten as soon as the simple little joys in life like food, warm and friendship were gone.

On nights that dropped below -30 the police would gather them up and take them to a shelter. They got food, a bath, someplace warm to sleep and something warm to drink, but once the cold and bad weather were gone they all ended up back on the street. Some thought it kindness that the King would open up shelters for such occasions. Others found it made them look like less than human. Given warmth, food and shelter by the Kings wishes as if they could only survive through him. They took it as insult and refused such kindness, inevitably sleeping through a cold, crisp night or freezing to death. While some of the financial secured homeowners frowned on the program. They thought that their tax money was better spent elsewhere. Not on foolish people who couldn't get their act together. They strongly believed that those that hit their downfall deserved nothing but a hard time and if they died in the act well then one less issue for someone else to deal with.

I thought it a kindness and possibly a way for many to learn that there is a better life out there for them. If they could pull themselves together they could have shelter every night, not just when the King orders the shelter doors open. On the cold nights, Cadence would participate in going with them, but I wouldn't, if it got too bad then I would go to my healer's house.

I began to move, slowly and quietly. Night came and with it a cold wind. Almost everyone was inside by now making the streets eerie. I made my way through the alleys and listened for any sounds and looked for any movement. Houses began to appear from the dilapidated buildings, smaller than the huge 20 or more floor buildings and more colourful. The neighbourhood wasn't as nice as my dad's, though there were some trees randomly placed on some lawns and some houses were bordered by flowers. The houses sat, planted to their foundations, some unstable and others not far from it. The paint on each house was old and washed out; the lawns were a lot more rugged looking with long, un-kept green-yellow grass. The sidewalks were cracked and uneven, some sunken while others were heaved up. The buildings that bordered this neighbourhood blocked a lot of sunshine or moonlight, so this neighbourhood was left in shadows most of the time, and the people living here matched that.

They weren't your happy, friendly neighbours. This street that I walked along was called Gunners St. because on this street there use to live a family who were all insane. It was a family of five, a wife, husband, one daughter and two boys. They didn't go to school, the husband had a job butchering animals, but was later fired when the animals he butchered were poisoned and so killed people. They kept to their house mostly, but sometimes you could see them all wandering around the streets, if they came across someone they were known for kidnapping that person and taking them home. The people would be discovered later in someone's attic with a bullet in their head. All but one boy was dead now, that last boy, now fifteen was now an assassin in the making. He wasn't extraordinary, but his insanity and his lust to kill more caused an eternal hunger that made him think only of killing. He didn't want them to feel pain, he just had an obsession with life and death, and he thought that life was what made people bad. By living you slowly became evil and so he killed people, mostly at a young age so they wouldn't ever become bad. The bad thing though was, he only killed the good people, those who were successful and as harmless or as innocent as a child. He was known as Angel, named by the people of Vale Darra and a little joke from the other assassins because of his reason for killing. He wasn't angelic at all with long dreadlock, black hair and dull brown eyes. He was creepishly skinny and walked with a bowed back. Most of the time you could see him, if ever you did, walking with his fists clenching and unclenching. He was tall too, standing at six foot four, but his slouched posture made him look smaller and his flesh hung from his bones like old clothes on a hanger. His skin was a sickly gray; his few remaining teeth were sharp, but crooked and black. Even I didn't like crossing paths with him as he was just too unpredictable and too insane to trust. I would have liked to kill him, but he did have his uses. Sometimes he could be convinced to do something for me and most of the time now he was monitored by the police.

I was going to visit Hoken. I didn't actually know the guy, but I wanted to check him out all the same and if I could kill him then I would. I had a very interesting way of tracking people I didn't know. It was sometimes difficult to do, but I had been working on my hunting skills so decided to hunt him down instead of getting more info on him first then killing him. With my Wish I could sense everyone around me, I could also smell them which at this moment wasn't all that great for me. Each person had a certain thing about them that set them apart from everyone else and this is what I used to track people with. If a person has come into recent contact with someone, that would also show up on them as well. So having studied the people who were talking about Hoken I decided on what path to follow to get to my pray. Sometimes I was misled, but sometimes I was dead on.

Myre and I walked down the dark street, a tabby cat walked out and hissed at us, then dashed off in another direction. I gave it no mind though Myre was annoyed by it. We made our way to a house much resembling a mansion that had fallen down ages ago and was now only two stories, but with an extra few feet that use to be a third story at one time. I crept to a window, but they were covered. With my Wish, I could see people moving inside and in other rooms and levels. There were only three people so it would be a quick job. One slouched in a chair that was way too small for him, another was leaning against a wall talking on the phone and the other was staring at a wall tilting his or hers head this way and that, brushing long hair constantly. It looked like a she and she was probably looking at her reflection in a mirror.

I walked to the backyard and found the back door unlocked with Myre as my faithful guide, I was able to make my way to the living room where the person in the chair was.

"That is the target" Myre's voice spoke in my head. I drew out a knife from inside my sleeve and slowly came up behind the person as Myre came and leaped on the sloth that must have been the man's Guardian. It made no noise as it went and the man didn't even flinch, he just sat, only breathing. I swiped my knife along his throat making a fine, clean line. Blood began to leak down his neck and stain his shirt. All the while he sat there staring listlessly at the TV, making not a sound. I dashed away and back outside, the night concealed me from any people watching. I easily made my way back to my home, this time I didn't make an appearance, but by tomorrow everyone would know of the killing.

CHAPTER #23

As months went by I began to see more of a pattern forming. There was no specific gender or age, it was purely a hatred for magic users. I began to come up with possible reasons for why someone would want to kill strong magic users thus destroying the world. Throughout it all I continue to kill, though seldom, for the most part I kept myself busy with trying to find out who was targeting strong magic users.

Cadence began to lose focus with everything and became snappish.

"I don't want to be here! I have other stuff to do you know!" He yelled at me one day. I hadn't even said anything, but still his outburst was predictable. Lately he seemed distant and distracted so I knew a blow up in my face was coming. We were in our little den, I making a sandwich when Cadence came stomping in through the doorway and confronted me.

"Ok well then Cadence go ahead and do whatever you like, cause I'm done with you," I said walking away from him with my food.

"Don't you walk away from me! What do you mean you're done with me, we're not finished here! Khireal! We are not finished here!" He said seething.

"No I'm not, but you are. I know you've been going off on your own, you've been having your own life and that's fine. I gave you that chance years ago and you didn't want it then, but supposedly you want it now. I know you've been dealing with other people, I know you hate me so why do you still follow me?" I asked him turning to face him. He flinched as if I had hit him.

We stood face to face, I a picture of calmness before a raging storm.

"I... I don't want to be here anymore," Cadence said his eyes downcast. He kept clenching and unclenching his hands, but his stance told me he wasn't looking for a fight.

"Fine you have never been chained here. You have always been allowed to go your own way," I told him simply.

"I don't want to be here anymore," He repeated. After that Cadence left. I don't know where he went to, but he left and by the way he ran off I had a feeling I'd never see him again.

I kept my focus on solving Vale Darra's problems feeling that if I just held on I could fix them. I became obsessed with the city and all its issues and I would do anything to further my attempts to save the failing city. I even got a job. I showed up at a historical building called Historica. A nice building with large towers and brown brick walls. I applied for the job as a translator and researcher and sat in an office translating ancient script for people, helping out with field trips and helping tourists who couldn't speak English.

I found that I actually enjoyed working with languages and history. It was a rewarding job that kept me out and about to hear anything going on and allowed me to keep an eye on everyone. I was one of few people that could speak and read ancient languages, languages that I actually learned from Midnight so I could communicate with him privately. When I wasn't in my office, I was either sitting on a bus or just leading people around talking to them and telling them the history of the city.

It was at this job that nine months later I found a ray of hope. My little hope came in an old journal written in 1382 by a guy named Dyras. It was hard to translate as it was in an old style of writing, but with patience I managed to understand it page by page. Dyras was a non-magic user, he feared magic, hated it more than anything. However, he fell in love with a women named Litith and she was the world's first magic user. Or so this journal claimed. She loved Dyras and did not fear Dyras's Wish, which is unknown, but supposedly he was the first person to be identified with a Wish.

Dyras was able to tolerate Litith's use of magic, but when one day a little boy died because of it, he could not tolerate it anymore and spent the rest of his life trying to kill his beloved Litith and any others that could do magic. Over time he focused on the strong magic users thinking if he could take out the strong strain of magic slowly, but surely, all magic would stop.

The journal had many pictures and even dates, some didn't make sense though. In the beginning the pictures dated from 1382 to 1406 then suddenly jumped to 1734 then to 1989. I had to use the computer at my desk to see if I could find the pictures and sure enough each picture that was dated in the past was an exact replica of the structure or scene it was capturing. I didn't know what to make of this, but I kept it to myself.

I also noticed how thin the paper was, which was unusual for an old book. Furthermore, this book looked nothing like the old ratty books that I had grown accustomed to. The front and back cover were in good condition and the pages clean and white with neat writing. The spine was not crinkled from people reading this book or the pages dog eared or crinkled. The historical books had very similar wear and tear, even ones that were not obviously popular reads showed similar signs of ageing and use. This one almost seemed like a replica of an older book that was written in the present then in the past. However, it was in the computer system as a historical book and so I gave up on puzzling it out.

It was on a snowy afternoon when I was standing in the square listening to the street rats sing that pieces started coming together. I had just got off work, being with a group of tourists that were sure they were going to see all that Vale Darra has to offer in just one day. The street rats voices carried as I came near them and the crowd around them stood hushed as they listened to their words. They were singing about dreaming of a world of peace, but they woke up to a cry. A cry that couldn't be comforted in this world of pain and sorrow. They went on to sing about the world falling apart and how this city was failing. They finished the song by praying for peace and singing to a being I didn't believe in.

People didn't know what to think, but they listened and as the music went on more people stopped in the street and listened to their voices. The streets were quieted for the minutes of the song, but from that silence, the music echoed through the street and as the sun streaked across the sky I got my ideas. Dyras only wanted a peaceful place, he feared magic because he could see its potential in being used for evil purposes. There must be a cult where people believed the same thing as Dyras.

I walked away from them and into the darkness of the alleys. The afternoon was growing colder and soon the police were walking around to take the homeless off the streets and to the safety of shelters where they would survive the night.

It took me an hour and a half because I had to keep taking detours so the police didn't catch me. Though once there, I slipped through the palace gates. I was skinny enough, which isn't exactly a good thing, but it did work to my advantage. I went across the snowy lawn towards a high tower dark in the moonlight. It was a large castle standing almost eighty stories high and stretched even farther then that lengthwise. It was a huge place with a property of twenty eight hundred acres. To the right of it were two stables. Each made to be mirror images of each other. They had stonework around the base, going a third up the walls and flat stones led into the large front doors. The rest of the barn was cedar. Each barn could hold twenty horses; large box stalls provided plenty of room to each horse. There was a main aisle going right down the center with four smaller aisles leading off to the stalls and dividing the barn into quarters. The stalls allowed the horses to view everything around them, with a sliding panel to conceal them if the stable master wished.

The loft stored the hay, while a room at the very back held the tack. Two more buildings off to the side of the barns held carriages and other necessary items. These were built in a similar fashion to the barns. In was in one of these buildings that the stable master and his hands lived. They had good living quarters, though still appropriate for people that also had other lives and may live elsewhere.

The castle door nearest the barn led directly to the kitchen. With two large ovens and a sink that was practically a bathtub, the kitchen was fully supplied with everything it would need. A large pantry stored the food and a large walk in freezer preserved anything that needed to be frozen. There was always something cooking there that kept that place smelling yummy.

I haven't even fully explored the castle as many places weren't even used. Many rooms were guest rooms and though the King did have regular guests, most still stayed empty year round. However, I was not here as the Kings guest tonight. I had a little more personal reason to be here. I was here to see Shirra. I hadn't seen her in a while, our different lifestyles didn't allow us to meet on regular occasions and even if they did, it was far too dangerous to meet each other. However, sometimes I couldn't help but end up here. Needing to be near her and just listen to her talk. I told myself that coming here on cold nights was a good excuse. And so here I was, smiling as each step brought me closer to her.

I was closer to her then any married couple could get with each other. It is hard to explain and can only be understood by feeling it, but giving your true name away, your name given to you by your Guardian, to another is even more than giving your life to them. It creates a bond between you two that can never be broken. A bond that allows you to feel what the other feels, even see what the other sees. It makes two people one within two bodies and yet it is even stronger than that. I feel everything she feels, know everything she knows and have a complete understanding of her. She too feels every feeling I have, experiences every emotion, knows all my thoughts, and feels my times of tiredness and times of strength. And each day I still marvel at how the bond works and how much I love her.

I have never regretted giving her my name, to this day I still owe more to her then my life and so I gave my name to her, showing my love for her through our bond, as I can never tell her in words. No thought or action could explain how much I love her, I would without thinking, die for her, take a bullet for her and protect her from any harm anyone wanted to do to her.

I approached the castle, always feeling myself relax as I got closer to Shirra. I grabbed an old vine that crawled up the side of the castle, gardens being plenty here as the castle was over taken with all the plants. I got to a part where the vine I knew wouldn't hold so I launched myself up and grabbed on to a higher bit then pulled myself up farther. I ran across walls to balconies, climbed more of the thick vine and leapt over areas that were weak. It took me only ten minutes to get to her room that was on the eighteenth floor, but I took an extra second to look back at the city before stepping down to the balcony I wanted. The city was all lit up, but the streets were spotless of people now. When the balcony doors opened up to reveal Shirra's personal maid who was more like a best friend to Shirra, I left the cold night and walked inside.

Not one alarm being set off though there were everywhere. Shirra had secretly recoded them to allow me to come in undetected. The alarms were set up to identify anyone who wasn't supposed to be there, so it was easy to fix that, hard though to keep it a secret. Shirra and Donta were the only ones to know about Cadence and I. They kept the secret well and Donta was good company as the maid had a motherly tone towards us. She was only twenty-five and she could be really fun, but at times she could be strict. Still, Shirra and her were close and at times they relied on each other, that being so I too relied on her as Donta relied on me. She didn't care to get involved with assassins, but recognized what I did as good for the health of the King.

I smiled at her and she quickly closed the doors. Shirra came into the room and threw her arms around my neck and gave me a kiss. I smiled and held her tightly wanting to never let her go.

"Hello come to sleep here and steal my food then leave me in the morning?" She teased.

"Yup," I said kissing her again, holding her tightly and kissing her until she gasped for breath.

"We still have a great deal of leftovers, we had stew and pie paste tonight, I will be back with some soon," Donta said ignoring us.

Shirra's room was a big room with silvery coloured walls. There was a huge walk-in closet that had all her clothes and jewellery and a great deal of shoes. The doors to the closet were right now shut, but they were made of stain glass that swirled in a pattern like butterflies and flowers. There was a nightstand by the huge bed piled with pillows, blankets and a very warm navy blue duvet. There was a lamp that turned on when you clapped and hung on one side of the bed over a nightstand. There was another door leading into a bathroom that was bigger than my dad's living room. It had a Jacuzzi and a shower, with a sink and a chandelier that hung from the ceiling adorned with small colourful crystals that flickered like little flames. It wasn't real fire, just a spell, but it made the bathroom light up with thousands of different light blue colours. I couldn't see everything clearly through my eyes, but in her mind, I could see it.

Donta soon returned with a steaming plate and I ate slowly, enjoying each mouthful as Shirra sat beside me leaning against me.

The food was gone too soon and before Donta went to bed, she took the plate and cutlery away.

"Come to bed," Shirra said and yawning I obliged. Snuggling up to her, I fell asleep within moments of putting my head down on the pillow and my arms wrapped around her.

CHAPTER #24

A tune I knew well sounded from my window and as I opened my eyes I could see the bird sitting on the tree not far from my bedroom window. It was a small bird with iridescent colours and I always seen it alone every morning though I didn't know what it was. I shoved the covers off of me and went over to the window to open the window. "Hello birdie," I said with a cheerful smile. I looked over to my bed where Khire slept. His blond hair covering his strange coloured eyes that I loved so much.

I watched him as he slept and it was times like this that I got to see just how peaceful he was. Everyone thought that Dusk was someone great in all ways, but Khire wasn't overly tall, though perfect height for me. His scrawniness made him seem more scrappy then dangerous though I knew better to judge appearance. It was his mind that was dangerous. In one of these rare times though, I could say I knew a more peaceful side of him. A side I brought out in him. I was the key to his heart, mind and soul. He could only be the lovable Khire I know with me, though I cherished every moment I could have him, right now I couldn't. I was to meet with my father and so I had to get ready for my day.

I gave Khire a big kiss to wake him.

"Good morning beautiful," I said to him smiling. "Hi," He said smiling back. He pulled me on top of him and kissed me slowly and in that moment I forgot what I had planned for the day. Nothing in the world mattered when I was with him. I wanted him and only him, I wanted to be with him and I wanted everyone to know that he was mine and only mine.

"Your breath smells bad," He said gently pushing me away, a warm smile on his lips.

"Well so does yours. I have to shower, want to come?" I asked tracing his lips with my finger.

"I think I'd rather sleep," he said squinting up at me.

"Nope I'm not allowed to sleep and neither are you," I said and tore the covers off of him. He groaned and instead of getting off the bed gracefully he rolled off the bed and stumbled after me.

It was funny moments like this that Khire's self-consciousness seemed to be non-existent, much to my liking. He was very protective of his body and didn't like just anyone getting near him. He didn't want to give the last part of himself that was truly his away. He lost his life to Midnight, he lost his love to being an assassin and lost any chance for a real life because of his past. The only thing he felt he had control of is his body and mind and so very few got to meet and understand Khire as he really is. He didn't have to guard his thoughts with me or pretend to be any different. He would however put restraints on us physically. Over the years I had worn him down, so every once in a while he would throw caution to the wind and fully relax with me. I understood him because I was in his mind all day every day, so it was silly that he wanted nothing physical when really I knew his body just as well as he did. I didn't see how his body was strictly his. It was partially mine to, just as mine was his.

One thing I loved was the smell of him and the warm water hitting him always made him smell even better. I tore off my clothes and before he could fully undress, I pulled his boxers down leaving him naked.

"Hey!" he exclaimed a little self-conscious. He turned on the water and got behind the frosted glass door. I walked in after him and he pulled me closer to him and kissed me. He smelled amazing and I kept taking deep breathes of him trying to keep the smell of him in my nose. Khire dumped a huge globe of shampoo on my hair and I let him massage it into my hair.

"Hmmm," I moaned trying to bring him closer to me.

"Focus Shirra," He said and started shampooing his hair.

I took the time to finish my hair and then shave, careful not to cut myself then using more soap then necessary scrubbed myself down. The soap smelled of pomegranates which was one of my more favourite scents. I then re-shampooed his hair. Making sure to get every strand and accidentally getting soap in his eyes.

"Shirra," He complained, swatting my soapy hands away. I pulled him under the water and rinsed his hair as he rubbed his eyes. I put conditioner in his hair and methodically made sure each golden strand was lathered with soap. Once I rinsed his hair, I tried to scrub him down to, but he became squirmy.

"Would you hold still?" I said, grabbing his ear to keep him from running away.

"Shirra, I'm pretty sure I can clean myself," He said annoyed while fending me off.

"Nope," I said and wrapped him in a hug. "I got you now," I said and gave him a kiss.

"You have some place to be," He said trying to sound serious as he kept kissing me back. With a sigh I tried to focus on my day.

Once finished, I got dressed into a warm, dark forest green blouse to bring out my green eyes. I pulled on a pair of black pants and then turned to the mirror to see my hair plastered to my face. Picking up the brush I forced it through my hair and bit my lip, trying to quickly get through the painful knots. With quick tugs I was able to get out all the knots and move on to brushing my teeth. My Guardian Lyteary, a polecat, waited patiently for me. She lay on the ground by my feet enjoying the white, shag carpet she laid on. With a stretch and a yawn she got to her paws and turned to look at me.

"I think you should put your hair up today," she said.

"You think so, mmm, probably, eh," I took a hair band from a drawer and brushed my hair into a ponytail and secured it with the band. My hair would take too long to dry so I usually never bothered even trying. I didn't really like my hair up, my face looked very pale and drawn back, but I would be outside and I didn't want to worry about it flying in my face all day. I shrugged at my reflection and left to go back to Khire.

He was sitting on the bed completely dressed, though still tired. With a yawn he got to his feet, before he could gain his balance I pushed him back down to lie on top of him and kiss him.

"You don't really need to leave yet do you?" I asked.

"Yes, sorry, I know I probably should stay, but I have a lot to do," He said sighing. He had a very nice voice, deep and a little husky, it was a voice I could listen to all day. I smiled down at him then kissed him, trying to make him breathless. Donta was just coming in and I knew I had to get going. With another sigh I left my love.

The halls were long, with paintings hung on both sides and a purple carpet stretching from one side of the hall to the other. I walked down the hall to a staircase that twined up and down to go to different levels. I went down and soon I came to the next level. Unfortunately what I had to do consisted of running down quite a lot of stairs so I wouldn't be late for my father, it was really a work out.

I always wondered why people of high standing always had stairs instead of elevators; you would think that with a lot of money they would have one. I guess the stairs were a good way to get them to do something physical, so it wasn't so bad. I was however a little breathless when I finally got to the last level and found my father and mother with my older sisters waiting by the door. I was sure my cheeks were flushed and my hair not as nice as it should be, but at least I didn't fall down the stairs and come out black and blue. I smiled a breathless smile and greeted them.

"Hello mom, hello dad....hello Isra and Vernaia," I tried to slow my breathing, but it just made me feel more out of breath.

Isra and Vernaia were always pristine, ready to go to a photo shoot at any hour of the day. Both had silky, brown hair and brown eyes. They were tall and slender, Vernaia with a little more of a figure then Isra. We all had the same round face with tanned skin, but they had softer skin while I was callused and scratched up a bit. I was more muscled and shorter than them and looked more like our father while they mostly resembled our mother.

They gave me a warm smile, use to my tardiness. I followed them outside Isra shaking her head at me while Vernaia looped arms with me. The sun wasn't warm and seemed very far away, but everything looked beautiful with fresh sparkling snow blanketing the ground. With the blue stonewalls of the castle against the light dusting of snow on the ground and trees and some icicles hanging in the windows, it started to look like a winter wonderland. This time of year was generally warm, sometimes cool, but the night had dropped below twenty setting a record low for last night. Not prepared for this weather already, my father had issued an order to get all the street people off the streets.

We came out of the front doors and I looked back to try and capture the beauty of the castle and the fresh snow. The front had pillars reaching up to support a veranda that wrapped around the entire castle and joined at the back to a garden where you could go out and walk around. There were three tall towers and two smaller ones. From each of the towers you had a view of the entire city. A forest covered the area from the castle to the city while in the distance the harbour showed where the kingdom's land ended. As it was winter, the trees that surrounded the castle were bare except for the evergreens that stood out sprinkled with snow and made the scene picture perfect.

A slight breeze blew ruffling the trees and wind chimes hanging from all the verandas. It was an old superstition that if the castle didn't have wind chimes on each level then there would be no life in the castle and the kingdom would fall to ruin. There was also a superstition about ghosts to, but as I was not superstitious in any way I found it was absurd. However, my father took such things seriously and so the constant sounds of the wind chimes became a usual sound to me.

Walking out a side entrance to the castle, we came to a garden where a cobbled road lead from the main highway down a tree lined driveway and circled the garden. This entrance was where most drivers came to drop off people or items. It was also where occupants of the castle would leave from. A path lead around the barn to a parking lot where we could get our vehicles then be on our way.

There were only six entrances into the castle, but rumour has it there were also two secret entrances that were still secret even to me. The castle was built to be a fortress for as many people as could fit, the gardens, verandas and statues were added years later. This being so, it was purposefully designed with few entry points, the windows had been smaller and there had been a lot less of them. Because of magic, the castle was able to be revamped and still remain relatively safe against all types of disasters.

The stones were weathered and sun bleached, standing the test of time for over two centuries. It was an old castle, with many add-ons and restorations over the years. Many more gardens were added, with outside patios, the old barn had burnt down many years ago and two new ones built. Balconies were added for most of the bedrooms, the front entrance redone to allow for bigger doors to be put in. The pathway was still the same winding pathway to the castle, but the old cobbles were taken up and new ones put down. The forest was thinned and the old guard towers around the property were torn down and rebuilt with more comfort in mind.

Statues that had stood for decades still graced the castle, placed in gardens and even in the forest. Why there was some in the forest I don't know, but if I had to guess, I'd say dwellings use to be there and the inhabitants were someone of significance. The history of this place dates back to the early 1200's with the first document of the castle dating 1232. Previous to that however, we have no knowledge of this area and the records from the 1200's tell us little of Vale Darra's former occupants. Unfortunately, as much as the mystery behind this place is intriguing and I want to dig up the dirt to uncover all the dark secrets, I have found very little evidence that this place was significant back then. Most likely the people before 1232 had very little reason to write everything down, or records were destroyed in some disaster. I signed, wishing Vale Darra had some momentous past.

Remembering I was with people and headed someplace I returned back to reality and realized I had been starring at the castle while everyone already waited in the carriage.

"Sorry," I apologized, hurrying to my seat.

"It's ok you looked pretty deep in thought. Care to share what has you so serious Shirra?" my father asked smiling.

"Just thinking about the history of this place that's all," I said shrugging.

"Vale Darra is a very old city, known for being peaceful and a place to find refuge. What else would you like to know? You've read the writings in the gardens, they all tell us about former inhabitants and what the buildings use to be for," He answered.

"I know that much, just speculating about other stuff," I told him, not really sure what answer I was looking for.

"Well maybe you should go to some of the historical libraries. Maybe they have something that will satisfy your curiosity," My father said patting me on the knee. I instantly perked up as I knew exactly what library I was going to visit.

I looked out the window, anticipating my visit to Khire's work. Scenery passed us as we made our way down the winding road towards the city. I loved driving in this carriage. It was blue silver, with large sleighs and a large passenger cart. Blue curtains bordered the windows while the benches were covered in warm blankets and cushions. The outside was covered in large plates of metal, made in the design like a log house. Some words were written around the bottom plate of the carriage, but the words were in a foreign language that no one understood now though I'm sure they had meant something to someone at some time.

The musher sat high on a cushioned chair with magical warmers in the seat and the wall behind him. He wore black thick pants with a white jacket over a blue shirt. Black gloves kept his hands warm while a hat with faux fur kept his head and ears warm. His name was Zeariah and he had lived in Vale Darra for only eight years now, but his Wish allowed him to create a magical force field around people so that no one could hear what the people in the bubble were saying. People couldn't even read their lips and so he became employed by my father and has served faithfully ever since.

The carriage wasn't the prettiest carriage we had, but it was the oldest and most comfortable. The two dappled horses that pulled the carriage were my favourite horses we had. Silver Rain and Snow Bell were a great team, well trained and well mannered. They were very smooth and not easily startled making the ride very enjoyable.

We passed people walking outside to go attend their chores. I waved and smiled at them in greeting. People bowed their heads to show their respect and waited for us to go by before moving on. Once we got to the center of the city the musher pulled over and helped us out. He then went off a little farther away to wait for us if we needed him. I followed my family up to a podium standing tall and old. It looked odd in the town, being made out of wood and carved with odd carvings that no one today understood. It was a typical thing to see around the city. Obviously the former residents of the city had spoken a different language, after the world became more developed and people began to use magic, Vale Darra began the changes that would allow it to become the city it is today.

The King walked up to it to stand behind it and deliver his speech. He stood very tall and proud, six foot two with a strong build, a big nose, ruby cheeks and peppered hair. He was every bit the joyful King and he cut a fine figure with his ironed black pants and white shirt with a blue blazer. On the breast, the Vale Darra crest with a sun peeking out behind a cascading waterfall. He had some medallions of honour as well as some badges on his sleeves from his years of service as Vale Darra's King. His crown, resembling a range of mountains, sat on his head and from experience as a little girl I knew that crown was far heavier than it looked. People gathered around to listen to his speech as he motioned for everyone to be quiet. Speakers were spread out throughout the city so that his speech would reach everyone.

"Citizens of Vale Darra! I will not act like nothing is wrong, I know we are in troubled times. And I wish I could tell you that I have an easy solution, but I don't. I don't know how long Vale Darra will be stricken with these acts of violence, but I assure you that I am doing everything in my power to help you. Know that I suffer as you suffer, I cry each tear that you cry and I tremble in fear the same way you do.

"I do not want this to continue, but I am starting to think this is beyond what we could even imagine. So if anyone, anyone at all, has any ideas or suggestions, please let me know. Any knowledge will help. I know it can be intimidating to confess that you may know something and so I offer you complete secrecy. You may come forward to Princess Shirra who has offered to act as councillor for this occasion. She will not require your name or how you may have come about this information and no ill will befall you for coming forth.

"I also please ask that you all give your time to help in any way either by signing up as volunteers or simply staying safe. There will be a curfew set in place between the hours of six pm and 7 am; no one is to be on the streets without permission. There are a few exceptions for police unites, ambulance, hospital staff, the army and the like. Children must be supervised at all times as well. There will be routine census's to assure people. A spell has been in place when everyone has settled down for the night and woken up each morning they have but to say their name. Anyone who does not do this and does not do so in a secure building will be taken into custody and fined or labeled as a missing person.

"These rules are put in place for your security and all of our peace of mind. If anyone has any questions please come up to the podium to my left and speak," The King announced. For the next while, citizens came up and asked questions, all answered professionally and thoroughly. They were all afraid and seeking reassurance though the King could give very little, but the people trusted him.

For the next little while I had people ask me questions as well, tell me things that they thought pertained to the situation or just ask what they could do. I answered each question being careful not to lead onto the fact that I knew far more than a princess should. Khire was in my mind, guiding me in each question telling me what to say so that I could gain as much true information without leading them into making up stories.

All too soon, it grew dark and I and the rest of the royal family loaded into the carriage to go home. We passed a frozen fountain, the angel had her head bowed, hair hiding her sad face, her hands reached out to the pool below her feet. Water that poured out of her eyes had frozen and made her face look distorted. She was called the Weeping Angel.

We passed more statues and people, cheeks and noses red as they walked shivering to go and find somewhere warm. I looked ahead as we passed under a metal frame that arched over the road. I looked back up to the sky and noticed a wispy white cloud slowly gliding in the sky. More were coming in from the horizon, though they were dark in colour.

"Shirra," the King said and I met his eyes.

"Yes dad?" I replied and smiled kindly at him. My other family members listened quietly as our King spoke.

"That boy you spend so much time with. That Khire fellow… I trust you and am very proud of you. He comes from a very honourable family, but I don't know if I trust him. I have heard that he can be very dangerous and not a man to be trifled with. I also ask you something that I want your full honesty on. Is Khire a spy for you and can he help this city?" I could feel my eyes widen and my mind went blank. Even Khire seemed speechless for a moment, but then his words flowed into my head and I spoke them aloud as if they were my own. I tried not to look at Jakk as I spoke though he squinted slightly as he looked at me.

"Khire lives on the street, I really wouldn't call him a spy, only he has been a source of information from time to time. He is just a friend to me and I to him. You don't need to worry about anything between us. He loves this city and he has a way with the street people and a way of hearing things, which he then tells me and in return I heal him. That is all," I said and he nodded.

"I would like to speak with him and pay him to be the King's spymaster if he is interested. He will be honour bound to this city and I. I will pay him very well for his services. I see him in my dreams as a great light surrounded by darkness and I know that he is important. I would not want to press him, but we are in hard times and I know that I need him to help this city in a way that I cannot," The King spoke, his eyes never leaving mine. Jakk was very still beside the King, watching me carefully. I got the sudden feeling that he didn't want his brother being the King's spymaster, but I wasn't sure if it was from protectiveness or something else.

Khire was very silent, thinking, planning till finally he came to the decision that he would love to save the city, but being the King's spymaster would not help him. It would also put too many restraints on him.

"I will ask him when next I see him. Though I know Khire very well, he doesn't do so well with rules. Nonetheless I will ask and see,"

I said, ignoring Khire. I thought it would be great, Khire would be in the castle more and I could see him whenever I liked and not have to sneak around as much, but it would also put us in a vulnerable position. I looked out the window again thinking how best to tell the King that Khire would not be his spymaster.

CHAPTER #25

The light dimmed as a cloud moved across the sun, and Vale Darra seemed to fade. People seemed worried about the weather, though some still walked the streets. I watched them from a chimney on a high roof. The wind was freezing up here, and I had lost feeling in my toes and fingers. I huddled next to the wall, but couldn't stay there much longer so looking around I slid off the roof and landed quietly in the ally. I walked around to warm up.

The King's words went through my head. Being his spymaster would free me of any charges held against me. It would allow me access to regular pay, which would be wonderful, and it would bring me closer to Shirra. However, I would have to pledge magical oaths to the King, binding and unbreakable oaths that I must serve the King and the entire kingdom for life. It would give the King a lot of power over me, which I didn't like. I did not want another master, though I thought highly of the King I didn't want to serve him directly. I also didn't like how close he came to guessing what I really am. An assassin working alongside a King is not anything new, most kingdoms had assassins, but I didn't want to be the first for King Esmir. He had multiple spies that served him well, I joining them would reveal too much of me to too many. Also my brother would be there and I didn't care to stand before him telling everyone all I've done.

I ran through the alleyways to try and create heat, and as I wandered through the streets I came to the nicer parts of the city. The streets were wide and snowy with only footprints marking it. I turned to look both ways down the street, but no one was near. Still I turned back and headed around where I could cross the street safely without being seen. My thin clothes weren't very warm, running was the only thing creating heat for me, but I hadn't eaten much today and running would make me hungry. I had gone to the bank to get out some money, but it appeared my money was being watched. So unfortunately I couldn't access it and Shirra couldn't put money into it without people noticing. Due to that I couldn't buy myself anything warmer, so I was left running around trying to keep warm.

After some time I ended up going to sleep with Shirra. Climbing in to her bed and snuggling in close. With a long kiss we talked for a little bit, but slowly I drifted off to sleep and anything Shirra said to me was lost in a dreamy haze.

☾

I was sitting at my desk when the bell chimed. I growled at it and got out of my chair. The bell positioned in every room went off when a murder was reported. Since most people died from being murdered and I was the head detective who dealt with homicide cases, I had to respond to the bell. I was newly appointed to detective, though had dealt with the Dusk case for many years. Still it was nice to officially be called detective. I went looking for my boss as usually he liked to be involved.

Ludah wasn't in his office, but instead was at the front desk. He was talking to three young boys in baseball caps accompanied by two adults who seemed shaken.

"We were just throwing rocks in the river, we didn't know what it was at first it just floated to the surface," One of the boys said excitedly.

"Fetcher there you are. These boys were standing on the bridge by the mall and believe they have found the body of a dead person," Ludah said to me and I sighed.

"Ok I'm on it," I said. While Ludah got any information he could from the boys I went out to investigate the scene.

The bridge was taped off to allow investigators to survey the scene. People who wanted to get to the mall were either grouchy and yelling at us or stopped to watch the excitement. A few left to take other routes to the mall, but for the most part there was a crowd.

"Ok get the tarps up!" I shouted and the crowd groaned. Quickly, magical barriers were put up to stop onlookers from seeing anything. Already a diver was positioned on the bank, an arm of the machine reaching out over the water ready to submerse itself and collect anything at the bottom of the river.

"Have you found anything?" I asked a lady in brown glasses who was writing things down.

"Yes actually, a body is definitely at the bottom. We have it held in place with magic so once the diver gets it up we can study it. There's not much to it, mostly bones," The women said shrugging.

"Ok," I said and sighed. This was going to be a long day.

It took an entire hour for the diver to collect all the body parts, or what was left of it anyway, from the bottom of the river. Once the body was brought up pictures of it were taken then the bones were dropped into a tank. The tank sat on a trailer pulled by a truck which was driven to the station. It was all very strategic; bodies were discovered regularly so it wasn't a surprise. About 60 people died in this river along this stretch each year, they were collected once every three months usually though some were missed or in this case due to funding cut backs we haven't been able to do a proper search in over a year.

I followed behind the truck and trailer with the tank, lights flashing all the way.

"Dispatcher connect me to Ludah please," I said into my radio.

"Right away Fetcher," A female voice said.

"Ludah here, what do you got for me?" Ludah asked sounding alert.

"We've recovered a body from the river," I reported.

"Ok bring it in and we'll find out who it is," Ludah said simply. It was a sad thing when reporting a death was boring.

Just last month someone had supposedly drowned in the river and the body was never found. Though I knew this body couldn't be the same body it made me realise how much time I devoted to my other duties and neglected others. I had not even thought about collecting the bodies in the river and wondered how many were down there that could put people's hearts to rest. I knew the investigators I left at the scene would make sure any other bodies were collected and brought in, but I knew that I should have been the one to make the call to collect the bodies not three boys.

I was looking forward to going home at the end of the day and sleep, I had tomorrow off so I was constantly looking at the clock and counting down the minutes. It was 4:36 and I had to make it to 7 o'clock. I sighed when I realized I still had stuff to do and not enough time to do it in.

At the station any bodies that were found were brought in to be investigated. Usually bodies were taken to the hospital, but murder cases or possible murder cases were not. This gave the doctors at the hospital more time to just deal with their job and gave the investigators easier access to the bodies. I parked my car and went back to my office. I would be noted in the next few days of the results and then I would have to make the newer cops go and tell the families of the persons death.

☾

CHAPTER #26

I wrapped my arms around Khire and pulled him tighter against me. I breathed in his scent and smiled with pure happiness. I was really warm from sleeping under the covers and I didn't want to move, but I wanted to be closer to Khire. I wrapped my leg around him and rolled on top of him, pushing his back against the mattress. He stirred slightly, but continued to sleep peacefully.

"Khireal," I said in a singsong voice. He didn't answer and so I whispered his secret name into his ear. His eyes opened slightly and he smiled drunkenly.

"Hi," he said looking up at me with his blue eyes. He couldn't see me clearly, but I knew he thought me the most beautiful person on this planet. His body was all tingly from me saying his name out loud and so I said it again. This time I sent shivers down his body and made him kiss me. I kept repeating his name in my head until he rolled on top of me and kissed me so long I couldn't breathe. I could feel his heart beating faster, his blood pulsing through his body, his mind was blank as the euphoria took over his body.

"I need… to… breath," I gasped and he laughed. He pushed himself up so he sat on my hips looking down at me.

"Good morning," he said huskily.

"Morning," I said smiling. I pushed him off of me and stretched. I always had a lot to do each day and so I couldn't waste it snuggling with Khire much to my dislike.

Donta came in with her hands already on her hips. "Do you know what you're going to wear Shirra?" She asked knowing I didn't.

"No," I said apologetically then leaped to my feet and went into the closet. Pulling random clothes from hangers I put them on. I came out wearing a pink fleece tank top with a cotton blue sweater and a black skirt. I smiled at everybody when I realized this then turned back around to get properly dressed.

The next time I came out I wore a long sleeved baby blue shirt with a very warm, black vest over top. Nice warm socks and long, dark blue pants.

"Better?" I asked and Donta rolled her eyes then returned to watering the plants in my room. I sat down beside Khire as he put his bowl of food he had been eating aside on the bedside table.

"What are you doing?" Khire asked.

"I have to go with my dad to some place in Hopkit," I said then yawned. I would have preferred to stay here, but I knew my father would wait no longer. I wrapped my arms around Khire, stole a long kiss then ran out the door. I took my stair exercises as I dashed down the staircase and finally came to the bottom where my father was just pulling on his jacket.

"There you are Shirra," He said with a smile. I smiled back and walked over to him breathless. A servant passed me a coat and I took it with a thank you.

I was breathing hard, but I pulled on my coat and tried to look respectable. I checked my reflection in a mirror and found my cheeks flushed, but other than that I was fine and ready to go out. My hair was in a simple ponytail again, but I didn't care to look like a Princess today. Before I left the castle I forgot I hadn't brushed my teeth, thankfully some great person invented breath mints and after a hand full of those I felt slightly cleaner.

I climbed into the waiting carriage after my father and we went off. It took us half an hour to got to our destination. People were rushing around frantic as the streets filled with the huge fluffy flakes of snow.

"What's going on?" The King asked flustered.

"My King, there has been a terrible tragedy the Queen of Tobberen was murdered along with her guards, and her squires," A servant who had run by, but had stopped when he noticed the King spoke hurriedly. The King looked thoughtful for a minute then spoke.

"It was Dusk wasn't it?" He asked, a note of anger in his voice. The Queen of Tobberen lived far off to the East, but was a valuable trading partner to us.

"Think so, Your Majesty," The servant said with a nod. With a wave from the King he ran off to return to doing whatever he was doing.

"We need to do something with this Dusk," The King said thoughtfully.

"Was it him? If I recall the Queen was a very strong magic user. She also had many books on magic," I said trying to get him to piece some of this weird puzzle together.

"Hmm so you think it's this new assassin or whatever he is?" My father asked and I shrugged unable to give him a proper answer.

I feared what would happen if he found out I knew Dusk and if he found out I was in love with him. It wasn't like I would ever be on the throne and I could just as easily remove myself from the line entirely by handing in my tiara and becoming a full time doctor, but I didn't feel ready yet to leave home. I was 22 years old so I should have a plan, but I always knew I would be a doctor. So I felt no drive to actually make the leap and become a doctor and leave my princess life behind right now. I had my whole life ahead of me, my schooling, getting my own house, there was so much ahead of me. Accept that I could never have Khire because he was an assassin and marrying him would put us both in a tremendous amount of danger.

"Well let's continue Musher," The King said and tapped the side to tell the musher to go. The carriage slid across the snow on its skies and in some minutes we were climbing out of it to walk up a walkway to a castle. This one wasn't as wide or as long as ours, but it was taller, with eight towers pointing at the sky. The clouds were very low here and the tops of the towers disappeared as they pierced through them.

I followed my father and a few servants into the castle then to a meeting room. This was going to be long and boring, but I was prepared. We all sat down and as more Kings and Queens came with a son or daughter we all greeted them. Once everyone was here the meeting started and I sat there listening to every word. It was general talk at first, discussing boundaries, old laws and criminals which lead us eventually to talk about Dusk. After three hours of going in circles it was all over and we all returned to our home kingdoms.

By the time I got home the last thing I wanted to do was sit, but lunch was being served and I wasn't excused to go eat it in my room. So I sat at the table in the large dining room with the rest of my family to eat lunch. There were portraits of late Kings and Queens surrounding us and talk of Dusk's newest victim to fill the silence. I was able to say not a word and the lunch ended fortunately quickly.

Finally I was able to leave and I headed up to my room.

"Gaaaa why can't anything be going right for a change! I wish we could just go find whoever is killing all these people and stop him!" I said as I came over and stood before Khire, arms crossed. I was tired and frustrated and just wanted a break from the hectic whirlwind of life. Khire looked at me, his head tilted to the side.

"How was the meeting?" He asked.

"Oh you know, annoying as always, we just talked about laws, and boundary lines. Then we got into a talk about Dusk, but it was just asking questions about what to do with you and no one answered them" I shook my hair as I pulled out the band.

Shirra came in and I watched her knowing she was tired and slightly annoyed. I listened to her speak then patted the side of the bed and let her lean against me.

"So I was wondering if we could go out and have some fun, you know, like normal people do?" She asked.

"Sorry, but I'm busy, I'm leaving again," I said putting an arm around her. "Again! Khire," She tilted her head and looked at me pleadingly. I shook my head and with a quick smile I got to my feet. She glared at me, arms crossed as I stared smiling down at her.

"It's just a week," I told her and she sighed. Before I could turn and leave she got to her feet and wrapped her arms around me then pulled me down onto the bed. I kissed her fiercely, holding her so tightly she squeaked. I could feel my arms around her ribs, feel the pressure on her ribs as if there were my own ribs and I smiled, loving the feeling of being so close to someone else.

"Well then be safe," she said, her voice muffled.

"Be back soon," I told her and walked swiftly to the veranda.

Once I opened the doors I turned to look at her.

"Remember in a week, I'll be back, make sure supper's hot," I told her.

"Sure street boy, now out and be gone," She joked as she made a shooing motion with her hands; I jumped off the veranda with Myre behind me. Ribbons, blue-purple, circled us, slowing us down until we hit the snowy ground lightly. We lunged across the ground to make as little tracks as possible.

We got to the front gate of the city and received a grey dappled horse that was more than happy to leave. His name was Dust, my brother had trained and raised him, Dust being born from one of my brother's, Shean's, mares. Dust smelt me, remembering my sent and once he was tacked up I mounted. He pranced and snorted when I held him back and let other horses and riders go. I nodded at a guard and left. Dust fought with me as he wanted to head straight into a dead run, but I held him back and got him into a choppy trot.

In a few hours we were both sweating as the day had turned unusually warm, but I only stopped for ten minutes when we found a watering hole. Dust nickered when we saw a deer and young fawn stare at us from across the water. The deer turned its head and eyed us suspiciously while the fawn kicked up its heels and played in the cold water. It would stop every now and then and look at us with one eye then go back to frolicking. Tail wagging and ears swivelling every which way as it walked around, bringing its feet up high as it came farther into the deeper water.

With a smile to myself I slowly drew back, the deer became alert, but surprisingly didn't bolt as I tightened all that I had loosened on the saddle and bridle then left. It was at that moment the deer and fawn fled and dashed off to the safety of the trees that were nearby.

Myre and I continued on, Myre jogging beside us as we made our way towards a small town known as Bogg. It wasn't anywhere near a bog, but it's first inhabitants were a family with the last name Bogg and so it came to be called Bogg. It was generally a friendly little town, but there was a gang there that I wished to meet. I left Dust at a stable that agreed to take care of him and walked into the streets. The gang was an open bunch, instead of waiting in the alleys to jump people they stood around a beat up picnic table that was situated by a fountain. The fountain was once nice, but now was a swimming pool for the homeless and so people could say little about it. They were in the lesser part of the town as most people preferred to stay away from the gang, so there were no eyewitnesses around.

I walked into the square and looked around confused as if I had taken a wrong turn and didn't know where I was.

"Hello, can you guys tell me how to get back to the town hall? I think I took a wrong turn somewhere silly me," I said walking up to them.

"Oh ya, we can help you out man," One guy said smiling.

"Great, I tell ya this town is like a maze," I said sounding relieved.

They walked slouched towards me wearing baggy stained pants and long t-shirts with the sleeves torn off. Their speech had a slight slur, but they wore enough jewellery to make you think they were rich. The one that approached me wore a black and grey cap sideways. He grabbed my shoulder with an overly large hand full of spiked rings and turned me to face him directly. His other hand had spikes on them as well, but I wasn't worried.

"Can I help you with anything?" I asked calmly.

"No man, we're cool," He smiled and as soon as he moved to punch I flipped out a small knife and drew it across his throat.

He fell to the ground surprised and before the other gang members could react, they too fell to the ground dead and bleeding from a cut across the throat or a stab to the heart. I looked at the people and wrinkled my nose, they stared shocked at the ground or sky, their eyes dull, but their blood stunk horribly as if it were toxic. With them finished, I left them to their rest, leaving them for people to find and know that they were dead.

Myre brushed against me and I stopped walking, I heard laughter and turned to see a skinny old man with white hair sitting on the ground laughing. I could tell that he was blind by the way he didn't turn his head to face me.

"I know you," He taunted and by the sound of his voice I knew he was crazy. I walked up to him and smiled. "I know you to," I whispered threateningly into his ear and with a quick swipe, he was dead. One more homeless person dead on the ground would mean nothing to the police when they found him later.

I turned and ran all the way to the main street then slipped into the stable that held Dust. With as much fuss as I could manage I complained about having come all this way to go to a meeting just for it to be cancelled. I got Dust and left in a huff. We galloped away towards a clump of trees and with no one watching us; we disappeared from Bogg.

CHAPTER #27

The next day I was in another town called Rambuck and it was times like this I marvelled at how big the kingdom was. The King ruled Vale Darra plus multiple dukedoms together creating Esmir's Kingdom. Rambuck was only a tiny little town situated on the side of a rocky hill and all the people were either loggers, shoemakers or farmers. Hundreds of acres spread out wide in all directions to allow for large herds of sheep. Some cows mingled together in clumps, but the fields were dominated by sheep. Some boys and their dogs sat or stood watching over the flocks. All the sheep were watched over by the entire community. When it came time to shear them, the owners would ride out and gather all the sheep into pens which would then allow people to sort them out to their proper owners.

I stopped Dust just before the trees gave way to clear plains and tied him to a tree. I ate a granola bar while he grazed and we waited for dusk. It didn't take long, but when I got up to move I was stiff and I had to walk around just to loosen my muscles. Dust was at this point board and nibbling on his reins.

"Stop that! If I come back here and find you gone I'll tell Shean," I threatened the horse as if he could understand me. Dust looked at me then stretched his long nose out looking for treats.

"I don't have anything for you, you be a good horse and stay here," I said then left him.

The stars were coming out as I moved towards the town. People hardly slept here so I got into the town later then I would have liked as I took a long time moving from brush to stone to building to get into the center of the town without being seen. Here I planted a bomb inside a building where people gambled, dealt drugs and prostituted themselves. It would go off later in the week. That done it was a simple matter of leaving and moving on.

I was moving at a fast pace, the third day going past me, but I made sure to slow down so that I didn't attract attention. The next place was a small city, heavily guarded, but I knew my way around it well enough and so I left Dust out of sight of anyone coming by road or anyone in the city. At this time it was early morning on the fourth day, but it was still dark and so I snuck up to the city. There were no walls, but there were cameras everywhere and so when I got to one camera I froze the picture. I'd fix it later, but for now, I had to stay unseen. I did that to several cameras this town being advanced in its technology. For some reason this town was always on high security as if the very King of Vale Darra himself lived here. There were very few mages in this town so this town depended on technology run on solar power or electricity more than magic.

I was coming up to a building that would be my target when a group of people walked onto the same alleyway I was on. I jumped behind a dumpster and waited quietly, Myre curled up beside me. They were talking, but I couldn't understand them as they spoke in a language that I didn't know. I pressed myself into the dumpster and brick wall that was at my back as they walked right past me without even glancing at me. Once they were out of sight I got up and went over to the building. This building was kept in great shape and it took a while for me to even find a way to get into it. The windows were locked and bolted, though there were no magical guards, this building was still difficult for me to enter without attracting attention. The front door was way to open and there were no loose stones that I could move to make a tunnel to get inside. I looked around and when I seen the garbage can, empty and waiting by the door I decided that was as good as any. I put a tiny bomb in the inside of the garbage can. When people came to work here they would carry it inside and it would go off later.

I left and circled around to another building. This one already had people working in it and so I found someone about my height with blond hair and pale blue eyes. Conveniently he came outside for a smoke. When he had his back turned I crept up behind him and knocked him out. Catching him, I lowered his limp body to the ground and though I wasn't happy about it, took off his jacket and put it on me. It was big and smelt weird. I wasn't going to go as far as completely undressing him so I dashed into the main entrance and slipped into an office close by. There were no cameras thankfully in here so I quickly stuck a bomb in a small hole in the wall that I had made in the back of a large closet and set the bomb, again it would go off when the others went off. I dashed out again and took off the jacket to put it back on the person. I quickly put the jacket back on him then left.

I spent the rest of the day resting to make sure Dust got rest, food and water as well as I and Myre. I checked on Dust constantly, but he was more than happy to stay where he was. It was hard getting out as day four turned to day five, people were everywhere, but I reset the cameras and managed to leave with only a few people seeing me. One woman, determined to make everybody want to tear out their hair stopped me before I could go get Dust.

"Hey, boy, help me. Don't be so rude!" She commanded and when I stared at her dumbly she advanced on me as if she were about to hit me, but I stepped back out of her swing and put my hands up.

"Sure, what do you need?" I asked confused.

"I need these boxes in that building," She growled.

She pointed to a warehouse and two-dozen boxes that waited to be placed in the warehouse. The boxes didn't look too heavy, but I didn't understand why I had to do it and so I looked at her.

"You stupid boy, do you not understand! Put those boxes in there! Now!" And with that I nodded and got to work, bewildered by this situation. She watched me, hands on hips, eyes narrowed.

"Who are you?" She asked cranky. She seemed to have no sense of personal information and no trouble asking questions and speaking her mind.

"Umm, I'm..." I started, but she cut in.

"What's the matter, forgot your own name, boy! Never mind just work!" I picked up the box that was heavier than it looked and slowly carried it inside.

She kept yelling at me and telling me what she thought of me though I glared at her and tried unsuccessfully to ignore her.

"Know what, your pathetic, you are as dainty and weak as a little girl," She told me looking at me with her arms now crossed. I wasn't as 'dainty and weak as a little girl' I was just tired.

"I should have gotten a man to help me, what a pitiful thing you are," She shook her head and when I stopped working she yelled at me and advanced on me to smack me in the head. I was so surprised I just stood there and dropped the box.

"Be careful with that! Don't you know how fragile crystal is? That box better have nothing broken in it!" She scolded and I sighed.

"Look, I have to go," I told her and she turned on me.

"Oh no you don't those boxes are not all in there," She said and I straitened up.

"I don't care! Do them yourself you fat whale!" I yelled back at her as indeed she was very fat. She looked shocked, but soon recovered.

"Why, you little twit..." Before she could go on I turned and left her. She continued to yell at me even when her voice cracked and I was out of earshot and eyesight.

"You handled that extremely well," Myre said out loud as he rolled his eyes.

"Shut up," I growled back and finally left the city and got Dust.

I had now wasted an entire day, but I mounted and road Dust hard to the next destination. This one was a day away, and so I was behind schedule, but I wasn't in any mood to dwell on that and so I got to the next town as the sun was setting on the fifth day. This town was a little place with a population of just 3000. People were scattered throughout the town and I walked right up to a building and went inside.

I was focused on getting the job done now and so I walked up to the person I would be killing tonight.

"Hello, I'm looking for a job," I said instantly friendly. He was a little set off by my forwardness, but shook my hand and welcomed me inside his office. He offered me a seat and I sat. He arranged a few things on his desk then addressed me.

"So why are you coming to me and why are you interested in here?" He asked me simply, sounding a little confused.

"I heard from a friend of mine that he got great business from here, I have just left my job, my employer was coming in drunk and I wanted to get out of that place. I like the friendliness of this place and knowing you have a great business I was instantly interested," I said. I kept my voice polite and soft, my posture a little stiff to signify that I was more for perfection while my smile told him I was friendly. He nodded along, but didn't entirely relax which told me I was coming off a little too harsh. I took a deep breath to try and relax myself, but found I couldn't just brush off my irritation.

"Tell me about yourself then," He said and I started.

"Well I come from Vale Darra, I like to spend my time working around the house, I don't have a family, but I'm fine with that. I like to take things apart to see how they're made, I tend to be the leader most often," I rambled on trying to sound polite and sure of myself.

"Great, great, great, now, what job are you interested in?"

"Oh, well.... Oh I'm sorry, by the way I'm Majeer," I said acting like I totally forgot.

"Right, I'm Mr. Gusher Hoover senior," I was a little surprised, but covered it up.

I was talking to the right name, but I hadn't realise there was a senior and a junior.

"Ok, well I'm interested in talking to people, I like to be on the road a lot, I am a great spokesperson, I have always been one going around trying to interest people in things,"

"So you want to be a salesperson," He said though not as a question. "Yes," I said.

"Well we already have a lot of people out in the field, but I can try you out. Do you have any questions?"

"Yes, if I were to work here what environment would I be in? Are there people here who like to bring their kids in? Would I be dealing with drama or anything?" I asked leaning forward. "Well my son, Gusher jr., comes in every now and then," That was who my actual target was I guessed because this guy seemed too clean cut. "The atmosphere is usually light, we have some pranksters who like to make their little acts, but I like to think this place is quiet friendly,"

"How did this place come about?" I asked resting my chin in my hand and my elbow on my arm rest. "Well I grew up in a very bad place and by the time I was twenty five I was pretty much on my death bed, but I decided to turn my life around and so I started this business. I wanted to help people master their own demons like no one was able to help me. It's been hard and I have been tied into some troubles lately, but I have finally cut off all strings that have attached me to my troubles. I let everybody go and hired new people, I gave them training and now I am in a better place. I just hope my son shapes up soon,"

"Why, if you don't mind me asking, what's up with your son?" I asked him and put some magic into my voice to make him want to tell me.

"Well he's a trouble maker, partying, getting in fights, he's recently been caught up in a murder case. I've been helping him and he's been coming here more and more often. I and my wife have got people helping him as well. We're doing so much, but I don't know what else to do," His voice dropped by the end and we both sat there in silence.

The one thing I loved about small town people was their openness, just a little magic and they would pour out their deepest darkest secrets to you in a heartbeat.

"Well can I meet him? I have some experience personally with a few issues with the police and the law. I've been on the streets and have managed to pick myself up. I can't promise anything, but I hear I'm pretty good at getting people to open up," I said smiling. He seemed not sure of what to say.

"Well sure," He said simply and after a quick phone call his son was on his way here. "This office is sound proof, I will leave and let you talk with him privately," He said with a nod, he moved slowly in a weird sort of trance as my magic took control of him, convincing him to tell me everything and leave without thinking this strange.

"Thank you," I nodded back.

He left and Myre and I waited.

"What are you doing?" Myre asked me.

"Look we're running out of time, let's just threaten the kid and move on," I told him. He nodded and rested his head on his paws. A boy walked into the room and waited by the door. I turned around and smiled. He was fat, with a big round sweaty face and greasy, long black hair. He wore a long green shirt with large jeans and sneakers.

I held back my distaste for him, fighting to keep the smile in place. "Hi," I got up and extended my hand. He shook it gingerly then went to his father's chair and sat down.

"You don't know me," He said after a while. "You don't know what I've been through, so what makes you so sure that you can help me?" His voice was tight and his eyes were cautious as he spoke.

"I'm not here to help you, I'm here to save you," I said putting my hands on the desk and leaning forward. "You don't smarten up and your gonna be filling your own grave real soon. I know what you do, I know where you go and I know who you hang out with. I know you and if for one moment you put one toe out of line, I'll cut that toe off. Got that?" I said harshly.

"Who are you?" The boy asked taken off guard.

"A very dangerous enemy or a very valuable ally, it's your choice which I'll be to you. Now listen, your little gang and drug-dealing business is over, you want out, I'm opening the door for you, but I will close it just as fast. Here is what you will do. You're going to let go of all the deals, pay them all off and walk away. Next you're going to go to your gang leader and tell him you're not part of his anymore and if he got a problem with that he can face you in a match. Tell him you got the shadows on your side. Then walk away without a glance at anyone, walk confidently and slowly.

"Leave them all and never talk to them ever again, act like they don't even exist. You're going to drop everything you do and start going to school again. You'll succeed and get a good job and at the end of the day you can still say your hearts beating.

"I'll be waiting for you to slip up, just once and I'll be after you," I said, my voice dark and deep. He was pale faced and nodded stupidly.

"What will you do to me?" He asked.

"I only give warnings once boy, you even so much as make one little mistake and you're going to feel pain like you've never felt it before. You'll be worse than dead when I finish with you. I'll make it a slow torture, so terrible you'll beg me to kill you. You'll experience a darkness where no light can exist," I said darkly and his eyes went wide, his face clammy and ghost white.

"Cut your hair and wear nice clothes, lose some weight and shower regularly. Be a person you take pride in, not a pathetic, greasy rat," I added. I was going to say some nastier things, but I remembered how I was when I was younger and fat. The last thing I needed was someone to remind me how ugly and fat I was.

I left him to think it over hoping he would listen and clean himself up.

"How'd it go?" His father asked me as I put on a smile.

"Good, I think he listened to me. Just be there for him, and treat him like an equal not as a kid or as a trouble maker. I think he needs a good friend not a father right now," I said and he nodded. I nodded back and began to leave.

"Hey don't you want a job here?" He asked as I started to leave.

"No, it's ok, I have some thinking to do," I told him and left.

I had other things to do now, the bombs had gone off and people were walking around talking non-stop about it as I went and left them to get Dust. Blowing up the buildings wasn't really a big deal. They were either the homes of drug dealers or public buildings that weren't certified to code anymore. They were all falling down anyway, but the owners insisted on fighting the police and saying they were ok. Blowing them up was the easiest way I could think of to resolve the matter. Now I could go home. I left, riding out on Dust. It would take me three days to get back so I couldn't stop yet.

Dust snorted as we raced across the flat ground, he was happy to be galloping, happy to really stretch his legs. His main flying, head up and tail held proudly, he galloped as the sun rose and crossed the sky. I slowed him when we came up to a well. Dust was sweating even though it was getting chilly. I took off the saddle and blanket, then slipped the bit and let him find whatever grass he could to graze.

Myre drank from the well and afterwards so did I. I didn't have any food, but I didn't care, I would be home soon and Shirra would have something prepared. I was thankful for this well, it was one of several wells placed around the countryside for travels who were lost or traveling by other means then a car. It was a little piece of paradise.

I sat there so long that a bird flew down and perched close by me to get some water. I watched it as it hopped and eyed me, head twitching. I didn't know what kind of bird it was and neither did Myre, but I continued to watch it for a while until it flew off again small wings carrying it up. At this point Dust had lain down and had rolled in the grass so when I got up I had to swipe the grass and whatever dirt I could off him. He pranced; ready to go for another go while I put the saddle blanket and saddle back on and tightened the bridle. When I mounted I put him to a trot and gave him his head though I still kept a light contact on the reins so he knew who was in charge. When he was younger he gave Shean a hard time, Dust was always trying to do what he liked, and though he was now eight years old and trained well, he still had that stubborn streak in him.

When I came close to Vale Darra, it had been more than a week since I had been here. I left Dust with a groom at the main gate and I decided to go to my dad's house. It took me nearly an hour to walk there, but I thought it would be nice to visit him. I knocked a few times on his door before he answered it.

"Well isn't this a nice surprise," My dad said happily as he greeted me. I smiled and said hi then walked past him to the living room.

"You look like you haven't showered in a week," Dad said bluntly and I frowned at him.

"I've been on the road," I said simply.

Even though I grew up in this house and even though I knew this house more than any other home, I still found it difficult to walk around in it. My Wish changed the house into a strange maze, my senses told me a lot of what was around me, but I couldn't see everything and sensing something that was right in front of you, but not being able to actually see it was disorienting.

I situated myself on the couch, sitting back and deep in the comfy cushions with Myre leaning against my side. I petted him absentmindedly as Dad sat down across from me.

"Did you hear about those bombs?" Dad asked, his eyes wide.

"I heard from a friend that some terrorist planted a bomb," I said shrugging not concerned.

"No one knows, but I betcha it was Dusk and there was more than one bomb,"

"Why would you say that?" I asked.

"I don't know, those places needed to be destroyed, they were no good, and though I don't really support Dusk, I don't blame him for destroying the buildings either," He shrugged.

"So Dusk hasn't been killing here?" I asked puzzled.

"He has, on the odd night, but you know assassin's they can be very mysterious in their ways. I'm sure he found a way to do it," and that was the end of that.

My dad wanted me to stay longer, but after two hours I said goodbye, he complained and grumbled, but I hugged him and left him still grumbling to himself. Standing in the entryway frowning with arms crossed and face set sternly and miserably. I waved at him as I walked away and with a huff and some other words he turned around, closed the door and left me to walk alone on the streets of Vale Darra.

Shirra was waiting for me and so I headed over to the castle, my stomach growling and anticipating the food I would get. Taking a long way so no one would see me, I circled part of Vale Darra and meandered my way to the tall castle. The sun came out, though did little to warm the chilly day.

The city was quiet, cars moving sluggishly through the snowy streets while people walked around trudging through the soft snow as they worked their way to their destination. I avoided meeting people or them seeing me by evading the busier streets and only crossed where the streets were less populated. I wanted people to see me so that they knew I was back, but I didn't want to seem suspicious and so I kept the sightings small.

When I finally got to the castle Shirra opened the veranda doors right before I even stepped foot on her veranda. She wrinkled her nose and immediately shoved me towards the bathroom to get cleaned up. After showering and getting into clothes that Shirra had bought for me I came out of the bathroom. She smiled and I walked in to sit on her bed. I was tired, but Shirra wouldn't let me sleep. She asked a bunch of questions till I crawled up to her pillows and fell asleep ignoring her. She shook her head and crawled up beside me, wrapping her arms around me, and snuggling close. She fell asleep even though she had little to do today to make her tired.

What felt like an hour was actually three and when I awoke, tiredness hadn't left me and I was very hungry. Donta came in and gave us food, steaming and delicious I ate faster than I should have before she managed to get the plate of food away from me.

"Slow down or it will just come up again," She growled. After that I ate slowly.

☾

CHAPTER #28

I snuggled into Khire as he dozed. Smiling, I slipped my hand up his chest and kissed him, waking him up.

"Hi," He said, his lips moving against mine.

"Good morning, Handsome," I said meeting his eyes. He smiled, a look of pure happiness that rarely came across his face. He turned onto his side and put his arms around me.

"What do you want to do?" He asked me.

"What do I want to do? Well I have a few ideas," I said sliding my hands lower. He smiled amused, but grabbed my arms and wrapped them around himself.

"You asked me what I wanted to do, why ask if we're not going to do it anyway?" I pouted. He snuggled closer, somehow, he was already as close as I thought he could get. He fit his body to mine and kissed me slowly. Melting into him I kissed him back.

Breathing hard, I stopped kissing him to take a breath. Not wanting to ruin anything I didn't want to talk, just make out, but I had to talk to him.

"So, what do you want to do today?" I asked.

"Mmmhhhhh," He said kissing my neck.

"Just stay here all day?" I asked tracing his face with my fingers.

"Mmmmmm," He said, eyes still closed.

"Go for a walk or a ride to the mountains?" I asked.

"Mmmmmm," He repeated.

"Go swimming at the beach?" I asked. I kept asking him different things, but he just kept saying the same thing.

"Ok let's do something besides this," I said and got up, pulling him up with me.

"Fine ok," He said rubbing his eyes.

I wrapped my arms around him and hugged him tight as he slid his arms around me. After a moment he began to pull me back to bed.

"Oh no we're going out," I said pulling him back up.

"Hhmm what?" He said grumbling.

We ended up on two horses going on a ride to the mountains. The Lost Mountains were small mountains covered with trees. I always wondered about the name. How a mountain could be lost was beyond me, but that's what they were called. It would take us at least two hours to get to the base of them, but that didn't matter. I just wanted to be with Khire.

It was on rare occasions like this that we actually went out. I knew the story of Khire and his ex-girlfriend and I never blamed him for what he did. He never meant to kill her, it was an accident. Still it troubled him that he could be so evil as to kill someone he so dearly loved. After losing Miranna, Khire became very protective of his things. If ever we went out, which we would do some times undercover, he would follow me around as if he were my personal shadow. And he was always asking me if I was ok or if I was comfortable or if someone was bugging me at work. I loved him, but sometimes he did get on my nerves.

It was funny how someone who killed people would be so huggable and caring like Khire. Also he was as honest as an assassin could be and he even had morals. He has had just about everything taken away from him. No say in his life, his job, where he could live, everything seemed chosen for him before he could even dream to think what he would want to be. Because of this he held on to anything he could control or keep to himself. The one thing he held dear to him, besides me, was his body. He said though he was beaten on a regular basis and he gets cut up all the time, his body still belonged to him and he still had say over his body. It was this strange fact that kept him a virgin, which I think absolutely absurd. I have talked to him about it telling him that I was in his mind, I felt everything he did, it wouldn't be stealing anything from him if we had sex. But he wasn't ready to let it go and so insisted on keeping it clean between us.

He was an assassin and I felt the dangerousness even as I knew the dangerousness of getting involved with someone like him. I knew the penalties when you dealt with death and as I knew right from the start I would enter into deaths games, I still know and still stand firm to my decision to remain with Khire. Already I have been out and helping Khire to kill the bad, I myself have slipped a poison into victim's drinks then smiled at them as if I were all charms. I have given information to aid Khire and I will continue to do so as I see that it is right.

People say that your mind is turned when you think of death, if that is so then so be it that my mind be turned. I looked at death with a new light when I entered into the world of the assassins and I continue to stay in that world for now until I die. As with anyone, once you're involved with one assassin, you're involved with the rest. I, though not really an assassin like Khire or Cadence, am still seen as a threat, someone another assassin could either call on for aid or see as an obstacle that needs to be taken out. I may not have the honour to say that I am an assassin, but I do have the honour to say that I am an assassin's assistant. It was the fact that I was the best healer in Vale Darra that made most assassins not bother to go after me. I was too valuable alive.

Snow covered the ground, though here and there rocks and dead bushes would emerge from the snow. It was mid-November and though the nights had been chilly, it was a nice day to go for a ride. The two horses we rode, a pretty flea bitten mare and a dun gelding, weren't particularly happy about leaving their barn buddies, but they willingly rode on. They tossed their heads after a little while, pulling on the reins and trying to turn around to go back home, but after a few minutes of fussing we convince them that we were in control and we didn't want to go back yet. We entered the forest at the foothills of the mountains and began a gentle climb upwards. "Well this was a good idea," Khire said smiling. I pulled off the blond wig and took out the contacts, putting them in a case as my horse slowed to a walk and walked behind Khire's mare.

"Ya I'm very happy I convinced you," I said smiling at the back of him as I stuffed the wig in a saddlebag.

We followed a deer trail along a winding path, using magic to push aside branches that drooped over the path. It wasn't even twenty minutes along the path when Khire stopped his horse.

"What's wrong?" I asked confused.

"There's hoof prints leading this way," Myre said as he began to follow the strange hoof prints. So my plan of spending time with Khire ended and I huffed, turning my horse to follow Khire.

"No this isn't fair," Khire said reading my thoughts.

"No it's ok, this person could be a lead," I said and nodded. This wasn't a typical trail that people went on so seeing someone had come by this way was intriguing.

"Well I can always check it out another time, for now it's just us," Khire said and turned back to the deer path.

"Thank you," I said sincerely.

We stopped in a large snowy meadow. Khire used some magic and spread the snow away from a spot to reveal dead yellow grass. He set a heated blanket down then unsaddled the horses and tied them to a nearby tree. I grabbed a bag from my saddle and brought it over to the blanket to set out our picnic. Sandwiches, carrots, grapes, melon, cookies and some bottles of water as well as one bottle of wine made up our feast. Khire sat down then patted his lap, letting me sit down and lean against his chest. He wrapped his arms around me and kissed my cheek.

"I love you do you know that?" He asked, whispering in my ear.

"And I love you too," I said smiling.

We stayed like that for hours, saying little, but just being with each other. I fed him some grapes and he fed me some cookies, which was rather messy, but it was cute.

"Get it in your mouth," Khire said shoving a cookie into my mouth.

"You're feeding me too fast, I'm going to get fat," I whined though smiling.

"So more to love," He replied and I shook my head. He pinched my stomach and I swatted his hands away.

"No," I said, but he wrapped his hands around me and hugged me tightly, still trying to shove another cookie in my mouth. I giggled and tried to get away from the cookie.

"Yup," He countered and eventually got most of the cookie into my mouth.

I poured some wine into a plastic cup and together we drank about half the bottle, me drinking most of that portion. Khire didn't like drinking and he certainly wasn't a wine person, but he drank some and I could feel his body relax as he drank more. I held his hands around me for a time and rested my head just below his chin.

"I want this moment to never end," I whispered.

"Me too. I want to love you the way you deserve. I just want to make you happy and give you everything. I love you," He whispered back.

"You give me more than I deserve, you make me the happiest person on this planet. You are everything to me and I love you back more," "No that's not possible, my love for you is far greater than yours for me. No one can love anyone more than I can," He said and kissed my neck.

"You have so much love, but I still got you beat boy," I said and let him kiss me more.

We ended up at some point lying down and falling asleep. It was already seven when we woke up and realized it was dark.

"We need to get back," I said, grabbing at things and trying to stuff them in my bag. I couldn't see anything, but I think I got the most of it. Khire grabbed anything I didn't grab then grabbed the two horses and tacked them up. We led them through the night down the trail. I was a little nervous, but Khire was confident enough and the horse he led seemed relaxed enough to follow. My horse had his head up and ears twitching each way, hearing things that I couldn't and spooking at things I couldn't see. He wanted to walk closer to his friend, but ended up pushing me aside.

"Slow down," I said to Khire and he slowed. The gelding sniffed Khire's horse's tail and relaxed slightly.

Slowly we made our way down the hill, Khire illuminating the way with a ball of magic shinning at the ground and into the forest. It cast a spooky glow and made the forest look dead and ghostly. I wanted to be standing beside Khire with his arms around me, but I knew that I was all right and should be able to stand on my own. I took a deep breath and held it a few seconds then let it out. Breathing in and out in a rhythm to calm me down and keep me from freaking out even as my imagination conjured nightmares in my mind.

"It's ok," Khire said calling from up ahead.

"I know, I'm just letting my imagination get the best of me," I said laughing slightly.

"Well let's just talk then. What do you think might be out there maybe waiting for us?" Khire asked.

"Wild animals," I answered.

"Ok I've taken on bears and wolves. Raccoons, bats, birds, squirrels, bees, bugs, rabbits, weasels and anything else out there I'm sure will leave us alone. Coyotes and foxes tend to be shy and if they decide to be courageous I'm pretty sure I can take on them too," Khire said easily.

"People," I said next.

"I can see them coming before they see me coming, I can move fast and kill them before they can kill you," He said confidently.

"Midnight," I said with dread.

"...He's another story," Khire said seriously.

We walked on in silence for another little while when Khire suddenly stopped.

"Why oh why do you keep doing that?" I asked slightly annoyed.

"There's a cabin here," Khire said surprised.

"What? A cabin? Why would there be a cabin here, this is King's Land no one's allowed to build on this land," I said confused.

"Well someone doesn't care about rules 'cause there's a cabin right here," He said and lead us over to it. It was a really small cabin, made of old wood that was rotted and falling off. Khire opened the door and shone the light inside revealing a wooden desk and chair and a wooden frame for what was supposed to be a bed. It looked unused with dust settled over everything.

Khire handed me the reins to his horse then went in to survey the place.

"We can stay here for the night?" He asked shrugging.

"Ummmm not really feeling the sleeping-in-the-creepy-cabin idea," I said shrinking away.

"Come on its safe and no one's been here for years. It will be safer than trying to ride down these mountains in the dark," Khire said crossing his arms. I sighed and nodded. Khire came back and took back his horse, leading her around to try and find a place to put them. Amazingly coming off the back of the cabin was a wooden roof supported by two walls. Some posts identified where two stalls were and some mangers showed where hay use to go.

"Well now this is perfect. Apparently whoever lived here had horses," Khire said smiling. He seemed to be really enjoying this while I on the other hand had a really bad feeling. Khire however had a point, we got this far in the dark, but it wasn't safe traveling down the mountain in the dark.

We tied the horses with ropes from our bags to the posts and untacked them then Khire turned and with the help of some magic cut up armfuls of grass and put it in the two mangers. The horses would rather graze, but they contented themselves to lipping at the grass. Next Khire set out to find them some water, which didn't take long as there was a stream nearby. Going back inside the cabin, Khire grabbed an old plastic bucket and started getting some water. Offering a bucket each to the horses; I watched him while smiling.

"I think I'd like living like this with you," I said dreamily.

"Maybe one day," Khire said smiling.

"Would you run away with me?" I asked him.

"I would run away with you any day you know that, but neither of us can leave Vale Darra in the state that it's in right now," He said as he walked back to the stream to get more water.

"How about after all this, would you run away with me?" I asked following him.

"Yes I will. After all this is over, once I stop this guy from destroying magic, and if we're both alive. I will grab you by the hand put you on a horse and we will ride off together. I will take you far away and we will never look back. We will get a little place and live together until the end of our lives," Khire said stopping in front of me as he was coming back from the stream.

I smiled and kissed his lips slowly.

"Perfect," I said and led him back to the horses. We offered them more water, but when they weren't interested anymore we left the bucket where both could reach it and went inside the cabin.

"Well I don't know what would be more comfortable, the wooden floor or the wooden bed frame?" Khire said smiling.

"Well we have a blanket and I call sleeping on you, so it's really your decision," I said hands on hips.

"Oh really what if I didn't want to be slept on, maybe I want to go sleep with the horses instead of you?" Khire said laughing.

He came over to me and hugged me, kissing me slowly. Very slowly and consciously I pulled off his shirt then undid his pants. He hesitated, but then pulled off my shirt and after a moment undid the button to my jeans. "We don't have to do anything you're not ready to do," I told him looking up to him.

"...No, but we can get a little closer," He said unsure. I laughed a little at the uncomfortable situation and he laughed as well.

"We're just sleeping it's not like we haven't done that before," I said pulling him to the ground as he grabbed the blanket out of the bag. He spread it out then lay down pulling me to him. I kicked my pants and shoes off then after a moment I took my socks off.

Khire pulled me closer to him and kissed my eyelids.

"Do you want to get a little closer?" He asked and I giggled.

"Oh dear Khire you are so uncomfortable right now. I had a great day, I will not ask of you that you are not ready to give," I said and laid my head on his chest.

"I just don't know how to start," He said after a moment, his voice had gone really husky and it sent shivers up my spine. Stupidly I began laughing, for some reason awkward moments made me laugh a lot and I just couldn't help it.

"Do I need to narrate?" I asked laughing.

"No," He said laughing slightly. "I … I'm just not good at this. I am very uncomfortable about this, okay? Let's just sleep," he said, and went silent.

"You sure?" I teased sliding my hand up his thigh.

I could feel how uncertain he was, but I was curious to see how far I could push him. I really wanted to have sex with him, it would be the perfect ending, but I knew he wasn't ready.

"Ummm we could try…," He said tensing as my hand slid up over his thigh and to his hip. I kept my hand on his hip and kissed his lips.

"Good night Sweetie," I said. He smiled and hugged me tighter in return releasing a deep breath as his body relaxed. I kissed him deeply one last time.

"I love you," I whispered and then whispered his name. His body tensed again then went warm as his magic began to race through his veins.

"I love you too," He managed as he took long breaths to calm his magic. I smiled happily, one day it would be right, until then I would enjoy him as much as I could.

At some point during the night we both woke up again.

"What? What was that?" I asked sitting bolt upright.

"Nothing it was me sorry I kicked the saddle bag and it fell over," Khire said sleepily.

"Oh," I said then backed away for him and pulled the blanket along to make him come away from the wall. He didn't like having his back to open air, but he followed me anyway.

"How's the comfort level, still working on it?" I asked before I nodded off.

"Shhhh," Khire said half asleep.

In the morning we heard birds singing and weak sunlight was streaming through the window and any crack it could find. I brushed my fingers through Khire's hair and breathed in his scent, loving the warm smell of him. I couldn't describe his smell, but at this moment it smelt amazing.

"You have a weird habit of smelling me? Were you a dog in your past life?" Khire asked jokingly. I playfully smelled him, being really loud as I rolled on top of him.

"Good morning beautiful," I said and he smiled up at me, his blind eyes not seeing me.

"Why won't you get your eyes fixed?" I asked suddenly.

"I don't know," He said truthfully.

"Well why don't you get it checked out?" I asked him and he nodded.

"Later," He said then pushed me off of him and got to his feet stretching. "Let's get going," he said and left the cabin. He checked on the horses and walked around the cabin to see if anything had come visiting last night.

I walked around inside the cabin and pulled on my cloths. I pulled out the one drawer in the small, wooden table and within it lay an old used pen. I pulled out the drawer a little more and accidentally pulled it out. The bottom of the drawer fell out and with that a book.

"What's this?" I asked picking it up. It was really old and wrinkling, but it was in pretty good condition.

"What's that?" Khire asked coming in.

"I don't know," I said and opened it up. It was in faded ink and in a different language, but the words were clear enough to read. Khire read it over my shoulder:

"I ran out to the field to pick flowers, it was a sunny day and mother was out in the town," Khire read slowly. "It's someone's journal or diary or something?" He said confused. I turned through the pages till Khire told me to stop. He read some of the words then took the journal from me. He flipped through it and kept reading more.

"This is Midnights journal," He said breathlessly. "Seriously?" I asked looking over at the journal.

"Ya," Khire said incredulous.

I listened to the words stream through Khire's head as he translated it and slowly a picture began to form in our heads.

"Midnight had a brother that looked just like him, his name was Josin. They grew up till Midnight was fifteen then Midnight left and came to live here in this cabin. He later found me and trained me, but… He never told me about his life as a boy," Khire said slowly.

"I guess he never had a great life either," I said shrugging. "Come on we have to go, let's read it later," I said and he nodded.

"Right lets go," He said and put the drawer back together and put it back in its proper place along with the old pen.

We tacked up the horses then headed out, following our tracks from last night back to the deer path then following it downhill. It took us a while, but an hour before we got into the city limits I put on the wig and the contacts. Khire said a spell so when people looked at me they wouldn't focus on me. I still looked like me for the most part, but no one would recall seeing the Princess Ride into the city dishevelled and with a guy.

"Rough night?" A guard asked Khire with a raised eyebrow and a smile.

"We lost track of time and decided to camp it," Khire said smiling. The guard smiled and nodded us through. We returned the horses to their stalls and walked to the castle.

Thankfully a forest green car came towards us and stopped right beside us. Already knowing who drove around in that colour car and that kind of car, I started to smile.

"Do you want a ride kids?" Temptress asked leaning over the passenger side as the window rolled down.

"Yes!" I cheered and jumped in the front.

"We found Midnights journal," Khire said first.

"Really?!" Temptress asked turning around to look in the backseat at Khire. Khire held up the journal and Temptress looked at it as if it held the answers to the world's most serious questions.

"Well let's get back to the castle and then we can get through it. By the way my little wayward Princess you have suddenly become ill due to some female problems. You have requested to see no one and have been staying in your room," Temptress said smiling at me.

"Thank you so much. I'm so sorry, we didn't know we'd lose track of time," I told her truthfully.

"You're welcome. Now serious question, did anything magical happen last night?" Temptress asked nosy. Her question was met by dead silence. "Oh my God what happened?" She asked looking in her review mirror and glaring at Khire.

"Nothing why are you looking at me?" Khire asked defensively.

"Well obviously. That's the problem you always do nothing. Do you need some help, like do you actually know how to have sex?" Temptress asked bluntly.

"Yes," Khire said folding his arms.

"Really tell me, what do you do?" Temptress demanded.

"What? Noooooo," Khire said shaking his head.

"Shirra my dear, what is wrong with your boy?" Temptress asked now turning to me.

"He thought about it, but it was awkward," I said shrugging.

"Awkward? It was awkward? What is he small?" Temptress asked confused.

"I am not small, I am perfectly normal," Khire said leaning forward to look at me sternly.

"Is he?" Temptress asked trying to whisper in my ear. I giggled and smiled.

"No he's fine," I said looking back at Khire who glared at me.

"Ok well how about this I will go and buy Shirra some lingerie and I'll even buy some wine, and all's you two have to do is actually do it. Ok does that sound like a good idea? Khire what flavour do you like?" She asked smiling.

"You know it's really all right, I'm sure we can figure it out," I said patting her hand. She waved her hand at me.

"Ya whatever I'll see what I can do," She said. She gave Khire a stern look. "I'll buy you a book to, help you get past the first jitters,"

"I don't have jitters and I don't need help," He growled.

"Sure you do or else you'd be having sex with her every night and you'd be giving me advice," "I don't think that would be possible," I laughed at her and she shrugged.

"No, I'll always give you advice, though I'll give Khire a little more. Say Khire how...,"

"Stop," Khire cut in.

"What? I didn't finish you rude little boy," Temptress said annoyed.

"You don't need to," he said and looked out the window trying to block out everything.

"Well whatever, you're just grouchy cause you don't know how to man up," Temptress said and shrugged again. I rolled my eyes, but smiled.

"You have no shame," I told her and she nodded.

"Nope I don't. Sex is very important to me, why would I be ashamed of that?" She asked seriously. I just shook my head in response knowing I would never win this conversation.

We arrived at the castle in record timing and Temptress got us in with little commotion. We traveled with some tourists then took a roundabout way to my room, running into a few guards that raised their eyes at us. At this point I had taken off my disguise.

"We had a tough night, thought the Princess would feel better after an early morning walk, but apparently not. Thankfully this young man here was gracious enough to help me escort the Princess back to her room," Temptress would say to the guards. I was very thankful to get back in my room and go for a shower. Khire was happy to wait for Donta to bring him some food.

CHAPTER #29

Supper was nearly ready and I was just about to pour the noodles into the strainer when the doorbell rang. I just got home from showing a house on a late Monday night and all I wanted to do was settled down for the night.

"Well it was almost an uninterrupted supper," I huffed, talking to my Guardian, Jain an Australian Shepard. I went to the door and opened it.

"Hello Khire," I said surprised. He stood outside smiling warmly at me though he looked cold in his light clothing. His hair, never kept nice, was ruffled though that was normal, and his cloths looked well worn. He seemed well rested and though skinny, seemed to be fine.

"Hey dad I got a job," He said looking at me.

"Oh, where?" I asked delighted.

"At Historica, I translate stuff and help tourists," He shrugged and I guessed it wasn't a big deal to him as it was to me.

"Well that's great! Come in I've just got supper nearly made and we can talk about it," I invited. I hugged him tightly and couldn't hide the big grin that stayed on my face the rest of the night.

He followed me inside to the kitchen. I took the noodles off the stove and poured them in a strainer in the sink. Khire sat patiently waiting on a stool.

"So how do you like it?" I asked him. "Are you working tomorrow?"

"Yes there's a tourist group coming in at three to go look around. And I like it, I like translating stuff and using different languages.

I've always liked working with languages," He said shrugging. I grabbed two plates out of the cabinet and scooped noodles onto both of them, giving Khire a heaping pile. I smothered both with sauce then took them over to the table where a plate of bread, some butter, parmesan cheese and a fork was already laid out. Khire helped himself to a piece of bread and buttered it then poured a dumping of cheese on his spaghetti.

"This looks great thank you," Khire said smiling.

"Good, tell me more about your job," I prompted.

"Well it's nice, my boss is really nice and strict, but fair. He works a lot, but he comes around every once in a while to check things out and make sure everything's ok. You'd like him," He said before taking a bite.

"Oh really, I'll have to meet him some day. What have you been doing lately?" I asked.

"Nothing really, just relaxing and focusing on work," He said shrugging.

It was a nice little visit and though I still asked if he'd stay the night and he still said no, I still liked him coming over. I also felt like he had taken a big leap by getting a job and telling me about it. I waved goodbye to him as he walked down the street then I closed the door. Feeling as if something huge was accomplished today.

The night wasn't too cold and the moon shone out clear as I made my way to the castle. Shirra and Caprica waited for me there so we could go over the journal. I was excited yet nervous about reading the words of the man I most feared and hated. Yet I wanted to see his written words and see what they said, reading the words that Midnight wrote with sincerity. It had taken me a week to finally decide to read the journal.

Once there I got up to Shirra's room and Donta let me in. I smiled at her then joined the two women sitting around a table drinking tea and talking.

"It wasn't supposed to mean anything, it was just a stupid thing I did," Temptress said her hands waving in the air.

"What?" I asked coming to sit down beside them.

"Adult stuff hun, you wouldn't understand. Would you like some tea?" Temptress asked gesturing towards the tea pot.

"No," I said and opened the journal that was on the table in front of me. The rest of the night we focused on reading the journal.

CHAPTER #30

Over the next three months more people known to be strong magic users died. I was with Shirra on Christmas Eve and Christmas Day as well as New Year's Eve and New Year's Day. We celebrated together and ignored the people dying all over the world. I had come no closer to figuring out how to stop this guy or cult. Midnight's journal told me many things, but nothing to really help me.

I worked five days a week at Historica and killed very seldom. I had to watch who I killed because I didn't want to disrupt the magic anymore and so it became a rare thing to see Dusk running along the rooftops. The citizens of Vale Darra were scared and tended to stay in their houses more than go out. The city suffered for it too, with a smaller inflow of tourists, businesses were suffering. I went out on a regular basis to survey the city, but would soon return to Shirra. I was spending a lot of time with her, spending every night with her and some days as well.

Shirra began to work more and more at the hospital then with her father. She also made a separate account that was strictly for her earnings as a doctor. I still didn't have access to my account, but Donta managed to access them and draw out some money. I had a lot in there which made me happy and I knew my job would bring in some more, but I was just happy to have something. Together Shirra and I got prepared to run away after this mess by buying clothes, shoes, food and anything else we could travel with to our new place.

We wanted to get away as soon as possible from Vale Darra, but we didn't want to leave the city in the mess that it was in. I accepted that this wasn't my fault, but I still felt obligated to fix it. And so we held on together and slowly the snow melted and the flowers bloomed. Tourism picked up a little bit, but not a lot, still it was better than it had been and so I was called on to work six days a week.

It was as I was sitting at my office, looking out my door, across the hall at the office nearby and listening to the TV play that I had an idea. The movie was a real old movie about a son and father who wanted to build a time machine and go to the future. They built this crude looking machine that blasted them back in the past to the dinosaur age where together father and son had to learn to survive. The machine then blasted them into the future where vehicles could hover and everything was run on technology. There were machines that could fly and everything was either voice controlled or motion censored.

"Myre what if Dyras's Wish allowed him to time travel? Does that sound possible? He has all those drawings of the past and future, he must be able to see the past and future somehow?" I asked Myre. Myre lifted his head from his paws.

"I guess it's possible, we don't know any limits on peoples Wishes," Myre said, head cocked to the side.

"I think that's it and that's how he's getting around. That's why I can't find him. It's all starting to make sense now," I said getting out of my chair with excitement. I paced the room as I thought about the possibility of dealing with someone who could time travel. I didn't know how to stop someone who could do that, but it was nice to know that I could be dealing with something like this.

Just then the little buzzer on my desk sounded an alarm meaning I had tourists here I had to translate for. With a sigh I left and went back to work, leaving my office and having done very little in it besides sleep or think. I met a group of Eastern people who seemed really happy to be here. I asked them the usual questions and after some paper work we left to tour around the city on a bus. It was a nice bus, comfortable, blue, cushioned seats with little tables and a washroom at the back. There would be a luncheon at twelve and after gift packages to hand out to the tourists. I truly thought it a great job and I liked working with the people. I had to memorize a lot so that I could answer any questions and talk about Vale Darra, but I really didn't mind that. It was an easy job that got my mind off of my troubles and problems.

That night I spoke with Temptress, Donta and Shirra about the possibility of someone being able to time travel. They didn't know if it were possible, but they weren't ready to just shove that thought aside either.

"If someone could time travel, then why wouldn't Dyras have destroyed magic already?" Donta asked.

"Many reasons I guess. Maybe Dyras is aware the world runs on magic and so is trying to slowly weed out magic so the world doesn't get destroyed. I also think he has a morality issue. He doesn't like killing anyone innocent so even if the person is a strong magic user, Dyras may not kill them because they haven't done anything bad. Remember this all started because he feared magic and then a boy died so I think Dyras might also be afraid to attack a magic user," I said to her and she nodded.

"Ok so then it should be easy to stop him then. Either make him so afraid to attack a magic user so that he doesn't or try to get him to understand magic is good," Donta said as if it were that simple.

"Mmmm not a good idea to scare people into thinking magic is evil, that might just cause more problems. And I think if Dyras hasn't realized magic is good now, he won't ever. I think we need to kill him," I told her and she sighed.

"But what will that do in the future or past? If he's time traveling then time might get screwed up if we kill him in the wrong time zone… or any time zone for that matter," Temptress asked.

"I don't know does anyone else have any other ideas?" I asked grabbing a cookie from a small plate and nibbling on it as I thought.

"What if we found a way to catch him when he's from the past, like his past form comes to the now and we catch him. We can magically convince him to go back to his time and not fear magic," Shirra guessed.

"You know how hard it could be to find an early form of him?" I asked her.

"Well I'm thinking he's getting smarter so he's going back in time and bringing his younger self back to the future," Shirra said though unsure.

"Ok and maybe he's also scaring away all the other assassins?" I said trying to tie in all options.

"Because assassins are magic users and know death magic so Dyras fears to kill them, but because he can time travel he might have found a way to get them to leave," Temptress said clapping her hands together.

"Ok great now that we have figured that out, how do you find someone who can time travel?" Donta asked bringing us back to the main issue.

"Well I think we should just… ummm what if we were to use a lot of magic in one spot. Like we bring him to us?" Temptress asked looking around at everyone.

"We could try that, but we have to be careful what magic we use because we don't want to scare him away," Shirra said.

"Ok so we will have to think of a place, can't very well start using a lot of magic in the city, you'll have the police on you," Donta said looking at me.

"We will go into the mountains. I will find a place that is suitable," I told her and she nodded.

"This isn't a great plan," Shirra said.

"I know, it has so many holes in it. So many ways for things to go wrong, but we don't have time," I told her.

The rest of the night we discussed possible spells to use, who would all be there or if only one person should go at a time. We didn't want to overpower Dyras so much that he wouldn't show, but we also didn't want him to come and just kill us. Also we didn't want him to find us then later on when we were alone, give him an opportunity to kill us then. There was a lot to think about, but we didn't want to wait any longer as more people continued to die each month and already magical instruments were starting to fail. We had to work fast, but working fast without thinking it through could kill us. We had never dealt with something like this and have never even thought of having to deal with a time traveler. We didn't know the rules or the problems with screwing with this guy, but we knew we did have to stop him. I worried however just what else we were stopping or starting and if it was still a good idea. I constantly worried about everything and each time I found it harder and harder to come to any solid conclusions. But eventually I decided if the guy was left to his own devices he would surely destroy us all. So killing him might bring peace and even that little possibly gave me reason enough to try anything to stop him.

CHAPTER #31

The sun was warm and the snow sparkled under it. We had been hit by an unusual snowstorm just last night allowing winter to hang on much longer than normal. I had ridden out to the mountains to look for a spot to do magic that wouldn't attract attention, unfortunately there were a lot of sensors around and I wouldn't be able to do magic around them without being caught. I had to go really far in order to get away from them all, but then I ran in to other issues. I didn't want to be too far from a town just in case something went wrong and I didn't want to have to spend hours getting there because that would make me tired and might attract unwanted attention from other people.

I gave up around noontime and headed back to Vale Darra. I gave the horse back and after a few words to the guards I left them behind. I heard that my brother had a new baby and though I liked kids, I also didn't like kids. Still I thought I'd be nice and go visit them. Tellnair wasn't at his house and so I headed to my dad's house. It took me twenty minutes to get there, but soon I was walking up the short walkway and knocking on his house.

"Hello," He said with a smile as soon as he saw me. He invited me in. "You just off work?" He asked.

"Ya," I said and rubbed my hands together to warm them.

"Well your brother and his wife are here with their baby, go see her," Dad said with a huge smile, every bit a proud grandfather. I nodded and went into the living room.

"Hello Khire," Mellony said.

"Hey, congratulations," I said as I sat down in a chair.

"Do you want to hold her?" She asked.

"Oh, no thank you," I sat back in the chair and shook my head.

"Come on," Tellnair picked her up and put her in my arms. She was very tiny and looked up at me with wide blue eyes. I stared down at her, not able to see her well other than a small fuzzy blue-pink figure, but I continued to stare down at her for a long while. She was very small and I couldn't help, but note how weak and defenceless she was. She was completely dependent on her parents for everything. And right now she was in the hands of a dangerous assassin. I was a little startled to think that that was the first thing I thought of when meeting my niece for the first time.

She lay in my arms silent and watching me with her wide eyes, she was chubby and her little fingers were stubby and short. Myre told me she looked quite a lot like Tellnair does with some of Mellony's features. I told as much to them and though Mellony smiled widely Tellnair sighed, but smiled warmly afterwards.

I couldn't imagine a better day. When first I woke to my wife in labour I was scared, but after getting her to the hospital and into the delivery room to wait out the time till my little baby was born, my excitement and happiness grew. Now I was able to take my little girl home today and my heart soared with pure happiness. I left work early and headed over to the hospital where my wife and my new baby girl waited. The doctors were smiling and wanting to see her as I took her from Mellony's arms and left. My brother stopped us before we left.

"Wait, ah isn't she cute. What's her name?" Aster asked.

"Sighann," I told him.

"Pretty, congrats," He said.

I let him hold her as Mellony left to go get some food.

"So what ya going to do?" Aster asked. He handed my baby back to me and I cradled her as I rocked back and forth. I could have put her in her carrier, but I didn't want to put her down.

"Uh Mellony has this whole thing planned, where gonna go around town to a lot of stores. She says she needs to buy more things for the baby, but I think it's to show her off," I shrugged, but smiled.

"That sounds like Mellony," He said and I nodded in agreement.

"And we are having a little party tonight, nothing really just some cake, you're invited, Mellony insists on having everyone at our house," I invited.

"Mmmm, well I have nothing going on and Darcie has nothing either and cake really sounds good, why not, it'll be fun," Aster said smiling at the baby in my arms. Darcie, his wife was also pregnant though she still had five months to go. I knew Aster was nervous, this was their first and as they were both doctors, they were really busy.

"Hey do you know where Khire is, I found everyone else and invited them, but I couldn't find him and of course he gave us no number to call him?" I frowned. Khire was someone I would have liked to have come, but he was near impossible to get a hold of or find. If he wanted to be found, he'd just find you instead.

"Ya sorry I don't know, but that kinda bugs me. Let's get him a cell phone for his birthday," Aster commented and I nodded in agreement.

Mellony came back eating a sandwich.

"Well looks like you went for the good stuff," I said as I watched her stuff her face. "I haven't been able to eat one since her, apparently she doesn't like sandwiches, so now I'm eating them to make up for it," She said with a smile.

"Anyway bye Aster," I said then turned to leave.

"Hey, did he invite you over tonight?" Mellony asked him.

"Yes he did," Aster replied.

"Good, now we can go, bye," She said giving Aster a kiss on the cheek then turning to leave.

We left the hospital and went over to dad's house to first show him his new grandchild.

"Hey dad, do you know where Khire is, I can't find him?" I said as soon as he opened the door. I handed over Sighann to him and his face lit up. This was his first biological grandchild and he was ecstatic.

"Oh I have no idea, I don't even know where the boy lives. Did everything go well; I thought you were picking her up two days ago?" He sounded worried.

"Oh, well we were, but Mellony got scared after she had a little cough, so she stayed there two extra nights. We actually just came from the hospital," I said as I sat myself on his couch.

It wasn't long until a knock came from the door.

"One sec," Dad said and left to answer it. I couldn't hear what he was saying, but soon he came back with just the person I wanted to see.

"Hello Khire," Mellony said.

"Hey, congratulations," He said as he sat down.

"Do you want to hold her?" Mellony asked smiling.

"Oh, no thank you," He shook his head as he sat back in his seat as if he were afraid of the infant.

"Come on," I picked her up and put her in his arms. He stared down at her for a long time as she starred back at him. I smiled to see him obviously taken by her.

"We're having a party at our house tonight, Khire, we'd really appreciate it if you came," Mellony said delicately as she came over to stand behind him.

She had a hard time respecting and liking Khire because he lived on the streets and was so scrappy. She was use to the more expensive ways of living and had a typical idea that everyone beneath her was beneath her and so not worth her time. With Khire though she was forced to acknowledge his existence and be nice to him because he's my brother. She has been getting better and letting him hold her baby was a big step for her. I was proud that she was coming around to liking Khire and watched them silently. "Sure," He nodded his head and looked up at her.

"Dad tells me you got a new job? How do you like it?" I asked, curious to hear his answer.

"Oh I like it, I've just been touring around people and stuff. It's a lot of fun and I really like working with all the different people. Some people I don't like, but I think everybody has that issue," He said shrugging then he handed Sighann back to her mother.

"Oh ya you'll have plenty of people you hate," I said smiling brightly.

"This one guy asked me all sorts of stupid questions, I ended up just making up a bunch of answers to satisfy him. Some people just don't like to shut up. I had one women pretty much narrate the whole trip, I even let her sit in my seat at the front of the bus because she insisted on doing my job," Khire said laughing slightly.

"Really?" I said glad to hear him laugh.

Dad sat down beside Khire and patted his hand to speak with him, "So what else have you been doing?"

"Nothing really, I've been going out to the mountains just to get away from the city and all its craziness," Khire said shrugging.

"I don't want you leaving the city, it's not safe," Dad said suddenly.

"Nowhere is safe dad, and I don't go alone, I bring friends along… most of the time and we stay on the Kings land," Khire said this time patting dad's hand.

"Still why do you need to get away from the city? What's wrong with the city?" Dad asked defensively.

"Nothing, I just… I don't know I'm starting to see myself as moving out of the city to somewhere else," Khire said slowly.

"You're moving?" Dad asked turning to face him.

"Yes, not right now, but I will be. I like it here, I really do, but I just want to try something new. I'm leaving for good probably, but it's not like I'm going to an entirely new planet," Khire said before dad could say anything.

"Where you going?" I asked him nicely to try and calm the situation.

"I don't know, somewhere," Khire said shrugging.

"Well I hope you find happiness and where ever you end up you keep in touch with us," I said and smiled at him. He smiled back then turned back to dad who still looked unhappy, but nodded along.

"Just be careful, it's dangerous outside the city," he said and Khire sighed, but stayed quiet.

"Now what do you want for your birthday?" Dad asked Khire.

"It's still months away," Khire said confused.

"I know, but if you're planning on leaving at some point I want to get you a gift," Dad said stubbornly.

"You don't have…," Khire started.

"What is it with you and gifts? Just tell me what you want Khire," Dad asked, his voice rising.

"I want everything to just be ok," He said simply.

"What?" Dad and I both asked confused.

"I want everyone to be happy and stop fighting for a change. I want everyone to realise that I don't need a gift to be happy or whatever. I like spending time with you, a birthday is just an ordinary day, it's not special, and people just make it special because we live in a world obsessed by material goods. How about instead of getting me something we just have a good day," Khire said simply.

You had to be proud and amazed by him, he was a rare person. Someone you don't meet just casually on some street. I liked him for what he said, but it is hard to understand different people, still I respected him enough to let it end there. Dad on the other hand was not. He paced around the room muttering to himself.

"What's wrong now?" Khire asked calmly.

"You're not normal!" Dad yelled and my wife took our now crying baby upstairs.

"Look, you had so much potential, you are so smart, I know you're smart. So why can't you just realise that you had so much and you threw it all away?" Dad asked.

"I didn't throw it all away, you think I have, but I do well with my life. You don't see it because it's the minimal, but my life makes me happy," Khire said still remaining calm.

It was a long frustrating discussion, but we came to a resolve of a sort near the end of it. Khire had to be more open about his life and dad had to be more welcoming and open to it. Also Dad was allowed to get Khire gifts, but he couldn't make a big deal about it.

"Now tonight we will be all together, let's be happy we have so much to be happy for so please don't fight," Dad said then turned to Khire. "Now, you, just answer the questions, where do you live?" Dad looked at Khire, watching him and waiting for an answer. I could tell he was upset, and as I listened to them speak I began to ask questions, but calmly.

"I was staying with a friend in Stonemill, but he recently moved out so now it's just Myre and I," Khire said and it sounded true. Stonemill rang a bell too; it was a part of the city, a small stone house settlement for either street rats or people with little money. It was cleaner than the streets, but still lacking in development.

"Ok, can you show me? I don't know, can we visit?" Dad asked he already wasn't enjoying the answers he was getting, but he was trying hard not to get too mad about it as he stared wide-eyed at Khire. The lines at the edges of his pale blue eyes and his mouth showed the strain he has held onto for years and just now they got deeper as he tried to stay calm and question Khire.

"It's Stonemill's dad do you really want to visit there? I do have a house, I got a bed, and I have clean food and water. I have the usual necessities for life, I don't have plumbing or electricity, but I have magic," Khire sat on the chair calmly, but he reminded me of a rabbit ready to bolt.

I wondered if I really should be worried about him more and if it was partially my fault for why he was the way that he was. I realized just how much I didn't know this Khire. I have said I didn't know him, but it hit me just how much I really don't know him. I studied him comparing him to the old Khire, the fat and ugly Khire that had lived with dad, but would always go wandering off to someplace. Now the young man in front of me was lanky, medium height and somewhat rugged. Through the years the weight dropped off and he became a very attractive looking young man, even for a street rat. He took care of himself in the sense that he could pass for a regular person on the street and not attract attention. Some people just have a natural rugged appearance to them and still be attractive and that was Khire. However, knowing he lived on the streets made me still think of him as helpless and poor and gave me the delusional thought that he needs us to fix his life. Maybe that delusion has made us miss the real opportunity to help him.

I had lost the conversation, but started to listen in again.

"Yes I do," Dad said with all the assuredness he could have. "But it's difficult,... you will just hate it," Khire said tiredly.

"I don't care," Now dad was mad and his stubbornness was stopping him from being the patient person he needed to be right now.

"Fine. Is that all you want to ask me, cause I have to go?" Khire got up, but dad got up to.

I was a little worried dad would be a little too aggressive with getting Khire to talk so I cleared my throat to draw the attention to me, but it didn't work.

"No, you're not going anywhere, you aren't even answering my questions," Dad growled. "Yes I am. Look I'm sorry to upset you, but please, dad you don't have to worry, I'm alright. I'm alive, I see you now and again, I spend time with you and my brothers. I'm ok," Khire went to leave, but dad grabbed him by the shoulders and shook him. "Yes, you are alive, Khire we understand, but I hardly know you! I feel like you're a stranger to me! All's I want is for you to just answer my questions, if you need help, just ask, please!" Dad's breathing was choppy and raged.

"Dad are you ok?" Khire asked. He took him by the arms and sat him down on the chair. "Look dad, I do understand, I know it's not fair, you don't know much about me, and I'm sorry. I wish I could be a really great son that was successful and had a wife and kids, but my life didn't go that way. I am your son, but I am older now, I can't stay here forever. You can't hold my hand anymore ok. You need to understand that I need to work things out on my own. I'm going to fail at times, but I will be ok. When I need help I know to come to you alright," Khire made sure dad nodded before saying goodbye to us then left.

"Well that was something," Mellony said after a moment. Dad looked at her annoyed.

"Dad, come on are you ok?" He was still breathing irregularly and I went to him to kneel in front of him.

"What has he got himself into?" He asked looking down at the ground. "He hates me,"

"He doesn't hate you. He loves you so much that he tries too hard to be successful and he gets discouraged at himself when things don't go his way. In any case, I'm going to find out some more stuff, ok," I kissed him on the top of his head then got to my feet. "I'm going to see what he's up too, Mellony could you stay here and make sure dad's ok?" I didn't want to leave him like this, but if I didn't leave now, I wouldn't be able to find Khire. She nodded and I left.

CHAPTER #32

The sun was setting, but I still had four hours before it would be completely dark and as I got outside and spotted Khire walking away down the street I ran behind a bush to hide. As he walked away I followed him bit by bit till soon we were in the city and I had to stop or I would look weird. I casually walked far behind Khire. Not too far that I couldn't follow him easy, but far enough that if he turned around I had some seconds to react and hide.

"What are you doing?" Fetcher asked very confused. He was dressed in his police outfit, which meant he was working and obviously was being obvious of me stalking our little brother.

"How is it that out of all the police officers I could run into I run into you. This is a city, you can't go work some other area? And I'm doing nothing, I just want to find out more about Khire and seeing as he doesn't talk much I'm following him, ok, now go away," I said and made a shooing motion at him with my hands.

"Ok, um, but you know, stalking is kinda frowned upon and I do have legal obligations to this city you do realise that right?" he said eyeing me suspiciously as he continued to follow me.

"Yes yes, and you would be an awesome detective if you left me alone. My wife just had a baby, we brought her to dad's house, she's real cute. Why don't you go see her? Dad wasn't in the greatest shape when I left either, why don't you go see how he's doing?"

"Why what happened?" He now sounded worried and a little annoyed.

"Oh nothing him and Khire got into a little bit of an argument, he was breathing oddly,"

"Well I guess it's pick on Khire today. Why are you following him again?" He squinted his eyes as he looked forward. Khire just turned a corner.

"I'll tell you later ok, go!" I said and with a weird look from him, he finally left me alone.

I ran to the corner and looked around it before turning it. Khire stood right there in front of me.

"Why are you following me, Tellnair?" He asked as he crossed his arms.

"Because I have a right to!" I said annoyed.

"Really, and who gave you that right?" He didn't sound upset, more amused.

"Well Fetchers a detective and he left me alone. Listen I just want to get to know you better…" "That's a little tricky to do when your stalking the guy and not right beside him just doing the old style and talking to me," again he sounded amused.

"Because that didn't work so I resorted to stalking….I wasn't stalking you as a creeper would do, I had good intentions," I pointed my finger at him and talked to him as if he were a little kid.

"Ok, fine, but if you want to ask questions than just ask, don't stalk me or whatever it is you were doing," He walked away and I kept pace with him. "Ok fine, first question, are you in danger?" I asked and he looked at me surprised.

"Well I guess, I live in Stonemill, it's a tad bit sketchy," he said after a moment.

"Right, well why don't you get a new place, get a place then you could have a wife and family, you could be successful. We would all help you," I said trying not to plead.

"No I don't want help I want to work this out on my own and I do have a place it's just…," He started.

"Not exactly the type of place you want to call home is it?" I jumped in.

"Awwmmm well it's complicated," He said shrugging. I nodded not understanding him at all.

"Well figure it out, how complicated can it be to decide to move? Again you know we will all help you and there's nothing wrong with help. Dad practically bought me my house," I said nudging him and he nodded smiling.

"Yes I realise that and thank you. I plan on moving some day, but outside of Vale Darra and I don't know where I'm going. I want to travel a bit," he said looking over at me.

As I was thinking Khire slipped away and disappeared. I knew I wouldn't be able to find him again so I turned back to go home.

"See now, talking to him works too," Fetcher said, coming over to me.

"What you stalking me now?" I asked looking at him from the corner of my eye.

"No, just watching you, would hate if my older brother got in a fight right in the middle of the street with my little brother," He said innocently.

"We weren't fighting. We were talking, jeepers is all you think we do is fight?" I lengthened my strides.

"No, but you look like you were going to get in a fight by the look on your face, you don't seem like a very pleasant person to be around just now," He said. I guess I looked mad, but I didn't care, and I certainly didn't care for the weird looks I got and how people moved out of my way. When I was caught in thought I had a bad habit of looking very serious almost angry, I didn't mean to, that was just my thinking expression.

"Sorry, I'm going back to dad's, remember tonight at my house," I said then left him as he nodded in agreement.

I got back to dads house and let myself in. "Dad, how do you feel?" I asked as I came into the living room. "Ok," He said and took a sip of water. "Did you talk to Khire?" "Ya, but we still have to talk some more," I said as I sat down on the couch again.

Later on I drove dad, my new baby girl and Mellony to my house and we laid Sighann in her crib to sleep. She looked very small in her round crib, as she slept breathing evenly. I turned away from her and looked at Mellony.

"I think its best that you don't ask questions. Khire will come to you when he's ready," She said crossing her arms, but she wasn't mad. She stood there leaning against the wall, her hair was up in a bun, but there were some brown strands hanging down in loops. She looked at me, eyes a steady, vibrant green and I looked back at her.

"I don't know it seems he needs help he just doesn't ask. I don't mean to be nosy, I just care about him," I went over to her and pulled her close. "You understand that, right?" I asked her looking down.

"Yes I do because you're a nosy person," She said jokingly. "But in all seriousness, I think Khire does need help and he knows it, but maybe he's not ready to tell us yet. Just give him some time, you never know maybe he will figure it out himself and then everything will be ok," She smiled at me.

"Maybe, I just hope it's nothing too serious," I rested my chin on her head.

"Maybe he's just scared you guys will reject him....Come on, let's start making this house look somewhat party like," She walked away towards the kitchen and began to unpack bags we had brought home yesterday.

We spent the rest of the day taping pink and white streamers to the ceiling, walls, tables and over the door ways. We taped silver and gold stars to the ceiling along with blown up balloons and after putting some on the walls we put some on the floor. "Ok, she's a baby, she doesn't really need all this stuff, but why not," Mellony said after we were finally finished.

"No she doesn't, she especially doesn't need that tier cake, but oh well, we can definitely take care of it ourselves," I said and sat down on the couch.

The sun began to set and become a red globe in a red, orange and blue sky. The clouds were purple pink and I got a picture of it. I was going to take another one when I heard a knock at the door. Mellony answered it though and I was able to get a quick picture before two of my brothers walked in. They walked slowly from the front entrance down the hall and turned left into the living room a little awed by the decorations. "Hey guys," I greeted.

"Hey," Jakk said while Shean just nodded.

Jakk and Shean looked almost like twins, both with brown hair and brown eyes. The difference between the two was that Shean was tall and lanky and Jakk was slightly shorter, but far more muscular. Shean was dressed in his usual jeans and t-shirt while Jakk was dressed in kakis and a long sleeve.

To my surprise, Khire came in some moments later and sat down on a couch across from me, he smiled at me and listened to the conversation. Slowly the rest of our family flowed in.

"So I was walking in the castle yesterday on duty," Jakk began. "And I noticed something. It looked like a gun placed in a wall. I told some other guards and we got it out. It was a pistol placed in the wall aiming outwards with a cord on the ground for someone to walk across it and trigger it off. Isn't that weird, no one noticed it before, but now everyone's freaked out and watching where they're walking. We did a whole castle search just to see if there were any more," He looked around the room and sat there on the couch beside Aster who looked at him wide eyed while Fetcher looked at him with squinted eyes.

You could see the training the people went through when it came to situations like this. I knew immediately Aster would be thinking if anyone got hurt and if so how to help them, while Fetcher and Jakk would be thinking who planted the weapons? What their motives were? Who else was involved? How long have they been placed there? And many other questions. Even Khire, the smartest one in the family would be thinking, though I didn't exactly know what the first questions that would pop into his head would be.

"Did it go off?" He asked answering my unasked question.

"No, I stepped on the wire, but saw the gun before I moved the wire. We used magic on the cord and then I moved and we got the gun out, so no one got hurt," Jakk said relieved.

"That's not good, has the King ordered investigators?" Fetcher was very concerned and we all watched Jakk, waiting for the answer.

"Yes, they came to the castle today, that's why I'm off today, the King told everyone to leave while they investigate. As personal guard I should still be there though," He grumbled.

"I wonder who put it in the wall; do you think it was Dusk?" Shean asked.

"No, Dusk is good, he wouldn't put a gun in the wall, he'd just go and shoot whoever he wanted. The gun in the wall is chancy if you want a certain someone then it's best to do it yourself and not plant a trap like that. That gun could have killed anyone meaning the person didn't want to kill a certain person, he or she probably just wanted to kill someone," Khire said. I was proud my brother was so smart, but I didn't like how his mind seemed dark at times.

"Maybe the person has people in mind, just all the people in the castle are his or her victims," Aster said though he didn't sound convinced himself.

"How high was the gun placed?" Khire asked. "Why does it matter?" Shean asked.

"Because if the gun was placed near the bottom then the gun would shoot someone's foot or leg, then the person who set the gun could just come and do whatever he or she wants with that person, maybe kidnap him for questioning. If it's placed higher than it could shoot someone in the side of the head and kill them," Khire said thoughtfully.

"Oh, that makes sense, ummmm….I believe it was just a bit higher than five feet from the ground," Jakk answered. I didn't know what that would do, Jakk was taller than that, so it wouldn't hit him in the head, but it seemed to mean something to Khire.

☾

When Jakk first said something, my mind instantly went to work trying to figure out who might have done it. When he said the height, I thought of Shirra, Shirra was about five foot four inches and if she had been walking she may have noticed the wire, she was smarter and quicker at things than others. Being with me for so long, she probably would have noticed it before she stepped on it, but if she hadn't and she had kept walking she would have been killed. I thought about this for a long time, but put on an act as if it didn't bug me as much as it really did. I didn't need my brothers talking to me to try and figure out what was wrong after dad had already fought with me. I didn't like that I had shared so much, but I hoped that he would take it as a sign to shut up and not ask so much questions.

I would one day like to tell my whole family who I am, but with the guy going around and all the other assassins it was safer keeping them in the dark. They were already in danger for just living. Me telling them would get the attention of other assassins even more and I didn't like my family being in the spotlight of other assassins. Also I feared what they would do and what I would do.

Sighann began to cry and Mellony left to go get her. She brought her back and everyone lit up with happy chatter. I made a few comments, but otherwise stayed quiet. We had cake and supper, which I greatly enjoyed and let myself relax a little. It was almost eleven o'clock when everyone began to leave. Though there was the curfew on, they wouldn't be going far and Fetcher would guide them all home.

"Khire, wait," dad said as I opened the door. He came out with me and we walked down the path to the street.

"Please don't say no, can you please just come back with me and stay at my house, it's really cold and I don't like you out there sleeping wherever you sleep?" He was nearly begging and with a huff I turned to him. "Sure," I said, it wouldn't be too bad, I would have a warm bed, but I still had some things to do. "But let me just do something first ok, I'll be quick, my roommate will be wondering where I am and stuff, I'll meet you at your house k?" He, slightly unhappy, nodded. I gave him a hug and left turning right when I got on the street. When I was out of sight, I changed directions and headed down an alleyway and ran to the castle.

The castle towered above the rest of the city and it was hard to miss as I came closer to it and looked around for anyone. I saw no one though and so after a check around the castle I went inside. I couldn't do a good check, but I could do a quick go over. I found no one inside that shouldn't be, but after searching the castle I was able to detect odd presence of magic in random locations, which ended up being stashed weapons. I carefully disabled every trap and took them away. It took me an hour to get all seven out and then leave to get outside and away.

I met Temptress at her house which was ten minutes away from the castle and gave her the weapons. She looked them over as I looked around for any people nearby. Everyone was asleep though and the only movement on the streets were dogs or cats moving around in backyards or alleys. Temptress told me all she could see of the weapons then she took them away and I left to go to my dad's house.

"Sorry it took so long," I apologized as I came in as soon as I got there.

"It's ok," He said as he went back upstairs. I knew he hadn't been sleeping because he was still fully dressed, but he was tired so I said goodnight and went up to my old room where I burrowed under my comforter and gladly fell asleep on my old blue blanket surrounded by an empty dresser, empty blue walls and empty shelves. All my things I had ether taken with me when I went to the streets or were stored away in the attic for safekeeping.

☾

CHAPTER #33

The sun was high in the sky, but it felt like it had been there for hours. The streets were crowded as usual and everything seemed to be going nicely. No one fought and I didn't have to deal with any disagreements, misinformed citizens or anything. I just walked the streets in my uniform, tall and serious and everything went smoothly. I smiled and waved at the people I knew and greeted others I didn't, I helped tourists find restaurants, hotels, the must see attractions or any other place. It was boring today, and it didn't help that the time went by slowly.

When the sun was three quarters across the sky I left the streets to head to my office to file some paper work and to go to a meeting. It took me almost forty minutes to get to my office with the streets so crowded then it took me ten minutes to file everything and an extra twenty minutes to collect all I will need for the meeting then get to it. The station was large, with large slabs of bullet proof metal as the walls. It wasn't the most welcoming place and it looked very cold, but it was imposing and that suited its purpose. The well-kept lawn added some greenery to the structure, but no trees stood nearby and the magical fence that wrapped the entire property was tall and near deadly with electricity. The interior didn't look much better. With slabs of stone acting as the floors and hardly any windows, the furniture was more for practicality then comfort. The whole layout was almost maze-like to confuse anyone trying to cause trouble. The walls were blue, the floor dark blue with black veins.

Having worked here long enough the maze of hallways made sense to me and so after some turns and a staircase, I came to the fourth floor where I took a right and entered into a meeting room. It was large with a long metal table in the middle, a projector on a stand that hung from the ceiling, a weaved sheet that you could pull down to project things on, a stand to put objects on and some windows to look out on the streets of Vale Darra. I greeted the people already in the room and waited for the rest.

When it was full we began.

"Your all probably wondering what's going on and what this meeting is about. Some of you were asked to bring records of assassin activity, ideas that did work and didn't work for catching them and anything else deemed important.

"As it is obvious this meeting is about Dusk. We've spent a number of years trying to deal with him and nothing has worked. Some of us feel we are at a losing battle while others think there's still a chance. In any case we are going to continue to try and catch Dusk and prosecute him when we are able to.

"So, I have had a few ideas floating around in my head and I have put them to action. I have a few new gadgets made up that should help. I also have a special guest here that will be working with us to get Dusk. Everyone I would like you to meet Mr. Cander Valasheen, he is a well-experienced private investigator and very familiar with assassins. Successful in his areas, he will be put in charge of this Dusk business.

"Now as for the new devices, this device here will set off a signal, point and aim at Dusk and it will disorient him. This gun here will shoot a metal net at him that will weigh him down. However, it won't stop him from doing magic so keep the first device trained on him. I also have here guns to shoot a poisonous dart, not strong enough to kill, but strong enough to immobilize a strong magic user. By strong I mean strong, shoot this at anyone else and it will kill them. There are also larger nets here that will be strung around the city high enough so people walking along the streets won't get caught, but someone jumping down from a building will be and a strong electrical current will jolt them and hopefully immobilize them and not kill them.

"Now as you can tell these are powerful weapons, used improperly and you could kill many innocent people. Therefore you will all be trained extensively on the proper use, technique and care of these weapons and only a few of you will be granted permission to actually use them," Ludah, my boss went on and on, explaining in depth the plan and the weapons and how he hoped it will turn out. Cander stood silently to his left, black skin, eyes and hair he looked in his late forties, but still well-muscled and fit. He had a very grim expression on and looked slightly over the heads of everybody. I didn't feel like he gave off an air of arrogance or superiority, just distrusting and mean. I thought he looked like a very capable man and was interested to talk to him about his work.

The meeting lasted an hour then we were allowed to leave to the training grounds where we all worked with the different weapons. After a few hours some left while others continued on until it was down to just six of us. It wasn't that the weapons were hard to use or learn, but we had to test each weapon on a dummy. The dummies used looked and acted exactly like real people. They walked or ran around, ducked and even evaded capture. We had to work as a team for some exercises and by ourselves for others.

It became very apparent very quickly that though these devices look harmless, they are very dangerous. One of my friends blew up eight dummies by accident trying to immobilize just one with one device that was supposed to turn all magic attacks back on the attacker. After waiting for the smoke to clear, the dummies were amped up magically to get an idea of what the device would do to a powerful mage. The results were less fatal, but still had the potential to kill a strong mage if we weren't careful.

I tried a device that sent out a signal that supposedly prevented a mage from using their magic just so long as I pointed it at them. When one dummy ran at me with a bat, I pointed and clicked the trigger. The dummy kept running, but did stagger and slow down which was our way of knowing that the magic was cancelled out. After a moment I switched to the net which shot out and quickly pinned the dummy to the ground. The net was made of metal and cloth. The metal strands threaded in the weave were sharp so as the dummy squirmed and tried to break free the net ended up cutting fake flesh.

The unnerving part was, when testing the weapons on the dummies we weren't using the full power of each weapon. When it came to Dusk, we were to use the full power, which was an uncomfortable thought. Some people didn't like the idea that we were willing to take such a huge risk to bring down one person, even Dusk. The fact that if someone accidentally took a common citizen for an assassin and used one of these weapons on he or she could kill them made many people decide to leave.

After a long day of working with these weapons the six of us signed waivers that said we would use these weapons only in extreme situations and only against Dusk or people believed to be Dusk or another assassin. Which really gave us a lot of leeway when you really thought how many assassins could be out there. We also were safe from being sued or charged for murder if we accidentally killed the wrong person. In the end, we were basically given absolute freedom from all laws and given the responsibility to act on our own however we see fit.

The next day I was assigned a place in the city I knew well so I quickly left and stationed myself there. I had the gun and the other weapons I got from the meeting strapped to my belt along with my ordinary weapons. I was positioned near an alleyway so I went and hid myself in the darkness as I waited for Dusk. The sun was shining till it finally disappeared and it began to get really cold. I still sat in a little cubby waiting while some snow gathered around me.

The moon was just starting to come up when I saw a silhouette on a rooftop across the street from me. I got ready, he was too far away and facing me, so I wouldn't be able to get to him without giving myself away. He came closer and walked along the rooftops of a house right beside me. I sprang up and shot at him, a large crack and a flash of light erupted from the gun startling him as well as me.

The net shot forward and fell on him pulling him to the ground. The aluminum roofing was slippery so he went sliding off the roof to the ground. He hit the ground with a thud and tried to get to his feet, but the net pulled him to the ground pinning him there. My Guardian, a tiger, leapt forward and his Guardian leapt to defend his Protected. It was a cheetah and against a tiger there was no way for the smaller cat to win, but the cheetah was very fast and not holding back. The cheetah dashed around and swiped at Faleash's flank then darted the other way and leapt at her head. Faleash swotted the other cat away and lunged at her. Faleash got him on his back and stood over top clawing at the other cat, but I called her off scared she would kill the cheetah. I went over to Dusk, carefully holding my real gun with the remote over the top of it aimed at him as I walked over to him. He groaned slightly and lay sprawled on the ground. I caught the smell of blood that told me he was bleeding, but it was too dark for me to see how badly he was wounded.

"Remain still," I cautioned him. As I got closer a gun went off and hit me in my thigh I gasped and grabbed my thigh as I fell to the ground on one knee. I faced forward, but Faleash was facing me and her eyes went wide then everything went black as something hit me in the back of my head and I lost consciousness.

When I woke I was in the hospital with a bandage around my head and one around my thigh. Aster came in and smiled when he seen I was awake. "So had an encounter with Dusk did ya, you're lucky you're a good guy and not a bad guy," He said as he checked the machines.

"How did I get here?" I asked, I couldn't remember anyone getting me after I was hit.

"Oh a homeless person called the police when he was walking and saw you lying on the ground. He said he was walking and then he just turned down an ally and seen you, he was a little concerned and surprised to see ya there. Anyway he called and some cops found you and brought you here," He said from where he sat in a chair. "How do you feel, your head ok?" He asked worriedly.

"Ya," I nodded then squinted as it sent shooting pains to my head. Aster saw that and got a needle to stick into the line. The pain slowly went away and the black patches forming at the edges of my vision left.

"You have some visitors; you think you're up for that?" He went to the door and pulling the blinds away from the window I could see outside my room into the hallway.

"Sure, bring them in," He opened the door and motioned for some people to come in. My boss and some other people followed him in.

"Hi, Fetcher feeling ok, we just came to ask some questions alright?" He seemed more worried than I expected him to be.

"That's fine," I said and he turned to a notepad and took out a pen from his breast pocket to get ready to write.

"Ok, tell me what happened," He said.

"Well I got to my position on Wheeler Ave and Old Main Street. There's two building close together with a wooden structure blocking the alleyway. I know from past experience that it's a great place to hide so I hide there. Just a bit after 8, Dusk came out and he walked along the rooftops towards me. He got close enough to me so I shot the net at him. It got him and brought him to the ground. He had a cheetah with him and Faleash fought with it. She got the cat on the ground and I moved in to Dusk, but then a gun went off and I fell. After that I got hit in the head and got knocked out," I told them.

"So either Dusk has a friend or he can do more than what we thought he could," Ludah said nodding as he wrote.

"Did anyone see anyone else besides me when they came and got me?" I asked.

"No, and we didn't even find much evidence of people being there," We thought about that for a long time.

"Faleash, before I went unconscious I saw you, your eyes went really wide, did you see anything?" I asked my Guardian. She looked at me and an odd emotion I couldn't recognize flashed through my head from her.

"No sorry, I couldn't see anything, just darkness," She said solemnly.

"Dads here," Aster said as he looked out the window again. Dad along with the rest of my family came in and as the room got crowded, my boss and the other cops left.

"How are you?" Dad asked coming over to me and kissing the top of my head.

"Fine, how are you?" I asked back

"I'm not the one who got hit in the head by Dusk I'm perfect," He said jokingly, but he was still very concerned.

"Well ya I guess you weren't, but really I feel fine. I think Dusk wasn't trying to kill me or really hurt me, I think it was just something to get away," I really believed this, but I didn't know if they would.

"Maybe," Aster said as he walked around the room checking things. I made myself more comfortable on the bed.

"When can I get out?" I asked him.

"Tomorrow morning," Aster said as he sat back down in a chair. I would have preferred to have gotten out now, but I wasn't in any mood to argue.

We talked, but it was mostly to fill the silence until they were kicked out and Aster had to get back to work. Everyone said bye and I said "bye" back as one by one they left, Khire was the last to leave.

"There's a man here by the name of Dyras, his wish is time travel and he's slowly killing all the strong magic users because he fears magic. He's scaring off all the other assassins to. I think you should leave Dusk alone for the now and focus on how to stop Dyras without causing too much trouble for the future," he said standing before me.

"Where did you get this information?" I asked him.

"I work at Historica and I found a journal, it has multiple pictures in it from different time periods. Also I believe I have seen Dyras, he's not overly dangerous, just smart and his Wish gives him a good advantage," Khire told me, hands clasped behind him.

"When did you figure this out?" I asked suspicious.

"Last night I was working late and figured it out. I've had the journal for some time, but it took me a while to figure out he's a time traveler. I might be wrong, but it's the only reasonable explanation," He told me frowning.

"Ok, I'll look into it, thanks Khire," I said and gave him a stiff nod. He said bye and left me to my own thoughts.

Within five minutes after he left I fell asleep, too tired to convince myself I needed to think this through now. The room silent, the closed window blocked out all the noises from the busy street below. So I let myself drift off telling myself I could solve everything tomorrow.

☾

We all seemed to drift towards dads house where we talked some, but soon after everyone began to go home.

"Hey dad I'm leaving again, but I'll be back soon ok," I heard Khire say. Dad looked like he would have said no, but he stopped himself.

"Just be careful and come here when you get back," He said instead. I left then so I didn't hear what else was said.

When I got home Julia was moving the furniture and cleaning the house.

"Hello Shean, can you do me a favour?" She asked. She was my fiancé, soon to be wife and soon to be mother in seven months. Currently she was in a state where she would move everything around in the house, clean it, then move everything around again and put everything in different places. She'd then forget where she put things so when we tried to find it we couldn't.

"Sure," I said as I went into the kitchen to get a drink of water.

"Um well my mother, with the smart brain she was gifted with at birth went on vacation spontaneously and just called me saying she's across the world. She has the house and she just left it. Could we take a trip over and make sure her cats and plants are ok and make sure that the house is locked?" She grunted as she shifted a table.

Her blue long sleeved shirt was wet and so were her pale cream coloured pants, but her hair was up in a small ponytail and though not neat, she looked like she had a good day. She also looked like she had a very busy day. The hardwood floors were clean and smelt like orange, the horse ornaments on the side tables that were usually blanketed in dust were once again black, brown and white. The rugs by the doorways looked clean too, though still stained in places and there were more pictures hanging up on the walls.

The kitchen looked like it also got attacked by her cleaning frenzy. It smelled strongly of lemons, the cabinets above the sink were a freshly painted light brown while the lower cabinets were an old dark brown. The fridge was once again a pure white with a few magnets on it. The biggest change was the island, which sat in the middle of our kitchen and was once an old wooden structure, barely holding itself together.

"Ah sure I guess," I said. She nodded.

"What did you do?" I asked looking at the island. I wasn't a fan of change and I didn't like things changing on me without me knowing about them first.

"It had to go, it's not safe for the baby. Relax it's in your office," She said and I smiled.

"Thank you," I said relieved, the island was old with some kids hand prints all over it. I was glad she didn't get rid of it. The new glass island that took the center of the kitchen didn't exactly scream child safety, but it was very nice.

"How's your brother?" She asked coming over to me.

"Fine, he wants to get back to work," I said and put my cup in the dishwasher. "Probably, that sounds like your brother," She walked away. "Ok, do you have anything to do? I just have to get changed. Do you want to start tacking up the horses?" She asked leaning on the door and looking at me.

"No I'll go tack them up," I said and began to leave.

Just then the phone rang. I picked it up and when the voice asked for Julia I handed it to her. "Ok........sure, when......oh I was just going to go out to my mom's........can it wait...fine one sec," She turned to me. "It's my boss, I have to work, but could you do it? I don't really want you going alone, but this can't wait and it will take me a few days. I don't like the thought of my mother's house being unlocked," She smiled pleadingly at me.

"That's fine," I said. Julia dealt with rehabilitating teens and adults who have mental disabilities and have gone to jail. Currently she was dealing with an eighteen year old and after three years was finally getting somewhere with him.

With a kiss goodbye I left and went to the stables. I got my horse; an appaloosa named Kieko and saddled him up. He was happy to be going out and so I had him tacked up and on the road in no time. He pranced all the way to the front gates, head held high and tail held up as he picked his feet up and made his way down the road as if on parade.

"What's gotten into Kieko?" A guard asked when I came up to them. Sairey my border collie Guardian sat watching Kieko amused and ready to go though patient enough to wait for me to chat a bit with the guards. "Nothing he's just excited," I said patting my horse on the neck. Keiko responded with a snort and a nod of his head. My Wish allowed me to communicate with horses, so he knew what I said and usually liked keeping up a constant chatter with me. Today however, he just wanted to run.

"Shean," I heard a voice say and I turned to see Khire and another person walking with two horses towards me.

"Oh, hi, where you going?" I asked him confused. I knew he did some ridding despite the fact he hated horses when he was younger, but I still never expected to see him on a horse.

"My friend and I found a cabin in the woods the other day, we're going exploring to see what else we can find," he said pointing at the person walking behind him. His friend was a gorgeous looking women who walked right up to me with a smile on her face. It took me a moment to think as I looked back at Khire then to the women. Khire wasn't ugly anymore, but I wasn't used to seeing him with women especially gorgeous women that look like they just strolled off the cat walk.

"Hi I'm Caprica," The women said one hand on her hip the other extended out to me. I shook it and smiled at her.

"Hi, I'm Khire's older brother Shean," I greeted her. "Has he told you about me?" I asked being funny. Khire smiled and shook his head.

"A little bit, but not much, you're a horse trainer right?" Caprica asked and I nodded.

"I trained that horse you got there actually," I told her. She looked surprised as she looked at her horse.

"Oh, it's a good horse," She said smiling enthusiastically. She had a lovely smile that lit up her face.

"Thanks, hey I have to go to my fiancés mother's house, if it's the same rout as you're going, why don't I join you until we have to split?" I said.

"Sure," Khire said with a shrug.

When we said goodbye and Khire and Caprica mounted we rode out, Khire in the middle and me on his left while Caprica was on his right. We talked as we rode Caprica filling most of the silence. "So you guys found a cabin in the woods and are going to investigate it?" I asked amused. I looked from Caprica to Khire and back again wanting to think my brother was a little classier then that. Khire looked at me dumbly for a little bit, then clued in.

"It's not like that!" Khire said frantically.

"Well it sure looks like something," I said laughing.

"Khire's too immature for grown-up stuff," Caprica said teasingly.

"I am not!" Khire said turning to look at her, face flushed.

"Really cause whenever I try and kiss you, you back away and cross your fingers saying 'stay away from me witch'," She said as she crossed her fingers, dropping her reins in one hand. I couldn't help but laugh at Khire who glared at Caprica.

"No I don't, and I'm not the one who's immature," Khire said defensively. Caprica just smiled and nodded.

"If you like you can join us?" Caprica invited.

"To explore the cabin," Khire added in quickly. Caprica raised her eyebrows at him, but stayed quiet.

"No, I'm ok thank you," I told her still smiling.

"Pity I had all these fun things planned. A party of three would have made it all the more fun," She said mischievously.

"Can we just stop talking?" Khire asked looking up.

"Why? Am I making you uncomfortable?" She asked pleasantly.

"Yes you are," He said looking at her.

"I'm just being polite grumpy. You know there may be a chance we get lost and then we have to camp outside in the woods surrounded by bears and wolves. It might get cold, we might have to..." Caprica started. "Stop!" Khire interrupted and I laughed.

"She's right, are you guys set up for camping in the woods if you have to?" I asked in all seriousness.

"Nope, I brought nothing. No food, no water, no sleeping bag or anything to start a fire. Khire you might actually have to hunt to feed me tonight. I like my rabbit a wee bit bloody please," The women said completely enjoying herself.

"Why did I bring you?" Khire asked turning to her.

"Because my dear you said you knew of a secluded cabin in the woods and there would be some exploring involved," She said winking at me.

"Yes, but exploring the cabin. I'm nosy and I want to see who lived there," "Yes well I'm nosy of people too and I'm far more fun than any hermit you'll come across," Caprica added. Khire looked absolutely bewildered by her, which sent Caprica into a fit of laughter.

"Well anyway, stay safe kids no foolish stuff ok," I said smiling. Khire turned his glare on me and began to say something before Caprica cut in.

"Oh don't worry I'm a big believer in safety first," Caprica said. Khire snorted and shook his head.

"Oh! Says the women whose broken more bones then she can count," Khire quipped.

"Heh, I like to live a little so what's the matter with that. You on the other hand don't. Maybe we should just go to this cabin and have some fun. I'm pretty sure I can change your mind about anything if you give me an hour," Caprica teased.

"Ahhh ya no I think I'd have a better time exploring the land not each other," Khire said shaking his head stubbornly.

"Oh Khire, Khire, Khire, my dear boy. One day you'll be a man," The women remarked. Khire shook his head completely embarrassed by her. I smiled at them. I had never seen Khire joke with anyone before and it was nice seeing Khire so comfortable with someone. He looked at me and I shook my head then decided to change the subject.

"You've become a better rider Khire, have you been riding a lot lately?" I said out loud, but spoke to his horse in my head. Knight, Khire's horse, told me Khire rode him some times and that he liked Khire because he was very light and went exciting places though sometimes scary men chased him and Khire had to use magic. I wondered at that last part, but didn't ask Khire.

"Ya, I've been going out now and again to the mountains," He said nodding in the direction of the tall peaks.

We chatted about random stuff for a little bit until we came to a split in the dirt path. One narrow path led to the mountains, the other, more traveled one, led to the neighbouring towns.

"I have to head off now, but it was nice meeting you Caprica. Bye you two and remember no funny stuff," I said and left them as I headed west. They said bye and went their own way. It was still hours from night and I planned to get home before the moon came up. I asked my horse to go into an easy gallop and within the next half an hour I was tying him to a post then went inside Julia's mother's house. It wasn't locked and her two cats were rubbing against me and meowing to be fed and petted. I found some food and poured a bunch into a pot. It would last them a week I hoped then I watered the plants, hoping I didn't kill them.

"I think the plants would survive better without me," I grumbled. I was never a green thumb, so I wasn't very good with plants; they always died in a week whenever I tried to water them. That taken care of, I locked up the house and mounted my horse. I rode off back home, it was only four o'clock in the afternoon, so despite the fact that I did little today, it was still a good day.

CHAPTER #34

When Shean left I was relieved, but disappointed, it was nice talking and spending time with him. I couldn't remember the last time we did that, but there was work to do. Temptress and I thought it would be a good idea to test our theory and so we headed out to the mountains. I decided that the best place to try it would be by the cabin. The fact that Midnight was able to build and live there for however many years proved that there was an area on this side of the mountains that either wasn't censored or was blocking the censors.

It was a long ride to get there, but I liked being with Caprica, she made anything and everything fun and always had a smile on her face. For the most part her conversations with anyone tended to stay around her, but today and after Shean left, she was focusing pretty well on magic.

"So I figure if we just use our magic to cast a lot of light that should be alright. Creating light isn't evil, it doesn't take a lot out of ya, but a beacon of light is kinda hard to miss," She said as she led the way to the cabin. She didn't know where she was going, but she was never a follower and she wasn't about to start being one.

"Ya we can start off with that and see if that works," I said nodding along. I was liking our plan of action less and less seeing as doing a lot of magic wasn't exactly a sure way to get at someone to kill them, but having no other better idea, I went along with it.

We got to the cabin and took the horses to the stream, tying them up there to get them out of the way. They were more than happy to get away from us, sensing our excited moods, they pranced and tossed their heads nervously.

"Ok let's stand on the other side of the cabin," I said and Caprica and I walked around the cabin. We found a little clearing and stood an arm's reach away from each other.

"Ok on the count of three I guess, one, two, three," I said and together we both pooled our magic together to create light. Our magic flowed out of us in a whitish light and shone blindingly around us. Creating light was sometimes a little hard to do and most assassins couldn't do it. All magic users could do some pure magic and some bad magic which created what was called tainted magic. That's why everyone had different coloured ribbons, the different colours came from the mixing of the two good and bad forms of magic. In reality there was no good and bad, it was just a way to differentiate between the two types. In order to create light, you had to pool your magic together and try to focus on the pure, good magic.

Some people could use the dark magic to create a dark purple light, but it usually took too much energy for the mage to do and eventually turned them mad. Temptress's light was slightly greenish while mine had a blue glow to it, but together we were able to create a bright enough light that anyone nearby could see. We also used enough magic for anyone looking for strong magic users to notice. We held the light for a full five minutes then let it fade. Temptress put her hands on her knees and panted, sweat coming off her forehead to drip in the snow. I looked around, panting and sweating, but remaining on my feet.

"Ok now we wait," I gasped and Caprica nodded. We both ended up sitting in the grass and snow trying to catch our breath and waiting for something to happen. "Ok my butt is wet," Caprica complained getting up and brushing snow off her pants. I got up as well and brushed myself off then looked around. I couldn't see or sense anyone nearby and began to feel like we failed.

"Let's try again," I said and Caprica nodded.

This time we only held it for about three minutes with about the same success as before. A buck came out of the trees and stopped to look at us. I could sense his heard nearby so he probably thought us some type of weird predator that he wanted to check out.

"You're a brave little deer," I told him and he eyed me with one black eye before swishing his tail and walking away. I walked around the cabin to try and stretch my legs, but I could feel myself getting shaky. It was hard for me to create light because I was a strong assassin and use to doing other magic. My magic was used mostly to create heat, strength and energy so it was hard for me to create light. Usually energy is given off as light, but as an assassin making light is not something we usually want to do and so we train to not create light.

"Ok that didn't work," I said when I found Caprica leaning against a tree.

"Well it was worth a try," She said and I sat down beside her.

"We can try something different tomorrow. Let's just sleep for the now," I told her and she nodded. We agreed on taking turns standing guard and as she was the most tired, I agreed to stay up and keep watch first.

That night it got really cold and we both ended up in the cabin using our magic to create heat. Our Guardians curled up with us, but I ended up alongside Caprica asleep. It was a comfortable sleep, but it was cold so we shivered and woke up a lot throughout the night.

"I'm freezing," Caprica said pulling me closer.

"I really don't think this is a good idea," I told her pushing her away despite how cold I was.

"S-s-s-hirra s-should thank me, it's either... spoon with me or b-b-become a popsicle," Caprica spoke, her teeth chattering.

"You have a point, but she still won't like it," I said loosing willpower to push her away. She was very warm and I knew if we shared body heat it would be a lot warmer.

Shirra was screaming in my head to stay away from her, but swearing and complaining to her on how cold I was, I got her to shut up and I pulled Caprica closer. She wasn't as warm as I thought she would be, but I felt a little better.

"You know I could solve your little issue right here right now," Caprica whispered into my ear.

"I th-think it's you that has a problem," I told her as I tried to stop my teeth from chattering so much.

"Well how about… I help you with yours then you… can help me with mine?" She asked trying to get closer.

"You know what I feel like I'm ok you know? Y-y-you know that f-f-feeling when you suddenly f-f-feel ok?" I asked her and she giggled. "Let's just sleep w-w-we have a long day tomorrow," I told her and restrained her hands though she still tried to wrap her leg around me and keep me uncomfortably close to her. I could smell old sweat on her, her natural body odour mixed in wasn't bad, but my senses were abnormally sharp and the smell of her was a little overpowering.

It was an interesting night, but we both got some sleep and as soon as the tiniest bit of sunlight streaked across the sky Shirra was shrieking in my head swearing and cursing at me.

"Ok I'm up," I said out loud. I got up and left Caprica asleep with her little white cat. I checked on the horses and decided they would be ok if I let them doze some more. They were warm standing side by side and protected from the wind.

"I should have just slept with you guys," I grumbled to them.

I walked through the trees around the cabin until I came to the stream. I used some magic and cupped some water in my hands to drink. The water was ice cold, but it flowed fast enough to not freeze over. It was the end of February and I looked forward to the coming summer, but up in the mountains, winter would last much longer.

"It is so cold here," Caprica said shivering as she came over to get some water.

"Ok let's try instead of using magic we open ourselves up to it. Let's try and find out Dyras's next target?" I told her and she nodded.

We returned to our earlier spot from yesterday and sat in the snowy grass cross-legged. Opening yourself up to magic was something all magi learned how to do. It taught control and how to calm your mind. And if you were good enough, you could even sense people from around the world, hear people speaking, feel things, see things and possibly manipulate the flow of magic. People who specialized in this used this power to see when earthquakes would shake the earth or when a storm was coming, but it could also be used for evil purposes. A strong magic user could over power a weaker mage and take control of the weaker mage's mind. It could even kill someone, but at the cost of both people involved. Still it was important to learn how to do when growing up so you know what pure magic is.

We breathed in deeply and slowly to let the world of magic envelop us. Despite what people believe about magic being alluring or able to trap people, that wasn't entirely true. It was appealing, but the magic was flowing and closed off to everyone. You could access it to feel, hear, see and possibly manipulate people to some degree, but you couldn't actually use it. I thought it was because it was pure magic and the little dark magic in everyone stopped people from using real pure magic. Some people believed it was once manipulated in a way to benefit humans, but even if it were true, that skill was now lost to us. I have some ideas that the magic wasn't manipulated so much as just used to sense the earth thus allow humans to better use the earth in a way that benefits humans. In any case, I know I can't manipulate the magic so I never bothered to try.

I sensed billions of people on the earth; I sensed tremors somewhere below, people steadying themselves for an earthquake halfway around the world. I heard babies crying, people singing, I felt heat, cold, and I smelt all sorts of different foods. I tried to focus on pockets of magic where I knew it meant strong magi lived, but I couldn't control where and what I felt, saw or heard. The magic showed me what it wanted me to know and so I just continued to try and glean something from whatever I got.

After a time I stopped the flow of magic and looked up to the sky realizing the sun was already down.

"I didn't get anything," I told Caprica.

"I think I got something. I think Dyras has been jumping around a lot, I felt a disturbance and I think he was time traveling. I don't know where he went, but it wasn't in our time," Caprica said holding her head. My head like Caprica's felt like it was splitting apart and despite the fact I knew we should try and get back into the cabin, I felt like my whole body was on fire and I couldn't move.

"We will look after you," Myre said and Caprica's cat, Tailo began to purr as she curled up beside her Protected.

We slept there and froze, but still miraculously managed to survive the night. Snow fell and we woke up covered in it, but our Guardians did their best to keep us alive. We were stiff and in a lot of pain, but we managed to get to the cabin and sleep the rest of the day. The next day we would travel back to Vale Darra, but for now we needed rest. And to warm up again, our magic was doing well to keep our organs warm, but our bodies were dangerously close to hypothermia.

A twig snapped and my senses went on high alert.

"Caprica?" I asked looking over to where she slept. Her face betraying just how tired she was. I could sense someone was nearby and though I was still tired I got to my feet. I nudged Caprica with my foot and she woke groggily looking around confused. Sensing the tension, she got to her feet and looked around. It hadn't been that long of a sleep, but my magic was still running strongly and my body had finally warmed up to a safe temperature. We both went outside and stepped into the early sunlight.

"Who's out there?" She called. We obviously had no surprise on our side, so no point pretending we didn't know someone was out there.

"Hello children, what a pleasant surprise," A voice spoke and my blood ran cold. From a cluster of trees over to my left came an old man with a black panther Guardian. The man looked haggard, but still capable of a good fight. The panther came closer to us, but the man stood back.

"Hello Sinth," I spoke breathlessly.

"Khire, my little protégé. How nice for you to come visit. You do realise this is my property you're trespassing on don't you?" Sinth looked nearly the same since I last seen him, his hair now more peppery and his face sunken, but otherwise he seemed the same.

"What do you want?" I asked, spreading my feet a little wider apart, readying myself to fight.

Caprica beside me looked ready to fight to, but seemed to hold herself back realizing that this wasn't any of her business.

"You know I never thought to see how you faired after I left you. We certainly didn't leave things settled now did we?" He asked with a smile as if recollecting a happy memory.

"No we didn't," I said then lunged at him. I didn't want to talk to him, I wanted to kill him. I brought a knife out from my belt and made a jab to his kidneys. He, though much older then I, was easily capable at dodging and getting a punch to my shoulder. I grabbed his wrist and threw him down on the ground, trying to pin him, but he kneed my in the ribs and pushed me off of him.

"I am not your enemy. I know you hate me, you hate me more than anything, but I am not your enemy. There are bigger things out there then me. I'm old, my time on this earth is short now. Khire you need to put your feelings behind you and start thinking about other things besides yourself," He said to me as he drew his own knife from his belt.

"I will deal with the other stuff once I kill you. I've waited too long for this. Your life is going to end right here right now by me," I said viciously.

All my hurt and fear came crashing back to me, those memories I tried to block, all those times Midnight was there in my life. Those years that made me hide in fear then later give in to him and kill people. I hated him for what he did to me. The wounds unable to be fully healed, were ripped open again. I fought him knowing that I fought him with the knowledge he gave me. With every twist, turn, jab, swing and punch I could remember each lesson he had taught me. I didn't think of fighting him in the present, it felt like I was fighting him in all time periods. From when I first learned how to use a knife to now. When I was younger Sinth would make sure I got things right as fast as I could. He made me practice for a few hours then fight me and if I didn't get it right he would use the technique he was showing me on me so that I could understand the pain. Pain was his way of teaching. It was the only way he knew how to teach.

He punched me, his fist going for my face, but I moved and managed to take it off the side of my head. His hand sliding past my ear, but he turned it into a hold and grabbed my hair then yanked. It hurt like hell and made me stumble back. I kicked out and managed to get him to let go, but he fell on me and stabbed me in my shoulder. "That's for stabbing me," Sinth growled in my ear. He was furious, but he was still in control. While my mind raced and tried to come up with attacks he hadn't taught me. I had plenty of years without him to pick up my own moves. I grabbed another small knife from up my sleeve and stabbed him in the thigh. He winced, but tried to stab me again in the heart. As he pulled back I rolled and punched his right arm, right at the elbow to make him buckle. Following through with the momentum I got on top of him and slammed his head into the ground.

Magic suddenly blasted out from him and slammed into my chest sending me flying a good several meters from him. I hit the ground hard, the wind knocked out of me, but managed to get to my feet just before engaging in battle again.

"Listen to me, stop this!" Midnight was saying furiously. He kept speaking, but my brain blocked it out. He sounded mad, like he had finally let go of his sanity, his eyes round and his movements turning frantic. He was getting desperate now, but I didn't stop. I had an opening to his chest and took it making a large gash across his chest. Blood seeped out of his wound and Midnight pushed me away, breathing ragged and sweat gleaning from his brow. My own breath was harsh and quick, but I was too focused on killing Midnight that I didn't take the time to try and calm my heart allowing me to think straight. The world seemed to fade away as the only thing that mattered now was killing Midnight. My master that had given me nothing, yet everything in the world. He had taken away my life in exchange for his. Making me into his little creation.

I screamed with rage and pummelled into him. My fists finding spots on his body he left unprotected.

"I have had enough. You won't listen then fine. It's your fault that you're too blind to see the true threat. You've always let your hatred for me blind you from the broader world. There are other people out there far more powerful then you or I Khire. You're going to need my help to defeat them," Sinth said. His face was red with rage.

"I don't need your help, I've never needed you!" I growled and swiped at him cutting his forearm as he brought his knife up.

I could tell when he used his magic as the atmosphere crackled with tension and the incredible energy radiated around him from his magic. He was a strong mage, stronger then I as his two brown ribbons zoomed around his body, creating sparks and melting the snow around us. I opened myself up to my own magic and then we were fighting again. This time everything was faster. We moved trying to outdo each other and kill the other. I was full of hate and furry, it sent me into a frenzy and I didn't feel my body starting to tingle with the amount of magic I was using. I couldn't stop, I had to kill him.

His knife bit deep into my side, but I managed to stab him back. The thick muscle at his neck now torn and bloody. I ducked under his arm and dragged my knife up his back, slicing the skin open as Sinth brought his elbow back and broke my nose. Blood spurted everywhere and my eyes began to water. Sinth pressed the attack and knocked me to the ground, slamming my head repeatedly into the now bloody dirt. I punched upwards, unable to put a lot of power behind it, but enough to get him to back off and I to roll away. I didn't get to my feet though, instead I lunged and brought my knife around, stabbing his right knee. His fist smashed me in the head and I had to fight to stay conscious. I was losing a lot of blood, my magic was burning through my veins like fire. My body felt past the point of being able to function, but I was too determined to listen to my own slowing heart to stop. I knew I didn't have much longer, but my mind was still screaming at me to kill him. Sinth got to his feet and tried to back up. His right leg was useless, but he got back far enough that I couldn't reach him. "Khire I'm sorry for everything I did! Please listen to me, it's not me you're after, you just think it's me," He said and seemed to almost plead, but I was past all rationality.

I roared and dove at him again as he brought his blade up. It caught me in my face and tore my skin creating a gash from my cheekbone all the way into my hairline. It stung and it fuelled my furry as I tried to stab him. He sent a vicious kick at my head and I just managed to dodge. He fell on the ground and that's when it happened. I was on my knees ready to lunge at him when he suddenly shrieked and something invisible tore him to shreds. I could feel a deep hunger feasting on his death as he was quickly torn to bits. Large claw marks gouged the earth and Sinth lay still in a bloody mess of broken bones and tissue strewn across the ground. It was a terrible sight to behold, my mind blanked at the horror of it all and for a second I forgot who I was and what I was, I just stared at what I couldn't comprehend.

I gasped, my breathing was ragged, my magic seared my veins, it was too much for me, but my triumph was sweet. I smiled and gave a funny laugh. I killed him. I finally killed him. I collapsed after that and the world grew dark as my mind let go of consciousness.

I woke a day later, I felt like I had been in a fire and pulled out before I could roast to death. My skin was torn and blistered. I could feel nothing, but heat and it hurt. I tried to get my bearings, but my mind couldn't focus on anything, everything was dark and nothing made sense. After sometime I slept again, fitfully, but a soothing sensation came over me and I finally was able to settle into peaceful sleep.

When next I woke I was in Shirra's bed, Myre was beside me, one of his ears was torn off and large scars adorned his side going down his back right leg, but otherwise he looked ok.

"Ok? I look a lot better then you," He told me shuffling closer to me. My body was sore, but I felt far better than I had.

"What happened?" I asked stupidly, my mind unable to piece things together.

"After you collapsed, Caprica called Shirra and she came. She healed your major wounds then she and Caprica brought us here. You've been out for a week," Myre said and I winced. A week?

Caprica came through the doors then and walked over to me.

"So Creature awakes," She said smiling.

"Creature?" I asked confused.

"Sinth was found a few days ago by city police. Their saying it's the work of a new assassin that they call Creature," She said and shrugged. "It fits," She said and it was then that I noticed that haunted look in her eyes.

"What's wrong?" I asked her.

"Nothing," she said, but not very convincingly.

"Caprica?" I encouraged.

"What happened out there? What did you do?" She asked me quietly.

"I killed him, I killed Midnight," I told her, awe struck to think that my life could finally start. "I finally killed him, I can live now," I rambled hysterically.

"How? You were kneeling there then suddenly Sinth was just torn apart, there were huge claw marks everywhere. How did you do that?" She said and this time I heard it. She was afraid.

"Are you afraid of me?" I could almost think straight now, but I still thought it strange that Temptress would fear me.

"What are you?" She asked so suddenly that it made me actually question myself.

"I'm Khire, I'm who I am meant to be," I told her, meeting her eyes and for once feeling as though those words were actually true. She nodded then abruptly left. I let her leave, she obviously needed some time to think, but I still didn't understand. What had happened?

"You attacked and killed Midnight, but not with your body, with your mind," Myre said and I looked over at him.

"How?" I questioned, very confused.

"It's your Wish. Your Wish doesn't just heighten your senses, it makes you animalistic. You have the instincts and senses of an animal, you're not a mere human. Humans are animals too, but lesser animals. Humans have grown dumb with age. They have lost their ability to be in tuned with nature and instead choose to control it. You are greater, you're more animal then other humans. You can become an animal," Myre said and I felt a weird stirring in the back of my mind. An imaginary growl of confirmation sounded in my mind.

I nodded, having nothing to say and let that knowledge sink in. It made me feel powerful and in control. I liked that feeling. I wanted to walk out this room and use that power, but as I sat up a wave of nausea over took me.

"Maybe not yet," I said and collapsed back down.

"You need time to heal. You let your magic control you and you didn't listen to me when I told you to stop," Myre told me sternly.

"I didn't even hear you speaking to me," I confessed and he nodded.

"I know. Now sleep, you need to heal," He said and laid his head on his paws and slept.

Vale Darra was the same when I had left, though I felt different and though the city hadn't actually changed, I still felt like something had. Maybe it was just my own self-confidence or the fact that I felt able to conquer anything. It was early in the morning and I was walking up the pathway to my father's house. I was tired, but able to move about without any pain or nausea now and all my wounds were healed. I decided to visit my father. The snow had piled around the front door so I grabbed a shovel at the side and shovelled it away. By the time my dad opened the door the snow was gone and I had replaced the shovel at the side of the house.

"Did you shovel?" He asked confused.

"Ya, the snow was in the way," I said as he invited me in.

"Well thank you, but you didn't have to do that, now, how was your trip?" He asked as he went into the kitchen.

I sat in the living room on the couch and waited for him to return. When he did he had two bowls of cereal, one he handed to me. I looked at him and shook my head, but he placed it in my hands and told me to eat it. I wasn't sure if I could keep anything down at the moment, but wasn't about to tell him that.

"My trip was good, weather got bad as we were coming back…." I started to answer his question when he interrupted.

"What happened to your nose? And we? You weren't alone?" He seemed surprised.

"Oh ya I had a friend with me and I just got in a little bit of a fight," I thought back to the ride that seemed so long ago.

"Oh, ok, where did you go? Should I ask about this fight?" He asked.

"To the mountains, I wanted to check out this cabin, but I couldn't find it. It wasn't anything to worry about, just a confrontation, I handled it," I shrugged and took a bite.

He thought as he ate his cereal and we sat in silence for a while. It was then that he noticed Myre.

"What happened to Myre?" He asked. Myre was clean looking, but now missing an ear, and he still looked a little scraggily with all his healing scares. Unfortunately, though Shirra could heal me and only leave very faint scares behind, she wasn't as good at healing Myre and so he would bare more scares then I.

"Oh, we ran into some trouble. Some wolves attacked us at night when we were sleeping. Myre's alright, aren't ya buddy?" I asked Myre and he smiled.

"I did my duty," Was all he said. My dad frowned, but let the subject go shaking his head and mumbling about fights and wolves.

"Is everything ok?" Dad sighed, but asked me.

"Yes," I told him and put my empty bowl on the table in front of me.

"You seem different," He said, studying me.

"I think the fresh air did me some good. Being stuck in the city hasn't been good for me," Was my reply and he nodded, but he still looked puzzled. I wasn't really sure what else to say so gently ran my fingers through Myre's fur and looked around. All the while my dad looked at me as if trying to work out a difficult puzzle.

We talked some more, but after some hours I said my goodbyes and left. I had work to do and with a new sense of worth I strutted down the alleyways as if the street people asleep in the boxes were my audience. My new sense of self empowering me to be fearless.

CHAPTER #35

Some days later as I was walking near the middle of the city, a place surrounded by taller buildings, when a gun went off. The whole crowd cowered and started screaming as everyone ran trying to get to safety. Another gun went off and another, though they weren't coming from the same place. They were shooting into the crowd and people where falling to the ground bleeding. I ran to a man and checked to see if he was ok, but he was already dead with a bullet in his head.

More people went down and the guns began to fire repeatedly, going off one after another until all you heard were guns firing and people screaming as they tried to save their lives. I got to an alleyway and into a house from the back door. Running up to a higher window I looked out at the guns and taking out a gun strapped to my leg I fired at them, magic hardening the bullets and making them explosive. The guns shattered and sent fragments to shoot out and rain down on the people. I couldn't get all the guns before they ceased, but I decided to destroy them all anyway. I stepped back out of view of the people below and looked for anyone near the guns. No one was close to them and they weren't mine. Apparently there was a new comer to Vale Darra and invading my territory. I growled to myself, Vale Darra was my city and I would not have some new person killing on my turf. I immediately decided to see him or her as a threat and so kill the assassin as soon as I got the chance.

I left the house and went back to the alley to make my way around to the other side of the street. The sun was high in the sky and ambulances were already arriving to load bodies, the dying or the injured onto stretchers. Police wandered the streets and told everyone to move along. They stretched police tape around the area affected and closed that part of the city. People were evacuated from nearby buildings and told to go elsewhere while people who had been involved were asked questions. A cop came up to me.

"Hello Khire, were you involved in any of this?" He asked. I looked at him for a second, recognizing who he was as a friend of my brothers. "Ok I just have a few questions to ask you," He started. "How do you know I was involved?" I questioned.

"You have blood on you, do you feel any pain?" He asked as he held up his clipboard to write on.

"No, I think I'm fine, it was just the people around me that were shot not me," I said as I thought it through.

"Ok, now tell me from the beginning, what happened?" He asked next. So I told him what had happened.

"I was just walking when the guns started firing, I ran into an alleyway and hid as everyone else was running around, though I did stop to see if someone was alive. A man went down right beside me and I checked to see if he was alive, but he was already dead so then I ran," I said honestly. The cop nodded and continued to question me.

Fetcher came limping overlooking panicked and worried. "Are you ok?" He asked placing his hands on my shoulders then hugging me. He pushed me away to arm's length and looked me up and down.

"I'm fine," I said annoyed. He still looked worried, but he let me go. The cop seemed to be done asking me questions. "Can I go home?" I asked. The cop nodded and I said bye and left. Fetcher followed me.

"What happened to your nose?" He asked trying to look at my face.

"A little disagreement between two people that I solved rather well. Are you going to follow me?" I asked irritated and stopped to talk to him. "What just happened here?" Fetcher asked me seriously.

"I actually don't know," I told him and he nodded.

"Do you think it was Dyras?" Fetcher asked.

"I'm not sure, I thought Dyras just hated magi. Shooting at a crowd of people is something different," I told Fetcher. I had a bad feeling that I was missing something.

"What am I supposed to do, this is a city. There's no way to protect everyone," Fetcher said frustrated. "Please just tell me what you know and I won't question you. I will do as you say," Fetcher suddenly said to me.

"I don't know any true facts and I already told you what I know. A guy named Dyras lived centuries before and I think his Wish is time travel. He has something against magic so he's trying to destroy all magi," I told him truthfully.

"Ok did you try using magic to find him?" Fetcher asked hands on hips.

"Yes, but all I get is a disturbance, nothing exact. He's moving around a lot and I think he's jumping around in time.

"Over the past two hundred years there's been a steady decline in magi and I think it's because Dyras is learning better ways on how to weed out all magic. He's responsible for a lot of unexplained events. Like years ago there was that mage group of seven strong magi who traveled the world helping people. They were doing really well when one of them accidentally destroyed a building and killed thirty people. A month later the seven people turned up dead and the police never found out who did it. There are a lot of other examples all never solved because Dyras would just time travel to some other place so he was never caught," I told Fetcher as he listened intently.

"How come he never stopped magic right when it started?" Fetcher asked.

"I think because it was still so new and he didn't understand it. It's taking him this long to figure out how to destroy it. He doesn't want to just go back in time because he's afraid of what he might change. I think he may have limits on how far he can travel. That's all just a hunch, maybe he's afraid of his past?" I had no idea why

Dyras wouldn't just stop the magic from the very beginning. Even trying to explain it was confusing.

"That doesn't make any sense," Fetcher said. "And how can we stop someone like that without destroying something else?" Fetcher asked me.

"I have no clue, but if we don't stop him he's going to keep destroying the world," I said shrugging. Either way something bad would happen.

"Ok I'll look into records to see if there's anything there that might help us," Fetcher said and with that we parted ways. "Oh Khire before I leave you, I just wanted you to know that some months ago we found Miranna's body," Fetcher said before I left.

"Where?" I asked slowly.

"Her throat was cut and she was chained to a rock then thrown into the river by the mall," He told me with a dark expression.

"Do you know who did it?" I asked.

"No, but when we talked to the family they didn't seem to want to know. There's no point trying to find a killer when there's so much more going on right now. I'm sorry, but we will just have to blame it on either a thug or an assassin," Fetcher said shaking his head and looking sad.

"That's alright, it was years ago, everyone's moved on," I told him and walked away.

I stepped into the shade of the tall buildings and made my way to my home. I found my old backpack and a duffle bag and packed the duffle bag with all my cloths I had. The backpack was filled with my weapons which I took out and put some of them on me. Two guns to my belt plus a short sword, two thin daggers up my sleeves and another curved sword strapped to my back. I put three grenades in a pouch on my belt along with extra bullets. Grenades made me nervous, but they were also effective so I decided to pack them. Magic concealed the weapons and made sure the grenades didn't go off. I had a few other knives strapped to my legs and bullets as well as a few short knives in my backpack. Some bombs were strapped in my bag as well and then I was set. I stashed my bags in an abandoned house near my own place then left.

I walked around the town always looking out for Dyras. I felt like even though I didn't know him, I'd still recognize him, but I didn't find him and nothing bad happened as the sun was diving down to the horizon and the moon was coming up. I spent the next three weeks searching the city for anything unusual.

On one occasion I came across two people fighting in an alleyway, on another I found a little boy running away from a house after stealing something from within. Creature quickly dealt with all three and I continued my hunt for Dyras. Every once in a while I sent out strong magic pulses to try and draw him or anyone in. Challenging nearby strong magi and purposefully making myself a target for assassins. Even during the day, I challenged the world. I will no longer hid in the shadows, but be active in the day as well. If I didn't like someone I came across then they were a threat that needed to be disposed of.

One night in early April while I watched from the rooftop of a building, I saw two guys walking around following a girl who looked very terrified and was trying to walk fast in her skirt and high heels. The girl bolted when the men started running after her laughing and howling at her. She didn't get far till someone jumped out from the ally beside her and grabbed her, pulling her into the darkness. The two men came to an abrupt stop and stared at the spot, then ran the other way as quickly as they could. I made my way over to where I seen the girl pulled in and entered the dark ally. The girl was lying on the ground with her blood around her, spilling out of deep gashes all over her body.

I looked around for anything that would tell me something and looked for the attacker, but found no one and no evidence or anything. Whoever was doing these killings was playing it safe and was really good. Myre sniffed around and came up with something.

I took a deep breath and closed my eyes, listening around me. I was getting use to the idea that I had heightened senses and so I let them find the attacker for me. I picked up a scent and a nearby heartbeat then began to follow it. I wound through the alleyways and after some hours was retracing my steps. The attacker wasn't just wandering, he used quick, long strides and his path wasn't straight, already turning the next corner right as it began and continuing to a particular spot he or she knew how to get to. Whoever did it knew the back streets of Vale Darra very well.

After a time of following the guy I stopped. I wanted to learn more about this attacker and so I let him be. I memorized his scent though and the sound of his heartbeat, it was very steady and rhythmic. He seemed very confident and at ease so he wouldn't be hard to recognize in a large crowd of people that from living here tended to be frightened. I had a target to hit in the meantime and decided to deal with it.

I returned back to the streets and looked around, no one was around so I crossed the street and walked through the alleys on the other side to make my way to a subdivision right on the outskirts of the city. I walked down the street, the moon shining down on me as I came to a house near the front with a small picket fence and a greenhouse. The house itself was small and simple shaped, two stories with a deck in the back. I went to the side widow and looked inside. No one was there so I pushed and it gave, swinging inward and opening up enough for me to squeeze through.

I got through the gap and came into the small, four-piece bathroom. I went to the door and slowly opened it then looked around and walked through the hallway down to the last bedroom. Two people lay sleeping as I walked up to the one on the right. I was only there to kill the husband, but looking at the two sleeping figures I instantly hated them both. I didn't know how to control Creature, but whenever I targeted someone Creature seemed to naturally take over.

I approached the figures intending to slash at them with my knives when I blanked out. My legs locked and suddenly I was watching the two people get torn up. I couldn't feel myself attacking the people, but I could smell the blood and feel their lives slipping away, which gave me pleasure.

When I was out on the street again I went up to the rooftops and walked across back to the city. The moon slowly rising above the rooftops. People started screaming and the police came out. I stood there a little longer enjoying their fright.

"They fear me," I whispered to Myre.

"They should fear you, you are better than them. You are death and power," He said and I smiled at him. When the first gun went off that's when I started to run. I quickly ran to the other side of the building and jumped down into the alleyway, disappearing into the shadows.

I continued to smile to myself, listening to the shrieks and screams of people yelling in fear of me. It made me feel dangerous that just the sight of me caused people so much fear. I wanted them to fear me, I wanted the world to fear me and know not to get in my way. I was better than everyone else, I was no mere human being limited by a weak sense of smell or hearing, even being blind I was still better then everyone. I was every bit Creature now, ripping people to shreds. I was the top predator and the humans were my toys to play with and kill. It was a great feeling of power that made me more courageous and headstrong.

The darkness crowded around me and all the smells swirled covering any sweet smelling sent with a fowl stench. I stepped around a turned over garbage can then stepped over a dead cat. It lay there frozen on its side and other cats I could see were hiding in the other garbage cans and dumpsters eyeing it jealously as I passed it. When I was some feet away they lunged at it and I heard the sounds of the cats fighting behind me.

The next day I found myself crouched behind a dumpster as a group of people entered a building. Music pulsed from the doorway every time the door was opened. After a few moments I decided to enter. Instead of sneaking in as I usual would, I decided that I could just walk in the front entrance. I could face down anyone I met in there and so casually walked through the door. This was a nightclub, most people here just looking for a good time. I looked around for anyone of interest, but saw no one. I walked around, staying along the walls and avoiding the maze of dancers in the middle of the room. When I reached the bar the bartender asked me what I wanted. I asked for whatever was strong and he quickly got me a drink. I put down some cash and took my drink. I drank the liquor, letting the liquid flow over my tongue before swallowing it.

Just as I was about to move to the other side of the room someone bumped into me.

"Sorry mate didn't see ya there," A guy said. He smiled at me and continued to stand before me. My mind registered who he was. The leader of a small gang and soon to be millionaire. I smiled at him disarmingly.

"No worries, the fault is mine," I said sweetly. Three guys came up behind me and stood surrounding me.

"What say you and I have a little chat. You look like the type whose looking for some action. I know just the type to satisfy you," He said.

"Sounds just the fun I need," I said and followed the group through a door at the back. We entered a room where a desk was set off to the side and shelves with books occupied the other walls. This was clearly an office. I turned to look around and smiled.

"I hope you don't think I've come here to do book work," I told the leader.

"Nah man, I just wanted to talk. I've got something here that might be of interest," He said and held up a small bag. My senses told me it was a powdered drug, something new to the market, but very strong.

"I'm not here for your crap, I want the good stuff," I told him and he smirked.

"Not to worry man, this is the best of the best," He told me and tossed me the bag.

"No I think I'd rather just kill you instead," I said suddenly.

They responded rather quickly, one guy threw a punch at me while two others pulled out pry bars. The leader laughed, enjoying himself as he backed up to let his men do their job. I pulled out two knives from my sleeves and smiled at the men around me. My glass falling to the floor to shatter into fragments. I sidestepped as one guy came to the side of me. My knife came up under his jaw and plunged into the soft flesh there. I quickly pulled out the knife and let the man fall to the floor. I plunged the knife into his back and side before turning to my next victims. The three of them ran at me at once and I lunged forward, catching them off guard. I killed another before anyone could cut me.

The leader got lucky and managed to cut my arm just as I was finishing off with his last guy. When I turned to the leader, six more guys ran in to assist him. I laughed.

"You know this is fun, this is just the type of action I needed," I said and shot forward at the leader. I drove a knife through his head then threw another knife at the nearest opponent. They didn't all rush forward, but instead tried to plan out how best to get to me. It didn't matter, they would all be dead soon anyway.

I growled at them as they moved around me. Widening my stance my vision narrowed and dimmed. The man before me shrieked in pain as I tore him to pieces. His leg was thrown violently into his buddy beside him and blood splattered the walls painting them red. I opened myself up and attacked the rest. Limbs were hacked off, torsos cleaved from legs. I beheaded a few and slowly disembowelled the others. When I was finished I stood in a room with 10 bodies littering the floor. Their blood pooling together. I walked casually to the door and left. Using magic to rid myself of their blood.

A cloud moved across the moon and all was plunged into darkness, the streets were cold and silent, the houses still as snow began to fall in large, white flakes. I looked up to the sky and the snowflakes came down to melt on my skin. It was cold and wet and as I looked away, the water slowly ran down to dampen my clothes. The snow was coming down steadily and was turning the ground to slush, sleeping outside would get us sick so Myre and I headed to Shirra's castle where we knew we would get food and someplace warm. Winter was being stubborn and refusing to give into spring, but soon it would give up.

The castle was dark and towering above us as we approached, but my attention was caught as I seen a figure dart from a bush and head towards the castle. I stopped and ducked down behind a bush and watched. He darted up the side and I moved, following him as he went up the side of the castle, using the old bricks as hand holds where the bricks were cracked big enough for fingers. I was able to get up faster, but I stayed behind so that I didn't get too close. He got to Shirra's bedroom and jumped onto the balcony.

When the door opened up to Shirra and her room, she had a few moments to react before the person lunged at her and something silver flashed. As he lunged I lunged as well and brought him down to the ground of the balcony just as he was about to cut Shirra. She stood watching, a large knife in her hands.

"Who are you?" I asked. The person struggled to get away, but finding he couldn't he reached over and stabbed me in the leg. Pain flared through my leg, but I ignored it, my magic pulsed in my veins to stop the blood from pouring out my wound. I disarmed him then pinned him to the ground.

"Well you're quick, quicker than I expected," A female voice said. It surprised me, but I didn't let it show.

"Who are you?" I asked again.

"She's got long black hair, dyed it looks, it use to be red. Blue eyes, pale skin, freckles, skinny, but very strong and she's wearing a long dark blue shirt with a vest of weapons and a belt of weapons with black pants

and black shoes," Myre told me all he could see of her as the moon came in and out of cover.

I put it to memory and waited. She seemed not to care about giving me an answer. I was going to ask again when she moved. She shifted slightly and kicked up, kneeing me in my groin. Gasping I curled into a ball trying to hold her and trying to stop her from hitting me again. She managed to wiggle loose and ran towards the railing. I flicked out my hand and my knife came out. With another flick I sent it flying into her back just as she got to the railing. She fell over it and fell to the ground far below. The assassin didn't move again and her body went black as she lay there dead. I was still slightly in pain, but I made myself get to my feet and make my way down to her body.

I looked at the weapons she had and broke them apart then put them back in their places, then took my knife back and cleaned it on her clothes. The blood was dying the snow, but more snow was falling now quicker than before and soon her body would covered by fresh snow. I used magic to breakdown her body so that it looked like an old kill.

Finding nothing that I could learn I went back up to Shirra's room and tapped lightly on the door. When Shirra finally opened she was wide eyed and scared. I entered the room with Myre behind me and hugged her as she stood there stiff and uncertain of what to do or how to react. I could feel that she wanted to cry, but no tears came and I continued to hold her for a long time.

Donta came in with a tray of food and gave some to Myre then some to me and asked if Shirra wanted some. Shirra shook her head then leaned her forehead against my shoulder.

"Who was she?" I heard her say.

"I don't know, but she's gone now," I said just as quietly. She nodded then brushed her hair away with both hands and walked over to sit on her bed. I went over to her.

"Are you ok?" I asked taking her hands. "It was just a scare, sorry to be like this," She said with a sigh.

"No its ok, its scary when you open a door and someone jumps out at you to kill you. You're ok now, so don't worry, just eat something," I said and knelt down before her.

"Food, no, but I will settle for a nice bath. Can you stay here?" She asked with a note of fear in it.

"Yes, we'll be here," I said and as she nodded. She got up and got her things to go for a bath.

I followed her in, placing my hands over the water as it poured out the faucet to check for any poison in the water. My magic flared a green light signalling toxins. "Ok," She spoke tiredly and pulled the cord leading to the plug to empty the tub. The water drained and she continued to run water as I used magic to draw all the poison out of the water tanks in the castle. After just a few minutes I was sweating and tired, I wasn't good at any elemental magic, but pulling poison out of liquids was something Sinth made me learn. It was hard because the poison mixed well with the water, but with some practise it was possible to separate them and so after some while I confirmed there was no more poison in it.

Shirra's movements were slow, her body tired after so much stress and a long day. I sat with her as she undressed and went for a bath. She spoke softly to me about her day, her voice gentle and calm. She finished too soon to be truly relaxed, but got out anyway feeling a little better. She got a warm, old shirt on; underwear and some fleece pants then went back into her bedroom.

I went and laid on the bed pulling her down with me and hugged her tightly to me.

"I love you, you know that right? And you know that I would never let anyone hurt you?" I asked stroking her hair with one hand and holding her to me.

"I know, but it's still scary. I… I wish we could just leave right now," She said miserably.

"But you know why we can't. We said we'd stay and fix the city then we'd leave," I told her slowly.

"But things are different now. Do you not see how you've changed? I'm in your head, but I still feel as if you're a stranger now. Khire I think we should leave now before anything else happens. Maybe if we leave the bad stuff will stop happening," She pleaded. "I can't do that," I told her simply.

"Why?" She asked getting up and sitting away from me to look at me better.

"This is my home," I told her steadily.

"No it's not, it's my home. You don't like it here and you've never wanted to stay here. You think this is your territory well it's not and I hate Creature. I don't love him because he's dark and evil. He's too wild. Where did Khire go, you know the boy I fell in love with. He was kind and wanted everything to be good. He'd recognize that he should just leave and go elsewhere. But you, you think you're all powerful and badass, that you have to prove a point to the world you are invincible. Well guess what, you're not and if it wasn't for me you'd be dead.

"I want you to look at me and tell me who you are," She said, she was fighting back tears and I could tell she had been holding this in for a long time now.

"What's wrong? I am Khire," I said sitting up now, hurt by her words.

"No you're not. Even Donta and Caprica think you've changed. You've I don't know... your just not who you were before you killed Midnight," "I killed him, he tormented me my entire life and all I ever wanted was him dead so that I could live for once in my life my own life. How do you not understand that? He held me back all these years and stopped me from being who I am, who I'm meant to be and now that he's dead you think I'm some terrible person!" I shouted and Shirra got off the bed.

"I know what you've been through because I've been suffering with you through it all, I know exactly how you felt when Midnight was alive and I know how relieved you felt after you killed him. But Khire, he never held you back it was you all this time. You held yourself back thinking someone had control over you, thinking Midnight ruined your life and made you this monster. It wasn't Midnight though, that's all in your head. When Sinth disappeared you started killing bad guys, you were trying to make Vale Darra a better place. Now look, Midnights dead and now you're running around as Creature. You know how many people fear you, are terrified to even go outside because they hear almost every day that some person was torn to pieces. Some person who maybe stole some food just to feed his family was torn up by some strange animal.

"Khire when will you stop and realise, it's been you all this time. You're a monster," She said and began crying. Those words sent chills up my spine. Mirranna said those same words to me "You're a monster" and I killed her. My head felt clouded and I could hear my breathing become harsh.

"I am not a monster!" I screamed at her. A knife was in my hand though I don't know how it got there, but I couldn't put it away.

"You would never hurt me, you would never do that to me," Shirra sobbed, her whole body tight with tension as she tried to hold back her tears, but she stood her ground. I advanced on her. "I had loved someone who said she loved me and that wasn't good enough in the end! I had to change to survive! If you really knew me you'd get that!" I screamed, tears were running down my face and though I tried to wipe them away and make them stop, they kept coming. "I love you and I will never leave you, but you have to let me in, you have to let me help you. Being here is what's stopping you from being who you are. It's great that you're finally confident in yourself, but you need to stop," She said and took a step towards me trying to reach out to me physically, magically and mentally.

I stood trembling, dropping the knife to the floor and trying to calm myself down, gasping in air. Shirra came closer and wrapped her arms around me. "Khire," She whispered then she whispered my secrete name. A sudden feeling of tiredness overcame me and I sunk to the floor nearly blacking out with the sudden overwhelming exhaustion. My body hurt for some reason like I'd been kicked multiple times.

She held me tightly and I sobbed into her shoulder as she told me over and over again that she loved me and would help me.

"I'm sorry, I'm so sorry," I begged. I felt so ashamed that I had pulled out a knife and so repulsed at myself that I would even think about hurting Shirra.

"It's ok, it wasn't you," She said soothingly. She sent some magic into my body, calming me down and making me sleepy.

"Let me in," she said and as I was drifting off to sleep a pink light blazed, lighting up the entire room. It hurt when it hit me, a wave of power scorching me from the inside out. I barely managed to stay conscious, but I was too confused to make sense of anything. Everything was pink and I could still hear Shirra telling me that she'll help me. I tried to move, but my body felt sluggish.

"What's happening?" I asked trying to find Shirra.

"I'm here, I'm right here with you, everything's alright just trust me," She said. I trusted her and let her take care of me, knowing she would help me.

Soon everything went normal again and I looked up into her green eyes. I felt a little strange, like I had been looking at the world through a cloud and now the cloud was gone and I could see everything in detail. I had no dark thoughts in my head, I felt like killing people was repulsive and I never wanted to put more blood on my hands again.

"I can see you," I said surprised. After all these years of being blind, being able to see again was strange. I stared up at Shirra taking in her features. Bewildered and awestruck, I reached up to touch her face. Her cheeks were wet from crying. I wiped them away wishing I hadn't caused them.

"You're so beautiful," I said and she smiled.

"Thank you," She said, her smile reached her eyes and made me feel warmer.

"I didn't know you were so beautiful," I mumbled. "It's nice to hear you say those words... I healed you, there was a lot of darkness in you and I took it out," She said before I reached up and brought her down to me so I could kiss her. I was a little rough and uncoordinated trying to hold her while I still lay in her lap, but I kissed her, taking her breath away and her fears.

I wanted to prove that I loved her more than anything in the world just then. Without even thinking I pulled off her shirt and tried to pull off her pants. The knot in the drawstring was hard to undo and finally after struggling Shirra tried to help me.

"No I can do it," I said irritated.

"Ok," she said and patiently waited while I sat up and struggled with a stupid knot. Finally I got it, ridiculously triumphant.

"Wow!" Shirra commented.

"Ok you know what wear different clothes next time," I growled.

"You do realise that you didn't have to undo the knot, these pants are loose enough to slide right off," She said smiling and trying to hold back a laugh. I looked at her annoyed, but then gave up. She sat up and pulled me to her feet with her.

"I love you and I want to be with you, but you don't have to prove anything to me you just have to be Khire," She said and wrapped her arms around me.

"I know, but I want to love you. I want to do better. I have to stay here and help this city, but I will help this city, I won't kill people anymore unless I have to. I have to help Vale Darra and I might die doing it, so while I'm still alive I want to live and I want to live as much of my life with you as I can. If we live I promise I will take you far away. I will marry you and we will start our life together like normal people,"

"We will never be normal," She said smiling.

"No, but we can try. I don't want you giving up your life for me just because you love me. That's not right. All these years you could have been with your family, you could have a life with a husband who's rich and doesn't kill people for a living. You chose me and so it's about time I chose you," I said and pulled her towards the bed.

"Ok then lets save this city together and then we can leave, but for now let's be together as much as we can in case we die," She agreed. She pulled me on top of her and kissed me happily.

"Ok," I said after a moment.

"I know you love me more than anything…" Shirra began.

"Stop, you are making me lose my focus," I said kissing her to get her to stop talking.

"Seriously *though,"* She said in my mind. *"I know you love me and love is really not all about sex despite what Caprica thinks,"*

"Let's not bring her into this please," I said out loud. "Besides I already proved I loved you by giving you my real name first. This is just extra," I said smiling.

Shirra had a fun time teasing me, I was too nervous and unsure that Shirra ended up taking over. She let her feelings for me flow through the bond to me. My magic flared, and suddenly I was way too hot. I tried to breath, but my body was on fire. This was not how I imagined this. I wanted Shirra, but I was having a hard time breathing and my body was overheating. Shirra didn't seem to mind and nor did she help me, but I really wished she'd give me a little air to cool down. I felt way too anxious and energized to be laying in a bed. Just when I thought my magic was going to burn me up Shirra sent her magic in my body. Suddenly I was on top again and kissing her fiercely. It felt like my mind was separate from my body as instinct took over and my body responded. I quickly agreed that I should have been with Shirra sooner.

After what felt like hours, but I'm sure was not more than one, I stopped, panting for breath. My magic finally calm now while my body was beyond tired. I wanted sleep, but instead I whispered Shirra's name into her ear and felt her body tremble. It felt nice to please her. I spoke quietly to her, telling her how our life together would be when we left this place. We'd live in a little blue house somewhere in a forest where there were no neighbours around. I imagined having a dog and even kids running around chasing it, running on chubby legs, trying to catch the dog and get their ball back. The dog would run, tail wagging triumphantly as it escaped easily from them. Shirra sitting on a swinging chair, reading a book with sunlight streaming down around her. A blue, cloudless sky that seemed bigger and more beautiful than the city sky here. I imagined it all and wished desperately we could have that one day.

CHAPTER #36

The day started sunny and warm, the snow was nearly gone, leaving large puddles everywhere. I sat on my couch staring at the TV as a reporter reported a murder of a women found in the alleyways and a man found dead in his bed when his wife woke up beside him and seen his throat cut. I stared at it, not really hearing or watching, but just staring. Several thoughts kept going through my head and I couldn't figure them out, but I knew I had to do something. The doorbell rang, but I didn't get up to answer it, the phone rang, but I didn't budge.

Soon I heard the door open and Tellnair call me. I didn't answer him, but he shut the door and came into the living room and sat beside me. "Ok Dad, why didn't you answer my knock and my phone call? What's wrong?" He asked sounding a little annoyed, but more tired that he had to deal with another problem.

"Did you hear the news about the two murders?" I asked still gazing at the TV.

I knew I looked bad, tired and puffy eyed, still not dressed and my hair not brushed, I hadn't even eaten breakfast. I just sat on this couch.

"Yes," Tellnair answered, worry coming into his voice.

"It has something to do with Khire," I said simply.

"Why do you say that?" He asked caught off guard.

"Because I know and I know Khire has been keeping something from me. There's a bigger picture and I feel like I should know what it is. I feel like I've just ignored it because I didn't want to see it," I stopped talking and silence filled the room. "Maybe there's a good explanation, maybe Khire's like a spy or something ok. It would make sense, he is really smart and always seems to be where he shouldn't be. Remember when he was little he was always off and he never told us where he was. Sometimes he came back soar or upset or something. We always wondered what he was up to, but he would just say some lame excuse. I think there is an explanation for this. We will just have to ask him and demand answers ok. Let's go look around, maybe we will find him," Tellnair said sounding like everything was ok and people weren't dying outside. He helped me up and to my room, up the stairs to my disliking. "I'm not an invalid I can take care of myself," I huffed.

"You're an old fuddy-duddy with too much time to worry about everything you have no control over. I think it's time we trusted Khire. He knows how to take care of himself. He's a good guy. And this bad stuff that's happening right now will blow over, you'll see," he said and waited for me.

Quickly I got ready, teeth and hair brushed, face washed and fresh cloths on, dressed warmly, but comfortably for a long walk. We left the house and walked down the street into Vale Darra. The streets were nearly empty, but there were some people walking around. It was about half an hour till we spotted Khire sitting on a picnic bench facing away from us staring at the castle that could just be seen above the trees and other buildings. A journal lay on the ground by his foot as if he had dropped it.

As we walked up to him, he showed no recognition of hearing us and as we sat beside him he didn't react. I grabbed the journal and looked at it. "Khire, what's this?" I inquired. I read the small writing, realizing it was more of a diary.

"I.... it belonged to someone I knew, but he's dead now," He finally said.

"Is everything ok? Why are you reading this?" I asked him confused.

"He had a brother, looked just like him," Khire said in a strange voice as if he forgot I was there.

"What? Who had a brother? Khire you need to back up a little. Whose journal is this?" I asked him handing it back to him. He took it and sighed. "There was a man I knew from when I was younger, he died not too long ago and left me his journal. I've been reading it to see what's in it. He had a younger brother named Josin, he was a trouble maker, he never did what he was told and he was always looking for more power. He hated when there was someone stronger then him.

"Growing up I use to talk to this man named Sinth, he was always following me around and telling me stuff then some day's he'd ask me to do other stuff and for that I hated him. But it wasn't him. It was his brother Josin who screwed up my life, Sinth was trying to help me because he knew his brother would come after me," Khire said and slouched. "And now Sinth is dead," He looked up at me and frowned. I realized the colour of his eyes were different today which confused me, but I let it go to deal with one issue at a time.

"You look so old," Khire said as if seeing me for the first time in years. His blue eyes looked up at me making me feel a little uncomfortable. "Well thank you son, that's what every old man likes to here nowadays," I joked. Tellnair snickered, but otherwise stayed silent.

"Why don't you go to the police about this? If someone's after you, you should get help," I told him and he nodded.

"There's also a man out there who fears magic, he's been going around trying to kill strong magi to try and destroy all magic, but the world runs on magic so now the magic is unbalanced. I've been trying to find him, but he's a time traveler. I've told Fetcher about him, but he's like a ghost. I don't know how to stop a ghost," He told me then laughed. "Ironic how I use to be a ghost,"

Tellnair was very quiet and still beside me, pondering his brother's words.

"Why do you have to do this?" I asked.

"I don't know, it's just something I feel that I should do," He answered quietly looking at his hands.

We sat there silent and thinking as the sun rose higher in the sky and the day warmed up. Fetcher came up to us and watched us for a time, hands on hips and not sure what to do.

"Ok, do I have to remove you three or will you just move. The streets are being closed and everyone is being asked to stay inside for the day while the streets are investigated for the killer," I looked up at him and he gave me a weird look as if I was someone new to him and I was slow. I slowly got up and Tellnair and Khire followed. We made our way to Tellnair's house where Mellony greeted us, looked at our faces then disappeared in the kitchen. We all sat on the couch.

"Is there something we can do?" Tellnair asked.

"No, I haven't found a way to stop him and I don't know how without possibly screwing more stuff up," Khire said frustrated.

"But…" I started. Khire shook his head.

Just then Mellony came in with a batch of muffins. She smiled and set them on the table beside the couch. No one made a move to take them and Mellony took Sighann from her crib as she woke up. She gave her a pacifier, but soon she began to cry and Mellony left to feed her. Khire kissed me on the cheek and hugged me, then he did the same to Tellnair then he left. I wanted to go after him, but I couldn't move as I stared at the floor, unable to respond to anything. Tellnair got up and walked quickly to the front door, but he walked back soon and started pacing the room.

"What can we do? How do you stop a guy who can time travel?" He started speaking, but I lost track of him. I watched him for a bit then left and went to my home. I had to keep living, Khire would come home one day, and when he did I will be ready for him and he will be able to stay with me. Till then I had things to do like eating, going to work, sleeping and doing activities I liked, like spending time with my family and going for walks.

☾

On an unusually cold April night I crouched on a rooftop remembering Vale Darra as it was, when it was still a beautiful city. It was green, alive and thriving, it was a huge tourist attraction and had the promise of becoming a mega city. Now however the city seemed to be in ruins. With all the killings going on, the people were in fear of even sleeping. The tourism slowed and the King was hard pressed to keep the economy running. People just about had enough of what was going on and they were starting to get agitated. Some were leaving the city, others were staying, but getting gun permits and having a gun loaded and ready at arm's length at all times. The policemen on duty were teamed up and more were recruited to guard the streets. The machines in the hospitals that allowed people to live, breath, monitor hearts and many more machines began to fail. People across the world began to believe God himself was killing them off as slowly the world was plunged into darkness. The magic of the world was slowly dying and with it every living thing on it as well.

I turned away and left to walk the streets to a small building divided into two stores, a pet store on one side and a jewellery shop on the other. I went into the pet store, after fiddling with the lock on the door. Animals in cages and tanks were asleep, but at my approach some awoke and begged for attention. A puppy stretched with a yawn then put his paws up on the cage and stretched his nose up at me as far as it could reach, giving a little whimper saying he wanted some attention. I picked him up and petted him, he settled into my arms comfortably and his tail wagged constantly side to side. As I put him down, he whined a bit louder than the first. I ignored him and moved to the stairs in the back as he gave a little bark.

When I got upstairs I was faced with the smell of alcohol. I moved down the small hallway to a door and the only bedroom. A person lay on a couch with the TV still on and a drink in the guy's hand almost falling out as he slumped on the chair. Arms splayed over the sides, head tilted to one side, wearing a dirty blue shirt and sweat pants, stained and old. He was a large man who had given up on life, ignoring the world and his charges down below. The man lay dead, seeming almost peaceful in his timeless slumber. I wasn't expecting him to be dead, I had thought to come here because he was a friend of mine, but I was too late.

I wished I could have seen all of life's beauty, not the ugly side, but that wasn't the world I lived in. I liked to spend every moment I could seeing everything and anything that I had missed, the sun, the sky, my family and Shirra. Even seeing the strangers on the street was fascinating, but all I was met with was sorrow and pain.

I went down the stairs slowly, the puppy reached up for my attention and I gave him a pet. "Sorry, pup, I can't even take care of myself let alone you," I told him and left. The streets were dead silent as I made my way up them and turned into a dark alley that never went straight for very long. This alley way was one of the few that were in good condition, so I could walk without having to worry about tripping, but it was wide enough for a car to easily drive down so I was still in view.

As I was walking four figures came round the corner up ahead and seeing me they turned their attention to me and made their slow, cocky way over to me. "Look what we got here, lost your way? We'd be happy to help you," One snickered. Their little talks they always did was really old by now, but I half listened to them anyway and stood there waiting for them to finish. They circled around me, but I was hardly worried, my mind was on other problems.

I took a deep breath to center myself. When they moved I moved around them, hitting them in certain spots that would numb them. They struck at me with knives and attacked me with an anger I wasn't expecting. After a moment I realized they weren't attacking me out of anger, but out of fear. They were terrified I was going to kill them. Terrified of the world around them. I breathed in raggedly, my emotions too high and I mentally tried to calm down, but I was feeling too much pressure and all I wanted to do was run from it or kill them now.

Shirra sent calmness to me and I took a deep breath, closing my eyes to try and relax.

"I won't hurt you," I told the four, opening my eyes as I stepped away from them. They watched me, trying to guess my plan, but I held up my hands and backed away from them. They slowly backed away from me then ran off, trying to find a safe place to go.

"I want a puppy," Shirra said in my mind and I smiled. I returned to the pet store and was greeted by the same puppy who had wanted me to pick her up. I picked her up again and left, taking her to a new home where she would be loved.

Some days later I was wandering through the labyrinth of the alleyways. It was strange relying on my sight for direction, looking for familiar things rather than relying on Myre to guide me, but now that I could see I wanted to use my sight, just in case I lost it again.

It was now a few hours till sunrise and I was still walking through the alleyways searching. The knowledge of Sinth having a brother seemed absurd for some reason, though Sinth being the good guy was more so. I didn't know if I should feel regret or relief from having killed Sinth now. I just knew my happiness of thinking I was free of him was over. I believed Shirra when she told me it was I that held myself back. Looking back I could see the truth in that, but I still felt that if I killed the man that ruined my life I would be better off.

I was also kicking myself for telling so much to my father and brother. My dad looked terrible. Having been blind I had always imagined the young, healthy, strong father I had when I was a little boy. I knew he aged as I to had aged, but it was still a huge shock at seeing him. Tellnair too looked far older. It wasn't just my family struggling though, the entire city was failing. I felt useless just walking around looking for danger, but I didn't know how to find Josin so I had no choice, but to wait.

A week went by and everyday was another day I searched for Josin. Every minute of my life I began to count, I could feel the world thrown into chaos. With such a magical imbalance people had to resort to a different way of living. Magi were hit harder though, their magic was thrown off balance as well, making them weaker for the most part, but with random uncontrollable flare ups. I myself felt weaker, much to my dislike, but it made me search for Dyras more.

I became more agitated and slept badly. I hardly ate and focused on finding the cities killer. Vale Darra was in a state where people thought that the city couldn't ever be saved, but I was determined not to give up on it. It was my home and it was a beautiful place, if I were to die I'd die with the beauty of Vale Darra restored.

CHAPTER #37

As time wore on the season changed to spring, the trees budding that later gave into leaves. Flowers popped out of the ground and the grass grew back green and lush. My birthday came and went with little recognition. I spent most of my time looking out for Dyras and Josin and trying to stay alive.

I stepped out into the weak light of the sun and onto the streets on a chilly afternoon. Everyone turned to look at me as they were all on high alert. I walked with the same rigid movement they had and made my way around the town, waiting and watching for anything to happen. Nothing did, and nothing did for the next days after.

I was beginning to think that all of us had failed as a human race and deserved to die, but then I would think of Shirra and I didn't like the idea of her dying. I decided I would save it, if only for her to live another day.

People sat in their houses watching the TV or doing some other activity while I stared out the window at the city far below. I was on the thirty sixth floor in the castle and had a breath taking view of the city. The King was going to a meeting along with two of his daughters. I stood a little longer then moved on down the long hallways following the long blue carpet down the hall and passing by pictures of Kings and Queens, Princes and Princesses of the past.

They smiled down at me, clothes neat and un-wrinkled, not sleep deprived, hair neat, teeth white, great posture with their crowns or circlets on their heads, their head held high and proud as their eyes twinkled.

I didn't look anything like that even on my good days. Right now I was wearing the same clothes I had worn yesterday, my hair was quickly brushed and so were my teeth, I hadn't eaten yet and my stomach made that well known sound that told me I was starving, my body making it known how tired I was.

I continued down the hallway then down the stairs and back down the next hallway robotically.

"Jakk! The King needs to speak with you. Go to his chambers," I heard someone say, the voice sounded familiar, but I didn't care to think who it was, he wasn't a danger so it was ok. I turned back to the staircase and went down a few floors to the Kings hallways where I began to tug my clothes straight and brush my fingers through my hair. I couldn't do too much about my appearance, but I walked in, back straight, head held high and respectful, voice calm and serious as I stood before the King to address him.

"My King," I nodded slightly.

"Ah, Jakk, we are going to a meeting, please join us," He said, not really asking, but still saying it anyway. "My pleasure Your Highness," I bowed and left the room to return to my rooms and get cleaned up.

Ten minutes later I had showered, brushed my hair and teeth again, redressed into better and cleaner clothes and was making my way down to the front door when a maid looked at me and stopped. In her hands she held a platter of food, grabbing a multigrain role still steaming, she handed it to me.

"Here ya go, you look like you could do with some food," She said smiling. I smiled back and thanked her.

"Thanks," I said and we parted. She continued her way around the castle doing her things while I went to the front door.

I was the first one there so I stood and waited for the rest to come. The King came next, dressed in a white shirt and a blue coat and vest over top with black pants and gold trimming around the hems. His crown was shining as the light caught it and sat upon his head straight. His face was wrinkled, his black hair speckled with grey and drawing back, but he held himself proud and walked firm and sure as he made his way easily across the floor to me. "Hello, Jakk, have you eaten?" He asked as servants ran around trying to prepare everything needed for the trip. "I had something Sire," I answered politely.

"Well we have some more food if you're hungry or thirsty please help yourself to our storage along the way ok," I nodded.

"That's very kind of you Sire," I said smiling.

The Queen Ahoura and Princess Isra arrived soon after. The Queen was dressed in a long flowing dress. It was silky and cream-pink in colour with floral designs running up the left side and along her arms. It was tight around her torso then poofed out around the hips. It was V necked to show off a necklace of pearls with a white gold chain. She had her hair piled neatly on her head with her white crown. She was smiling, wrinkles appearing at the corner of her eyes. She came forward and greeted her husband like any normal person would, showing love for her husband and kindness towards me as she came over to me and took my hands in hers. Her hands were very small in mine and looked very fragile.

"You look stunning Your Highness," I kissed her hands and she nodded her head.

"Well thank you Jakk you are a true gentlemen. Please take care of them for me?" I gave her a reassuring smile.

"Always, Your grace," I bowed my head.

Isra smiled at me, her big, white smile that always touched her green eyes. She had her brown hair up the same way as her mothers, but she wore a long peacock blue dress with silver floral designs along the hem and her fingerless gloves. Her dress was also tight around the torso then flowing out from the hips. Her shoulders were covered by a thin peacock blue scarf that she held secure around her neck with one hand. Her circlet was placed on her head showing that she was next in line for the throne. I took her other hand and kissed it as well. "You as well Princess, you look absolutely picture perfect," She smiled bigger at the complement. She was always one to look her best and liked complements and attention on her. I was good at saying complements and staying on the good side with people because I was a people pleaser so she enjoyed me near.

Princess Shirra rushed down the stairs breathless, hair flowing behind her in loose curls and dress flowing out behind her. She stopped before us and greeted everyone a little flustered. She tried to fix her hair then stood tall and straight to try and look a little more presentable. Her dress was different, snow white and smoky green. The top was tight with a strip of smoky green down the front and went down into a short dress. The bottom just reached her shines and was jagged with the fringes smoky green and the rest white. She had a bow around her middle that tied up at the back, with straps around her shoulders and three quarter gloves that ended in again the same smoky green colour. Despite being flustered and trying to catch her breath, she had the natural beauty that only few women could truly capture. I always thought it funny how flustered she always was. She wasn't exactly punctual and always ended up rushing everywhere, doing things last minute and seeming to always be on her feet, but that was Princess Shirra. She had a bit of a frantic personality and seemed a little oblivious to some things around her like there was always something that distracted her.

I smiled kindly at her when she was finished greeting everyone else. "Hello Jakk, how's your family?" She asked. Her voice was breathy and a little deeper then what you would expect for a women, but it was still pretty.

"Good," I said simply.

"How's your father?" She asked me as she gave one last glance in a nearby mirror.

"Fine," I said.

"How's he doing with Khire gone?" She asked.

"He's a bit upset and a little stressed, but he'll be ok," I said. "Oh, where's your brother? Khire right?" The King asked turning to me when he overheard me speaking to Princess Shirra. I didn't want to say too much, one thing not to do was call all the attention to yourself when you're with royalty. It was their time not yours so I answered it quickly and short.

"Yes, Sire, Khire. He left somewhere, no one knows, but that's him, he's always been one to leave then come back at some time, Your Majesty" I shrugged to show Khire leaving meant little to me.

"Oh, well I hope he's ok and returns soon, please tell me when he does," The King said kindly. I smiled back, not surprised by his kindness as he tended to be more concerned with others then himself.

When everything was ready we left the castle and wandered outside towards the waiting vehicle. We were riding in a bullet proof, anti-magic stretched car. Not quite a limousine, but close enough. I looked around, investigating everything and climbed in last after the royal family got in and settled. With a last check I climbed in and buckled in. I was in the back with three other guards and two in the front, one driver the other, passenger.

It took us two and a half hours to get to our destination and I looked out the window looking out for any potential dangers. There were none and once we reached our destination and the vehicle stopped I climbed out checked one more time then helped everyone out. The two Princesses and the King climbed out and we circled around them then walked towards a huge building, not a castle, but made to resemble one.

It was tall with several pillars shooting up towards the sky. It was rectangular in shape with an open court in the middle to provide for a large, flourishing garden. The outside had thick walls while the first floor had no interior walls so that you could stare out to the garden or go outside and look up to the sky. The rest of the floors were where people worked. There was a great hall where the royals would gather and speak and there were bedrooms to sleep in, bathrooms, a kitchen, some offices to do work, three libraries and several other rooms, all large and spacious. In total there were just over a hundred rooms in this building and each room was adorned in rich carpets, paintings, and everything else to fit royal standards. It looked more like a museum with its décor of exotic plants and statues, but it was actually an office building for royal affairs.

We walked into the entry and turned left to walk down a hallway to a staircase that went along the wall up to the higher levels. We took it to the twenty-eighth level then went down the hallway to the Grand Hall. One side was completely made up of windows that looked out on the garden. There were already guards lined up along the glass, looking in different directions so I and the other guards with the King and his daughters took our places, standing a few feet off to the side of where the royals sat. There would be four other royal families here, usually there were anywhere above ten, but we didn't want to make such a great gathering just in case someone tried to pull something and put them all in trouble.

Some minutes later we had everyone here and the meeting started. I half listened, but my most attention was directed to looking outside for anyone then looking around the room for anyone who would be a danger to the royals. No one was out of the ordinary so everything was going fine. The minutes were ticking by excruciatingly slowly, but the meeting continued. Servants came in at lunchtime and gave the Royal families food, it made my stomach growl a bit, but I ignored it and continued my search.

Princess Shirra was sitting on her chair full attention on the rest, her sister doing the same, but now and then smiling at a Prince down the table who was smiling back and mouthing words to her. They were going to meet after the meeting on the top floor, second door, as I read his lips and she nodded slightly. I would have to stop them from meeting up, but later. I wasn't here for them to get aquatinted and right after the meeting we were going to leave and head straight home. I kept it in mind to carefully watch the two as I investigated others. The other Kings and Queens talked, expressions serious and shoulders tense. Their children showed the same seriousness, the youngest being fourteen. They were all dressed nicely in different colours and styles that tried to hide the hardships they faced in their own kingdoms. They sat around the long oval shaped table. Twelve royals, twenty three guards nearby and another sixteen around the room with servants coming and going. Many other people were working in the building, mostly making sure every room was clean.

I looked back out the window and looked through the glass to the other side where there were more windows into other rooms. Those rooms weren't all empty, but the people I was able to see I confirmed them as workers here and not a threat. They typed on keyboards and stared at their computers doing whatever they did while some went around cleaning, watering plants, talking to people or taking papers to other rooms to do work with. Before coming here I had gotten a list of the workers with their pictures so I was able to identify everyone by name.

I looked back around the table, but only five minutes had gone by and the meeting was still going on, nothing changed. I continued to look around the room then turned my attention to outside then back to the room. Nothing was changing, everyone was going around, smiling, working, talking and planning, writing, discussing, copying papers, and then as the clock hit two o'clock and I turned to look out the window something shattered. The large window that stretched from floor to ceiling not far from me, cracked and a small hole appeared. I looked towards the royals and now a King, I didn't know, stared blank eyed at everyone, still and slightly slumped. People started screaming and rushing to their feet, the Kings wife shook her husband then let out a high scratchy scream as she discovered him dead. The guards acted at once as we circled around the royals and moved them out of the room where there would be no windows.

I looked back out the window and there right across to the other side, on the roof was a figure I recognized well. It was Dusk and he stood there holding a large gun, his stance showing a cockiness and pride. He walked away and I lost sight of him as the rest of us left the room headed down the hallway to a room, bullet proof and with no windows. There was a camera outside the door so anyone inside could see who was outside and was then able to open the door and let them in if they so choose to. The door could only be opened a certain way, so anyone who got into the room would have to have authority.

The royals went inside along with some guards, but most stayed outside, some stood by the door while the rest left to patrol the entire building. I stayed by the door while others left, leaving eight of us to guard the door. It was fine if you were dealing with an easy opponent, but I had a bad feeling and I knew someone else was going to die.

The minutes dragged on as if in slow motion as we looked around in every direction, waited for news to be able to move the royals to their vehicles and get them back home, but no news came. It was hours and still we had not seen a servant, a guard or anyone. I walked over to a nearby window and peeked around the edge. There was a guy walking around in the garden with a gun. He had on dark clothing with a short sword and a few knives on his belt. He had dark shaggy hair and brown skin. He was tall, but skinny and scraggily. I couldn't see anyone in the other rooms, lights were on, computers still running, but no one else was about. I decided to call everyone dead; we had not seen any one and so that being so we were on our own.

I walked back over to the other guards and gave them my observation. They nodded and we made a plan.

"Ok, you guys stay here, I will call the police and get them here ok," I said after deciding that back up hadn't been called yet. I returned back beside the window, being careful to not be in any view of anybody and took out my cell phone to dial the police searching for signal. This building was a lone structure so the closet place was Vale Darra and standing beside the closed room where the royals were, all signals were lost, so I had to walk around a little.

A voice sounded on the other end.

"The police..." I'm sure they had a very well prepared speech, but I wasn't in any mood to listen to it. I did recognize the voice however.

"Hey this is Jakk..." I started to say.

"Oh ok, here's Fetcher," She said in her light, daisy voice and I huffed as I waited for Fetcher to finally take the call. I hadn't intended to get transferred to him, but apparently the dispatcher assumed I had nothing better to do then dial 911 to talk to my brother. As soon as Fetcher picked up I spoke. "Fetcher we're at the Great Hall, there's been a killing. We have the royals in a secured room and we have sent guards out, but that was almost two hours ago and we have not seen anyone. "I just saw a man walk across the garden room armed with a gun, I think it was Dusk, I saw him on the roof too, but he's in the building now," I said quickly. It was best to give all information just in case I were to die he would at least know everything.

"Ok, we're on our way," He said. I told him the floor we were on and what room. I heard screams come from behind me.

"What's that?" Fetcher asked. I turned to see the guards all gazing inside the room, the door wide open. I walked up to them and looked into the room and gasped.

"Jakk, what is it?!" Fetched growled, hating how one sided this was.

"The royals are all dead, wait.... Let's check, I think there's some missing I don't see..."

We entered the room and looked over the bodies. It was then that we discovered the huge hole. It was in the floor, and went to the next level then went outside to let the sunshine stream into the dark room and light up the gore on the floor. Blood was dripping down the hole, some bodies slumped over it, but they were dead, obviously they weren't the ones we were looking for. I had to leave the room to call Fetcher back.

"The King, Princess Shirra and Princess Isra are missing, the rest are dead. There is a huge hole down to the next level then to the outside," I explained to Fetcher. He swore, which wasn't very uncommon, and I could hear the sound of a car speeding and sirens blaring.

I stayed on the phone telling him anything else I discovered right till he arrived and got up here. He came with over eighty police at his back. More were to arrive from the other surrounding areas. They surrounded the area and moved in, everyone staying in a group and staying in contact by use of a radio.

Fetcher came up to me and began asking me questions, which I answered to the best of my knowledge. Other cops questioned the other guards, but soon we were making our way down the hole and out the other hole in the wall. The landscape stretched before us and as we looked down at the ground below we could see holes in the wall where people may have climbed up the wall. We left that room and ran down the hall, down the staircase to the ground level then outside and went to where the little holes stopped. We looked at them as they went up all the way to the large hole in the wall far above. We couldn't get all the information we wanted right there, but we pressed some mould into a hole and waited for it to dry. By now investigators arrived along with other people who had a certain Wish that may help us.

We were getting nowhere with following the kidnappers and murderers, but we did discover some things like the type of weapons used and that there was more than one person involved. The sun was diving down quickly towards the horizon and it was getting dark. We left the sight, police taped, to return at a later time.

I was driving passenger side in Fetchers cruiser, looking out the window to see if I could see anything. Nothing out of the ordinary appeared which didn't surprise me. I knew they would be long gone and would probably make some type of appearance or something to demand something for the return of the King and his two daughters. I felt angry with myself and kept clenching my hands and jaw.

Fetcher was glaring at the road, seriousness and work edged into his expression. "Relax," I told him even though I was tense myself and he took no recognition that I had spoken. I repeated myself and this time he gave me a quick glance, but didn't loosen up.

"I know this is hard, but being stressed won't help us, you may just go into a fit then we'll have to send you to the hospital and we'd be one person short," I explained.

"Things are getting way to out of hand," He sounded very upset, his voice rising slightly. I could still picture everything and I couldn't get it out of my head. Whenever I closed my eyes I could see the blood and the bodies, all those people I never knew, but someone else did and they loved them. They were all dead, all set to be buried in the ground and get appreciation from worms. My stomach clenched and I felt suddenly sick.

"Are you sure it was Dusk?" Fetcher asked all of a sudden.

"I saw him, I'm sure of that. I even know what he looks like now," I told him and explained his appearance.

"Ya, but you never know, an illusionist could have been his Wish, remember we don't know Dusks Wish. We have no idea what all he can do, we know some thing's he can do, but he always manages to surprise us. Just think for a second, there was more than one person that was involved with this, maybe Dusk was there, he just had to kill the King and only the King, but then other people… other assassins were also there and killed the rest then kidnapped the family members. Dusk doesn't kidnap people, he kills them and leaves them where they fall," "I don't know, I don't see any motive in that," I said sceptically.

"Maybe Dusk plans to ransom," Fetcher seemed determined to settle the matter right now.

"Ok here's a thought, maybe it was Dusk, but maybe all these years there has been two people at work. You know, working together so well so that we would think it was just one great person. I've noticed something about Dusk. He looks the same, when you see him up on the rooftops, he always looks the same, his silhouette I mean. For some reason whenever people think of Dusk they think, big, strong, muscle guy, but when looking at his silhouette, he isn't very tall, he's skinny, nothing great about him. Another thing, there is a difference in the stances," He was talking, but at that he lost me.

"What?" I asked confused.

"When you see him and he's just staring down at us do you ever notice the way he stands? It changes. I've noted two different stances for Dusk, one he is standing before us with his left hand on his hip with his right hand just limp at his side, the other is him with his arms crossed and all his weight on his right hip. Do you never notice that? Let's make this easy and just say right handed people stand more on their right hip then they do on their left. Most people use their dominant hand for everything that they do. That's different for Dusk, either he is ambidextrous or there's two, ones a lefty and the others a righty," Fetcher said excited.

"Look I have videos of him on my video recorder," Fetcher said and tapped the mounted screen on the dash and videos of Dusk came up. I flipped through them until I came to some pictures that were of him standing. There were two different stances. "Honestly I haven't noticed, but that is interesting to think about. It would make sense, but wait, we've always seen him arms crossed, and weight on his right hip, the other one hasn't been seen as long. So maybe there was one Dusk, but at some time there became two. Look at this. Here is two pictures with Dusk standing against a chimney, that chimney stack is four feet high, look where it comes up to on this Dusk and this Dusk. One is taller than the other," I said and continued to look through the videos and pictures.

"That all makes sense, now though, the next question why all the sudden change to the evil side?" Fetcher asked.

"Well that's another thing, I saw Dusk, I am sure of it, but if Dusk is two people maybe they split, one is still killing the bad guys while the other is killing the good," I explained and it all seemed to fit.

We were entering Vale Darra and we drove to the police station to change cars. We were going over to Tellnair's house tonight to watch something he was excited about, so we headed over to there and parked, saving our conversation for later. I would hear from my boss as soon as he had something for me, but for now I had to sit and wait. "Hey guys, have a good day?" Tellnair asked meeting us at the door.

"Work," We said together and walked in, Tellnair giving us weird looks.

We sat down on his couch waiting for the rest to show, already dad was here, looking worried and distressed, but better than he had in weeks.

"Hey dad," I said sitting beside him. "Hello Jakk, what did you do today?" He asked. I didn't want to tell him, the news wasn't confidential seeing as the news would get out and everyone would realise three members of the royal family were gone, but he had so much other things to worry about he didn't need any more. "Nothing much," I told him nonchalantly.

"Your keeping something from me, what happened?" Having Khire gone and him worrying about him seemed to make his senses better.

"Nothing," Dad gave me a very worried look.

"Tell me," he demanded. "Well I went with the King, Princess Isra and Princess Shirra to their meeting today and I think I saw Dusk at one point up on the roof. He shot and killed a King then we got all the royals to a safe room and sent guards out to investigate only they never came back. I called Fetcher and they came over as we opened up the doors to get the royals out and take them to safety. Only when we opened the door we found them all dead, all accept the King and his two daughters who are now missing. Most of the staff and guards are dead. We found some survivors, but not many," I explained.

Dad had a look of pure horror on his face and I was nervous he would have to be sent to the hospital as his face paled and his hands began to tremble. "You were in danger, you could have been killed?" He said looking at me with his eyes wide. I got a bit annoyed at how everyone seemed fixated on my safety when the King of Vale Darra and his two daughters were now missing and other royals were murdered. My brothers were around me watching, all but Khire who had yet to return.

"Yes, but I'm ok, I and Fetcher got out of there with not even a scratch, we'll be ok. There's three members of the royal family missing and one is our King," I patted his hands and grabbed them hopping he would calm down. He sat there watching me for a long time. "Khire's gone, I don't know if he's coming back and you two were out there with murderers, I could have lost you both!" Dad was not calming down as tears came to his eyes.

"It's my job! The King is gone!" I said angry. "And Khire isn't dead, he will come back," I said without a doubt.

"How do you know, you haven't seen him, you don't know where he went, no one knows where he went. He could be bleeding somewhere out there calling for help and we will never know till we got a phone call from the morgue asking us to come identify him! It's been months since we've seen him last, he usually comes back to me after a few days maybe a few week, it's been months!" Tears were coming, streaming down his face as his voice rose.

"Ok first off even if Khire was in trouble he would never call for help," I said trying to make a joke. "Jakk's right, Khire is very capable of taking care of himself. Out of us all, he is the most likely to survive this. Dad you need to calm down and relax, you're getting too in over your head about this," Aster said with authority. "I was never a good father to him, he was always on his own, always sad. I don't even know him, he's like a stranger to me. I'm a horrible father!" Dad seemed to be a little unstable, but I couldn't comfort him. He needed Khire for that. And as much as I could tell my father that he was a good dad to Khire, I couldn't. Truth was, he hadn't been that great, but nor had Khire been a good son.

Dad wasn't a youngster anymore, his health was failing and him getting in a panic was not helping it. He already seemed to have aged ten years in the past months. "Dad, you are a great father to us, we all grew up and are so successful, everybody in Vale Darra knows our names because we are so successful and good. Khire had his own ways, but he's just as good. You were and are a great father," Aster said coming over and kneeling before dad. Dad turned to look down at him. Aster smiled at him reassuringly and dad calmed down a little bit.

"You have nothing to worry about, Khire is very smart, he knows how to take care of himself and you know he won't do anything that he knows he won't survive. He will always fight for a chance to live no matter how small. He wouldn't put himself in a situation that he can't come out of," Aster continued.

"No he won't, but with all that's happening, maybe someone got to him?" Dad was calm now, but still sniffling and very upset.

"Again, we would sense it, ok. Have just a little bit of faith in Khire, we may not agree with how he lives his life, but I think we can all agree he's very good at surviving it. Now let's all settle down, we're here for a reason so let's get to it ok?" Dad nodded at him and we all tried to settle down and watch TV.

CHAPTER #38

The building was a black shadow against the dark sky as we came near, the moon hid behind clouds high above us. Khire rode determined and serious towards it. I wanted the King and his daughters to be safe, but the wind was cold and I was shivering in my saddle uncontrollably. My horse was running with long strides, eating up the land, but making the cold wind blow harder in my face. It wasn't too cold, but I hated being even slightly cold and so I still complained. Nevertheless, I was determined to ride out with Khire to the Resort for Royal Affairs. Khire said he felt when Shirra got hit and fell unconscious, she wasn't awake right now so it was hard for him to figure out where she was. For now, he wanted to investigate the scene of the murder and kidnapping.

We stopped and tied our horses to a post then went around, getting inside and looking around, going over every inch of the building then doing the same for the outside. We found the huge hole and the smaller holes in the wall. We found blood sprayed everywhere, dried now, but not the bodies; they were picked up yesterday and taken to the morgue already.

As I was walking I noticed something glittering in one of the flowerpots. A small knife lay forgotten in the dirt and as I picked it up I looked around looking to see where Khire was.

"Khire," I called quietly and he came over. He took one look at the knife and nodded.

"That's Cadence's knife," He said certain. I to recognized the small blade and felt a little angered at Cadence's betrayal.

There wasn't too much Khire could find, but Khire did pick up on things we've seen before and afterwards we got together and talked. We finished looking over the building and were now sitting on a tree trunk in the nearby forest with the horses tied to a tree, grazing nearby.

"Ok, so there was more than one person," Khire started. "And they knew what they were doing, they obviously weren't new at killing or kidnapping. They left nothing much behind for us to find and figure out who they are. Also they had a good plan and knew well enough where to be at what time. And Cadence is involved," I added.

"Yes, so we've confirmed them as assassins and good ones," He said and I nodded.

"How's Shirra doing?" I asked him. He looked a little uneasy. I never told him I knew about the bond, but he knew it was important to find Shirra and I wouldn't betray him. Still it was uncomfortable talking about something such as that.

"She's hurt, but alive, she doesn't know where she is. Let's go look at the bodies and see how they were killed," He said and we left and returned to Vale Darra.

I returned the horses to the stables when we got back to the city, while Khire snuck in and we ran through the alleys all the way to the morgue. The moon was just setting by now so we snuck in and got down to the bodies easily with not a soul nearby.

We uncovered the bodies and looked them over finding where they were cut, how they were cut, and how deep. When we were finished, the sun was coming up, but we did learn something's. There were signs that the people fought back, some nicks and scrapes told us some tried to overpower the murders. Unfortunately they couldn't and were killed. The wounds weren't deep, but would still bleed a lot confirming the killers knew what they were doing.

I sat on a stool as Khire looked at the bodies again. He was talking, but quietly to himself so I turned my attention to other things. I was hungry and having worked a lot this past few weeks I had a lot of money and was ready to spend some to make my stomach stop growling.

"I'm starving, I'm going to get us some food, but I'll be back soon ok," I said as my stomach growled loudly making it known just how hungry I was. Khire nodded and I left.

The night was cold, but I was happy to be moving to somewhere I could get food. Cops were out and about looking around for any trouble. I avoided them easily and made my way to an emergency grocery store that was open during the night for citizens that needed food. The cashier still on till wasn't happy to see me come in and I apologized for waking her up as I ran around the store collecting some food. The shelves were stocked with food, most of it comprising of foods that could be stored for months or years if needed, but some held meat or produce. I grabbed what I wanted then brought it to her and she un-happily rung it through, told me the total, took my money, then in a monotone voice said good morning and goodbye. I took my bags and left the store, looking back at the unhappy cashier.

"Jeepers, never go to you again," I said to myself as I rushed down the streets then ran down an alley way and snuck back into the morgue.

Once in I settled back into the stool and began to pull out food and split it equally into two parts, one for me the other for Khire. He was staring at the bodies, serious faced as he stood with his back to the wall of drawers filled with other bodies.

"What have you discovered?" I asked before I took a bite out of my sandwich. It had four types of meats on it, lettuce, some sauce of some kind and some cheese.

"Well not overly much, the cuts are clean and true, there not just skims or nicks, so the guards and royals may have put up a fight, but who ever got to them was really good and fast to make their cuts.

"I think we're dealing with more people to," Khire said after a moment

"Umm, we already confirmed that," I said hoping he didn't get hit in the head when I was gone or somehow lost his memory.

"No I know, but I think we're dealing with even more people, ten at least. The whole was made by an explosion, but the people would have heard it, so that means someone was already in the safe room when the royals and guards were put in there so that they could kill the people, but one person couldn't do it alone, he'd need help. I think it was an inside job with outside help. At least one person outside to blow the whole. The whole was hit from the outside and blown inside, so someone had to be outside, while there was another person on the roof then in the garden. The guards, servants and the rest who weren't in the safe room were killed by someone, probably the one who was out on the roof and if it's the same person, the one out in the garden. Which was probably Cadence. The other guards were waiting outside the safe room and so couldn't hear the blast, by the time they checked they were already dead or gone.

"They were put in the safe room at two o'five. Then the guards checked them two hours later and found them dead, at that time it would be about four o'five, and the blood was still wet, but they were dead for at least twenty minutes before that," He kept watching the bodies and soon I was finished my sandwich and was eyeing his. Instead I grabbed it and took it over to him, he took it without looking at me, but he didn't eat it.

"Ok, so there are more than two guys, ten for sure, but why would they do that? I don't see why they just captured the three of them, I mean, it was a room with royalty, whoever it was could have captured all of them then they would get an even bigger reward. What were their motives?" I started to think, but I couldn't come up with an answer that I could say.

"To get at me, they only captured them three because they know I'm involved with Shirra and to make it worse they captured her sister and father as well. This is all on me, I think someone's toying with me," He said gravely. So far it all fit.

"Ok so I think this is Cadence's idea and Josin's idea. Cadence is a stupid boy who has a tendency to follow anyone just so long as he gets something out of it. Maybe he teamed up with Josin?" I said as I pulled a chair over to Khire.

"I think so, but give me some more time," He said and we left, him finally taking notice of his sandwich. "Thanks for the food," He said kindly. "No problem, though the cashier wasn't happy," I said looking around.

"Probably not," He said with a hint of amusement in his voice. He started eating as we wound our way through the alleys.

"You don't have to be alone, I'm not asking for anything, but why don't you just come to my house?" I asked him.

"Thank you Caprica," He said and we headed off to my place. It was a little two story white house in a nice suburban area of the city. Nothing special, but a little piece of peace for the wary person.

CHAPTER #39

The night had a slight chill to it as I stared out on my porch looking out for my brother. Dad was now staying at my house and we were all helping him any minute we could, but we couldn't do much. It was Khire he needed and right now Khire was gone, somewhere where we had no idea.

I really hoped he was ok, I had been coming outside each night for the past week, but every night was always the same, no Khire. I sighed and headed inside as the moon shone down from the middle of the sky. There were no clouds so the moon shone down without flickering out and in and the stars twinkled high overhead down at the world.

I went to the couch where dad sat watching TV, Aster was sitting beside him and as I came in he looked up at me questionably. I shook my head and he turned away disappointed. I went over to the crib where Sighann slept and picked her up, she made a noise, but kept sleeping and I sat down on the chair with her in my arms. She slept peacefully as I looked down at her and I wondered about the future. I could see she had a part of me and her mother in her, but who would she be most like. I liked my family, but I hoped she was more like her mother for some things, I didn't like Khire going off and I certainly wouldn't like my daughter going off when she got older.

The TV show we were watching ended and a news report came on.

"Hi I'm Linda Tawfen. The Queen Ahoura of Vale Darra has announced a state of emergency. New laws have passed making people be in their homes by five pm, you can come out at seven am and must report daily to a police officer with an officer being assigned to each family living in Vale Darra and the surrounding area. People must now go to work and will not be paid for absences, sick days or holidays and taxes are rising as more and more people are losing their jobs. Already we have twenty two thousand people without a job and some five thousands evicted from their homes as they are unable to pay for bills.

"Queen Ahoura is giving three thousand dollars to people living on their own and eight thousand five hundred for people with a family. Her Royal Highness is also working to make new businesses and train more people to be police officers and investigators. Already there has been almost ten thousand people signing up for training dealing with military, police, investigators and undercover agents and more," The news reporter, a women in her late thirties with short brown hair and green eyes spoke with her clipped voice as she sat, hands clasped before her, resting on the table with a pile of papers neatly piled in front of her. She wore a black jacket and brown shirt underneath which seemed to add to the professionalism, but I knew she was new. She had a hard emotionless face, but you could still see in her eyes she was very affected by the news she was telling. Chances are everyone was and so we were going to have a hard time till this ended.

"It is said that this will last five to eight years and maybe longer to fully recover from this downfall," She said as if reading my mind. That was a long time, too long and all the while people will just keep dying and probably disappearing. Something had to be done, but no one knew what exactly was happening. People were dying at an extreme rate, and the police believed it was the work of more than one person.

I thought about it a little more as I listened to what the reporter had to say, none of it was good, it was all about prices rising, deaths climbing, and more laws that pretty much put everybody under strict rules that they had to follow. She even mentioned that the police or investigators won't be charged with any act of murder if they shoot someone who is on the streets. I felt bad for all the people who didn't have a place to go, they would have to hide or risk getting shot and killed for just having no home to go to.

We were staying inside anyway, but it wouldn't help the ones with no home or in an emergency where someone needed to get somewhere. I kept thinking about all that had happened, but I was never as good at piecing things together like Fetcher, Jakk or even Khire. They all seemed to have an extreme gift on taking some information and being able to expand on it till everything made sense.

I looked out the window to the dark street. The night was cold and dangerous, I held onto my daughter afraid for her future and what was to come. Fearing that these last minutes with her would be all the time we had.

CHAPTER #40

The night was so still it seemed nothing was alive, no movement, no sounds, no wind, and the moon and stars added little light to the gloomy city. We had turned on all street lights and buildings to keep Vale Darra lit, but we could only do that for so long, with the depression, we didn't need to be dealing with a huge electricity bill, so now everything was black, all light seemed to be gone. I stood on a street staring around me waiting and watching for any life, but nothing stirred. There was electricity in the air and I knew something soon was going to happen. I didn't know if it would be today or in the next week, but something was building up and soon it would burst.

Suddenly a motion to my left, I whipped around, pivoting on my foot and bringing my gun up to point at the movement. It meowed then hissed at me and I saw the cat run away furious. I blew a sigh of relief, but that didn't release any tension, the night was dark and dangerous. There were other police officers spaced out throughout the streets, not being far away from another one, just in sight so that when something happened we were ready.

"Cool down Fetcher, its ok," I said to myself to try and reassure myself.

It was a cold summer night and my fingers were freezing in the thin gloves I wore. I turned and looked to my right, nothing again, but the moon was heading down and in five hours the sun would rise. People wouldn't be coming out of their homes till seven, but we had to stay out here all night and day. There were very few officers to take over positions so sometimes we were left standing guard for two days, eating little and drowsing the odd times during the day.

I turned to my left, the sun was not near rising, but it was warming up so as I stood there feeling crept back into my body. The standing was long and tiring and I was hungry and exhausted, but I stood there not moving or falling asleep except for the sweep of my head to check around me.

It was as the sun was coming up, beams of light streaming through the buildings and waking up the city from a restless, cold slumber. As I was turning my head to look back to the left that I noticed a building off to my far left, which had figures standing in the windows. The curtains were closed, but they just stood there, though there was something funny about the way they stood, their figures looked wrong, as if they were standing upside down.

I could do nothing though, this was my post and I wouldn't and couldn't move from it, so when someone came to relieve me I made a call to the office. "Hi it's Fetcher, ya I'm stationed on Petter Street and Collden Wood Street and I have noticed figures in the windows of a building. I have noticed them for an hour and a half now and they have not moved, there standing behind curtains so I can't get a proper look at them, but I think there strung upside down from the ceiling,"

"Well then you'd be right Fetcher, you know your brother always told me I had to be careful with you? You are too smart to be left alive, say could you kill your brother?" A creepy, dark voice came on the other line. I was thinking, when I had answered the phone it was Marthlin who answered, what happened to her and who was this guy talking to me now? I didn't answer for a long time.

"Who is this?" I asked, my voice breathless.

"Well I'm a great friend of your brothers, he's such a good boy, he makes me so proud of what he's become. I gave him so much and though he's against me, I marvel at all he does. You really don't realise who you're dealing with, but I'm sure you will find out later.

You're smart, you can see something's wrong, you can feel it too. Tell me, does it feel sickening to you?" The voice was excited like the person was enjoying himself. I couldn't stop listening as I was stunned where I stood beside my car that I had parked in an ally not far away. That voice, I recognized it as something I heard a long time ago, pictures of people killed, their bodies cut up then thrown from windows in the night. People screaming as blood would seep down building walls and paint the streets in red, the bodies emptied of blood. He liked stringing up his victims or making them jump from high buildings. It wasn't who I thought it would be though, Khire and I thought it was Midnight, but I knew this wasn't Midnights work.

I looked frantically around searching. I couldn't stop myself from panicking, I could hear that voice echoing all around me, laughing, I knew he was nearby, he could see me and I was in view of him. If he shot me I'd be dead in seconds, but no shot came and the voice sounded again. "So let's see how long it takes you to figure out my little game, Fetcher Sashess, let's see how many people will scream bloody mercy and their blood rain down until you figure out who I am," It sounded challenging, but also like the person was very much enjoying this. "I already know who you are Suicide," I said to the guy. He was an older assassin who made few kills then would flee before he was caught and reappear somewhere around the world. He tended to kill people by hanging them with a belt or rope so it always looked like a suicide. He also had a tendency to make people jump out of tall buildings.

"Very good," He said sounding pleased.

"I have a question for you," I said to buy me some time to think.

"Sure, go ahead," He responded, sounding amused.

"How can you kill all of these people?" I asked. I could not understand how someone could have such power over another to make them kill themselves.

"Ah well my Wish allows me to do that. You see when I was a little boy I use to write stories, typically about people I hated. I would write about a person who bullied me getting stung by a wasp and dying or a little girl falling out of a window of a tall building. After sometime I realized my wishes came true. I have since learned how to do such things without having to write them all down, so you see it is quite easy for me to say 'Martha go leap out that window' and Martha will do so," He said and I grimaced. "What a horrible power to grant you," I commented with great distaste.

I went to the trunk of my car, took my extra gun and extra bullets then shut the door and walked towards the building at a slow and determined pace. It loomed up in front of me and as I drew near it the sense of something bad grew stronger, I could smell a horrible stench and knew instantly it was blood. I was outside, not even six meters from the six-floor building and yet I could smell blood as if I stood in a puddle of it. I reached for the main door and slowly pulled it open. Blood was smeared everywhere as if someone had purposefully smeared it everywhere. I looked inside, the building was lightening up with the morning sun, but I couldn't see all the way to the back, no matter I crept inside. Something told me I wasn't going to die now, I was a part of a plan and my job wasn't finished yet so he would keep me alive until it was.

The main floor was empty other than the desks and appliances hotels usually have. I went to the elevator not intending to use it, but to just see if it worked. It did, it opened right as I came near it, though no one was inside. I wouldn't take the sign though and so went to the staircase and started climbing them, slowly and always looking around.

I got to the first floor and left the staircase to go out in the hall. My heart was beating fast, my blood pounding through my veins. I was breathing quicker and deeper, so I calmed myself, but that sense of dread grew and grew until I kicked open a door and lunged inside yelling and holding my gun out in front of me.

"Freeze! The police!" My yell echoed in the silence after. I was met with nothing, but blood smeared on the ground as if several people had been dragged.

I slowly made my way to the first bedroom, it was on the left of me and there was a door, but I easily pushed it aside. Then the first thing that I did was shoot. My gun went off with a loud crack, adding another echo to the silence.

Before me hung a body, upside down from the ceiling, a thick chain tied around the women's ankles and running up to the ceiling. She had long blond hair that was now streaked in dried blood, and dressed in casual clothes as if she were doing everyday things. Her eyes were open and staring blankly at the floor.

I couldn't stand the sight as I ran to the other rooms to find men, teenagers and children in the same position, they were all hung before the white curtains of the windows. And as I went through all the rooms in the hotel and finding people hung upside down by a chain from the roof, I still had that bad sense, but I knew this wasn't it.

After I returned back to my car and sat down inside it, I needed information and I had found nothing other than the dead bodies. Now I turned on my car and drove away driving up and down the streets and every so often I found a building with still figures in the window. Then I would stop and investigate inside, going to each room and checking out each victim. I would look at the bodies and find any identification on them where I would write it in my book along with other information I thought useful. I didn't have anything to break the chains that hung them up so I had no choice but to leave them dangling there.

The sun was moving across the sky and was soon sinking below the horizon though I was still going building to building, already on my second book, the other had two hundred pages and I had used it back and front with all the information I had collected, even inside cover and inside back cover.

It was getting too dark and I was too tired to go on and far too hungry. I went home where I gathered anything I might need and left to go to my brother's house, in times like these it was best to be in a crowd and off the streets. I would have one day and two nights to rest, but then I would have to work again and so I planned to spend it with my family. When I got there it seemed everybody else thought the same, all but Khire was there. "Fetcher…… what's wrong?" Shean asked his eyes wide and face pale. I must have looked like death, but I had information I needed to share. I needed people I could trust and I needed answers, my family was the only people I could ask since I already came up with the conclusion that they were a part of the guys plan.

"I was at my post last night, but as the sun started coming up I seen some figures in the windows of a nearby building. My post was taken over by someone else so I went to my car and called in to the office. At first it was a women I knew, but then it went to another person. The person who has been killing all those people and I think who holds the King and his daughters hostage," I told them all about the people strung up and they all looked horror struck as I told them everything he said and all that I had been doing. I felt like the only expressions on people's faces these days were either sorrow, pain or horror. I was dreadfully tired of looking into someone's eyes and seeing that.

"That sounds familiar to me," Jakk said thinking hard. "I have heard of the same things done by an assassin who use to kill people long ago, but no one has heard of any victims done by him in over ten year, so why is he doing it again?" He thought about it, but it wasn't him that gave the answer.

Dad was the one to answer that. He spoke in a haunted voice, his eyes sleep deprived and dark, his face worn and his clothes wrinkled.

"He's after Khire. I got a call just the other day, from the same guy," Dad stopped talking and the room fell silent.

"But what does this guy have to do with Khire, like what did Khire do. I don't really know Khire, but I can't see him doing something that would cause an annihilation of the people of Vale Darra," Tellnair said.

"Khire believes there is a man named Dyras who has a thing against magi. Dyras has the power to time travel and he's here trying to kill all strong magi. That's why a bunch of magical items are failing because there's an imbalance. Khire thought Midnight was also here killing people, but he was wrong it's an assassin named Suicide," I said sure of myself.

"Well in any case I think it's safe to say Khire is alive. I think if someone was after Khire he wouldn't keep killing people if Khire was already dead," Jakk said at first not hearing himself until he finished speaking.

"We have to find Khire!" My dad shot to his feet with a cry of desperation, but Aster and Tellnair shot up too and before he could get anywhere they grabbed him by the arms and sat him back down.

"Dad, we can't, we won't ever be able to find Khire. Vale Darra is huge and the world even bigger, you can't find him even if we were to all help, ok. If we can find Khire then so can this killer person ok, for Khire's safety, let's not look for him. He'll come home, don't worry, Khire will find his way back no matter what," Aster said calmly and dad nodded his head.

No one knew what to do, I wanted to tell Khire its Suicide not Midnight, but I knew I would never find Khire and I didn't think it would be a good idea to try. We turned the TV back on and made our self-watch it thinking if we can't help our city we could at least support it by watching the news.

"We're here to you live, just five minutes ago a body dropped out of a twenty sixth story building. More and more are jumping out of the other windows and buildings all around us have figures in the windows, some are moving and opening up windows to jump out others haven't moved at all.

"We have the entire area surrounded, but will it be enough? We're taking you to Vill Waelock in the sky…." The girl stopped talking and the cameras changed to a man in a helicopter above the city. The city looked like a sick gory movie with the sun casting red beams of light on the city and people jumping from windows.

"The person must be still in there, the killer has to be still in the building," I said shocked.

The camera got a close up shot of a girl about twelve holding the window frame and staring down, fear clear on her face. She took a step and her body plunged to her death below. You could see more people following her and now there was a pile at the foot of the buildings.

"I have to go there and stop this," I got to my feet and checked my gun. I still had the extra bullets I had gotten before, but there were so many people, there had to be more than one killer.

"We're coming with you," Tellnair said as they all got to their feet. I would have said no, but if it wasn't them it would usually be more officers and I knew I wouldn't be getting any of them to help me.

Just then something somewhere exploded. We all dove or fell to the ground and waited for the ground to stop moving. The house shuddered, but stayed standing, luckily.

"Ok we are staying inside until I can get an idea of what's going on," I said and began calling my office. I couldn't get through so I started dialling people's cell phones. Someone had to be alive and able to help or tell me what was going on. My family sat quietly on the couch trying to either think of some way to help or think of something to cheer us up. Tellnair and Aster rocked their babies to sleep while Julia sat cradling her large belly. Jakk's kids huddled around their mother, old enough to know fear, but young enough to not know what to do.

I watched them all trying to plan my next move, but nowhere in my training did anyone mention this. I felt a little unsure of what I was to do and couldn't find the courage to just run out there guns shooting. I took a deep breath and tried to think of something that could help me. Was their someone I was missing who could at least tell me what was going on? Were there already police forces out there trying to stop the people from jumping to their deaths? And most importantly, how did one guy have the power to force that many people to kill themselves? The longer I stood here the more unanswered questions I came up with.

CHAPTER #41

The moon shone down from its peak in the large sky. The cold wind tore at my face, but I stayed vigilant and waiting on a tall building. People were jumping from buildings, hanging from ceilings and everywhere chaos was in full swing. Names went through my mind as I watched down below many assassins fighting. There were more than I had thought, but they all came. It was becoming an assassin war, this killer, this person who has been so destructive had made a lot of enemies, but also alleys. His alleys were here causing terror and death, but his enemies, my alleys were here trying to stop them. I watched as people I knew were slain, cut down and trodden on as if they meant nothing to the world. I ground my teeth, but stayed where I was. It wasn't them I was after, I was after their leader. I was sure I knew who it was, but I stayed ready for anything. It was directly at midnight that an explosion went off far to my right and a shadow appeared before me.

A man stepped out of the shadows and I immediately thought it was Midnight smiling at me maliciously, but then I had to remind myself that Midnight was dead and that this was his brother. Being able to see now, I recognized his face. He was older, but still capable and deadly. A large scar ran from his right temple to his lip, drawing up his lip into an ugly smile. His pockmarked face made him hideous, but it was the fact that he was standing in front of me that scared me the most.

"Well hello old friend," He said with a smile. I had wanted to deal with Dyras first, I wasn't sure if I could survive a fight with Josin, but I wasn't given a choice on who I would fight first.

"What are you doing here?" I growled.

"What am I doing here? Why this is my home, I grew up here a long time ago as a little boy. I have such terrible memories of this place, but it is what keeps me here," he said with a shrug. "It's what's keeping you here as well,"

"No, I stay because I choose to stay. To protect this city and everyone living in it," I told him defiantly.

"But nonetheless you're trapped here and you'll always be trapped here. See that was the problem with you. You never had any imagination, never enough willpower to reach out and grasp everything. You have so much potential, but in the end you're just the same as everyone else,"

"I've never claimed to be anyone great, I've never wanted anything other than to be like everyone else. But I'm not. I'm not the same as everyone else and imagination is dead to me. I don't need to imagine how I'm going to kill you, I already know how Josin," I said and I saw a little surprise in his eyes as I said his name.

I yelled, jumping at him, magic propelling me forward. We clashed, sword to sword and sparks flashed. It was a fast frenzied dual that left us panting and gasping for air. But we continued. I jumped him again and this time got lucky, cutting his ribs, furious, he sidestepped and brought his hilt up and bashed me in the head with it. Dizzied, I tried to move as he swept his sword down and caught me on the thigh. I fell to one knee, but managed to dive forward and stab him back just above the knee. He screamed in pain and furry and grabbed my hair with his hands then with magic, threw me across the rooftops. I tumbled to a stop against a wall that stopped me from going over the edge. Getting up, I threw a knife at my old master. He grabbed it out of the air and threw it back at me. I didn't have the precision right now to grab it, still dizzy, I avoided it instead and rushed him.

We collided with a loud clash as I managed to bring up my sword to meet his. My momentum knocked him off balance and I ended up on top of him. I tried to pin him under me, but he had a lot more muscle on me and so pushed me off and ended up sitting on my hips, sword pressed to my throat. I used one of my hands and my sword to try and push his sword away as I tried to wiggle loose. The blade cut into my skin slightly at my throat, but before he could slice my throat I managed to push back enough and quickly jab a small dart-like knife into his right eye. Screaming as he swatted at his face, he fell backwards and I got to me feet, breathing hard, blood dripping from my throat. My heart beat fast with adrenaline, my blood pulsing through my veins. The night seemed to quiet in the last minutes of this fight.

☾

We were still in the house, I was still trying to get a hold of someone. We seen people outside, but we were too scared to join them. We heard fighting around us, people yelling, screaming, crying.

"Fetcher I've been thinking, you know when we were younger we would go out a lot and would always find Khire hanging out with this old guy?" Jakk asked me.

"Ya I've seen the same guy I think," Shean said standing up. "He's creepy looking, old, balding, has a lot of scars," Shean said gesturing with his hands.

"Ya him, I asked Khire one day why he hung out with an older man like him and Khire would say cause he had to and no one else would hang out with him," Jakk continued.

"So…?" Aster asked.

"Well do you think Khire's involved with this like little more in-depth then we had first thought?" Jakk asked simply.

"Like do you think Khire's an assassin?" Tellnair asked.

"My son is not a murderer, he would never do anything like that!" Dad yelled at us furiously.

"Dad just listen, it all makes sense, but it's no one's fault… well I guess technically its ours. All the signs were there. Khire never wanted to be alone, he got upset easy, he was quiet and always going off. We thought he was just going off as he pleased, but what if someone was threatening him. Fetcher, there are a lot of stories of little kids used by assassins as tools. Most don't become assassins, usually they are only used once, but what if Midnight saw something in Khire. Khire liked helping people and because he was neglected he looked for anyone's attention," Jakk said and everyone looked at him.

"It's something to think about," I said nodding gravely.

"And so what? What if Khire is an assassin? What if he's Dusk?" Tellnair asked everyone and we fell silent.

"I will still love him," Dad said stubbornly.

"Can you? Can you look into his eyes and tell him you love him even if you knew for sure he was out there killing people?" Aster asked hurt.

"Yes I can, because I may not know him very well, but he has a good heart. He was dealt an unfair hand in life and it's not his fault. If he is Dusk he is killing bad guys that should be killed. He's doing something that should be done, but no one else has the guts to do. He's risking himself to save others. That to me is a hero," Dad said looking at Aster and Aster nodded.

"Ok would you still love him if he were Creature?" Aster asked.

"I would," Dad replied, meeting Asters eyes and challenging him to judge him. Aster backed down, but it was obvious that while Dad approved of Khire as an assassin, Aster did not.

"Princess Shirra has to be in on it to," Jakk said randomly. "The King has spies, everyone knows that. The spies have noticed Princess Shirra and Khire spending a lot of time together. The King thought maybe they were hooking up, but I told him Khire was unstable because of Miranna," Jakk said and that reminded me of Miranna.

"I found Miranna's body. It was in the river by the mall, her throat was cut," I told them all sadly.

"And do you think Khire killed her?" Aster asked.

"Aster!" Tellnair yelled.

"If he's an assassin he could do anything!" Aster said defensively.

"Aster's right, but I don't think Khire did it because he is an assassin. If anything he did it by accident because of his training as an assassin, but talk to anyone and Khire loved that girl more than anything. It was at the same time that Dusk stopped killing everyone. Remember, there were two years that Dusk seemed to have just disappeared. I think Miranna was a good thing, but she died somehow," I said and this time Jakk nodded at me.

I went over to the window to look out, but I could see little.

"But what, I'm sure the man I saw at the Royal was Dusk," Jakk said and I nodded.

"Yes but remember we think there's two Dusks. They split now so maybe Khire's Dusk and the other one is Creature?" I said thinking it through.

"No, Khire would be Creature. Have you never noticed how cat like he is? Khire's always been sneaky and quiet. Always prowling around where he shouldn't be. At first I thought he was just like that like some people are, but Khire is very animal like. It must be his Wish. Khire is Creature," Aster said. We all nodded, not having a reason to contradict that.

It was a little appalling thinking Khire as Creature. Creature hasn't been in the news long, but he tore his victims up to shreds and even I didn't have a very good opinion on someone who did that.

"I can't say that I love or accept him, but I don't think its right to just reject him. If he is an assassin, it's because he was forced into it. Everyone knows once you're an assassin, you're always an assassin. Midnight trained Khire and now Khire has no choice, so he kills bad guys, he's trying to make things right," Shean said from where he sat.

"Actually I think Suicide is Khire's master. Khire said a while ago that someone he knew died, but he had a brother. Khire seemed shocked that he had a brother. I bet Suicide is Midnights brother and they look identical and Midnight is dead," Tellnair said. He seemed almost happy and I gave him a weird look.

"What? I'm not smart enough like you guys are to figure out all the little connections, but I'm proud of myself to have made that connection," He said with a smile and I shook my head.

"I've noticed bullet wounds on him, he doesn't know that I know, but I know he's tried to kill himself," Aster said sadly. "I took a course on suicide and learned how to sense someone who was hurting himself. I know Khire has never wanted to be alive, I just thought it was because he hated us,"

"Trying to kill yourself and killing bad guys doesn't make killing any less of a crime," Shean said sighing.

"No, but it's good to know that if he is Creature, he's wanting a way out. He doesn't need to be killed, if he will cooperate. He can be put in a special home where he can live out the rest of his life and still do normal things, but not be behind bars or in the ground," I said and rubbed my face.

"Ok well what do we do?" Tellnair asked confused.

"Don't know, but Khire's out there trying to fix things," I said and sat back down to think.

"I just wish Khire knew he didn't have to do this alone," Dad said quietly.

"Well Khire always thinks he has to fly solo," Shean said sighing.

"What do you think he will do once he comes back and he finds out we know what he is?" Julia asked.

"Run maybe," Aster said easily. "Assassins run,"

"I will tell him I love him and want to take him some place safe," Dad said. He seemed a little ignorant in all that Khire would have done as an assassin, but I wasn't about to educate him.

☾

Chapter #42

Isaac stood nearby, creepily watching as Josin and I tried to kill each other. The ground was slick with blood, my head didn't feel any better and blood kept flowing into my eyes, but I couldn't even swipe it off my face. I had to keep my guard up now as Josin was in a frenzy to kill me. Hard quick hits, constantly raining down on me as he attacked me.

"Everything I did for you and this is how you repay me? You ungrateful, worthless piece of street trash! I gave you life, I taught you how to live, how to survive and you try to kill me! You'll never kill me, I'm too strong even for you. You think you've won because you figured everything out, but you haven't!" Josin was screaming at me, voice thick with rage. I was too confused to figure out something was off here, but I began to lesson my attack until we ceased fighting all together.

"You made me an assassin! You took everything from me, my life, my family, my love, you made me into a monster! You did not save me! I feel dead because of you, my heart beats, but that means nothing!" I screamed back, nearly collapsing to the ground.

"Khire you don't understand, there's more going on than you think. You see Midnight was my brother, he was very kind and caring, he never wanted to be an assassin either. Our father made him though, our father was a great man, he was a simple thief, not much of an assassin, but he was very smart. He knew this world would only be kind to those that fought and be devastating on those that were weak. He made both Sinth and I assassins. I took to it rather well, you see I like power, I want to be the most powerful being on this planet," He said with a little laugh as if it were a pleasant thought.

"Dyras?" I questioned.

"I made that up to make sure you had something to focus on while I went about my business. I couldn't have you meddling with my plans and so I wrote a book to make it look like some time traveler was trying to kill magi. It worked really well, you became fixated on finding him, even involving your brother. But it's been I all this time. I will be the most powerful, most deadliest mage and I won't let anyone stop me," He spoke with such assertion it sounded like something he had repeated often. I swore at him and lunged forward just as I heard someone scream, a high piercing scream that cut through the cold, crisp night and stopped my heart.

Shirra's scream stopped me and Josin shook his head.

"You could have saved her, you really could have, but now it's too late," He said and with that he lunged at me and drove his sword into my heart. I stared down dumbly at the weapon in me then met my old masters eyes.

"I tried to save you from the world," Was the last thing I heard Josin say before my mind went blank.

I don't know what happened after that, but suddenly I was crawling across the rooftop, dragging my body. Josin lay behind me, cut to ribbons. Isaac gaped, horror struck, at the massacre. He hadn't moved, he hadn't turned on his master, he stood by loyal as ever as he watched some invisible force tear his master's body apart. That same invisible force left large gouges in the ground making it look like some overgrown cat had attacked the man now lying dead on the cold ground.

I didn't care; all feeling was gone from my body. I had maybe half an hour, maybe an hour if I was lucky. If I could just find Shirra I could die beside her. I could sense her nearby, in the next building over ironically enough. It was the hardest journey I have ever made. I got down to the main floor just to get to the other building and climb down the stairs. I wasn't able to stand which made this whole thing that much harder.

I could almost count my breaths now as my body slowly gave in to deaths wishes. I was nearly to Shirra when my body started to shutter, it couldn't go on any farther, it didn't want to go on, but I was almost there. Finding some type of strength from somewhere I managed to get down to the basement and to a small room. Shirra lay on the ground badly bleeding. She was unconscious, but miraculously alive. I crawled beside her and curled into her, giving into my inevitable death.

☾

The town was dead silent, and it seemed that everybody was waiting outside a building as I watched from afar. The assassins fought on and I watched as many died, there were few of them left and soon all battles ceased as the sun began to rise. I didn't join in the fighting, instead I stood patiently watching.

I watched as Khire and Josin killed each other than somehow Khire crawl away leaving a strewn body behind. I didn't see what had exactly happened, but some invisible force tore at Josin till he was nothing, but pieces. I was horror struck at what I saw and even more so when I saw Khire was still alive. I didn't think he'd get far, but he made it into the building I stood on and I assumed to Shirra.

"I can go finish him off?" I asked my master.

"No Cadence, leave him be, he'll be dead soon anyway," Duke said smiling. I nodded not liking it, but obeying nonetheless.

☾

Jakk and I drove through the streets when the sun finally came up. We drove to where the fighting was worst and got out to scout around. I could see something bloody had been dragged from one building to the next and so we fallowed the trail into one of the buildings. It went down stairs, but we heard some noises coming from upstairs and so we went up the stairs to see what was up there.

The building was silent and ghostly, besides the blood, nothing was disturbed. We followed the noises, holding our guns out until we approached a door to a closet. Jakk stood aside and reached for the handle, unlatching it, he slid the door open and two people burst out screaming. Jakk recognizing them first, grabbing the King before the King could swing his broom at me. Knocking him to the ground, Jakk began to talk to him to get the King to relax. Princess Isra was too terrified to do anything, but weep on the floor. I went to her, kneeling and wrapped my arms around her, the only thing I thought to do. She relaxed into me and slowly her sobs turned to hiccups until she quieted completely.

"Jakk?" The King said confused.

"Your both safe now, you'll be taken to the hospital," Jakk said, blabbering about being safe and getting help. The King relaxed and began to talk to us about what happened. It seemed to calm him down and so we listened intently.

"Shirra was taken somewhere else," The King said to us after a moments pause.

"We'll find her, Your Grace," Jakk said simply and the King nodded.

"I'm going to go see what happened downstairs," I told them.

"We should stick together," Jakk said slowly.

"I know, but what if Princess Shirra's downstairs?" I said getting to my feet.

I took my cell phone out of my pouch on my belt and tried calling the detachment, finally I got through.

"Hello Fetcher, why haven't you been picking up your phone?" Ave, a desk assistant, asked.

"It hasn't been ringing I've been trying to get a hold of you this whole time, but I couldn't get through. Well, whatever I have the King and Princess Isra, Princess Shirra has yet to be found, but it is believed that she is somewhere in the same building I am currently in," I told her. I then told her where I was, the situation if anyone was hurt and that there was bloody drag marks leading down into the basement of the building. She released three squads of nine to come and get us and escort us to the hospital while others secured the area and found the missing princess.

"Ok we have help coming, let's just stay situated here until they get here," I told everyone and we settled down to wait. Princess Isra whined a little about wanting to find her sister, but I told her that we needed to stay here and that people will be coming to get her. Once again it was a waiting game, but this one was shorter and a lot less intense.

When the police arrived we took them downstairs to the waiting vehicles. Jakk went with the King and Princess, but I stayed behind. Ludah who had gone with a squad downstairs to the basement came back to me. Taking one look at his face I instantly felt sick.

"Princess Shirra dead?" I asked. He nodded and took a deep breath.

"Along with someone else," He said gravely.

"Who?" I asked unsure.

"I'm so sorry, but... it's Khire," He said and I looked at him a minute longer confused.

"What?" I asked.

"Khire's dead, I'm so sorry, he has too many wounds, there's no chance to bring him back. It looks like he hasn't been dead long though. Maybe half an hour," He told me.

"Half an hour, that means those drag marks are his, he must have just gotten down there as Jakk and I were coming in. Had we gone downstairs we could have saved him, we could have maybe saved them both," I said. Ludah patted me on the shoulder.

"Go home and relax, its over. It's all over," He said and I nodded because that was the only thing I could do.

Without looking I climbed into my cruiser, someone tried to take my keys from me so that they could drive me home, but I said no. Just as I got into my car paramedics brought the bodies up. There were four of them, two humans and two Guardians. For some reason I smiled, it was rare that a Guardian chose to die alongside their Protected. The two white sheets covering the bodies were already red from blood. I wanted to see Khire one last time, but decided remembering him as alive was a better memory. I drove away to deliver the news to my family.

☾

I awoke to a very cold morning, my body felt strange, like it didn't want to move the way it was supposed to. I raised my head to look around and instantly got attacked by someone.

"Oh my little one sleep," a kind voice said and I turned to her, she was just a blur, my eyes were still trying to open, but they were clearing and slowly after a week I was able to see. I stared up into a face covered in fur. It was a serval and she was watching me with interest. I tried to flee, but managed an awkward stumble instead.

"Well that was a good try, but your legs aren't ready for any mad dash away from your mother yet. Give them some time to grow strong and soon you will be a proud serval like your father," the female serval said. "My father?" I asked very confused.

"Yes, your father. He's a handsome cat, the best one there is," She said pleased.

I was too confused to say much else and so I kept quiet. Each day I spent moving around, trying to get my legs to work properly, they were so small and wobbly I couldn't get them to move as I wanted them to and it was very frustrating. I hissed each time I fell over and each time my mother, for that's what the she-serval was, would lick me and encourage me to try again. After some time I grew hungry and would nurse from her then sleep against her warm belly with my litter mates.

It was a little time after that when I finally became good at walking that I started having dreams. I dreamt I was a human, I was a hunter and my prey were other humans. I didn't get it, but after some time I asked my mother.

"Momma, I'm having bad dreams. I'm a human, I'm not a serval in them," I said with fear. Humans were scary and I did not want to dream of them.

"My dear, in your past life you were a human. I knew you were special right from the moment you were born my little one. The Gods Matsa and Katsa smile on you as you will serve as Guide to a human.

"As a human you may have been evil or corrupt in some way so when you die you become a Guide. Humans call us Guardians, but truly we are their Guide. They are evil and need guidance from those more intelligent then them. You were once a human and now you're reborn into a serval. After sometime your memories will return from when you were a human and then you'll find your human with whom you will bond to. With your memories it is your duty that you will lead your human to a better life. Do you understand my little one?" She asked fondly.

"No," I whined and snuggled against her.

"In time you will," She said and began to clean me.

It was a simple life I had, but soon I had this nagging feeling of being in the wrong place. I was still too young to leave my mother so I told myself I'd stay with her until I was old enough to go on my own. But the feeling wouldn't go away. I became distracted easily and found myself wondering away from my family for a time then having to race back to them. After a little while my mother hissed at me and though I was still too young, I knew it was time for me to go. I said goodbye to my brother and sister then scampered off.

The days were hot and I wasn't a good hunter, but I found water regularly and so drank. As I journeyed I began to remember my time as a human. I was a little boy growing up in a big city; I was different from the rest, not excepted in any social group. I was a loner and an outcast and it made me hate everyone, but I did have some happy times in my life. A beautiful female, a women, fell in love with me, but I killed that love and so much more after her. I was an assassin and I only wanted death.

I couldn't believe how evil I was, it made me fear myself. How could I have been so cruel? I thought to myself that I better be a good Guide so that my human would not be as evil as I was. Then I began to have memories of my own Guide when I was a human. A cougar named Myre. He was a great and loyal friend, but he was corrupt, he should have helped me lead a better life, but he couldn't let his old human life go. He too had been a killer, a murderer, but not an assassin. He had done some horrible things and instead of those memories helping him to be a better person in his second life, he used them to make my human world full of darkness, pain and death. I don't know what happened to him after I died, he had died beside me, but I don't know what happens to corrupt Guides that don't save their humans and die. I felt a sad longing for the big cat who had been a loyal friend. At the same time though I promised that I would not be like him. I would help my human to be a better person as the serval Gods commanded us that those that are chosen lead the corrupt into light and life. I would do so and be the best Guide I could be.

The next day I found myself in a small town. It was a small little place, but teaming with life. I wandered the streets staying hidden as best I could. I was searching diligently for my human. A little boy I thought to myself. It was that night that I finally found him. It was the happiest moment of my life. He sat on the ground in ragged clothes. Not a clean spot on him. He was skinny and small only twelve years old, but seemed still too young to be on his own. His blond hair was long and filthy, his clothes torn and dirty. His knees that showed because of his pants being so ripped were cut and bruised from falling. He was crying to himself feeling lost and forgotten. He did not know where his parents were, he had never even known them, but after the day that he had, he wished he had someone to hug and to show him kindness.

I brushed up beside him and purred.

"Who are you?" He asked me startled.

"I am your Guide, your greatest and most loyal friend. I will lead you to a better place and I promise to give you a home," I told him and he smiled. His right eye was blue while the left was a brilliant green. "Hello Nyxx," I said to the boy and his smile widened.

"Hello," He said timidly.

"My name is Khire," I greeted and lay beside him to warm him, comforting him like no one had ever done.

☾

"I'm stepping aside so that my daughter can take the throne and be a better ruler for you then I could be. I confess that I haven't been the King I wanted to be, I haven't been the person I thought I was. I've fooled you all, even myself.

"My daughter, god rest her soul was not the daughter I wanted her to be. As some of you may know a few months ago, Princess Shirra's body was found, alongside her was someone else. Someone we all knew and feared. We had specialists extract their memories and we've found that Shirra had been aiding Creature for years. Creature died beside her. They loved each other and he wanted to protect her and so he protected everything about Vale Darra. He killed those that wished others harm, but he was still evil and corrupt. He is dead now though and will never haunt our streets again.

"I'm saddened to tell you all this, but though we all feared and hated Creature we also needed him. He helped us by watching over us only wanting to do good. He was never given a choice on what he was to become, he hated killing, but it was a part of him, a part he could never turn from. So he tried to be good, he only killed the bad guys and thus thought himself worthy of living. He tried so hard to gain acceptance and only wanted to make the world a better place. He knew he was not a good person, he knew he deserved all the hardships this earth can deal out and he faced so many demons in his life. But he has left this world and this city that he so loved.

"My beloved people, this city is in worst shape now than when he was alive. It's not a mess I wish to give to my daughter, but I feel that I have failed you and so I resign and remove myself from the throne so that I cannot do more damage. Princess Isra will make a great Queen and will help resurrect this city.

"I hope you all will be loyal to her as she finds her strengths and be kind to her when she faces her weaknesses. She is ready for the thrown and so Princess Isra please step forward and kneel before me," I spoke, sadness in my heart, but hoping I was doing the right thing.

Princess Isra came forward, dressed in the white robes that are usually worn by an unwed princess about to be pronounced Queen. She knelt before me and looked at me. So much like Shirra, my chest tightened and I was lost for words. "Father, my King, I am ready for the throne and will honour your great kingship by being the best Queen I can be," Princess Isra said, her voice ringing through the city center clear and strong. It brought me back to the moment at hand.

"Princess Isra, I King Esmir of Vale Darra, abdicates from the throne and thus gives to you the honour of serving this city as servant, as guide, as friend, as mother and as Queen. From henceforth the wellbeing of these people is on your shoulders and you are responsible for them until you choose another heir. I pronounce you Queen of this city, in its state, giving you only a shell of the city it can be, but with hopes that you will raise it as if it's your own child. Be strong and wise, brave and loyal and serve your people with an honest heart.

Princess Isra, you are Queen Isra of Vale Darra, the first of your name," I set the crown on her head.

The crown sat on her head, shrunk to sit properly and gleamed a pure silver with thousands of tiny sapphires adorning the top. It was a beautiful crown, the top was in the shape of mountains, the silver representing rock for strength, the sapphires for beauty, the blue for life, healing and everything good. The new Queen smiled at me, she looked so beautiful as she stood up and turned to face her people as their new queen.

"My people I am honoured to be first your servant then your guide, your friend and mother and then your Queen. I shall start by being honest with you.

"My youngest sister, oh how I love and miss her. Shirra was not evil, she was a great person and she was an amazing person. She seen strength and potential in everyone and did her best to help others. She saw an ally, a tool in which she could befriend to better protect her people. She was not afraid to mar her own name for the sake of her city, though it may seem wrong and evil of her to do so. But she had nothing, but love for her people in her heart and that is why she collaborated with Creature, an assassin that we all learned to fear. My beloved sister turned a dangerous enemy into a guardian and in doing so made this city a better place.

"We all know that even though Creature was evil, he did make Vale Darra safe. Because of him, we did not have the trials and turmoil's that most other cities face. He kept the greater darkness at bay, he wanted only to protect those he loved.

"I ask you all to remember Shirra not for the bad that she did, but for the good that she's done. She was a great healer and for that we will miss her. She was a loyal and kind friend, she wanted no glory for herself and just wanted to be a fair and honest person. She worked as your doctor and a servant, earning her way in life just like many of you do. She walked a path that's hard to follow, but she stuck to it with the best intentions.

"I also will give to you the true identity of Creature. Khireal Dakerie Sashess was born into this world being placed into the arms of a nurse. His mother died during labour, she had cancer and delivering a baby was too much for her body to handle. Khire since birth struggled to find his place in this world. He wanted to make his family happy, he wanted everything that people want in life, love, happiness and worth, but what he found was none of that. An assassin named Josin used him and tricked him. Josin was power hungry and wanted to use Khire for his own good. Josin's brother Sinth who is famously known as Midnight tried to save Khire and so taught Khire all he knew. As such, Khire became an assassin, he fought and screamed and cried about it, but in the end he became what even he feared to be. He was an assassin and killing others was all he knew though he did try to find other ways to make his life worthy. Khire could never truly be what he thought he should have been. He had a good heart, he was very intelligent, with dreams and hopes. He loved to study magic of all kinds and learn knew languages. He loved history and learning about different cultures.

"But Khire was lost to the darkness and he could not fight it. His last days were spent fighting and defeating Josin. Josin will no longer be able to hurt any of us again. We can all rest assured that though the darkness is not gone, we have made it through some of our most weakest times and still prevailed. We do not have Khire and Shirra to help us, from this day on we must go on without them. I know we can be a great city if only we learn how to work as a team. We are as strong as our weakest person, as intelligent as our simplest of people, and as helpful as our most lost. And after going through what we just went though I know we are all strong, intelligent and helpful.

"It will take some time, but we will find that in time we will be together. And I promise to stand strong when you are weak, to not let fear capture me, and to be the best person I can be. Thank you my people for your love and loyalty, I am yours till the day I die," Princess Isra finished and the crowed that had been so quite the entire time erupted into cheers.

I wanted to cry for the loss and for how proud of her I was, but I told myself I must remain strong. My guards were still around me and I wanted to be seen strong with them. Some of them would become Queen Isra's guards while the older ones would retire. One of my personal Guards Jakk would also be retiring. As it was his brother that was Creature he was not allowed to continue to serve as royal guard. I felt sorry for him, he was as devout and good hearted as they come, but he understood why he had to leave. He stood beside me stone faced.

When a few months ago it was discovered who Creature was, Khire's family was called in and given the option of reading his memories, some did, some didn't. I know Jakk did and he told me he did not hate his little brother, he mostly hated himself. His family was still healing from being told about Khire. Jakk's father had suffered a heart attack and so is in a long-term facility where he will be cared for. Tellnair was sad and left with his family to go on vacation, needing some time to get away and think. Aster didn't read Khire's memories, he despised Khire now. He continued to work at the hospital and would not talk about Khire to anyone. He didn't even go to Khire's funeral where he was cremated alongside Shirra. Fetcher was also removed from position and now works with helping troubled kids. Shean still works with horses and though he didn't like what Khire had done, he still loved Khire and wished him well.

I had read Khire's memories and felt sad for the boy. He was a good person and I wish I could have helped him maybe, maybe given him something positive in his life to help him. I hoped that he found rest and wherever he is now, he was happy. If death be the end to everything then at least he wouldn't suffer any longer, but if there were something after death, then I hoped Khire be given a better chance in the next life.

The rest of the day was spent feasting and commemorating past Kings and Queens and people speaking their pledge of loyalty to Queen Isra. It went on for the rest of the week as well. After a little while she released a book on Shirra and Khire's memories. She wanted her people to know their struggles and know what kind of people they really were. She didn't want to hide anything from them and so was as honest as she could be. Some years after her coronation she married a prince from a far off land. He was a good Prince. Prince Mica and together Queen Isra and King Mica ruled Vale Darra and the story of Creature and the Princess became legend.

EPILOUGE

Nyxx and I traveled around the world, we had grown from a little boy and his little cat to a young man in his twenties learning about the world and learning to see the goodness in everything with his Guide. It was some time until we traveled to Vale Darra, it had changed so much and it hurt me to see just how much was different. It was better for the city though. Queen Isra and King Mica were good to their people, the city was glorious and people were happy here. Nyxx wanted to stay, but I said that too many memories hurt me here and so we left. I led him to a good and happy life. He was a good person and he wanted to learn as much as he could. Together we learned languages, learned about magic, wrote books on magic that were published and became teaching manuals for young magi. Nyxx became famous and well liked. He was important and traveled everywhere and people would great him with open arms and kind smiles. He met a woman and fell in love with her. Together Nyxx and her as well as her Guide and I lived happy in a small little town in the mountains. We remained there and it was there that I found my purpose in life. My first life was memories and learning, but my second life was the one that mattered. How I used my first life to help others gave me a better sense of everything and I learned that though life is hard, the lessons you took from your hardships were worth it.

Printed in the United States
By Bookmasters